SWEDEN

SWEDEN

Matthew Turner

THE MANTLE
New York

Composed in 10.1/13 Adobe Caslon Pro with Gill Sans display at Hobblebush Design, Brookline, NH (www.hobblebush.com).

Cover design by José Lucas.

ISBN 978-0-9986423-1-4

Printed and bound in the United States of America.

First edition, 2018
10 9 8 7 6 5 4 3 2 1

THE MANTLE
21-33 36th St.
Astoria, NY 11105
mantlebooks.com | @TheMantle

For Trev and Renée

PROLOGUE

Tokyo, November 13, 1967

Makoto Oda cleared his throat noisily, casting a hush over the large meeting room on the second floor of the Gakushi Kaikan hall. He peered out over the sea of reporters and news photographers, several of whom had left their seats and were crouched in front of the table where the Beheiren co-founder sat flanked by two fellow members of the group's organizing committee. A camera flash went off, blanching the trio's faces, and for a split second, viewed against the gilded folding screen directly behind them, they took on the appearance of ghostly icons.

"Let's get underway then, shall we?" Oda said. The voice, high-pitched and almost frenetically paced, was all the more jarring coming from someone so tall and sturdy of frame. "My name is Makoto Oda and I'm the representative of the Citizens' Federation for Peace in Vietnam, otherwise known as Beheiren. To my right—" Oda gestured to the man, several years his senior, in black half-rimmed glasses sitting next to him "—is Doshisha University professor Shunsuke Tsurumi. And to my left is Beheiren's secretary-general, Yūichi Yoshikawa."

Yoshikawa, who at thirty-seven was just a year older than Oda, acknowledged the introduction with a nod of his prematurely balding head, which glinted in the harsh lights now trained on the table from the back of the room.

A few of the reporters jotted down the names, though most were already familiar with the Beheiren organizers and sat motionless, eager for the press conference to get underway. They had been told very little. Four U.S. servicemen had deserted in protest of the Vietnam War, and an announcement about the incident would be made at five o'clock that evening. Tensions were high in the nation's capital. Just the day before, Prime Minister Eisaku Satō had flown out to Washington for talks with President Lyndon B. Johnson. In a repetition of the scenes that marred his departure for South East Asia the previous month, thousands of helmeted, staff-wielding student protestors had descended on Haneda airport intent on preventing him from boarding his plane.

"As you know," Oda continued, "four sailors from the aircraft carrier USS *Intrepid*, currently docked at Yokosuka, have deserted. These young servicemen oppose the Vietnam War. The reasons behind their actions are outlined in the film we are about to show. We, the concerned citizens of Beheiren, as representatives of the anti-Vietnam War ideals of all the Japanese people, wish to declare our strong support for the courageous actions of these four servicemen. After the film we will be happy to answer questions."

Oda nodded to someone at the back of the room. The lights dimmed and a 16mm projector whirred to life. Some in the audience did a double-take as an image of Oda holding up the October 31 edition of the *Asahi Evening News* appeared on the makeshift screen at the front of the room. The next shot showed four smartly dressed young foreigners in military regulation haircuts, one sporting a moustache, sitting beside Oda. Each had a large handwritten nametag pinned to his chest.

The four—Craig Anderson, John Barilla, Richard Bailey, and Michael Lindner—took turns reading statements explaining why they had deserted. They spoke articulately and confidently, declaring it a crime for the U.S., a technologically advanced country, to be involved in "the murder of civilians" and "the destruction of a small, developing, agricultural country" and calling for the total withdrawal of American forces from the region. They then described their duties on the *Intrepid* and the circumstances of their desertion.

After the statements had been read out, the film continued with Oda asking questions of the deserters. High-profile Beheiren backers, among them well-known writers and university professors, appeared briefly to show their support for the deserters' cause. At times, despite their superior age and experience, the Japanese in the film looked more nervous than the Americans. The film lasted around forty minutes, the final frames filled with a creased sheet of paper bearing the handwritten message: "This isn't the end; it's just the beginning."

No sooner had the lights come on again than a barrage of questions erupted from the assembled journalists.

"One at a time, please," Oda pleaded, before pointing to a reporter in the middle of the room.

"Are the film and sound recording genuine?"

"Yes," Oda said, directing a sharp glance at the questioner, "they're real."

"Why aren't they wearing uniforms?"

"It's customary for deserters to destroy their uniforms," Tsurumi replied calmly.

A foreign reporter jumped to his feet and shouted in English, "Are the four still in Japan?"

Unfazed, Oda, himself switching to English, replied, "We don't know for certain."

"If the authorities demand that you hand them over, will you comply?"

For the first time since the conference began, there was hesitation among the Beheiren representatives. Then Oda slowly leaned forward, clasping his hands together on the table in front of him, and said calmly, "Beheiren is an organization based on firm principles. We're committed to upholding those principles, even if they conflict with the law. Above all, we have every intention of finishing what we've started."

CHAPTER 1

Yokohama, March 1968

A taxi pulled up in front of Yokohama Station and the rear door popped open. From under the large canopy that jutted out over the station entrance, Harper watched as a young man in a gray suit got out and set off toward them. The man looked up, and for a brief moment their eyes met. Harper tensed as the man's eyes darted from Harper to Yumi and back again. But just as quickly he looked away, and moments later the stranger strode past them into the station.

Harper relaxed and allowed his gaze to wander. Beyond the busy forecourt directly in front of them was a separate paved area where taxis waited in orderly queues, and beyond that still an area reserved for buses. Four modern ferro-concrete buildings, in addition to the station building behind them, fringed the large station square, actually pentagonal in shape. All were of a similar height, around eight stories tall. Skimming over the signboards with their incomprehensible Japanese writing, Harper's gaze eventually came to rest on a large clock attached to the façade of the department store to his left. Ten past twelve. Without thinking he glanced down at his watch to confirm the time before looking across at Yumi.

Yumi had not spoken to him at all during the taxi ride from her apartment, and only sparingly since. He had attributed her quietude to nerves, but as he looked into her eyes now he saw not nervousness, but determination. Aware that he was staring at her, she looked up at him and smiled. He opened his mouth, but before he had a chance to speak she turned away, her attention drawn back to the forecourt. Following her gaze, Harper saw that another taxi had pulled up. In the back seat a middle-aged man in a baggy gray overcoat and black beret leaned forward and spoke briefly to the white-gloved driver. He then got out and without hesitating made a beeline for Harper.

"Mr. Harper?" the man asked, his head swiveling to the left and the right.

"Yes."

"Come with me."

Harper looked at Yumi. She nodded and they both stepped forward. But the man, his head steady now, held up a hand and muttered something to Yumi in Japanese and she halted.

"What is it?" Harper asked.

"He says I can't come."

"What?" He eyeballed the man. "Listen. I'm not going without her. Do you hear me?"

The man frowned. "It's out of the question."

"No," Harper said, his eyes narrowing. "You listen to me. Where I go, she goes."

The man hesitated. "All right. But we must move quickly. There may be people watching us."

The man led them over to the waiting taxi and they got in, Harper and Yumi in the back. After speaking to the driver in Japanese, the man turned to them and said, "Listen carefully and follow my instructions."

They left the station square and drove two blocks before turning right and then right again. The man had the sun visor down and every few seconds Harper noticed him checking the mirror. A few minutes later they arrived back in front of the station, but instead of stopping they drove straight past and out of the square via a different road. They turned left into a side street and pulled up behind another taxi.

"Follow me," the man said. "Quickly."

Harper grabbed Yumi's hand, holding it tight until they were inside the other vehicle. The man in the beret barked an order to the new driver, who swiftly put the engine in gear and pulled away.

Once they had rejoined the main road, Harper turned to Yumi and raised his eyebrows in a mock look of consternation. She smiled hesitantly before turning away. Normally she would have laughed, raising a hand to cover her mouth in the manner that was now so familiar to him. He was reminded of how much she had changed. Usually carefree and relaxed, in the last few days she had revealed an inner strength that only increased his admiration for her.

It was Yumi who had suggested they contact Beheiren. Two days ago, sick of being cooped up in her apartment, he had insisted they go out. They ended up in a bar in Chinatown, where a fight broke out. When the Shore Patrol turned up they had to make a run for it. Later, back at Yumi's apartment, they sat across from each other at the table in the tiny kitchen-slash-dining room, Harper still pumped up on adrenaline and unable to relax. Yumi had given him a cup of green tea. It would help calm his nerves, she said. But he found the bitter drink unpalatable and could only manage one or two mouthfuls. He set the half-empty cup on the table and stared at it, slowly turning it on its axis. After a while he stopped and looked up.

"What are we going to do, Yumi? They saw my face. The Shore Patrolmen saw my face."

"You must stay here. Until they stop looking for you."

"But they're not going to stop looking for me. Not now."

She lowered her gaze, then stood up and went through to the next room. Moments later she came back holding a sheet of paper. Harper immediately recognized it as the flyer he had been handed by an anti-Vietnam War demonstrator outside Yokohama Station a few weeks earlier. She placed it on the table in front of him and pointed to a name at the bottom. "This group, Beheiren. They might be able to help you."

"Behei-who?"

"In English they're called The Citizens' Federation for Peace in Vietnam."

"And they help deserters?"

"They smuggle them out of Japan, to neutral countries. They were the ones who helped the Intrepid Four escape to Sweden."

"The Intrepid Four?"

"Four American sailors from the *Intrepid* who deserted at the end of last year. Beheiren helped them get to Russia on a passenger ship."

"Russia? So this group, Beheiren, they're communists?"

"Some of them are communists. Some are Buddhists. Some are

even Christians. They're just normal people who want the Vietnam War to end."

Harper looked down at the cup and gave it another couple of turns. "How do you know so much about these people, Yumi?"

She hesitated before answering. "I knew you couldn't just stay here forever. When I saw the name on the flyer I remembered the Intrepid Four. I asked some people I know if Beheiren still helped deserters."

He looked up, a stern expression on his face. "You told people I'd deserted?"

"No, I didn't tell them about you. Don't worry. They're people I trust. Friends."

Harper picked up the flyer. At the bottom he made out the word "Beheiren" in Roman letters. Next to it, what looked like a telephone number.

"I suppose it wouldn't hurt to contact them. Just to see if they can help."

She stood up and walked around to his side of the table. Standing behind him, she leaned over and put both arms around his neck and kissed the top of his head. "I'll phone them in the morning. Don't worry. It'll be okay."

The next morning, when Yumi announced before leaving for work that she was going to call Beheiren, Harper had second thoughts about the whole idea. Deep down, he still found it difficult to accept the situation he was in. Just hearing the word "deserter" made him flinch. After talking it through, though, he was forced to admit it might be his only hope.

Harper was emphatic that Yumi not use the phone in the apartment, and so just before nine thirty they went out to a nearby pay phone. They squeezed into the booth together and Yumi dialed the number. After a brief conversation in Japanese she placed her hand over the receiver and explained to him in English that someone from Beheiren could meet them the next day in Yokohama. Harper nodded. The man on the phone told them to be waiting in front of the West Entrance of Yokohama Station at noon. Then he hung up.

The man from Beheiren glanced in the mirror one more time before returning the visor to its original position. Satisfied that they weren't being followed, he settled back into his seat and gave what Harper assumed were new directions to the driver, who nodded in reply.

Harper wasn't sure what to make of all the spy shenanigans. On the one hand he felt relieved that the Beheiren people were taking security seriously. On the other hand he was reminded of the gravity of his situation. He had been in plenty of tight spots in Vietnam, but this was different. For a start he had to put his faith in people he knew nothing about. On top of that, there were no reinforcements to call if things went wrong. No air support or artillery to radio in. He took several deep breaths, reminding himself to stay calm.

They drove for around twenty minutes before eventually pulling up beside a construction site. The man from Beheiren waited for the taxi to leave before leading Harper and Yumi over to a wooden hut that stood in one corner of the site. The hut was about the size of a shipping container and had a single door and one small window. The man stood in front of the door and looked around cautiously before knocking three times. The door opened and another man, slightly older than his colleague and sporting a beard, poked his head out and looked first at the man in the beret and then at Harper and Yumi. The bearded man frowned and said something in Japanese to his associate, who replied curtly before pushing his way into the hut.

Harper knew that it was Yumi's presence that was the source of the friction between the two men. For a moment he was afraid that he had made a mistake by insisting she come with them, that he had jeopardized the mission. After a few seconds, however, the man with the beard looked at Harper and Yumi, tilted his head, and stepped aside, motioning for them to enter the hut.

Inside, the bereted man was sitting at a wooden table in the middle of the hut, which apart from the table and four chairs was completely empty.

"Please," the man said, looking in the direction of Harper and Yumi, "sit down."

They did as he requested, taking the two seats on the other side of the table. They were soon joined by the man with the beard, who sat next to his associate. There was a moment's silence. Then the man in the beret leaned forward slightly and said, in English, "My name is Ōe."

"Like the novelist," Yumi said.

The man regarded Yumi. "Yes. Like the novelist." He nodded in the direction of the bearded man. "And this is Mori."

Mori looked across the table at them and smiled.

The man who had introduced himself as Ōe now directed his attention to Harper. "We would like to ask you a few questions. These are standard questions we ask all the people who request our help, so please don't take offense."

"I understand," Harper said.

Ōe removed a sheet of paper from his coat pocket, unfolded it, and placed it on the table.

"First, do you have an ID card with you, or something else that substitutes as an ID card, like a liberty card?"

"I have an ID card."

Harper pulled out the card and handed it to Ōe. The Japanese man studied it carefully. "Lance Corporal James Earle Harper," he said before looking up.

"My friends call me Harpo."

Their eyes met, and Harper thought he saw the beginnings of a smile form on Ōe's lips. But the Japanese man quickly looked down and jotted something on his sheet of paper before returning the ID card to Harper.

"Thank you," Ōe said. He then referred again to his sheet of paper. "Are you on R&R from Vietnam or a crewmember on a ship which is presently stopping at a Japanese port? Or do you belong to an American base in Japan?"

"Neither. I was wounded in Vietnam. I was flown here and admitted to the 106th U.S. Army Hospital at Kishine for treatment."

"So you have been to Vietnam?" Ōe asked.

Harper nodded.

"Is there any possibility of your going there again in the near future?"

"I was ordered to return to Vietnam earlier this month. I was about to get on a plane when I...when..."

Harper hesitated. Sensing his discomfort, Yumi reached underneath the table and placed a hand on his knee.

"I understand," Ōe said. "So, why did you desert? What was your motive to take such drastic action?"

There was that word again. There would be no hiding from it now. Harper remembered something Yumi had said about Beheiren not helping G.I.s who only wanted to stay in Japan to be with their Japanese girlfriends. He thought carefully before answering.

"I decided not to go back because I no longer support the war. I am no longer willing to kill or be killed there, or have anything to do with the American war effort in Vietnam."

Ōe scribbled something on the sheet of paper before continuing. "How is your physical condition? Do you have any illness or injury?"

"A-1, according to my doctor at Kishine. Though I still get pain in my legs from time to time. From the shrapnel wounds."

"Do you have any venereal disease, like gonorrhea?"

Harper instinctively glanced across at Yumi, and noticed she was doing her best to hide a smile. "No, I don't have any venereal diseases."

"Have you ever tried drugs, such as LSD or marijuana?"

"Yeah. I've tried LSD and marijuana."

"Are you a habitual user of marijuana?"

"No."

"Are you a habitual user of any other drugs? Do you have any drugs with you now?"

"No and no."

"What do you think you will do from now on? What sort of help are you expecting from us?"

Harper thought for a few moments. "I heard you can get people out of the country. To a neutral country like Sweden."

"And that is what you want?"

Harper looked again at Yumi before answering. "Yes, that's what I want."

"You understand that if you are granted asylum in Sweden, there is a chance you may never set foot on American soil again."

This was something Harper hadn't considered. Certainly not at length. It occurred to him that it was something he should take some time to think over. He was mindful, though, of the need to maintain a cool exterior, and above all to convince the people from Beheiren that he was trustworthy.

"I understand," he replied. But even as he said this, images of his mother and father and younger brother and sister flashed through his head. Then his mind turned to how his family would react to the news that their son and brother was a deserter, to the names ("faggot," "commie") people would use to describe him, names he himself had used in the past to describe others in his situation. He thought about these things, and the prospect of never returning to America didn't seem so bad.

Ōe now looked up from his sheet of paper and addressed Harper directly. "We would like to make one thing clear. While we will do our best to get you away from the war, we need your complete cooperation at all times. You must agree to follow our instructions from now on."

"I understand," Harper said. He added, again without thinking carefully about the full consequences, "I'm willing to do whatever it takes to make your job as easy as possible."

When the interview was over, Ōe and Mori told Harper and Yumi to wait in the hut—in ten minutes a car would arrive to take them back to the train station. They further instructed them to contact Beheiren by telephone the next morning, by which time a decision would be made as to whether the organization would help Harper.

After the two Japanese men left, Harper turned to Yumi and said, "What do you think?"

She looked down at the table, deep in thought. Then she turned to Harper and said, "I think it's the only chance you have."

CHAPTER 2

Shinji Masuda closed his eyes and thought of Chet Baker. With his youthful good looks, mellow horn playing, and seemingly effortless crooning, Baker seemed destined for stardom. The major recording companies, keen to see a white musician succeed in a field dominated by black men, gave him all the support he needed. And when the movie moguls came knocking, promising to transform Baker from the pin-up boy of West Coast cool jazz into the pin-up boy of Hollywood, stardom seemed within his grasp. But he made just one movie before turning his back on Tinseltown in favor of the less glamorous life of a touring musician, after which it was all downhill for the one-time Prince of Cool.

These days Baker mostly played flugelhorn. He had lost his teeth—knocked out in a fight after a drug deal went wrong according to one story, removed due to decay brought on by years of heroin use according to another—and with them his embouchure, and so for the time being at least his trumpet-playing days were over. Whichever story was true, Baker's drug habit (he had started using heroin in his twenties) was ultimately to blame for his dramatic fall from grace.

The story of Baker's decline was all too familiar to Masuda. He despaired at the toll drug abuse was taking on the American jazz scene. Not only had it cut short countless careers, but it had also directly or indirectly claimed the lives of some of Masuda's favorite musicians. Among them Charlie Parker, who was just thirty-four when he passed away, but whose body was so ravaged by drugs and alcohol that the coroner who performed the autopsy on him estimated his age at between fifty and sixty. And John Coltrane, the latest to go, just forty when he succumbed to liver cancer in July 1967. Even the great Miles Davis had at one time been a junkie.

One of the reasons Masuda so admired Clifford Brown, the young trumpeter who played with Art Blakey before forming his own hard-bop combo with Max Roach in 1954, was because "Brownie," as he was affectionately known, never took drugs and drank only in moderation. When he first took up the trumpet in high school, Masuda spent hours memorizing Brown's solos on "September Song" and "Lullaby of Birdland" from Sarah Vaughn's eponymous 1954 album. He had found the record in his father's collection at their home in Tokushima. These days, Masuda still tried to emulate Brownie's rich, warm tone. He had more than half a dozen of the trumpeter's records of his own, which he kept in a suitcase in his one-room apartment in Minami-Senju. Among them was *Clifford Brown and Max Roach at Basin Street*. Recorded in early 1956, it was later hailed as one of the greatest hard-bop recordings of all time. Like Chet Baker, Brownie seemed destined for stardom. But *Basin Street* was the last album Brown and Roach made together. In June that same year, Brown's life was tragically cut short, not by drug abuse or alcoholism, but in a car crash that also claimed the lives of his pianist, Richie Powell, and Powell's wife, Nancy. Brown was just twenty-five years old.

A train pulled in, stirring Masuda from his reverie. Buoyed with expectancy, he jumped to his feet, anxiously scanning the passengers as they got off. Several carried newspapers or weekly magazines, but none the *Asahi Graph*. As the crowd thinned, a feeling of disappointment washed over him, and he sat down again.

He took off his glasses, closed his eyes and pinched the bridge of his nose with his thumb and forefinger. After holding this pose for a few seconds, he replaced his spectacles and looked at his watch. 9:43. His instructions were clear. He was to meet the JATEC operative, alias Higuchi, at 9:30 a.m. on the outbound Chuo Line platform at Tokyo's Shinjuku Station. He knew nothing about Higuchi's identity, only that they would be carrying a copy of the latest issue of the *Asahi Graph*.

As he waited for the next train to arrive, Masuda cast his mind back a fortnight to his meeting with Yūichi Yoshikawa at the Blue

Mountain coffee shop in Ginza. It was at this rendezvous that the Beheiren secretary-general had revealed to him the existence of JATEC and invited him to join the secretive group. The fact that Yoshikawa had insisted they meet on neutral turf and not at the Beheiren office was the first indication that something out of the ordinary was afoot. Masuda remembered entering the coffee shop to find Yoshikawa and another Beheiren heavyweight, Hajime Sekiguchi, sitting at a table in the far corner of the room. Masuda walked over and greeted the two men and sat down. They ordered coffees and exchanged pleasantries until their drinks arrived, whereupon Yoshikawa leaned across the table and said in a hushed voice, "We've been contacted by another group of deserters."

Masuda sat up, eyes wide open. "How many?"

"Three," Yoshikawa said.

Masuda looked from Yoshikawa to Sekiguchi and back again.

"We've found somewhere for them to stay for the time being," Yoshikawa said. "But that's the easy part. Getting them out of the country will be a lot harder this time. We need to find a new route. Using the *Baikal* again is out of the question."

As the Japanese press had reported soon after Beheiren's November 13 news conference, it was aboard the *Baikal*, a Soviet passenger ship that sailed between Yokohama and the Russian port of Nakhodka, that the Intrepid Four had fled Japan. Masuda had been involved in the operation from the very beginning. He had been in the Beheiren office working on a mailing campaign when Yoshikawa received the phone call that would change the organization forever.

The caller, who identified himself as a university student, said he was with four young American sailors from the USS *Intrepid*, an aircraft carrier that had docked at the U.S. Navy facility at Yokosuka the previous week after a tour of duty in the Gulf of Tonkin. The sailors had gone AWOL and were refusing to return to duty. They wanted to know if Beheiren would be willing to help them.

At the mention of the word "deserters," everyone in the office, Masuda included, stopped what they were doing. Their eyes remained glued on Yoshikawa as he repeated the information coming over the phone and jotted down the details on a notepad.

"We've got to tell Oda," Yoshikawa said after hanging up. There followed a flurry of phone calls to members of Beheiren's "cabinet." Shunsuke Tsurumi was at his home in Kyoto. He didn't have a phone, so they sent a telegram instead. It read, "DESERTERS HAVE SHOWED UP STOP CONTACT IMMEDIATELY STOP BEHEIREN STOP" Looking back, Masuda realized it was foolhardy to send such sensitive information across a cable, but they were amateurs and completely naïve about such matters.

A rendezvous was organized and, after taking custody of the Americans, Beheiren arranged billets for them while they made plans to smuggle them out of the country. Their final destination would be Sweden, where the government granted asylum to Vietnam War deserters. Late in October, the four were taken to a secret location where they were filmed reading statements and answering questions. Twelve days later the quartet slipped out of Yokohama aboard the *Baikal*.

With so much attention focused on Beheiren following the Intrepid Four's escape, it hadn't taken long for the media to work out the details of the quartet's travel arrangements. Masuda felt a sense of relief when the news broke. He was one of only a handful of people who knew the whole story, and the pressure to keep it secret was almost unbearable.

"Which brings us to the topic at hand," Yoshikawa said. He took a sip of coffee and glanced at Sekiguchi before continuing.

"One of the founding principles of Beheiren is that it should be completely open. But helping deserters requires a certain level of secrecy. So we've decided to set up a separate organization, an underground cell within Beheiren, if you will, that will concentrate exclusively on sheltering deserters and smuggling them out of Japan. Oda and Tsurumi will oversee the operations, and Sekiguchi here will be the liaison. He's at home most of the time so he can be contacted easily. And we'd like you to be involved."

Masuda tried in vain to hide his astonishment, looking slack-jawed at Yoshikawa and then at Sekiguchi before regaining his composure and directing his attention back at Yoshikawa, who was still speaking.

"You'll take instructions from Sekiguchi. You won't be working alone, of course, but for security reasons you won't be told who else is involved unless absolutely necessary. As we learned during the *Intrepid* episode, helping deserters from the U.S. military isn't a criminal offense, but it's a different matter for the deserters themselves. For them, the stakes are incredibly high. In fact, it wouldn't be exaggerating things to say that lives are at risk. As you know, American deserters can't claim political asylum in Japan. And under Japanese immigration law, once U.S. military personnel have left the armed forces they can be arrested as illegal residents. So they really have only two options: lie low and live with the constant fear of being caught, or try to get to a neutral country. That's where we'll come in."

Masuda nodded. "So, does this new organization have a name?"

"We're calling it JATEC," Yoshikawa said.

Masuda gave a puzzled expression.

"It wasn't my idea," Yoshikawa said, casting a sideways glance at Sekiguchi.

"It stands for the Japan Technical Committee for Assistance to U.S. Anti-War Deserters," Sekiguchi said, speaking for the first time.

"It's important to stress that we won't be offering assistance to just any American who's gone AWOL," Yoshikawa continued. "They have to be opposed to the Vietnam War. If some besotted G.I. wants to desert just for a girl, we won't help him. We're not a marriage bureau."

"Fair enough," Masuda said. "So what are we going to do about this new group of deserters?"

Yoshikawa shot another glance in the direction of Sekiguchi before responding. "We haven't decided for certain. But chances are we'll be calling on your help some time in the next few weeks. You'll have to be prepared to go away at short notice."

"Go away? Where? For how long?"

"That, too, is uncertain."

Masuda nodded. He would have to arrange to take time off from his job at the record store in Shinjuku, but the owner had always proved flexible in the past, and Masuda was sure he wouldn't have a problem this time.

"One final thing," Yoshikawa said. "We're assuming the telephones at the Beheiren office and at the homes of the most high-profile members are tapped. Given the clandestine nature of JATEC's activities, as a security measure we'll be using aliases over the phone and in the presence of deserters. Sekiguchi here has chosen the names of famous writers for this purpose. From now on, you're to refer to him as Endō. You'll be known as Kawabata. You'll be informed of the aliases of the other JATEC operatives as and when the need arises."

Two weeks later, Masuda arrived at work to be told by the record store owner that someone named Endō had phoned requesting that Masuda contact him immediately. It took him a few moments to place the name. When he did, he quickly excused himself and went out to the phone box on the corner and rang Sekiguchi at his home.

"This is Kawabata," Masuda said when the JATEC liaison eventually answered.

"Who?" Sekiguchi replied.

"Kawabata," Masuda repeated.

"Kawabata?"

The line went silent. Masuda didn't know what to say. Then Sekiguchi spoke again.

"Oh, it's you Masuda."

Masuda sighed. He wondered how long JATEC could survive if someone like Sekiguchi, who was in a position of responsibility within the organization, couldn't come to grips with such basic security measures as using aliases. It brought home to him the fact that, coming as they did from the worlds of literature and academia, even JATEC's leaders were amateurs at this game.

"The packages we discussed a couple of weeks ago," Sekiguchi said. "They're ready for immediate delivery."

This time it was Masuda who was momentarily confused. Then he realized that the "packages" Sekiguchi was talking about were the three new deserters.

"Immediate delivery? When? Where to?"

"You'll be leaving tomorrow morning," Sekiguchi said.

"Tomorrow?!?"

"That's right," Sekiguchi said matter-of-factly. He then went on to give details of the time and location of the rendezvous before finally wishing Masuda good luck.

Even before he hung up Masuda was starting to think of how he would explain his sudden need for an extended period of time off to the store owner. Perhaps a family bereavement. Despite the inconvenience, however, he couldn't deny that a part of him was looking forward to his first assignment as a member of JATEC, and he had an extra bounce in his step as he made his way back to the record store.

Masuda was so absorbed in his reverie that he hadn't noticed the figure approaching from the other end of the platform. Only when it was so close it cast a shadow over him did he look up. When he did, he recognized the shadow's owner immediately.

"Well," Sakurai said, "if it isn't the boogie-woogie bugle boy of company B."

"It's the trumpet," he said. "I play—"

"Yes, I know. You play the trumpet. And boogie-woogie is for fuddy-duddies."

They both smiled.

"But what are you doing here?" he asked. Then he spotted the magazine under her arm and everything became clear. Except when he looked closely he saw that it wasn't the *Asahi Graph*, but the rival *Mainichi Graph*.

"What is it?" Sakurai said, following his gaze. "Oh, this," she added, casually holding the magazine in front of her. "I couldn't get the *Asahi Graph*. Sold out."

There was an awkward pause before they looked at each other and laughed.

She was wearing a checked shirt and jeans, her hair swept back in a ponytail. The style was a legacy of her time as an exchange student in Oregon, the fruits of which also included near-fluent English and an unusually forthright manner.

A few years older than Masuda, Sakurai joined Beheiren soon after its inception. It was Sakurai who had greeted him the day he first visited Beheiren's Tokyo office in the central city neighborhood of Ochanomizu. Masuda had only recently arrived in Tokyo, having quit university in Nagoya and moved to the capital to chase his dream of becoming a professional jazz musician. One of the first things he had done after finding a place to live and a job was to hire a trumpet teacher. Once a week he traveled by subway and on foot from his apartment in Minami-Senju to Ochanomizu, a journey of just over twenty minutes, for a private lesson in a tiny room above a music store on Meidai-dōri. It was while exploring the area around Ochanomizu Station after one of these lessons that he spotted a Beheiren banner in a window on the second floor of a multi-tenant building overlooking the Kanda River. He was familiar with the organization from their activities on campus in Nagoya, and had even been on one or two marches organized by the local chapter. Curious, he climbed the stairs to investigate. The door opened into a small one-room office cluttered with makeshift shelves full of books and stacks of cardboard boxes. In the middle of the bare concrete floor was a large wooden table around which sat a dozen or so people, mostly around Masuda's age, folding newsletters and stuffing them into envelopes.

Assuming he was there to help with the mailing, Sakurai invited Masuda to join in. He immediately felt at home among the other volunteers, a number of whom were university dropouts like himself. Sakurai brought him tea and sat next to him as they worked, patiently answering his questions about the organization.

She told him how Beheiren had been formed in 1965 by a group of intellectuals and artists, including the writer Makoto Oda and the philosopher Shunsuke Tsurumi. Disillusioned by the existing anti-Vietnam War movement, which was dominated by the Japanese Communist Party and other groups associated with the Old Left, they aspired to form a new, grassroots anti-war movement made up of ordinary citizens. The new group would have no national head-quarters and no paid staff. They would actively seek donations but require no membership dues. Beheiren's aims were simple: peace in Vietnam, self-determination for the Vietnamese people, and an end to Japan's complicity in the war.

They had begun by holding rallies and marches once a month in Tokyo. Their numbers were small at first, but they soon grew, and before long new branches were forming and events being held in other cities around the country. Toward the end of 1965 they launched their newsletter, *Beheiren News*. They placed full-page advertisements denouncing the war in *The New York Times* and *The Washington Post*. Public meetings and teach-ins were organized up and down the country, from Sapporo in the north to Okinawa in the south.

Masuda became a regular at the Beheiren office, quickly earning the trust not only of Sakurai and Yoshikawa, but also of Oda, Tsurumi, and the other members of the organization's "cabinet" that met there from time to time. Not long after Masuda became involved, Beheiren began distributing leaflets to American sailors outside the U.S. Navy base at Yokosuka, just south of Tokyo. The leaflets urged the sailors to take action to stop the war, such as writing to President Johnson, holding meetings in their barracks, engaging in sabotage, and deserting. The leafleting was symptomatic of a desire on the part of Oda in particular to broaden Beheiren's activities to include direct action as well as the usual marches and meetings. Masuda thought this probably stemmed from frustration at the lack of progress in achieving Beheiren's aims, although the influence of Howard Zinn and Ralph Featherstone, the two American anti-Vietnam War activists who had recently toured the country at the invitation of Beheiren, may also have been a factor. Whatever the reason, the leafleting soon spread to other U.S. military bases around the country, and ultimately led to Beheiren's involvement in the escape of the Intrepid Four.

"I see you've brought your bag," Sakurai said now, nodding in the direction of the rucksack on the seat next to Masuda.

"Yes, as per instructions. So, am I allowed to know where we're going?"

"Kami-Suwa."

"In Nagano Prefecture?"

"In Nagano Prefecture."

"How long will it take us to get there?" He noticed she wasn't carrying an overnight bag like he had been instructed to bring.

"Around four hours. But that's just the beginning of it. You're going to be doing rather a lot of traveling in the days ahead." She glanced at her watch. "Well, Kawabata, we'd better get going. We've got a train to catch."

He stood up and shouldered his bag. "Lead the way, Higuchi."

CHAPTER 3

Eddie Flynn looked straight ahead as he approached the main gate at the U.S. Navy base at Yokosuka, resisting the temptation to glance across at the sentry box to his right. He was wearing a freshly laundered white Navy uniform—on the outside there was nothing to distinguish him from all the other American military personnel who exited through the gate daily. But there was one important difference. Unlike the others, Flynn had no intention of returning. This made him extremely anxious. So anxious he was sure the people around him could read it on his face. To make matters worse, the money he had stashed in the bottom of his right shoe made him walk with a slight limp. It was a relief when he made it past the gate, and it was all he could do not to break into a run.

With the base behind him, Flynn continued walking straight ahead until he came to Route 16. He crossed the busy four-lane highway and continued on, following the same route he had numerous times over the past week, the last earlier that afternoon when, after withdrawing all his money, he had headed into Honcho to look for a rucksack large enough to hold a change of clothes and a few other essentials. Honcho, or the Honch as it was known to those around the base, was Yokosuka's main entertainment district, a warren of narrow streets and lanes lined with bars, cabarets, and cheap hotels, along with hardware stores, souvenir shops, and other family-run businesses. "If you can spell it," they said of the Honch, "they sell it." And sure enough, in less than half an hour Flynn had found just what he was after: a sturdy canvas rucksack with two large outside pockets.

He had the rucksack slung over one shoulder now as he wandered through the Honch, past the gaudily decorated bars with their ridiculous sounding names: Snack Honey, Diamond Horse-shoe, Bar Swallow. Most had signboards outside listing the names of the ships docked at the navy base along with dubiously worded welcome messages. "Welcome come from Vietnam US hero," read one. "Make you second home. Inexpensive drink. Just step in." Another bar welcomed patrons with a large sign bearing a picture of three drunk cowboys, two of them propped up against a large wooden barrel, the third drinking from a whiskey jar. "This is a good bar—but not a great bar," it read. "We feel like home with shitkicking music."

Flynn looked up as he approached the neon archway marking the entrance to Broadway Avenue. It was still early in the evening, and though they were illuminated, the colorful fluorescent tubes barely stood out in the twilight. Below the archway, the centerpiece of which was a neon Statue of Liberty, hung a row of candy-striped paper lanterns that swung gently in the evening breeze.

After passing under the archway, Flynn turned left and continued walking until he came to a bar called Big Lucky. He went in and took a seat at the far end of the counter and ordered a beer. The barman, who had been busily polishing glasses when Flynn entered, turned and took a chilled glass mug from a refrigerator and filled it with beer from a tap and set it on top of the counter.

Flynn took a swig and looked around the bar. It was on the small side, almost austere compared to some of the other establishments in the area. Being early in the evening, it was still quiet. The only other patrons were a couple of sailors in uniforms identical to his. They sat at the counter flanked by a pair of bargirls in shimmering dresses, and were so enthralled in a drinking game of some kind that they were oblivious to his presence.

Further along sat another bargirl in a red dress. The low neckline revealed what looked like a generous cleavage, though Eddie had been in Yokosuka long enough to know that what you saw was generally not what you got. Flynn realized the girl was looking at him, and turned away nervously. His eyes came to rest on a large sign on the wall to his left. "The following practices will not be condoned by this establishment," it read. There followed a numbered list of eleven banned activities, among them "Picking nose at table," "Scratching nuts with swizzle stick," "Failure to button pants" and "Wiping ass on curtain." "Failure to comply," the notice ended, "will result in a fine of 500 yen."

Flynn smiled and took another swig of beer. Out of the corner of his eye he saw the woman in the red dress stand up and walk toward him. She planted herself on the stool next to his, turned to him and said, "Hi, what's your name?"

Flynn looked at her. With all the make-up it was difficult to tell her age, but she looked old, maybe in her thirties. Then again, he thought, it was probably the kind of job that aged people fast. Just like the military.

"Eddie," he said. "My name's Eddie."

"Hi, Eddie. I'm Naomi."

Flynn took another pull of beer. He felt his cheeks redden.

"Have you been in Vietnam, Eddie?"

He didn't answer right away. Eventually he said, "Yes. I was on a hospital ship."

"A hospital ship?"

"A hospital, on a ship."

"Ah, a hospital. So you're a doctor?"

Flynn laughed. "No, I'm not a doctor."

"Not a doctor? So what do you do? You're not a nurse, are you?" She giggled and looked over at the barman, who smiled as he continued polishing glasses, holding each one up to the light to check that it was clean.

"I'm a Seaman Apprentice. I did general deck and administrative duties."

Flynn considered telling Naomi exactly what he had been doing on the *Respite* before they sent him to Yokosuka. That he had been collecting dead bodies and taking them to the morgue. But instead he turned to her and said, "I don't mean to be rude, but if you don't mind I'd like to be alone." Naomi looked down, her lower lip protruding in a pout. Then, without saying another word, she stood and returned to her stool at the other end of the bar.

Working on a hospital ship off the coast of Vietnam was the last thing Flynn imagined he would end up doing when he enlisted. He had grown up on a potato farm in Bingham County, Idaho. He liked the farm, so much so that he fancied owning one himself one day. As a kid, he had delighted in the feel of the dirt under his fingernails, the wide-open fields. But he grew tired of the treatment dished out to him by his father, who would beat him for the most trivial of misdemeanors. With two older brothers ready and willing to take over the farm when it became too much for his parents, Flynn saw no reason to hang around. So when a Navy recruiting team showed up in town one day offering him the chance to travel and see the world, he decided to enlist. He had looked forward to visiting Italy. Or maybe Spain. When he graduated from boot camp and learned he was being posted to a hospital ship, he felt cheated.

The *Respite*, a Haven-class hospital ship, had been brought out of mothballs and sent to Vietnam in 1966 when it became clear the medical facilities on land would be unable to cope with the rising number of American casualties. U.S. forces had almost complete control of the air space and seas along the coast of South Vietnam, so the wounded could be ferried safely in helicopters directly from the battlefield to the *Respite*, where they were attended to in conditions that rivaled those at the best hospitals on land.

Flynn was initially assigned to the triage area next to the flight deck at the vessel's stern. Helicopters bearing the wounded came in day and night. One minute he would be relaxing on the weather deck. Then a speaker would crackle to life and after muffled blasts from a boatswain's call a nasal voice would announce, "Flight quarters! Standby to receive emergency patients!" The next minute he would be rushing to the stern along with all the other personnel on duty.

They were images he knew he would never forget. A UH-ID Huey descending out of the darkness and into the corona of light surrounding the *Respite*. Up on the flight deck, a Landing Signal Officer in a red satin vest guiding the chopper in, first waving two flashlights and then crossing them above his head to indicate to the pilot that he was in position to land. Young corpsmen in navy blue trousers and light blue shirts scrambling onto the flight deck to unload the stretcher-born wounded and ferry them down the ramp to the triage area. The Huey taking off to make room for the next one.

Flynn soon got used to this routine. At busy times it would be repeated every five or six minutes, each chopper delivering up to four stretcher patients or nine walking wounded for treatment on the hospital ship. Flynn's job was to strip the newly arrived patients of any weapons or ammunition they might still have on them. They were usually checked before they were medevaced out, but occasionally patients arrived with grenades in their pockets or even embedded in their bodies, which, understandably, made the medical staff nervous. He was pretty sure he had been given this detail so that his nemesis, Petty Officer First Class Henry Dawkins, could keep a close eye on him. For some reason, Dawkins had taken an immediate disliking to Flynn, and was constantly reprimanding him for even the slightest mistake. He had already spent one brief stretch in the brig for insubordination. Anyway, perhaps it was the pressure of being watched all the time, but it didn't take long for Flynn to slip up big time.

It was late at night, and a Huey had just come in with a full load of four stretcher patients. As the first two stretcher-bearers descended the ramp from the flight deck, Flynn focused his attention on the figure they were carrying. Usually, the first thing that struck him about newly arrived patients was the smell. The majority of the wounded were medevaced straight from the battlefield, so their uniforms and boots were covered in mud. Having grown up on a farm Flynn was used to the smell of dirt, but the mud here was different. It gave off a peculiar fetid odor. But the first thing he noticed about *this* patient wasn't the smell: it was that both his legs had been blown off at the knees. Flynn could tell pretty quickly he didn't have any weapons on him. He was a radioman. He knew this because he was still clutching the black handset in his left hand. All he would have been carrying was a sidearm and possibly some ammunition for the other Marines in his platoon, but all his gear had been stripped off him in the field. He also had a beard, which struck Flynn as unusual.

In the triage area, a senior surgeon looked at the radioman and quickly determined he needed to go straight to the operating room. He was waved through, and Flynn turned his attention to the next casualty. Lying face up on the second stretcher was a black Marine. He was unconscious and had shrapnel wounds to most of his body, though his legs seemed to be the worst hit. Flynn glanced at his face only briefly, but he was struck by his serene expression. Like one of those statues of the reclining Buddha, an impression that was reinforced by the large eyelids, elongated ears, and wide mouth.

Like the radioman, the black Marine had been stripped of his equipment before being loaded into the chopper. His boots and trousers had been either blown off or cut away. All Flynn had to do was check he wasn't carrying a sidearm or any grenades. He had finished checking and was about to tend to the third patient when he heard a clunk followed by a clatter. Something solid had struck the wooden deck and was rolling away.

Flynn spun around. The dozen or so nurses and corpsmen in the triage area had all stopped what they were doing and turned their heads in the direction of the noise. They froze, tracking the grenade as it continued to roll along the deck. Eventually it came to rest against a bulkhead. The medical personnel resumed their duties, almost as if nothing had happened. Flynn, too, had turned his attention back to the third patient when he heard a loud voice behind him.

"Seaman Apprentice Flynn!"

Flynn stiffened. He slowly turned around and regarded the owner of the voice. "Yes, Petty Officer Dawkins."

"What did I tell you about checking the pockets of incoming patients for grenades?"

Flynn felt the eyes of everyone in the triage area on him. His cheeks quickly began to color, and he looked down sheepishly at his feet.

"Do you want to kill us all?" Dawkins shouted.

"No, Petty Officer Dawkins."

"I can't hear you, Seaman Apprentice Flynn."

Flynn looked up. His face was burning now, and he found it difficult to meet Dawkins' gaze. "No, Petty Officer Dawkins!"

Dawkins' eyes held his for what seemed an eternity. It was as if he knew how uncomfortable Flynn felt, and was determined to prolong the agony.

It was almost a relief when Dawkins finally said, "See me as soon as you get off duty."

The remainder of the shift passed without incident. But it was no consolation for Flynn, who was preparing himself mentally for yet another dressing down from Dawkins, and yet another spell in the brig.

"Another beer?"

Flynn looked up. It was the bargirl, Naomi. She had returned to sit on the stool beside him. She seemed younger than before. Prettier too. He looked down at his empty tankard. Was it his second or third?

"Sure," he said. "And get one for yourself, too."

Naomi smiled and gestured to the barman, who took Flynn's mug and refilled it. He poured Naomi a glass of something from a large bottle and set it on the table, together with a small plate of peanuts. After taking a sip of her drink, she looked at him and said something in Japanese, smiling and tapping her cheeks with both index fingers. Flynn thought she was making fun of his reddened face, but the beer had lightened his spirits, and he didn't take offense. He simply looked at her and shrugged his shoulders. The barman leaned across and interpreted.

"Freckles," he said. "She likes your freckles."

The barman made no distinction between the R and the L, and it took Flynn a while to work out what he was saying. When he did, he turned to Naomi and smiled and nodded. She raised her glass and he reciprocated, slowly raising his beer mug and clinking it against her glass before knocking back another mouthful. She reached over and placed her hand on his thigh. He looked down at the hand, confused as to whose it was and what it was doing there, then placed his own hand on top of it. Though not large by any means, his hand completely enveloped hers.

Flynn had just one friend on the *Respite*. Wayne Huerta was one of the ship's one hundred and forty-five corpsmen. The two of them would spend hours together on the weather deck, sometimes swapping stories of home over a cigarette, sometimes just staring quietly out at the South Vietnamese coast. And so when Flynn was released from the brig to find that Huerta had been transferred off the *Respite* to a combat unit on land, he was crestfallen. As if to rub salt into the wound, Flynn himself was relieved of his duties in the triage area and given a new detail: the morgue.

Working in the triage area had desensitized him to pain and suffering. Flynn had seen not only men, but women and children, too, with gunshot wounds, fragmentation wounds, burns, and other horrific injuries. Often they were missing limbs. But nothing had prepared him for spending his entire working day with the dead. He could think of no other job that could as completely destroy the soul.

Conditions in the morgue itself were horrendous. The floor was regularly covered in a thick layer of gelatinous blood, sometimes up to his ankles. He was continually slipping, at times ending up on all fours, his hands and clothes covered in the gooey red jelly. After his first day he wondered how he would cope. His coworkers used humor to get by, laughing in the most inappropriate of circumstances, showing no respect for the dead. They saved the worst treatment for the bodies of Vietnamese that turned up from time to time.

To make matters worse, just a couple of weeks after he started working in the morgue, the North Vietnamese initiated the Tet Offensive, ushering in one of the busiest periods in the *Respite's* history. The offensive began on the morning of January 31, 1968, with Charlie launching attacks up and down the country in a bid to spark a general uprising they hoped would bring the South Vietnamese regime to its knees. The worst fighting took place in Hue and around the combat base at Khe Sanh. It lasted for months, and there was an almost constant circulation of choppers transporting wounded from the battlefield to the *Respite*, and from the ship to hospitals on land. Personnel worked twelve-hour shifts to try to keep up with the demand. The morgue was full to the point of overflowing, and Flynn and the others in his detail were run ragged.

Flynn learned early on not to look at the faces of the bodies that came in. It was one of the survival mechanisms he relied on. But one day while moving a shot-up body, one of three that had just come in, the sheet covering it slipped off and for some reason his eyes were drawn to the face. He recognized it immediately. It was Huerta.

Flynn never really recovered from the shock of seeing his only real friend on the *Respite* lifeless. After that, not only did he avoid looking at the faces of the dead, but he was unable to look at the faces of the living. He wandered around the ship with his eyes downcast, looking up only when spoken to, but never making eye contact.

It was around this time that he began taking drugs. Marijuana at first, and then Binoctal, which worked faster and provided a better high. It also dulled the senses, making it easier to cope with the stresses of military duty. Binoctal had originally been developed in France as a headache remedy. It was sold as a prescription drug in Vietnam, but was widely available on the street. Before long, Flynn was addicted.

After each long shift in the morgue, Flynn would head to the weather deck and sit and look out to sea and dream of home, of the potato farm in Bingham County. His reverie was ironic, given that he was once so eager to leave home. It was while sitting on the weather deck one evening, thinking about Huerta and the conversations they had had, that Flynn recalled his friend mentioning the Navy's drug user support program. He remembered Huerta saying that all you had to do was prove you were addicted to drugs and the Navy would send you stateside for treatment. Could it be his ticket home? With Huerta dead, Flynn would have to find out about the program from someone else. It would have to be someone he could trust. He knew that if word got to Dawkins that he was using drugs, he would really be in trouble. Though he couldn't imagine anything Dawkins could do to him that was worse than his current detail.

The next day he went to the ship's chapel and spoke to one of the Navy chaplains. Flynn wasn't particularly religious, but his parents had brought him up to respect men of the cloth and it was customary in the Navy to see a chaplain if you wanted to discuss matters of a delicate nature that you were reluctant to discuss with other officers. He had also grown to admire the chaplains for the way they comforted the dying in their final moments, something he had witnessed all too often since boarding the *Respite*.

The chaplain listened intently, nodding from time to time, as Flynn explained that he was addicted to Binoctal and wanted to get clean. That he had heard of a support program that offered not punishment but treatment and rehabilitation. After asking a few questions about Flynn's background and experience on the *Respite*, the chaplain said he would look into it and contact Flynn in a day or two.

The next evening Flynn returned to his quarters at the end of a hectic twelve-hour shift to find Petty Officer Dawkins and another NCO he didn't recognize going through his belongings. He was ordered to stand at attention while they completed the search, which to Flynn's surprise turned up nothing. It seemed that someone else had got to his stash before them. Before he left, however, Dawkins informed Flynn that he would have to receive "treatment" for his drug dependency. *The drug user support program*, Flynn thought. He showed no emotion, but he scored this as a small victory against his foe.

Flynn's initiation into the program involved being given a test dose of pentobarbital to determine his tolerance. He was then given daily doses of oral pentobarbital, which were gradually reduced. Once he was clean, Flynn began seeing a psychiatrist and attending fortnightly group therapy sessions. He doubted they had any effect, though they did give him a chance to escape work in the morgue, which was still as hectic and demoralizing as ever. They also offered another glimmer of hope—that of securing an honorable discharge by reason of unsuitability, which, according to a corpsman he was talking to at one of the therapy sessions, was not uncommon among participants in the program. Could his drug problem actually be his ticket back home? The only problem was that drug possession was an offense, and he had already used up his one chance of getting treatment without fear of punishment. The next time he was caught with drugs it wouldn't be the brig, but prison.

It seemed that Dawkins was also aware of this. Every few days he would show up in Flynn's quarters after he finished work and search his belongings. During one of these searches Flynn asked what he was looking for. Dawkins laughed and told him he knew he was too weak to stay clean, that he would be back on drugs sooner rather than later, and that Dawkins would be there to bust him.

For Flynn this just provided another incentive to stay clean. The longer he stayed off drugs, the more frustrated Dawkins became, and nothing gave Flynn greater satisfaction than to see his nemesis frustrated. But Dawkins' intimidation was taking its toll on Flynn's fragile state of mind, and one day he snapped, lunging at Dawkins after he had confronted him on the weather deck and pushing him toward the wooden guardrail. If a nearby seaman hadn't intervened, Flynn may well have pushed Dawkins overboard.

The incident earned him another spell in the brig. When he came out, the psychiatrist he had been seeing for his drug addiction called him in to a meeting and told him he was being sent to a mental facility for an evaluation. For a moment he thought he had done it. He thought he was going home. Only later did he find out that the clinic was in Yokosuka, Japan, not in the States.

When the *Respite* next put in at Da Nang, Flynn was transferred to the Air Force base and put aboard a flight to Yokota air base in Japan. It was a nighttime flight, and the thing he remembered most about it was the silence as they prepared to take off. Not one of the passengers spoke. He knew they were all thinking the same thing: Thank God I got out alive!

From Yokota, Flynn was taken by bus to the U.S. Naval Hospital at U.S. Fleet Activities Yokosuka, where he was admitted to the Mental Health Unit. A discharge was just a matter of time. Next stop, the good ol' U.S. of A. Or so he thought. But the psychiatrists had other ideas. According to them his problem wasn't "inaptitude," "unsuitability," or any of the other character flaws that would have earned him an honorable discharge, but "aggression." He laughed when they told him. He was in the military, and he was too aggressive? Then he realized they were serious. The treatment they prescribed was more therapy. A month after arriving in Yokosuka, he was pronounced fit to return to duty. He was told he would be flying back to Vietnam the following week.

During his final few days at the hospital, for the first time since arriving in Yokosuka, Flynn was free to come and go as he pleased. He became a regular visitor to the Honch, where he drowned his sorrows most evenings and frittered his money away on bargirls. It didn't take him long to decide he wouldn't be going back to Vietnam. He would simply buy a rucksack, fill it with enough basic supplies to last a week or two, and walk out the main gate. What he would do after that he had no idea. He would just take things as they came.

CHAPTER 4

It was dark by the time Harper and Yumi got back to Yumi's apartment. They were both tired after the interview with Beheiren, and after a simple meal they bathed and went to bed. But the knowledge that it could be their last night together inflamed their passion. They made love urgently and with abandon. Later, when Yumi was asleep, Harper lay on his back and looked up at the ceiling. He closed his eyes and tried to go back over the day's events. But the drowsier he got, the less he was able to control his train of thought, and his mind wandered. Back to the Nam. Back to Hill 842. Back to the day it all began.

They had set off from the camp at dawn, humping down the hill looking for enemy mortar nests. There were twelve of them in the patrol. In charge was the new platoon leader, Second Lieutenant Lloyd Muller. They were about halfway down when the point man called the patrol to a halt. He had spotted what he thought was a mortar tube in one of the few remaining clumps of thick vegetation at the bottom of the hill. They spread out and hunkered down in three groups in three adjacent bomb craters. The suspected mortar position was out of range of any of the weapons they carried, so Muller, who was crouched in one of the craters with his radio operator, Eldridge, and a corpsman, Briggs, had radioed through the grid coordinates to the forward air controller and requested an air strike. All they could do now was sit and wait for the Phantoms to show up.

From the large crater that he shared with five other members of the patrol, Harper looked down into the valley below. To describe what he saw as a lunar landscape would be a disservice to the moon.

The moon was beautiful, but there was nothing beautiful about the Khe Sanh Valley. Not any more. The B-52s had seen to that. Operating out of Andersen Air Force base in Guam, the massive Stratofortresses were an almost constant presence in the skies above Khe Sanh. They flew in at thirty thousand feet, so high they were invisible and inaudible to those on the ground, each laden with up to twenty-seven tons of 250-, 500-, and 750-pound bombs. These sorties, many of which took place at night, wiped out whole NVA units. They also left the valley cratered and barren of vegetation.

In the distance, Harper could just make out the gray airstrip beside Khe Sanh Combat Base, the focal point of Marine activity in the area. Originally constructed by U.S. Army Special Forces in 1962, KSCB now served as what the top brass referred to as "the western anchor" of the military's presence in Vietnam, though Harper thought the metaphor was a bit over the top, given that the base's defenses had yet to be truly tested. The high ground around the camp had been taken from the NVA in a series of so-called "hill fights," battles that left one hundred and fifty-five Marines killed in action and four hundred and twenty-five wounded. Harper wondered if anyone was keeping a tally of how many Marines had died or been wounded defending the hills since then. He doubted it.

A movement in the crater below caught Harper's eye. He looked down to where Lieutenant Muller was nervously awaiting the arrival of the Phantoms. Harper knew almost the moment he set eyes on the new platoon leader that he was another greenhorn glory-seeker. And if there was one thing Harper had grown to resent during his time in Vietnam, it was the goddamn greenhorn glory-seekers. Of course, he also resented the leeches, the trench foot, the jungle rot, the C-rations, the Bouncing Bettys, the Punji sticks, the rednecks, the rain, the mud, the dust. And the gooks. They all hated the gooks. But at least everyone knew whose side they were on. With the greenhorn glory-seekers you could never be sure.

Muller was part of a group of a dozen replacements that had been choppered up from KSCB about a week ago. Most newbies had no idea how perilous life was on top of the hill. They would saunter down the ramp of the CH-46 and stand there, just asking to be picked off by NVA snipers dug in on the slopes below the camp.

And so the company CO had set up a team whose job it was to tackle the replacements as soon as they reached the edge of the ramp and bundle them into the nearest trench for safety.

Harper, who had been a linebacker in his high school football team back in Redville, Mississippi, had practically begged to be assigned to this detail. He relished the chance to show off his tackling skills, and was known to perform the task with a little too much enthusiasm. Anyway, when he spotted Muller at the end of the ramp in his freshly laundered utilities, new flak jacket, and shiny boots, he took an instant dislike to him. He pushed past the other members of the detail and launched himself at Muller, wrapping both arms around his waist and shuffling him into a trench beside the landing zone where he wrestled him to the ground. For good measure he grabbed the back of his helmet and pressed his face into the mud. Officers always removed their insignia before heading up to the hills around KSCB, so Harper had no idea at the time that Muller was a lieutenant.

A few days later, Muller got back at Harper. They were getting ready to go out on an early morning patrol. Everyone was busy strapping on ammo and smearing carbon on their faces. Except the brothers, of course. Orders were that everyone had to blacken their face, but there were orders and then there was life on the hill. The entire time Harper had been on Hill 842, nobody had told him to put goddamn carbon on his face. But that didn't stop Muller coming over and motioning to Harper and another black Marine sitting beside him and telling them to blacken up. When Harper complained, Muller said, "Orders are orders. You don't expect special treatment, do you?"

Harper was seething inside, but he knew there was nothing to be gained by making a scene. Not all of the brothers on the hill would have backed down so easily. With the Black Power movement gathering strength back home, some of them were eager to stir things up with the chucks. Harper had heard the rumors about black servicemen smuggling mortars back to the States one part at a time, where they were going to be used in some kind of "insurgency."

But that was all bullshit as far as Harper was concerned. He didn't have time for movements. He remembered how a few years ago a group of "community organizers" from the Student Non-violent Coordinating Committee had turned up in Redville, which they were using as a staging area for their so-called "Freedom Summer" campaign. The community organizers, mostly white college kids on a mission to "save the Mississippi negro," went around all the houses in the area urging people to register to vote, and to hold on to their land. Most of the landowners in the area were blacks who had bought small farms as part of the New Deal. They had a strong community, and knew how to look after themselves. So when the SNCC turned up on the doorstep at the Harper household, Harpo's father sent them packing.

Now some cat by the name of Stokely Carmichael, one-time chairman of the SNCC, was calling for Black Power. Frustrated by their commitment to non-violent tactics, even in the face of violent repression, Carmichael had left the SNCC and thrown in his lot with the radical Black Panther Party. Like Martin Luther King, Jr., Carmichael was an outspoken critic of the Vietnam War, which was another reason why he had such a strong following among the politically minded brothers in Harper's company. But to Harper, the Panthers were just another movement, stirring up more trouble. Harper had no intention of rocking the boat. He preferred to follow the advice his uncle, a World War II veteran, had given him before he shipped out. "Do what they say," he had said. "That way, you'll make it."

Anyway, Harper had proved himself to Muller on that early morning patrol, displaying his proficiency with the M-79 by lobbing a couple of grenades into an NVA machine gun nest at near maximum range. There was no more bullshit jive from Muller after that. Even so, Harper's opinion of Muller didn't change: he was still just another goddamn butterbar.

Harper felt a nudge in his arm. He opened his eyes and looked up into the bearded face of Raymond Rhodes. Rhodes was one of a handful of men who had been on the hill with Harper since he arrived two months ago. For a moment he wondered if he looked as bad as Rhodes did. The beards, of course, were also against orders. Water was in short supply at the camp because—like everything else, including ammo, rations, and replacements—it had to be choppered up from KCSB. The little water on hand was needed for drinking, cooking, and cleaning wounds. So the CO banned shaving.

"What's up, Ray?"

"Don't let the lieutenant catch you sleeping, man."

Harper smiled. "I wasn't sleeping, I was just resting my eyes."

Their laughter was cut short by the sound of the first Phantom. Harper turned his head in the direction of the noise and quickly spotted the aircraft bearing down on the plateau. Within seconds the high-pitched drone had built into a guttural roar. The Phantom rolled and straightened again, white vapor trails streaming in tiny corkscrews from the tips of its angular wings. Two Mk 82 Snake Eye bombs dropped from the plane's underbelly, their petals springing open to slow their descent and give the pilot time to get the low-flying aircraft clear before they detonated. Harper tracked the projectiles as they glided down. Even before they hit the ground, triggering explosions that metamorphosed into contorted gray mushroom clouds and sent out threads of gray smoke and debris, he knew they had missed their target by several hundred yards. Moments later the second Phantom came in, its payload missing the target by an even greater margin. Harper looked down the hill at Muller, who was watching the same scene from his own crater.

He waited for the noise of the explosions to die down and turned to Rhodes. "Goddamn idiot got the coordinates wrong."

"I dunno, man. Could be those jet jockeys who fucked up."

"No, the lieutenant can't read a goddamn map, that's the problem."

Harper looked again at the hole where Muller sat and saw him exchange words with his radioman. The lieutenant then turned around and surveyed the other members of the patrol. His eyes came to rest on the lone machine gunner, a brother from Memphis, Tennessee by the name of Nelson, who was crouched a few yards from Harper and Rhodes.

"Nelson, get down here," Muller shouted.

Nelson shouldered his M-60 and scrambled over the lip of the crater and down to where Muller waited, his assistant gunner close on his heels, struggling under the weight of the M-60's tripod and the extra ammunition, which he carried in cloth bandoliers slung across both shoulders.

Harper strained to hear the conversation in the crater downhill. "Can you reach that mortar position, Nelson?" Muller asked. "I can try, lieutenant."

Harper frowned. "Goddamn glory-seeker's going to get us all killed," he muttered, his eyes fixed on the lieutenant.

Working as one, the result of hours of training and combat time together, Nelson and his AG quickly set up the M-60 and within seconds were pumping out 7.62mm rounds in the direction of the suspected mortar position. Later, Harper would recall hearing a faint pop down in the valley. It should have warned him that a mortar round was on its way. But for some reason he ignored it. Seconds later it landed about fifteen yards downhill, the explosion showering Muller and those around him with red earth and other debris.

Nelson stopped firing and ducked as the rest of the patrol clutched their helmets and threw themselves on the ground.

"Keep firing, goddamnit!" Muller yelled.

"Yes, Sir!" Nelson replied, standing again over the M-60 and recommencing fire.

Incensed, Harper poked his head over the crater rim and yelled at the top of his voice, "Goddamnit, lieutenant, we're drawing their fire. We've got to move out before they zero in on our position."

Muller turned around and looked up the hill at Harper. His gaze darted from Harper to Nelson and back to his radioman, as if he was unsure of what to do. It was then that the second mortar round landed, much closer this time, the blast knocking Harper off his feet. When the last of the earth thrown into the air by the explosion had settled, Harper got up gingerly, his ears ringing, and peered down into the hole below.

It was obvious that Nelson and his AG had taken the full force of the blast. Both lay motionless. Nelson's face was a bloody pulp. A large piece of shrapnel stuck out of his neck. It had hit the jugular vein, and dark red blood was streaming out.

His AG, who had been sitting with his head and torso exposed to direct the machine gun fire, was dead or unconscious. His left arm had been torn off above the elbow and his other arm had been shredded by small pieces of shrapnel. The frayed stump of his left arm was twitching. Blood was seeping through his soiled utilities.

Briggs and Eldridge were both conscious and moving. The corpsman had been hit down his left side and was struggling to get to his feet. Eldridge was clutching his bloodied right arm, and at the same time checking to see if his radio was still working.

Muller was lying with his back to Harper, so it was unclear how badly he was hit, but he, too, was conscious and moving.

Harper's first instinct was to rush down and help. But as he got to his feet, Rhodes, who had also been surveying the carnage in the crater below, grabbed his arm and pulled him back.

"No, man," he said. "You can't go down there. It's too dangerous. We've got to wait for back-up."

Harper looked behind him at the two Marines in the largest of the three holes, both of whom were crouched by the side of the crater holding their helmets in one hand and their M-16s in the other.

"We ain't going to get no back-up unless someone radios for help," he said.

"Eldridge can do it, man. He's not hit that bad."

"Yeah? How's he going to do that then, telepathy? The prick twenty-five has had it."

As if to confirm this, Eldridge had unharnessed the radio's heavy battery unit and laid it on the ground next to him. He still clutched the black handset, but the long spiral cord attaching it to the battery had been severed.

"Listen," Harper said, "we have to get the wounded back up to this hole. And fast. Those gooks are zeroing in as we speak, and the next round is going to land right on top of them."

Harper looked imploringly at Rhodes. He would have preferred to have his buddy's support, but he was prepared to act alone if necessary. Before Rhodes came to a decision, however, they were interrupted by a voice from the crater below.

"Harpo!"

It was Muller. Harper froze.

"I'm hit. Help me, man."

Harper looked at Rhodes, who looked right back at him.

"Harpo! Can you hear me? Harpo!"

"Shit," Harper said. "Why the hell's he calling for me?"

"Don't go, man," Rhodes said.

After a brief moment of silence, they heard Muller calling out again. "Harpo! Help me, Harpo!"

"Shit," Harper said.

After setting his M-79 on the ground beside him, he unclipped his ammo bandolier and placed it next to the grenade launcher. He glanced once at Rhodes before crawling on all fours over the edge of the crater and all the way down to the smaller crater where the wounded Marines lay.

He stopped and looked over at Muller, who was still calling out.

"Harpo! Over here, Harpo."

Ignoring Muller for the moment, Harper crawled over to the far side of the hole where Nelson and his AG lay and checked their pulses. Nothing. He then turned his attention to Briggs and Eldridge. Briggs had shrapnel wounds to his left arm. Most of the sleeve had been torn away.

The corpsman looked up at Harper. "Hey, Harpo."

"Hey, man."

"Hey, did you ever play doctors and nurses when you were a kid?"

"Yeah, sure. Why?"

"Because you're going to have to play doctor now. I'm not much use without this arm."

Harper glanced down at the bloodied limb and slowly nodded.

"Listen," continued Briggs, "I want you to take my medical supply bag and go check out Eldridge and the lieutenant."

"Don't you need something on that arm, doc?"

"It's okay. It can wait. Go check out the others first."

Harper was pretty sure Briggs' arm wasn't okay. But he knew he wasn't going to get anywhere arguing with the corpsman, so he did as he was told and took the green medical supply bag and started crawling toward the lieutenant.

Just as he reached Muller he heard another tube pop down in the valley. He knew he had only seconds to get to safety. There were shouts of "Incoming!" from the Marines uphill, but by that time he had already dropped the medical supply bag and was crouching and grabbing the lieutenant under the armpits and lifting him up in a fireman's carry.

He spun around and set off up the hill. But as he crested the crater rim the mortar shell landed behind him, the explosion knocking him to the ground. The last thing he heard was Rhodes calling his name.

CHAPTER 5

From Shinjuku Station, Masuda and Sakurai rode a Chuo Main Line commuter train as far as Takao. The trains heading in the opposite direction toward Tokyo Station were still fairly full, but few people were heading out of the central city at this time of the morning, and the car they sat in was practically empty. Still, though they talked about Beheiren, they avoided any mention of their mission for the first quarter-hour of their journey until they had passed Nakano and Kōenji Stations, by which time they had the car to themselves. Sakurai, who had been sitting next to Masuda, moved across to the seat opposite, looking around to confirm they were alone before leaning forward and addressing her co-conspirator.

"We're picking up three packages. Two of them are eighteen, one's nineteen. They're all Privates First Class in the Army. We've decided to keep them together until we can arrange to get them out of the country. Ideally we'd separate them, but with the convention in Kyoto less than a month away, we just don't have the resources available at the moment."

The convention was a gathering of peace activists from around the world being organized by Beheiren. Masuda knew all about it, because he had been helping arrange accommodation for some of the overseas delegates when Sekiguchi had contacted him.

"In fact," Sakurai continued, "we struggled to find anywhere for them to stay at all. Then Ōe remembered there was a vacant house down the road from his family home in Saku."

"Ōe?"

"Another JATEC operative. You'll meet him later today."

Masuda nodded.

"So, we've been hiding them in Saku for the last week. Actually, I've just come from there."

Sakurai paused, looking off into space as if she was thinking hard about what to say next.

"And?" Masuda said, eager to hear more.

When she eventually looked back at him, her expression had grown serious. "I'm afraid you're going to have your work cut out for you. They're not like the Intrepid Four at all. They behave more like high school students on a school trip. It's as if they're unaware of the seriousness of the situation they're in. When Ōe and I drove them to Saku, we timed it so that we'd arrive late at night, hoping to keep their presence a secret. But the next morning a group of children gathered outside, keen to see the foreigners. We did our best to keep them in the house, but they wouldn't obey our instructions, and were continually getting into trouble. One day we noticed they were missing. We later found them riding around on children's bicycles. Goodness knows where they got them from."

"They sound like quite a handful."

"That's not the half of it. They have no respect at all for Japanese etiquette. The house we stayed in was very old, and the bath was the kind where you had to light a fire underneath to heat the water. Naturally, because the three were our guests, we invited them to bathe first. Well, you wouldn't believe the state they left the water in. We'd explained how you're supposed to wash yourself outside the bath before getting in, but they took no notice. When Ōe went into the bathroom he found the water full of soap. Not only that, but they'd added so much cold water it wasn't even lukewarm. Needless to say, after that Ōe and I made sure we bathed first."

"I see," Masuda said, understanding now the reason for Sakurai's gloominess. "But if they're in Saku, why are we heading to Kami-Suwa?"

"We've decided it's too risky keeping them there any longer. So we're moving them. Ōe is driving them to Kami-Suwa as we speak. We'll rendezvous with them there tonight, and tomorrow you and I will take them by train to Nagoya. From there we'll travel by rental car to Nara. After that you'll have to look after them on your own for a while, I'm afraid. You'll be escorting them by train to Kagoshima, and then by ferry to Suwanosejima."

"Suwanosejima. Where's that?"

"It's one of the Tokara Islands, about a hundred and fifty miles south of Kagoshima. There's a commune there run by a group of hippies called the Tribe. Have you heard of them?"

"No," Masuda said.

"They were originally based in Shinjuku, and used to call themselves the Bum Academy. Anyway, they've agreed to look after the packages on Suwanosejima until the convention is over, at which time we'll be able to concentrate on arranging their escape."

A silence descended over the two JATEC operatives. Masuda looked out the train window at the passing scenery, which grew increasingly bucolic the further they journeyed from Tokyo, but his mind was busy imagining what lay in store over the coming days. A part of him was unsettled by Sakurai's description of the three's behavior in Saku, but another part of him was convinced Sakurai was exaggerating so he would be prepared. There was also the possibility that they had taken advantage of her because she was a woman. Masuda was thinking what a model of decorum the Intrepid Four had been in comparison, when an announcement came over the public address informing them they were about to arrive at the train's final stop, Takao. Masuda and Sakurai quietly gathered their belongings and made their way to the nearest car exit.

The next train took them as far as Kōfu. There they ate lunch before boarding another train for the third and final leg of the day's journey. It was late in the afternoon when they pulled into Kami-Suwa Station on the shores of Lake Suwa. Masuda followed Sakurai out of the station building and across the road to a coffee shop where they sat at a booth and ordered coffees and waited for Ōe and the three Americans to arrive.

Masuda had finished his coffee and was sipping from his glass of iced water listening to Sakurai talk about her experiences as an exchange student in the U.S. when he heard the door to the coffee shop open. He looked over to see a Japanese man in a beret enter, followed by three young Westerners. Masuda recognized Ōe as an older volunteer at Tokyo's Beheiren office. He had a reputation as a sourpuss, but the expression on his face as he approached the table where Masuda and Sakurai sat was even more severe than normal.

Masuda cast his eyes over the deserters as they drew up behind Ōe. His first impression was that they could easily have been mistaken for a group of high school students. All three wore jeans and T-shirts. Their hair was short and neatly trimmed. One was tall—around six foot three inches, Masuda estimated—and well-built. The other two were of average height for Westerners. One was thin and wore glasses, while the other had unusually pale skin.

After greeting Masuda and Sakurai, Ōe turned to the deserters and pointed to the next booth and the three sat down and immediately began talking loudly among themselves. Ōe nestled into the leather bench seat next to Sakurai, across the table from Masuda.

"Any problems?" Sakurai asked.

"No more than normal," Ōe replied. He then looked across the table at Masuda. "No doubt Higuchi has filled you in on events so far."

"Yes. I gather they're a real handful."

"It's imperative that someone is watching them at all times. We mustn't let them out of our sight, not even for a minute."

Masuda looked behind Ōe and saw that the waitress, a young woman who was probably a high school student, had arrived at the table where the three deserters were sitting and was trying to take their orders. The thin bespectacled American was talking to her, repeating the same phrase over and over, prompting laughter from his compatriots and a look of confusion from the waitress. At first Masuda couldn't make out what he was saying. Then he realized it was Japanese. *Ojō-san, kirei.* Miss, you're pretty.

The waitress was becoming visibly agitated. Noticing that Masuda was looking in her direction, she shot him a look of desperation, imploring him to intervene. By this time, Ōe and Sakurai, too, had taken notice, and Ōe got up and went over to calm the waitress and settle the orders.

Sakurai turned to face Masuda and rolled her eyes. "Those are the only words of Japanese I've heard pass their lips. It's as if they have one-track minds."

That evening the group took two rooms at a *ryokan* on the other side of the railroad line, just a few hundred yards from the edge of Lake Suwa. Having ensconced the three Americans in one of the rooms, Masuda, Sakurai, and Ōe sat around the table in the other sipping green tea. Masuda looked across at Ōe. He seemed relaxed, relieved at having been freed temporarily from the responsibility of looking after the deserters. Then, sitting up as if suddenly remembering something important, he reached for his bag and pulled out three red notebooks and placed them in front of Masuda.

Masuda responded with a puzzled expression. "What are these?"

"From now on," Ōe replied, "each deserter will have a notebook. In it we'll write personal details about them—their name, which branch of the military they belong to, their rank, likes and dislikes and so on. It's to make it easier for us to look after them when they're being moved around from place to place. Since you're going to be responsible for looking after these three from now on, I thought I'd hand them over now. It goes without saying that they mustn't get into the wrong hands. If it looks like you're going to be detained at any stage, destroy them."

Masuda picked up one of the notebooks and opened it to the first page. He began reading aloud. "Richard Santiago. Born 1949. Age eighteen. Private First Class, U.S. Army."

"He's the thin one with glasses," Ōe said. "He doesn't talk much, but the others look up to him. Usually, if you can keep him under control the other two will fall in line. The tall one, well-built, is Eugene Roberts. The other one, the one with the pale complexion, is Michael Sullivan. Anyway, the information is all there. I suggest you familiarize yourself with it as soon as you can."

"Thank you," Masuda said, gathering the three notebooks into a single pile, "I will."

"One more thing," Ōe added. "Other than the destination of the current leg of their journey, the deserters are not to be given details of where they're going or who's going to look after them. This is to prevent information falling into the wrong hands in the event that they're captured. It's also to protect people like the hippies on Suwanosejima who've agreed to accommodate them. The last thing we want to do is make things more difficult than they're already going to be."

"Understood," Masuda said.

"Now," Ōe said, looking at his watch, "I suggest we take our baths early, before the Americans have a chance to get in ahead of us. Unless you like your bath tepid and soapy, that is."

The next morning the Americans were at the center of yet another commotion, this time in the *ryokan* dining room where they refused to eat the raw eggs that came with their breakfast. It was Santiago who instigated the boycott, and Santiago who settled it by calling over the waitress and demanding they be served fried eggs instead.

After breakfast, they finished packing, paid the bill and walked the short distance back to the train station. Ōe bought six tickets to Nagoya at the ticket counter and led the way through to the platform where they stood in two groups of three, a few yards apart, waiting for the train to arrive.

It was as they were standing on the platform that Masuda, who had been keeping an eye on Santiago since the incident in the dining room, noticed the American scratching his crotch. It began with one or two cursory swipes, but before long he was raking the front of his jeans in so vigorous and blatant a manner that it was clearly more than a simple itch.

By this time some of the other people on the platform had noticed and were giving them sidelong glances, but when Masuda looked at Ōe, the older man tilted his head to the side and raised his eyebrows as if to indicate that the deserters were no longer his problem. Masuda looked briefly at Sakurai, but given the nature of Santiago's affliction he decided that the onus was on him to investigate, and so reluctantly he sidled over to Santiago and asked in a hushed voice, "Are you all right?"

"It hurts," the American replied. "I'm afraid it might be serious."

This was the last thing Masuda wanted to hear.

"Do you know what it is?"

Santiago didn't reply, but the way in which he cocked his head to one side suggested that he had an inkling. Masuda looked over at Roberts and Sullivan, who were obviously aware of the topic of the conversation. In the end it was Roberts who spoke.

"Go on, tell him."

"Tell me what?" Masuda said.

Santiago hesitated before speaking. "After I deserted, I spent a night with a bargirl in Yokosuka. I think I caught something."

"You think you caught something?" Masuda repeated.

"He's got the fucking clap," blurted Roberts, making no effort to hide his glee.

Masuda quickly looked around to see if anyone had heard, thankful that the conversation was taking place in English.

"All right," Masuda said, trying to remain calm. "Leave it with us."

Masuda walked back to where Ōe and Sakurai were standing.

"I think it's gonorrhea," he said, "or some other venereal disease."

Ōe and Sakurai both stared at Masuda. After a while, Ōe shifted his gaze to Sakurai. "The bath," he said.

"What?" Sakurai asked, her attention still focused on Masuda as she struggled to process the information he had just given them.

"At Saku," Ōe said. "We bathed after him. In the same water. He didn't wash himself before soaking."

The significance of what Ōe was saying slowly dawned on Sakurai. For a moment her face seemed to register a combination of fear and surprise. When she eventually spoke, however, there was a note of skepticism in her voice.

"But you can't catch gonorrhea from sharing the same bathwater. Can you?"

She looked from Ōe to Masuda. She seemed to be imploring him to offer some words of reassurance.

"Of course you can't," Masuda said. "It's only transmitted through sexual intercourse."

Even as he said this, Masuda was casting his mind back to the night before, relieved that he had heeded Ōe's advice to bathe before the Americans.

"So what are we going to do?" Sakurai asked.

"We should proceed to Nara as planned," Ōe said. "We'll get in touch with Tsurumi in Kyoto. He'll know what to do."

Tsurumi was Beheiren co-founder Shunsuke Tsurumi. It was becoming clear to Masuda that without Tsurumi it would be difficult, if not impossible, for JATEC to operate. It was Tsurumi who had arranged accommodation for the six of them in Nara for the next two nights. And it had been Tsurumi's idea to send Masuda and the three deserters to Suwanosejima. According to Ōe, he had contacts within the hippie group that ran the commune there. If anyone could arrange for Santiago to be treated with the utmost confidentiality, thought Masuda, it was Shunsuke Tsurumi.

As the train wound its way through the Kiso Valley, Masuda peered out the window at the cascading water in the river below and at the steep, forested valley wall on the far side of the gorge. Here the Chuo Main Line followed the old Nakasendō, one of the two main routes linking Tokyo and Kyoto in the Edo period, stretches of which still survived in their original form, complete with stone paving. Mostly, however, it had been destroyed, a casualty in the battle between the river, the railroad, and Route 19, the main highway connecting Nagano and Nagoya. Such matters were far from Masuda's mind. He was thinking about the morning's events and pondering the challenge that lay ahead. Ōe and Sakurai were only traveling with the deserters as far as Nara. After that they would be his responsibility, and his alone.

Even before Santiago's revelation that he had a venereal disease of some kind, Masuda had felt uncomfortable about the three new "packages." Perhaps Sakurai's forewarning—that they were going to be a "handful," as she put—was playing on his mind, but the previous night when he read the statements the three had made to Beheiren after deserting, he found them unconvincing. They seemed to contain all the right sentiments—resentment at the way young men were conscripted straight out of high school, just as they were ready to embark on a new life, and sent off to kill on behalf of their country; confusion at being ordered to murder other human beings, something they had been told all their lives was wrong. But much of it didn't ring true. Even more disturbing was Roberts' admission that after five months in Vietnam he had reached the point where he didn't want to leave, that he had come to enjoy "hunting VC," as he put it.

Masuda was already questioning the wisdom of his decision to become involved in JATEC. When Yoshikawa and Sekiguchi had invited him to join the group, he accepted without hesitation, excited at the prospect of helping a worthy cause and at the promise of an adventure. But the reality of what he was getting himself into was beginning to hit home. As well, he was already missing his music. One of the benefits of his job at the record store was that he had access to the latest jazz LPs from America, which he was free to play on the store's hi-fi stereo. After work and on his days off, when he wasn't practicing his trumpet, he would while away the time at Mokuba, Village Gate, or one of the other jazz coffee shops in Shinjuku, listening to records and discussing the latest sounds with other fans of the genre. The city's vibrant jazz culture was one of the reasons he had moved to Tokyo in the first place. And now, for how long he did not know, he was leaving it all behind.

The remainder of their train journey required transfers at Shiojiri and Nakatsugawa, and it was early in the afternoon when they arrived in Nagoya. Masuda was asked to look after Santiago, Roberts, and Sullivan while Ōe and Sakurai went to organize a rental car. He got the impression that this was a kind of dummy run, that Ōe and Sakurai were testing him to see if he could cope with the deserters on his own. Masuda led his charges across the street to a movie theater, where together they inspected the billboards. One was advertising the new John Wayne movie, *Green Berets*. Masuda turned to the three Americans, who all responded with thumbs down.

"What kinds of movies do you like?" Masuda asked by way of small talk.

"Blue movies," Santiago said, smiling lecherously.

"You and your dirty mind, Santiago," Roberts quipped. "Haven't you learned your lesson?"

Roberts and Sullivan both laughed.

Santiago looked menacingly at Roberts. Then he said, "At least I didn't kill anyone."

The laughter stopped.

Roberts looked sheepishly at Masuda and then back at Santiago. "Shut the fuck up."

Masuda was having trouble following the conversation, but he sensed things would quickly get out of hand if he didn't intervene. "You killed someone in Vietnam, is that it?" he said to Roberts.

It was Santiago who answered. "Not in Vietnam. In Yokohama."

"You killed someone here in Japan? A Japanese?" Masuda said, unable to hide his dismay.

"Not a Japanese. An American," Roberts said. "An MP. And I don't know for sure that I killed him. It was after I deserted. They raided a bar I was in. I had a knife. I guess I wasn't thinking straight. He came at me as I tried to make a run for it. I really don't know if I killed him or not…"

"And you haven't told anyone about this?" Masuda asked. "Anyone in Beheiren, I mean."

Roberts was gazing down at his feet now. Gone was the cocky G.I. who just moments ago was goading the ailing Santiago. "No. I guess I didn't think you'd help me if you knew."

"Okay, okay," Masuda said. "Let me handle it."

Masuda wasn't actually sure how he would handle it. But of one thing he *was* sure: the chances of things going smoothly over the coming days had just gotten a whole lot slimmer.

CHAPTER 6

Flynn blinked. Where was he? There was something familiar about the white walls, the bright lights. He was back on the *Respite*, back in the morgue. But something was wrong. He was running, or at least trying to run. But his feet were leaden, trapped in the thick layer of gelatinous blood that covered the floor, and try as he may he couldn't make any headway.

Exhausted, he stopped trying to move his legs and relaxed. As soon as he did, the tightness around his ankles slackened. He moved one foot backward an inch or two, then the other. It was tough going, like wading through molasses, but he realized that if he walked backward he could at least move. He looked over his shoulder to see where he was going. It was then that he saw the body on the gurney.

It was covered head to toe in a white sheet. Was this what he had been trying to run away from? He kept walking backward until he was just a few feet away. Then, turning and reaching back with one hand, he gripped the edge of the sheet and pulled it down to reveal the face.

Flynn's relief when he woke up and realized he had been dreaming was short-lived, as he quickly became aware of a dull but persistent pain in the front of his head. He was forced to close his eyes again as the light seeping in through the curtains stabbed at his retinas, increasing the pain to an almost unbearable level.

After three or four attempts he managed to keep his eyes open long enough to take in his immediate surroundings. Lying on the bed next to him was the bargirl from Big Lucky. He tried to remember her name. Didn't it start with N? As he looked at her face, she moaned and turned the other way, the bedclothes slipping down to reveal a naked shoulder. The smooth, honey-colored skin aroused him. But then he saw the round, pitted scar on her upper arm, the result of a vaccination of some kind, and his ardor waned.

Flynn looked at his watch. It was a few minutes before nine. He rubbed his eyes and rolled over and looked out across the room. Scattered across the floor were a red dress and several items of women's underwear, as well as his own clothing. He tensed for a second but then relaxed as he spotted his rucksack on a chair, the fastening still closed. But something was missing. It took him a moment to realize what it was. When he did, panic seized him.

He threw back the covers and jumped out of bed. Scrambled across the floor on hands and knees, wildly throwing clothes aside. He searched under the bed. Nothing. Crossing the room, he flung open the sliding doors and looked around the kitchen, the only other room in the apartment not counting the bathroom. Only then did he notice the small sunken area by the front door. There, next to a pair of red high heels, were his own black shoes, neatly arranged. He knelt down and picked up the right shoe and looked inside. Nestled in the bottom was the wad of banknotes. Relieved, he removed the money and went through to the bedroom and stuffed it into one of the side pockets of his bag.

After using the bathroom, he found his boxers and T-shirt, put them on and went back into the kitchen. He turned on the faucet and splashed water on his face and put his head down and drank until he could drink no more. Back in the bedroom, he unbuckled his rucksack and took out the change of clothing. Slacks, a short-sleeved shirt, a light jacket. Once he was dressed, he picked up his white navy uniform and stuffed it into the rucksack.

He looked across at the bargirl, who was still asleep. Naomi. Yes, that was her name. He tried again to remember last night's events. But everything from around the moment she sat next to him for the second time was a blank. How did he get from the bar to Naomi's apartment, if that was in fact where he was? What, if anything, happened afterward?

Removing the wad of money from the rucksack's side pocket, Flynn pulled out a ten-dollar note and walked over and placed it on the small wooden table beside the bed. He shoved the remaining money into his front trouser pocket, shouldered the bag, and turned and headed to the front door. As he was passing the kitchen he noticed a small refrigerator and stopped. Inside he found a loaf of sliced bread in a plastic bag and a packet of wiener sausages. He took the bread and sausages and put them in his bag.

The door opened onto the second-floor balcony of a run-down apartment block in a residential neighborhood. Never having strayed more than a few hundred yards from the Navy base, Flynn had no idea where in Yokosuka he was.

At one end of the balcony was a set of stairs. He descended them and found himself on a narrow, unpaved street lined with houses and cheap-looking apartment buildings. To the left the street went uphill. To the right it went downhill. He turned right.

After walking for a few minutes, he decided it was too warm for his jacket, so he stopped and took it off. He unbuckled his rucksack, pulled out his white Navy uniform and stuffed the jacket inside. He rolled the uniform into a tight bundle and walked over to the side of the road and rammed it into a culvert before quickly continuing down the hill.

Soon Flynn came to a busy four-lane highway, which he assumed was Route 16. He turned right and continued walking. He passed several people coming the other way, ignoring them until he saw an old Japanese man approaching. When the man drew near he asked, "Which way to U.S. Navy?"

The man tilted his head to one side, his brows knitted.

"U.S. Navy base," Flynn repeated, louder this time. "Which way?"

The man seemed to understand now. He said something in Japanese and pointed in the direction Flynn had come from.

"How far?" Flynn asked.

"Hmm, one mile," the man said, holding up one finger.

Flynn thanked him and set off in the opposite direction, the same way he had been heading. Behind him he heard the man say, "No, no, no," but he ignored him and increased his pace, keen to put as much distance between himself and the base as possible.

He walked for another mile or so before stopping by the side of the road. From the information the man had provided, Flynn concluded that he was indeed on Route 16, some two miles east of the base by now. He tried to visualize a map of the surrounding area. He knew that Yokosuka was on the eastern side of the Miura Peninsula. Flynn calculated that if he continued walking east he would reach the end of the peninsula in a couple of hours. Alternatively, if he turned around and followed Route 16 in the opposite direction, he would not only have to pass the Navy base at Yokosuka, but eventually he would reach Yokohama, where there was an equally heavy American military presence. There were other U.S. military bases west of Tokyo, including the Air Force bases at Tachikawa and Yokota, the Navy air base at Atsugi, and the Army base at Camp Zama, but these were many miles north of his present position, and so were of no immediate concern.

After thinking for a few minutes, he decided the best course of action would be to leave Route 16 and head south, crossing the peninsula before doubling back and heading west along the coast to Kamakura. An advantage of this plan was that Kamakura was a popular tourist destination, meaning he wouldn't stick out as a foreigner. He thought it would take him a full day to reach Kamakura. There was every possibility that he would bump into MPs or local police along the way, but given that he wouldn't be reported AWOL until later in the day at the earliest, there was only a slim chance they would be on the lookout for him. It was a chance he was willing to take.

Half an hour after leaving Route 16, Flynn bade farewell to Yokosuka and began ascending the hilly backbone of the Miura Peninsula. Not since boot camp had he pushed himself so hard, and his legs soon began to ache. He also felt blisters forming on the soles of his feet. His Navy issue shoes, the only part of his uniform he had kept, were fine for Navy work, which largely involved standing around and walking short distances, but were clearly unfit for the kind of long distances he planned to cover in the days ahead, and he regretted not buying a pair of hiking boots before making his getaway.

Despite these misgivings, he was in a far more positive frame of mind than he had been in for weeks. The road he was now following was relatively quiet, and for increasingly long spells the only sounds he could hear were natural sounds: water rushing along the narrow irrigation channel beside the road, birds and insects in the trees around him, frogs in the rice paddies, his own labored breathing. The effects of his hangover still lingered, however, and he had to stop several times to drink from the channel by the side of the road, bending over and scooping up water with both hands as he had done as a child.

Just after noon the road flattened out. Confident that the worst of the climb was behind him, Flynn decided to stop for lunch. He left the road and found a patch of grass out of sight of any passersby, unshouldered his rucksack and sat down. He took out the bread and wiener sausages and, using his lap as a makeshift table, balanced two of the tiny sausages end to end on a slice of bread and rolled the bread up to make a hot dog. He took a bite. It could have done with ketchup and mustard, but having walked what must have been well over five miles on an empty stomach, his body was grateful for what sustenance it could get, and he wolfed down two more of the "hot dogs" before placing the remaining bread and wiener sausages back in his rucksack. He stood up, brushed off the crumbs that still clung to his trousers, picked up his bag, and rejoined the road.

The road undulated for a mile or two before descending toward the town of Hayama on the western side of the peninsula. Flynn's thighs still ached from the ascent, but the climb down through the valley past stands of pine trees and bamboo, terraced rice fields, and the occasional wooden farmhouse was far less taxing on his body, and he made good progress. His feet made loud slapping noises as they struck the pavement, the beat at times frenetic as he broke into a jog-trot on the steepest parts of the descent.

The terrain became flatter, and soon he was in Hayama. The main road turned inland after passing the town, so Flynn left it and followed a side road down to the waterfront. All he had to do now was follow the road along the coast a few miles and he would be in Kamakura.

Not long afterward he got his first glimpse of Yuigahama Beach. Apart from the odd rambler and beachcomber it was deserted. The tide was out, and the vast expanse of dark sand beckoned Flynn. But he was exhausted from his traverse of the peninsula and it was nearly dusk, and so he pressed on, eager to find somewhere to eat and a place to spend the night.

On a side road near the northern end of the beach he came across a small cluster of restaurants. He spurned those offering Japanese food, eventually choosing a place called Sea Castle that professed to serve German cuisine. The menu included bratwurst and sauerbraten, but also more familiar fare, such as fried chicken and pork chops. Flynn ordered roast beef and a tuna fish sandwich, which he washed down with several glasses of beer. As he was leaving he asked the proprietor for directions to the nearest accommodation. A few minutes later he stood in his socks in the reception area at the Kamakura Hotel, where he agreed to a price of twelve hundred yen for a Japanese-style room without meals. When the kimonoed receptionist asked him how long he intended to stay, Flynn told the truth and said he didn't know.

He was shown to his room by a maid, who returned a short while later to inform him it was time for him to take a bath. He wandered through the hotel's maze of corridors before eventually finding the bathroom. After washing himself, he stepped gingerly into the deep wooden bathtub. The water was so hot it was uncomfortable at first, but as he got used to it he relaxed, and before long he felt the aches in his legs and the tension in his shoulders wane. Flynn returned to his room to find the futon had been removed from the closet and laid out on the *tatami* floor. He slipped under the covers and within minutes was fast asleep.

CHAPTER 7

The morning after their rendezvous at the construction site, Yumi left Harper alone in her apartment to phone Beheiren. When she got back she told him they had agreed to help him, and that the two of them were instructed to go the following afternoon to a restaurant near Tokyo Station, where someone from the organization would be waiting for them. From there Harper would be taken to a safe house. Yumi then went to work, leaving Harper alone in the apartment.

It took him less than half an hour to pack. He first set aside the clothes he would wear the following day, including a jacket, tie, overcoat, and the fedora he had bought at Honmoku. Then, in a cream overnight bag Yumi had given him, he put a spare pair of trousers, a spare shirt, underwear, socks, and some toiletries. The rest of his clothes, including his utilities, he folded neatly and left in a corner of the room. Later he would tell Yumi to burn them.

He had intended to spend the rest of the day reading a spy novel he had been given by a fellow patient at Kishine. But he found it impossible to concentrate and after realizing he had read the same passage three times, he set the book down and stretched out on the floor. He looked around the room, and was suddenly struck with the foreignness of the *tatami* and the paper room dividers. Not for the first time he felt the urge to pinch himself to make sure it wasn't all a weird dream. It didn't help that for much of the time between his getting wounded and his arriving in Japan he had been pumped full of morphine.

Of the events immediately following the mortar attack he recalled very little. He remembered the first two mortar shells landing and crawling down to check on the stricken Marines, but then there was a blank. The next thing he remembered was pain. It coursed through his entire body. And darkness. He tried to move but couldn't. And then he heard voices. Rhodes telling him to hold on. Telling him he was going to be all right. Someone slapping bandages on his legs. A stab in his upper arm as someone administered a syrette of morphine. And then nothing.

When he regained consciousness he was in a bed. A real bed with white sheets and a proper pillow. A beautiful, round-eyed maiden in a white dress and white hat was bending over him, touching him. For a moment he thought he had died and gone to heaven. And then the pain hit him and he knew he wasn't in paradise.

The nurse told him he was on a hospital ship called the *Respite*. It seemed just like a normal hospital, except that all the patients were in narrow, bunk-style, two-tiered beds. After a while the doctors came around. They told him he had serious tissue damage in his legs from the shrapnel, but that he would be able to walk again. He asked what had happened to the other members of his patrol. They told him that three Marines had been medevaced out with him that day. A corpsman with serious shrapnel wounds like Harper, who had pulled through. A radioman with leg injuries. The surgeons had done their best to save him, but he had died an hour after they got him off the operating table. And a lieutenant with minor shrapnel wounds, who was expected to make a full recovery. The goddamn greenhorn glory-seeker, thought Harper.

At first he was bandaged all over from neck to foot like a mummy, but later they dressed just his legs and a few places on his arms and back. They cleaned his wounds and changed the bandages once a day, and though they gave him morphine whenever they worked on him, the pain was almost unbearable. He kept reminding himself he was lucky. At least he still had his legs.

After four days on the *Respite*, Harper was choppered to the Naval Support Activity Hospital at Da Nang, and after two days there he was transferred to the 12th U.S. Air Force Hospital at Cam Ranh Bay. Each time they shifted him they gave him another shot of morphine, so he remembered very little about moving from one hospital to the next.

At Cam Ranh Bay the painful routine of cleaning his wounds and applying fresh bandages continued. He still couldn't move his legs. The pain eventually subsided. But as the soreness left him, the boredom set in. One of the few sources of relief was a television, on which Harper and the other patients in his ward watched American shows and sports, but without the commercials. Maybe he really *was* in heaven.

Things at the 12th U.S. Air Force Hospital stuck to a fairly predictable routine, so Harper was surprised one morning just before Christmas to see people in the ward scrubbing floors and walls and shifting beds about. Patients were being moved out of Harper's ward and new ones moved in. Harper waited until all the action had died down before asking one of the nurses what the fuss was all about. She was his favorite nurse, a sister from Memphis who seemed to have a soft spot for him and went out of her way to make sure he was comfortable.

"We've got a very important visitor coming this morning," she said.

"An important visitor? At this time of year, that could mean only one person."

"Come on, now. Don't tell me a big grown-up boy like you still believes in Santa Claus."

"What, you mean Santa Claus isn't real? Next you'll be telling me the Tooth Fairy doesn't exist."

She laughed, the whiteness of her teeth accentuated by the ebony of her face. "We're under strict instructions not to divulge his identity."

"Goddamn, he must be real important. Some top brass dude. It's not General Westmoreland, is it?"

"I told you," she said, running the tips of her thumb and forefinger across her mouth, "my lips are sealed."

"Goddamn, it *is* General Westmoreland, I know it."

She laughed again. "What I *can* say is the person who's coming has a little present for you. It seems that lieutenant whose ass you saved recommended you for a medal."

The lieutenant. Hell, Harper thought, maybe that greenhorn glory-seeker wasn't so bad after all.

Harper was woken by a commotion at the entrance to the ward.

Moments later, the room was filled with newspaper reporters and photographers and doctors and nurses, all rushing to take up their positions. Then a figure in dark trousers and a khaki short-sleeve shirt, his graying hair trimmed short and slicked back, swept into the room accompanied by a gaggle of generals and aides. Harper pinched his arm to make sure he wasn't dreaming. Still he couldn't believe his own eyes. It was his commander in chief, President Lyndon B. Johnson. LBJ himself.

Harper watched as the president made his way down the aisle, stopping to shake hands and chat briefly with each patient. The wounded soldiers smiled from ear to ear as LBJ approached, but Harper was determined to stay cool. After all, this was the guy who got everyone in this mess in the first place. It was Johnson who had overturned Kennedy's decision to withdraw soldiers from Vietnam and instead escalated the war, eventually ordering the full-scale commitment of ground troops in 1965. And weren't there some questions about LBJ's own military service during World War II? Harper had read somewhere that he had been awarded a Silver Star for his role in a bombing mission in New Guinea, despite records showing he was just an observer on the plane, little more than a tourist, and doubts over whether the plane even reached the target. Even the official citation was lukewarm, declaring that LBJ evidenced "marked coolness in spite of the hazards involved." Shit, if Harper got a medal every time he had evidenced "marked coolness" he would struggle to stand under the weight. But then LBJ was an officer, and everyone knew that it was different for officers, that they all recommended themselves for medals to boost their careers. And the higher the rank, the worse it got. So while the enlisted men ended up in hospitals and body bags, the officers got decorated.

And then there he was, the commander in chief, right beside Harper's bed. He was taller than he expected. LBJ bent over Harper and took his hand. Harper looked up at his face, and was surprised to see what appeared to be a look of genuine concern.

At the foot of the bed, the newspaper reporters and cameramen jostled for the best positions, settling into a roughly semicircular formation. Camera flashes went off and shutters clicked as an aide picked up a sign hanging from the end of Harper's bed and announced, "Lance Corporal James Earle Harper, Redville, Mississippi."

The aide continued to read the details of the citation, but Harper wasn't listening. He was still pondering the absurdity of the situation he found himself in, lying in a hospital bed in the Nam surrounded by newsmen with the President of the United States holding his hand.

When the aide finished speaking, LBJ looked at Harper and said, "How are you doing, Son?"

"I'm doing fine, Sir," Harper lied.

"That's the attitude! Tell me, where are you from, Son?"

"Redville, Mississippi, Sir."

"Ah, Mississippi. The Magnolia State. Well, I'm sure everyone back in Mississippi is wishing you a speedy recovery."

"Thank you, Sir. It's nice of you to say so, Sir."

The small talk over, it was time for Harper to be presented with his medals: a Bronze Star and a Purple Heart. After pinning the medals to his gown, LBJ shook Harper's hand and smiled and motioned to a Vietnamese man standing next to him whom Harper hadn't noticed until now. The man had a neatly trimmed mustache and was dressed impeccably in an expensive-looking charcoal gray suit, white shirt, gray tie, the works. In fact, Harper couldn't recall seeing anyone dressed so sharply since he had left the States.

"I'd like you to meet Marshall Ky of the Republic of South Vietnam," LBJ said.

So this was the notorious Air Marshall Ky, thought Harper. Ky was a leading figure in the junta that had ruled the country since 1964. Formerly prime minister and now vice president, Ky was not only despised by the locals, who heckled him on the rare occasions when he appeared in public, but mistrusted by personnel at all levels of the U.S. military.

Ky leaned over and shook Harper's hand. "Thank you," he said. "We all appreciate your sacrifice."

Harper had a few things he wanted so say to the vice president, including that he resented getting his ass shot-up to keep him and his corrupt buddies in power, but with his commander in chief by his side and several other top brass (including General Westmoreland, who seemed to be keeping a low profile) in the room, he thought it wise to keep his thoughts to himself, and so he simply nodded.

And then, as abruptly as they had appeared, LBJ and his entourage swept out of the ward. Only when they had gone did Harper notice that someone had stuck a handwritten sign on the wall opposite his bed. It read simply MERRY CHRISTMAS. A few minutes later Harper drifted off to sleep. He dreamed of Santa Claus. Except the Santa Claus in his dream was beardless and wore not a red suit but dark trousers and a khaki shirt.

It was early in the New Year when he was wheeled out onto the air strip next to the 12th U.S. Air Force Hospital at Cam Ranh Bay, strapped to a stretcher and slotted into a rack inside the belly of a waiting C-141 Starlifter. The aircraft could accommodate up to eighty wounded in stretchers stacked three high, and it was filled to capacity that evening. On the return flight from Japan it would carry supplies and reinforcements back to Cam Ranh Bay, fresh meat for the grinder.

Just under five hours after taking off, the Starlifter landed and taxied to the casualty staging facility at Yokota Air Base, west of Tokyo. It had been cool during the flight, so cool that Harper had to ask for a blanket but, even so, the rush of cold air that swept through the aircraft as the massive cargo doors at the back opened was a shock, and Harper clutched the blanket tightly to his shoulders as he was carried out, still strapped to his stretcher. He had been moved about so many times in the last month he was often uncertain where he was, but if there was one thing he was sure of now, it was that he was no longer in the Nam. He was back in the World.

Together with three other patients from the same flight, Harper was transferred to one of several waiting UH-1D Huey helicopter ambulances. It was still early in the morning, and as the Huey gained altitude, one of the Army medics onboard motioned out one of the large windows on the right side of the aircraft.

"Welcome to the Land of the Rising Sun, gentlemen," he shouted, his voice barely audible above the drone of the engine.

Though he still found it difficult to sit up, Harper strained to look out the window, where, under a clear blue sky, he saw the almost perfectly symmetrical cone of Mount Fuji, its snow-encrusted slopes colored an ethereal orangey pink by the early morning sun.

Minutes later the Huey began to descend. It cleared a tangle of high-tension wires and swooped down and landed on a tiny helipad surrounded by gray buildings, most of them four stories tall, the nearest of them so close Harper swore he could have reached out and touched their cinder-block facades. The big side door of the Huey slid open and Harper's stretcher was passed into the hands of four medics in white uniforms with Army-issue olive green field jackets over the top to protect them from the cold. They carried him to the reception area, their varied gaits causing his body to bob like an apple in a tub at Halloween. Along the way they passed a sign that read: KISHINE BARRACKS, 106th UNITED STATES ARMY HOSPITAL, UNITED STATES ARMY, JAPAN. When they stopped, another figure appeared by his side and proceeded to leaf through his medical records.

"Marine?"

Harper looked up at the doctor, noticing the raised eyebrow. "Yeah," he said. "Is that a problem?"

"No," the doctor replied. "It's just that we don't see many Marines here. You guys being so tough and all."

Before Harper could think of a suitably sarcastic response, the doctor was called away to tend to another casualty who had flown in on the same chopper. Harper couldn't see who was talking, but he figured it was one of the medics.

"Burns to forty percent of his body, major. Plus he's got a head injury. An AK round. It went in near his right eye and came out near the left temple. Blew away the left side of his head."

"Okay. Get him up to Neurosurgery right away. We can deal with the burns up there."

"Shall I put in an IV?"

"No, send him straight up."

Hearing this made Harper feel lucky. He later learned the kid was carrying detonators in his rucksack when he was hit. They blew up, setting him ablaze.

Harper was eventually loaded onto a gurney and wheeled into a building and down a corridor to an elevator. As they were waiting for the car to arrive, Harper asked the medic, "That kid, is he going to make it?"

"As long as he makes it through the neurosurgery he should be fine," the medic replied. "Burns always look a lot worse than they are. Major Simpson, the doctor who saw him, is the chief of the Burn Unit, so the kid's in capable hands."

"The Burn Unit?"

"Yep. Serves the whole of the Far East. We get sent patients from all over. That squid in the Philippines who singes himself on a barbecue? He ends up here."

The elevator car arrived and the medic wheeled Harper in and pressed a button.

Harper said, "But most of your patients come direct from the Nam, right?"

"Yep. Up to forty a day. They come in at all hours. If the choppers come in at night we just bring out the fire truck and whatever other vehicles are available and use their headlights to light up the chopper pad. We treat around a thousand patients a month."

"Where do they go after they leave here?" Harper asked.

The elevator stopped and when the doors opened the medic wheeled Harper out into a corridor.

"Home," the medic said, "or back to Vietnam."

Home for me, thought Harper. Oh please, let it be home.

CHAPTER 8

Masuda waited until noon the following day to reveal to his colleagues that there might be a cold-blooded killer in their midst. They were in a restaurant by the side of the Meishin Expressway, around half an hour into the three-hour drive from Nagoya to Nara. Sakurai reacted with horror, but Ōe's face showed no emotion. After a brief discussion, Ōe suggested they keep the matter of Roberts having stabbed and possibly killed an MP in Yokosuka to themselves for the time being. Masuda and Sakurai agreed, and nothing more was said about it for the remainder of the journey.

This still left the problem of Santiago's medical condition. Toward the end of the meal, Ōe slipped away to phone Shunsuke Tsurumi at Doshisha University. When he returned he summarized the conversation for the benefit of Masuda and Sakurai. Immediately upon their arrival in Nara, Ōe and Sakurai would drive Santiago to Tsurumi's house in Kyoto where a doctor would examine him. The results of the examination would determine what they would do next.

Two and a half hours later, Ōe brought the rental car to a stop in front of Musubi no Ie and cut the engine. Located in Nara's western suburbs, the unassuming two-story guesthouse looked completely at home in the leafy residential neighborhood. As they got out of the vehicle, the double-glass doors swung open and a middle-aged couple emerged. The man introduced himself as Kimura and the woman standing behind him, who bowed demurely, as his wife. Together, Kimura explained, they ran Musubi no Ie.

Although the Kimuras knew the three Americans were deserters, a cover story had been concocted to hide their true identity from the other guests. If asked, they were to explain that the three were exchange students from the U.S. Ōe had informed the Americans of this before they arrived. He had also emphasized how important it was for them to keep a low profile during their stay, although based on their record to date, Masuda suspected Ōe, like himself, held out little hope of these instructions being followed.

No sooner had they been shown to their rooms than Ōe and Sakurai were off again, wishing Masuda luck before bundling Santiago into the rental car and setting off for Tsurumi's house in Kyoto, some twenty-five miles north of their present location. Masuda spent the rest of the afternoon relaxing in his room, but he grew increasingly nervous as dinnertime approached. All the guests ate together in a communal dining room, so if anything were to go wrong during the meal the consequences could be disastrous. He needn't have worried, however. Roberts and Sullivan hardly spoke throughout the meal, and no one at their table paid them much attention. Later, as Masuda got ready for bed, he realized that it was probably because Santiago was absent.

It was late the next afternoon before Ōe, Sakurai, and Santiago returned from Kyoto. Masuda heard the rental car pull up and went outside to greet them. Santiago was the first to get out. He barely responded when Masuda asked him how it went, scratching his crotch and mumbling "okay" before sidling past him and straight up to his room. Masuda turned his attention to Ōe and Sakurai, who had been standing in front of the vehicle during this brief exchange.

"Well?"

"He'll be fine," Ōe said. "It's gonorrhea. Nothing a dose of penicillin won't cure."

"You got some, then?"

"Not without some difficulty," Ōe said, glancing over at Sakurai.

"The doctor who saw him at Tsurumi's house wouldn't write a prescription," Sakurai said. "So the two of us spent this morning going around pharmacies trying to find someone who'd give us the penicillin without one."

"In the end it was just a matter of coming up with the right story," Ōe continued. "At the last pharmacy we went to, Sakurai explained that we were visiting from out of town, and that she had lost the penicillin her doctor in Tokyo had prescribed. I'm not sure if the pharmacist really believed us, or if he just took pity on us, but after asking something about allergies he went out the back and returned with what we needed."

"He needs to take it every day until it runs out," Sakurai said. "We've stressed to him that he mustn't stop taking it even if the symptoms disappear, but it might pay to remind him occasionally."

"Understood," Masuda said.

"By the way," Sakurai said, "Tsurumi would like to see you tomorrow."

"Tsurumi?" Masuda said, surprised. "Tsurumi wants to see *me?*"

"Yes. He has something he wants to give you. You're to meet him in front of Kyoto Station at three in the afternoon."

In his gray jacket and gray trousers and with his brown leather satchel slung over his shoulder, Shunsuke Tsurumi looked as nondescript as the scores of businessmen shuffling past the entrance to Kyoto Station, and it wasn't until he had approached within a few yards and signaled to him by raising one arm that Masuda recognized the Beheiren co-founder.

"Sorry to keep you waiting," Tsurumi said.

"Not at all," Masuda replied.

"Let's go then, shall we?"

And with this, Tsurumi promptly turned and headed off in the direction from which he had come. Masuda followed.

The older man walked quickly, maintaining a gap of a yard or two between himself and Masuda, turning his head occasionally to make some remark or ask a question but giving Masuda little opportunity to reply. When they came to the streetcar terminal on the far side of the station square, Tsurumi pointed to one of the streetcars and they boarded it together and found seats at the back.

Seconds later the streetcar lurched forward and soon they were traveling north along Karasuma-dōri, the enormous wooden structure of Higashi Hongan-ji temple coming into view on their left. Masuda had visited Kyoto as a high school student and was familiar with its geography and its history. Unlike Tokyo, central Kyoto was flat and laid out in a regular grid pattern, as had been the city's predecessor, Heian-kyō, which was modeled on the Tang capital of

Chang'an and served as the nation's capital from 794. Heian-kyō had been surrounded by walls on all four sides, with entry and exit gained through a series of gates. The largest of these gates, Rashōmon, was just to the south near where Kyoto Station now stood, although nothing of it remained today. The fact that most of the streets in central Kyoto still ran either north-south or east-west made it relatively easy for visitors to find their way around, with the mountain ranges to the east, north, and west serving as landmarks in the unlikely event that they did lose their bearings.

Masuda knew better than to mention the deserters on the crowded streetcar, and so other than responding to the occasional question from Tsurumi he remained silent for the entire ride, which took them north past Doshisha University to Kita-Ōji-dōri, and then west as far as Daitoku-ji temple.

As soon as they got off the streetcar Tsurumi was off again, crossing the road and leading Masuda up a side street with the mud wall of the temple compound on their left. Soon they came to a large wooden gate, which they passed through into the temple grounds.

Inside the complex it was as if they had been transported back in time. Gone were the ugly concrete buildings and utility poles sprouting tangles of electricity and telephone wires that blighted Kyoto, replaced by ancient wooden structures and trees that, together with the mud walls, shut out the traffic noise from outside and reduced the temperature by several degrees. A column of monks in black robes and conical hats stopped by the side of the path and bowed their heads as Tsurumi and Masuda passed.

As they continued on, Tsurumi explained to Masuda the history of Daitoku-ji. Founded in the early fourteenth century as a small Zen monastery, its fortunes rose and fell over the following centuries, as did those of most temples and monasteries in Kyoto. This was especially true during the Ōnin War of 1467 to 1477, when Heian-kyō was the scene of intense fighting among rival warrior clans sparked by a dispute over who would succeed Yoshimasa Ashikaga as Shogun. Daitoku-ji benefited in particular from the patronage of a number of powerful warlords, including Nobunaga Oda and Hideyoshi Toyotomi, as well as from its association with the legendary tea master Sen no Rikyū. Eventually Daitoku-ji grew into a sprawling complex covering some fifty-seven acres and including more than twenty sub-temples and gardens in addition to the main buildings, which included a Buddha hall, a Dharma hall, and the abbot's quarters.

Presently Tsurumi and Masuda came to a compact, single-storied wooden building in a shaded corner of the compound. They climbed the steps to the entrance where they removed their shoes before announcing their arrival. Moments later the sliding door opened to reveal a figure dressed in *samue*. It came as no surprise to Masuda to be greeted by someone wearing the cotton work clothes favored by Buddhist clergy, consisting of simple trousers and a wrap-around top, both made from the same traditional indigo fabric. What did surprise him, though, was that the man was a Westerner.

After an exchange of pleasantries in Japanese, Tsurumi and Masuda were ushered into the building and through a small room with *tatami* flooring to an almost identical room, where a Japanese man sat cross-legged at a low wooden table. The room was sparsely furnished and almost totally devoid of ornamentation. In fact the only decorative elements were an *ikebana* arrangement and a hanging scroll in the *tokonoma* at the far end of the room. As he sat down at the table next to Tsurumi, Masuda strained to make out the calligraphy on the scroll, which was written in the flowing *sōsho* style.

"*Cha zen ichimi*," the Westerner said. "The way of tea and Zen are the same."

Masuda looked across the table at the Westerner. "Yes, of course," he said, embarrassed at not having recognized the famous phrase, and at having it explained to him by a foreigner.

"Masuda-kun," Tsurumi said, "allow me to introduce Gary Snyder."

"Pleased to meet you," the Westerner said.

Masuda regarded Snyder, who had sat down next to the other man on the far side of the table. Masuda guessed he was in his late thirties. He sat with his legs crossed and his back ramrod straight, the posture of someone who regularly practiced Zen meditation. Aside from this and his clothing, however, his appearance could not have been further from the stereotypical image of a Buddhist clergyman. His wavy hair brushed the collar of his *samue* and completely covered his ears, and he had a neatly trimmed beard, a rarity among Japanese in any line of work, let alone the clerically inclined. His face was tanned and creased, more indicative of a life outdoors than one cloistered in a place of prayer. But the thing Masuda noticed above all was his eyes, which radiated both warmth and a peculiar intensity, as if Snyder were looking into Masuda's soul.

"And next to him—" Tsurumi motioned to the Japanese man sitting next to Snyder "—is Kazuma Hattori."

"Please," Hattori said, smiling broadly, "call me Pran."

"Pran?" Masuda said.

"It's Sanskrit."

Pran was a few years older than Snyder and considerably shorter, the difference in height obvious even as the two men sat cross-legged at the table. But the Japanese man looked stronger, his forearms tanned and sinewy from regular outdoor physical activity of some kind. His hair was even longer than Snyder's and looked somewhat unkempt. Like Snyder he sported a beard, but unlike Snyder's it was long and wispy, which combined with his short stature gave him the appearance of a mountain goat.

"Would the two of you care for some tea?" Snyder asked. "We only have barley tea, I'm afraid."

"Yes, thank you," Masuda said.

Tsurumi, too, nodded his assent, and Snyder poured two glasses of cold tea from a pitcher and passed them over to his guests.

Snyder sat back and took a sip of the tea and looked across at Masuda and said, "You're probably wondering what we're doing here."

Masuda smiled.

"As you can probably tell from my appearance—" Snyder raised his arm and indicated his hair with on open hand "—I'm not a practicing member of the clergy, although I have studied Zen as a layman, here at Daitoku-ji as well as at another Zen temple, Shōkoku-ji. These days I spend less and less time in Kyoto, but when I do visit, the abbot is kind enough to allow me to stay here."

"Your Japanese is fluent," Masuda said.

"Thank you, but I'm nowhere near fluent. I studied written Japanese and Chinese when I was a graduate student at Berkeley, but it wasn't until I came to Kyoto in 1956 to study Zen that I made any real progress with the spoken language."

"1956? There can't have been many Westerners studying Zen at that time?"

"No, there weren't many." As he spoke, Snyder played with his beard, twisting tufts of it between the thumb and forefinger of his right hand. "Most of us were involved with the First Zen Institute of America, one of the first centers for Westerners studying Zen in Japan, which was established here at Daitoku-ji by Ruth Fuller Sasaki. Aside from studying Zen and helping other Western students of the faith, Sasaki's main focus was on preparing for publication the writings of her late husband, the Zen master Sasaki Sokei-an. A part of this work involved translating the Chinese Zen classic *Lin-chi Lu* into English. Unfortunately, Mrs. Fuller Sasaki passed away last year before the translation could be completed. Having been part of the original team that worked on the translation in the 1950s, I was asked to help complete the job. At the same time I've been helping the Tribe establish a commune on Suwanosejima, which I believe is what brings you here today."

"So I believe," Masuda said, glancing across at Tsurumi. "But I'm curious as to the link between your Zen studies and your involvement with the Tribe."

"The link is Pran here," Snyder said, gesturing to the man sitting next to him. "Pran is a man of many talents, but it was as a poet that I first came to know him. In 1961 I traveled from Japan to India, and on the ship was an Australian writer who showed me a book of Pran's poems that had been translated into English. He suggested I get in touch with Pran when I returned to Japan. We eventually met in 1963, when Allen was staying with me here in Kyoto."

"Allen?" Masuda said.

"Allen Ginsberg."

"Allen Ginsberg? The poet?"

"Gary himself is a poet of some renown," Tsurumi said. "He counts among his friends not only Mr. Ginsberg but also Mr. Kerouac."

"Jack Kerouac? *The* Jack Kerouac?"

Tsurumi smiled. "Gary was the inspiration for Japhy Ryder, the main character in Kerouac's novel *The Dharma Bums*. Isn't that right, Gary?"

"I hardly think 'inspiration' is the right word," Snyder said, grinning. "And Jack certainly employed a good deal of poetic license in his depiction of me. But yes, Allen and Jack are good friends of mine. Although having been brought up a farm boy surrounded by chickens and cows, and being so passionate about the outdoors, I always felt like I was the odd man out among the Beats, most of whom were city folk from New York."

"Gary read one of his poems at the famous Six Gallery reading in San Francisco in 1955," Tsurumi said. "That was the meeting where Allen gave the first ever recital of his epic poem 'Howl.'"

Masuda nodded and looked across the table at Snyder, feeling a new sense of reverence for the unassuming Westerner in monks' clothing.

"Anyway," Snyder said, eager to get back to the subject at hand, it seemed, "Pran and I soon found we had many interests in common besides poetry, including anarchism and Vajyarana Buddhism. Pran was living in Tokyo's Shinjuku district at the time, and he began to attract some young Japanese followers who coalesced into a group called the Bum Academy. Members of the group later set up a commune on a plot of rural land in Nagano Prefecture, at which point they adopted the name the Tribe."

"So why the move to Suwanosejima?" Masuda asked.

"Pran first heard about Suwanosejima several years ago when he was traveling through the islands between Kyushu and Okinawa. He arranged to be taken there through an acquaintance in Kagoshima, and ended up staying a week in the home of one of the islanders. He was so impressed he later suggested to the other Tribe members that they set up a commune there. Pran and a few others went down to the island in May last year and started building an ashram. I went down for the first time two months later, in July."

"So will you be traveling with us this time?" Masuda asked.

"No. Unfortunately I have other business to attend to in Tokyo."

"Gary's wife has recently given birth to their first child," Tsurumi said.

"Oh. Congratulations," Masuda said.

"Thank you," Snyder said, smiling warmly. "Anyway, Pran here will be accompanying you on the ferry from Kagoshima."

Pran, who had been listening intently to the conversation, took the mention of his name as a cue to join in. "A group of us are meeting up in Kagoshima and catching the ferry on Friday. So it makes sense for you and your—" he paused, trying to think of the right word "—your 'guests' to rendezvous with us then."

Masuda turned to Tsurumi, a look of concern on his face. "Friday. That's four days away."

"Plenty of time, then," Tsurumi replied matter-of-factly.

"I understand they've been a bit difficult," Snyder said.

Masuda glanced at Tsurumi, who nodded to indicate that they could discuss the deserters in confidence in front of Snyder and Pran.

"They've been a handful right from the beginning. I've only been with them for the last two days, but in that time we've learned that one of them has gonorrhea, probably the result of an encounter with a prostitute in Yokosuka after he deserted, and that another stabbed and possibly killed a man, an American MP, in Yokohama."

Masuda looked at Snyder and Pran, expecting them to react with surprise at this news, but neither of them showed any emotion. Masuda concluded from this that they already knew, and that the person who had told them was sitting beside him.

"But what concerns me the most," Masuda continued, "is that they appear to lack any genuine anti-war sentiment. One even wrote that he enjoyed killing the Vietnamese."

Snyder, who had been looking down at the table as Masuda offered these last comments, looked up. His smile had disappeared, replaced by a look of concern.

"The thing you have to remember," the American said, "is that they're still very young. I think Shunsuke said they were eighteen and nineteen? So they're barely out of high school. At that age, they're not prepared for the things they're put through, starting with basic training, where they're stripped of their individuality and any values they may have learned at home, and taught to follow orders and kill. That's even before they reach Vietnam, where they face situations even a grown man should never have to face. Sure, they may have made mistakes, but in a sense they're just as much victims of this war as the Vietnamese."

"One thing some of the younger Japanese involved in Beheiren fail to appreciate," Tsurumi said, "is the courage it takes to even speak out against a war one's country is directly involved in, let alone take some kind of action. Such is the hold the state has over us that to do so is regarded as unpatriotic. Many of us who lived through the last war will always regret that we didn't do more to oppose it. So perhaps we're compensating by doing as much as we can this time. If that means forgiving the transgressions of some of those we're helping in order to further the anti-war cause, then that's a price we're prepared to pay."

"One of the things that attracted me to the Tribe," Snyder said, "is that its members are exploring alternatives to the state, and to the nuclear family, which has to be the most barren family unit that has ever existed, and has proved ineffectual as a counterweight to the excesses of the state, patriotism included. Another thing that attracted me is that, unlike many of the so-called hippies in America, who come from privileged, middle-class backgrounds and are secure in the knowledge they can always run back to their families when things get too difficult, the members of the Tribe know that by making the decision to live the way they do they are in all likelihood cutting themselves off from their families forever. They've all had to learn how to survive on their own at the bottom of society, and now they've come together to share their knowledge and skills and live cooperatively as a tribe, with none of the materialistic drive of the outside world."

Masuda nodded. Listening to Snyder and Tsurumi speak, it was clear to him they had discussed these matters in some depth. He wondered about the nature of the relationship between the two men. Turning to Snyder, he said, "Tell me, how was it the two of you became friends? As far as I know, Tsurumi is neither a Buddhist nor a hippie."

"Ah," Snyder said, "but he *is* a seeker after truth."

Tsurumi chuckled at this remark.

"Since I was a young man," Snyder continued, "I've been

interested in social justice. At Reed College in Oregon I identified as a radical, but I had what some might call individualist-bohemian tendencies, which didn't endear me to the other radicals, most of whom were communists. Ironically, I was probably the only real proletarian among them. Anyway, while the other radical students were studying Marx, I was reading the work of the Russian anarchist Kropotkin. I was also inspired by the Industrial Workers of the World, or the Wobblies as we called them. They were a radical union that had a strong following among the lumberjacks and other forestry workers in the Pacific Northwest, including in Washington and Oregon where I grew up and went to college.

"Given my interest in social justice and my involvement in the literary scene, when I came to Japan in 1956, as well as studying Zen I made a point of seeking out like-minded radicals, poets, and artists. Unfortunately, the artists and poets were square beyond belief, while the radicals were mostly Marxists and far too doctrinaire for my liking. I was more into anarchist politics. When I met Shunsuke, I found that he shared my aversion to Marxism. Like me, he'd been an enthusiastic reader of Kropotkin in his youth, and this acted like a vaccine, rendering him immune to the influence of Marxism for the rest of his life."

Tsurumi smiled, apparently approving of the medical metaphor.

"Another thing we have in common," Snyder continued, "is that we've both fallen foul of the FBI on account of our political beliefs. In my case, the FBI investigated me when I applied for a passport to come to Japan in 1955. This was at the height of the Red Scare. My application was originally declined, presumably due to my political activism, and only after Mrs. Fuller Sasaki intervened was I given a passport. Shunsuke was treated far more harshly. As you know, he studied at Harvard before the war. After the war broke out he was detained by the FBI, who suspected him of being an anarchist, and sent to a POW camp. He was eventually repatriated to Japan. But his victimization by the U.S. authorities didn't stop there. After the war he was invited to teach at Stanford University, but due to his outspoken opposition to nuclear weapons he was denied a visa. He hasn't been back to America since."

"Perhaps it was all for the best," Tsurumi said, looking across at Snyder. "If things hadn't turned out the way they did, our paths may never have crossed."

Snyder nodded before looking at his watch. "You must all be hungry," he said, looking around the table. "It would be my honor to prepare a simple meal for you. I have some bamboo shoots and *shimeji* mushrooms, and plenty of rice in the cooker. What say I whip up some *mazegohan*?"

"Sounds excellent," Tsurumi said.

"Actually," Pran said, "much as I'd like to stay, I'd better be going. I have another matter to attend to."

Pran stood up, whereupon Masuda and Tsurumi and Snyder also rose to see him off. Before leaving, Pran turned to Masuda and said, "It was a pleasure to meet you. We'll see you in Kagoshima on Friday. Tsurumi will give you the details of where and when to meet us."

"I look forward to it," Masuda said.

It was getting dark by the time Tsurumi and Masuda left Snyder's lodging. An evening shower had passed while they ate their meal. The sudden downpour had cleansed the earth and the air and this, as well as the encounter with Snyder, meant that as he walked through the temple compound with Tsurumi at his side, Masuda felt considerably more optimistic about the days ahead.

As they approached the temple gate, Tsurumi turned to Masuda and said, "Over the years, many Westerners, among them potters and poets, artists and scholars, have come to Kyoto to study Zen. They tend to stay for only a short time and gain only a superficial understanding of it. Some stay longer and learn more, but unfortunately there's a tendency among these Westerners to reach a point where they proclaim to know everything there is to know about Zen. They convince themselves they no longer need to study. A few even claim to be authorities on Zen. Gary is different. Not only has he studied longer and more assiduously than the vast majority of Westerners, as well as a good number of Japanese practitioners, he is humble about his achievements. He understands that one's progress in Zen is one's own business, and not something one should discuss in public. For this I admire him greatly."

They had exited the temple compound now and were heading down the lane toward the busy main road. Just before they reached the end of the lane, Tsurumi stopped abruptly.

"I almost forgot," he said.

As Masuda looked on, Tsurumi opened the flap of his satchel and pulled out a bulging white envelope.

"This should be enough to cover your travel expenses," Tsurumi said, proffering the envelope to Masuda, "as well as those of our three guests."

Masuda accepted the envelope with a bow and slipped it into his back pocket.

"You'll also find a shopping list in the envelope," Tsurumi said.

"A shopping list?"

"Of food and other things you and the hippies might need on Suwanosejima. There are no stores on the island, so you'll have to buy them in Kagoshima before you board the ferry."

Masuda nodded.

"Keep a note of how much you spend and what you spend it on," Tsurumi added. "For Beheiren's records."

Then, hearing another streetcar approaching, the two men turned and set off again in the direction of Kita-Ōji-dōri.

CHAPTER 9

Flynn lay low for the next few days, spending most of his time at the Kamakura Hotel and venturing out only in the evening for dinner. After a week, confident that any search for him would have been scaled back, he mustered the courage to go out during the day. In the days that followed he explored Kamakura much as any normal tourist would, visiting historical sites, rambling in the hills behind the town, and strolling along the beach. At the top of his list of sights to see was the Kamakura Daibutsu, the giant bronze statue of the Buddha whose image was already familiar to him from postcards in the souvenir shops around Yokosuka, and the nine-hundred-year-old Tsurugaoka Hachimangu Shrine. He was fascinated by the shrine, and spent hours wandering through its sprawling gardens with their ponds and arched bridges and little sub-shrines, and exploring the museum tucked away in a quiet corner of the grounds. The museum was full of all manner of artifacts, from portable shrines, hanging scrolls, and Noh masks to suits of armor, bows and arrows, and other war relics. For despite its numerous temples, shrines, and other religious sites, Flynn learned, Kamakura was originally a military town, established at the start of the feudal period by the shogun Yoritomo Minamoto as Japan's capital. During this period, even the beach along which Flynn liked to stroll in the evenings served a military purpose, as an archery and horse-riding ground.

Flynn became a regular visitor to the museum. If he got there early before the day-trippers from Tokyo arrived, he usually had the place to himself. And so he reacted with a start one morning when, thinking he was alone in the building, he felt a presence behind him as he leaned over to examine an ornately decorated samurai helmet.

83

"They say it was worn by Yoritomo Minamoto himself," a voice said.

It was unmistakably the voice of an American, but still Flynn did not turn around. Only when he was sure the voice was addressing him did he look over his shoulder. He saw a young man around his own height and a few years younger than himself—a mere boy, Flynn thought—dressed in slacks and a short-sleeved shirt almost identical to his own. Even his hair was the same fair color as Flynn's, though whereas Flynn still sported a regulation short back and sides, his doppelgänger wore his hair fashionably long. It was parted on one side and combed over to the other, the combed-over part so long it hung down over his forehead, covering one eye. Occasionally the boy would give a little flick of his head to remove the bothersome hair. This mannerism, along with his pouty lips, gave the boy a foppish air.

"The helmet, I mean," the boy said.

Flynn directed his gaze back at the helmet in front of him. From the crown there extended two massive prongs, like antlers.

"Not the most practical of designs," Flynn said.

"True. But I imagine it scared the hell out of his adversaries."

Flynn focused his attention back on the boy, turning around this time so that his whole body faced him.

"I'm Brad," the boy said, extending his right hand.

Flynn hesitated before reciprocating. From his weak handshake, hairstyle, and rounded shoulders, Flynn gathered that he wasn't in the military. He was too young, anyway. Flynn relaxed.

"I'm Eddie," Flynn responded.

"Are you on shore leave?"

Flynn immediately tensed again. He shot an accusatory glance at the boy. "Who said I'm in the Navy?"

"I could tell the moment I saw you. I've lived around Navy guys all my life."

Flynn's eyes narrowed. "You're too young to be in the Navy."

"My dad's an officer," the boy said. He flicked his head before adding, "Over at Yokohama."

Flynn smiled. "Ah, so you're a Navy brat."

"Yeah," Brad said, chuckling self-consciously, "I guess that's what you'd call me."

"How old are you?"

"Sixteen."

Flynn reckoned he was fifteen at the most. "Are you here with your parents?"

Brad flicked the hair out of his eyes again, but this time instead of looking back at Flynn his gaze stayed focused off to one side. "No, they're back in Yokohama."

"What about school? Don't they have a high school for Navy brats in Yokohama?"

"Yeah. Nile C. Kinnick High School. But everyone calls it Yo-Hi."

"Yo-Hi?"

"Short for Yokohama High School."

Flynn nodded. "So why aren't you in school?"

Brad looked at Flynn briefly but looked away again without replying.

"You're playing hooky."

The boy didn't respond.

"Don't worry," Flynn said, "I won't tell anyone."

"It's not that."

"It's not what? You mean you're not playing hooky?"

Brad flicked his head again. It was starting to annoy Flynn.

"Have you run away?"

Again, the boy didn't answer.

"That's it, isn't it? You've run away from home."

Brad still didn't answer, but he looked at Flynn now, and the look confirmed his suspicions.

"Did your father treat you bad? Is that why you ran away?"

Brad silently nodded. Then he said, "They don't understand what it's like, having to move from place to place. Having to make new friends each time."

"I ran away from home once," Flynn said.

"Really? How long for?"

"Two nights."

"What made you go back?"

"I ran out of food and got hungry."

Brad laughed.

"How long since you left home?" Flynn asked.

"Three nights."

"There you go. You've done better than me already. Where are you sleeping?"

"On the beach."

"On the beach?"

"Yeah. Why not? It's not that cold."

"Yeah, I know, but—"

Flynn heard voices. He looked behind Brad to see a young Japanese couple, honeymooners by the look of them, at the entrance to the museum.

"Come on," he said. "Let's get out of here."

"What about food?" Flynn asked as he and Brad made their way through the garden toward the entrance to the shrine grounds, which was marked by a towering stone *torii*.

"What do you mean?"

"What are you doing for food? Have you got enough money to feed yourself?"

"Food isn't that expensive. Not if you eat the local stuff, rice balls and so on."

"Rice balls?"

"Yeah. They're not just rice, you know. They have different things inside them. Fish, pickled plums, that kind of thing. And they come wrapped in seaweed."

"Seaweed?" Flynn made a face.

"They actually taste pretty good. And they fill you up better than sandwiches. They're cheap, too."

"I'll have to take your word for that. You're not going to get me eating seaweed."

"Suit yourself," Brad said.

"What are they called, anyway, these rice balls."

"*Onigiri.*"

"*Oni*-what?"

"*Onigiri.*"

Flynn repeated the word several times until Brad indicated he had the pronunciation right. By this time they were nearly back at the entrance to the shrine.

"Hey," Flynn said, "all this talk of food is making me hungry. What say we grab some breakfast? Proper food, I mean. No seaweed."

Brad didn't reply, but Flynn guessed from the long face he made that he wasn't too keen on the idea. Maybe he didn't appreciate Flynn making fun of his Japanese food fetish. Then again, maybe there was another reason.

"My treat, of course."

"Yeah?" Brad said, grinning from ear to ear. "You're on."

It was still mid-morning, and most of the restaurants in the area were closed. But they found a café near Kamakura Station that was open and went in. They sat down and the waitress came with two glasses of iced water and set them on the table. Flynn looked at the menu and ordered toast and pancakes along with a coffee for himself and a soda for the boy.

When the waitress left, Brad looked across the table at Flynn and said, "You're not on shore leave, are you?"

Flynn stared at the boy for a while before answering.

"I guess you could say I've run away too."

The boy's eyes lit up. "You've gone AWOL?"

"Shh!" Flynn said.

The waitress returned with their drinks. Flynn took a sip of his coffee, waiting until she was out of earshot.

"I was in the hospital at Yokosuka. I thought they were going to send me home, but instead they ordered me back to Vietnam."

Brad took one of the straws from the container on the table and placed it in his glass and drew a mouthful of soda. "Why were you in the hospital?"

"Malaria," Flynn lied.

The boy looked up suddenly, his eyes wide open. The straw was still in his mouth, but he had stopped drinking.

"Don't worry," Flynn said, "I'm fine now. Besides, it's not contagious."

The boy resumed drinking. He drained his glass, slurping the last drops.

"What'll you do when it rains?" Flynn asked. "At night, I mean. You can't sleep on the beach in the rain."

"I don't plan to stick around here much longer," the boy said, pushing his empty glass to one side.

"No?"

"I reckon I'll head west."

"West, eh. Like the pioneers."

"Like the Joads," the boy said. "I reckon I'll head to Kobe."

"Kobe? Why Kobe?"

"It's a port, and lots of Westerners live there, so I won't stick out. Also, they say if you know the right people you can buy a passport and get on a ship out of the country."

Flynn saw the waitress coming over with their meals, and motioned for the boy to stop talking. As the waitress set the plates down on the table, Flynn thought about what the boy had said, and for the first time since walking out of the Navy base at Yokosuka a plan began to form in his mind.

When the waitress had gone he said, "This port, Kobe. How far away is it?"

The boy swallowed a mouthful of pancake. "About three hundred miles."

"And how do you plan on getting there?"

"I don't know. Walk, I guess. You can't hitchhike in Japan. No one stops for hitchhikers."

"Walk? That'd take weeks. Isn't there a train?"

"Yeah, but trains cost money."

Neither of them spoke for some time. Then Flynn said, "How long has he been beating you?"

Brad raised his head, a look of confusion on his face. "Beating me? Who?"

"Your father."

"My father? My father doesn't beat me."

"I thought you said…" But Flynn wasn't sure what the kid had said. "Oh, forget it."

They ate in silence for a while. Then the boy stopped chewing and looked at Flynn. "Hey, why don't you come with me?"

The same thought had already occurred to Flynn, but he didn't let on. He still wasn't sure if he could trust the kid. He decided to play his cards close to his chest. "Walk three hundred miles? Not likely."

The boy looked disappointed. Then his eyes lit up. "How much money have you got?"

"Why?"

"I dunno. Just asking, I guess."

"Not enough to pay your train fare to Kobe, if that's what you're thinking."

"Maybe I can get some more money," Brad said.

"Yeah? How?"

"I've got some saved."

"How much?"

"Enough. I'd need to go back to Yokohama to get it, though."

Flynn thought for a moment and said, "Won't we attract more attention traveling together? What if we're stopped by the police?"

"That's no sweat. The police question me all the time. I just tell them I'm over from the States visiting relatives at one of the bases. If they ask for my ID I say I've left it at the place where I'm staying. Works every time."

Flynn thought again for a few moments. "Okay," he said, trying to sound as authoritative as possible, "here's what we're going to do. This afternoon you'll go back to Yokohama and get your money. Have you got somewhere you can stay there tonight?"

"Yeah."

"Good. Tomorrow morning you'll come back to Kamakura. What's the earliest you can get here?"

"I dunno. About nine, I guess."

"OK. I'll meet you in front of the station at nine."

"Then what?" Brad asked, flicking the hair out of his eyes.

"Then we catch the train to Kobe."

Back in his hotel room, Flynn sat on the *tatami* floor and counted his money again, placing the notes in a pile in front of him. Once he paid the hotel bill he would barely have enough left for the train fare to Kobe, let alone food and accommodation when he got there. Luckily, he had no intention of going to Kobe. He'd take the kid's money and run. It wasn't that he disliked the Navy brat. Much as he found his head swiveling and pouting annoying, he thought he was basically a good kid. It was just that he didn't trust anyone these days. Knowing kids Brad's age, Flynn imagined he would be babbling to his friends in Yokohama as soon as he arrived, telling them how he had met a *bona fide* deserter, and how they were going to run away together to Kobe. It would just be a matter of time before the kid's parents found out, and with his father being a Navy officer, the chances were high that they would alert the Shore Patrol. It wouldn't take the authorities long to put two and two together, and within days every goddamn SP and policeman in Kobe would be looking for him. Maybe even ONI—the Office of Naval Intelligence.

Flynn still hadn't decided exactly how he would play things the next morning. But right now he needed a drink. He folded the money and shoved it in his pocket. It took him less than three minutes to walk from the hotel to the Sea Castle, where the proprietor greeted him by name and showed him to his usual seat by the window.

"Beer?" he asked.

"Yeah," Flynn said. "Make it a large one."

The next morning, Flynn got up early and packed his rucksack before paying the hotel bill and setting off on foot for the train station. It was still a quarter to nine when he arrived. He found a coffee shop with a view across the square to the station entrance and went in and sat down. When the waitress came over he said he was waiting for a friend. He sat sipping his iced water and looking out the window.

It was busy, but mostly with commuters entering the station to catch trains to Tokyo. There were only a handful of people arriving in Kamakura at this time of the morning, and nearly all of them were Japanese. Flynn was certain he would have no trouble spotting the kid. He continued sipping his water. The waitress had just come over to refill his glass when he looked out the window and saw two Caucasian men exit the station. He glanced at his watch. It was just a few minutes before nine. Though the men wore civilian clothes, Flynn could tell straight away from their bearing that they were military.

He froze, his eyes fixed on the two men as they wandered around in front of the station entrance, scanning the surrounding area.

Flynn had seen enough. He drained his glass, picked up his rucksack and hurried out of the coffee shop, holding his hand up to hide his face as he passed through the door. He turned right and walked along quickly until he came to a side street and ducked into it. The side street led to the busy main road that ran through the center of Kamakura. When he reached the avenue he glanced over his shoulder to make sure he wasn't being followed, turned left and continued walking north in the direction of the Tsurugaoka Hachimangu Shrine. Only when he reached the shrine entrance did he slacken his pace. Instead of entering the shrine, however, he followed the road that skirted it. He knew that if he followed this road far enough it would lead to Route 1, which would take him all the way to Tokyo, some thirty miles to the northeast.

He thought about the journey ahead. On foot he calculated that he could reach Tokyo in two days, three at the most. To save money he would sleep rough. From now on, no more hotels and no more drinking. No more fancy Western restaurants, either. He might even try some of those rice balls with seaweed the kid told him about. He racked his brain, trying to remember the Japanese name for them. *Oni*-something. "*Onigiri*," he said out loud. "That's it. *Onigiri*."

A woman stopped to look at him quizzically. Flynn walked on quickly.

"*Oni-giri, oni-giri*," he repeated, the beat regular as a metronome, every second syllable coinciding with a step. "*Oni-giri, oni-giri*."

CHAPTER 10

The train lurched to the left and then to the right as it left Kawasaki Station. Harper clutched the sides of the cream-colored overnight bag to prevent it falling off his lap. He had placed the bag on the seat next to him on boarding the green and orange car at Yokohama, but a surprisingly large number of passengers, mostly businessmen in suits of various shades of grey, had boarded at the next stop, and he had transferred the bag to his lap to make the space to his right available. To his left, Yumi sat motionless, her unfocused gaze directed at the waist of the passenger standing in front of her.

The ward at Kishine was much like all the other wards Harper had been in over the previous month: whitewashed walls, the smell of piss and disinfectant, round-eyed nurses in starched white uniforms and sensible white shoes that squeaked on the linoleum floors, guys in pale blue pajamas with missing limbs and shot-up bodies like his own.

He was put in a bed at the end of the ward. Once the medic had left, the patient in the bed next to his, an Air Cavalryman named Bunny Lerner, introduced himself. As usual when an Air Cavalryman and a Marine got together for the first time, there was plenty of jiving and joking about "Army pussies" and "jarheads." Lerner didn't seem to be joking, though, when he complained of how the Cav seemed to spend half their time extricating Marines from some sticky situation or other. It wasn't long, however, before both men realized they would get along just fine, and Lerner, who had been at Kishine for two weeks recovering from a gunshot wound to the leg, set about explaining the ropes to Harper.

The hospital, he learned, had been operating at its present

93

location at Kishine Barracks since the end of 1965. The barracks had been built in the mid-1950s to house various U.S. military facilities that were previously scattered around Yokohama's commercial area. On the site were a movie theater, a swimming pool, and a snack bar with pool tables. There was also a mini exchange where patients could stock up on the usual little luxuries from back home, though the main exchange was down by the harbor at a place called Honmoku. Harper was looking forward to getting back on his feet so that he could check it out. And as his doctor explained when he came to check up on him later that afternoon, getting back on his feet was simply a matter of time. As well as lots of physical therapy.

"And what then?" Harper had asked.

"Don't worry," the doctor replied, "they won't be sending you back to Vietnam. As soon as we get you walking again we'll get you stateside. So it's up to you. The harder you work, the earlier you'll get home."

That was all the encouragement Harper needed. In no time he was out of his wheelchair and on crutches, accompanying Lerner down to the snack bar where he whiled away the time chatting with the other patients, watching them play pool and listening to the latest tunes on the jukebox. He pushed himself during the physical therapy sessions, reveling in the challenge and the variety it added to the hospital routine.

Though he enjoyed the interaction with the other patients, it was the weekly visits from students at the local high school for children of U.S. military personnel, Nile C. Kinnick High School, that Harper looked forward to more than anything. He and the other patients played cards and talked with the students, and the more Harper heard about life outside Kishine, the more eager he was to get out and see for himself what Yokohama was like. He pleaded with the doctors to let him have a day out. Eventually, after Lerner assured them he would look after Harper, they relented, and one cold Thursday morning in February the two recovering soldiers climbed aboard a Navy shuttle bus bound for Honmoku.

Harper and Lerner chatted on and off during the bus journey, but Harper spent most of the time staring out the window at the unfamiliar landscape passing in front of him. It was different from

Vietnam in so many ways. For a start, there were far fewer bicycles and motorcycles. Instead, the narrow streets were crowded with an assortment of vehicles ranging from boxy automobiles and commercial vehicles to handcarts and three-wheeled trucks piled high with all manner of wares. Eventually they joined a major road that took them along the waterfront, past busy shipyards and piers, and around the edge of a bluff to the U.S. Naval Area at Honmoku.

It was just before midday when they pulled up outside the Navy Exchange. From the bus stop they made their way on foot past the parking lot to the main store. Harper was struck by the predominance of large American automobiles, all chrome and tail fins. It was almost as if he had been dreaming and woken up outside a shopping center in some small town back in America. In addition to the main store, which looked just like any family department store back home, there was a cafeteria, a bakery, a garage, a barbershop, a laundry, a bowling alley (with the latest automatic pinsetters, according to Lerner), and a movie theater. Across the road from the exchange was a large housing complex consisting of scores of white two-story buildings surrounded by neatly manicured lawns.

"That's Seaside Park," Lerner said. "It was built during the occupation. After the U.S. War Department decided to let dependents of military personnel join them in Japan, they realized they needed to accommodate these families and educate the kids, so they built housing and schools. A lot of prime real estate along the waterfront was handed back to the Japanese in the 1950s, but there are still some big housing areas run by the U.S. military, including this one, one further up the road past the high school, and another one even further up the road in a place called Negishi."

"But the occupation ended in 1952, didn't it?"

"Under the Security Treaty with Japan, we kept the right to maintain military bases on Japanese soil. We still have around a dozen big bases here, as well as over a hundred other facilities."

"Hey man," Harper said, "much as I'm enjoying the history lesson, I came here to shop. Let's spend us some money."

Harper had a list of all the things he wanted to buy, but as the two of them went to enter the store a uniformed attendant stopped them.

"Only Navy and Marine personnel allowed in," the attendant said.

Harper and Lerner looked at each other.

"I'm a Marine, man," Harper said to the attendant. "First Marine, First Division."

"I need to see your ID, Son."

"My ID? My ID's back in Vietnam."

"I'm sorry, Son, no ID, no entry. That's—"

"What the fuck?" Lerner interjected. "This man's a goddamn war hero. Can't you see he's been wounded? He's a Marine."

The attendant, a white guy in his thirties, glanced at Harper before turning back to Lerner. "Rules are rules."

Lerner took a step forward, fists clenched by his sides. "Fuck you, motherfucker…"

Harper had never seen Lerner so angry. Afraid that things were getting out of hand, he quickly hobbled forward and placed one of his crutches in Lerner's path to stop him getting any closer to the attendant and placed a hand on his shoulder.

"It's okay, man. If they don't want our money we'll go somewhere else."

Lerner continued eyeballing the attendant. "Fucking rear echelon motherfucker!" he spat.

Harper grabbed Lerner's sleeve and pulled him away. They turned and headed across the parking lot, away from the main store. Like Lerner, Harper was seething inside. He thought of his black buddies back in the Nam, risking their lives while white guys like the attendant got it easy in places like Japan. But if there was one thing he had learned over the years, it was to know when to put up a fight and when to back off.

As a child growing up in a predominantly black town in rural Mississippi, Harper was hardly conscious of being black. It was only when he moved to Washington, D.C. after graduating high school and got a job at a truck repair shop that he started to experience racism. Once or twice after work he had been caught alone in a white neighborhood at night and been attacked. But there was nothing he could do about it. He had to deal with white people all the time as part of his job, so he couldn't afford to get angry in front of them. He learned to keep it down.

Harper and Lerner rode a streetcar to a shopping area in another part of the city. Once Harper had bought all the things on his list, they returned to the Navy Exchange and watched *Doctor Dolittle* at the movie theater.

It was dark by the time they made it back to the hospital. A thick fog had rolled in, enveloping the hospital and the surrounding area in a cold, damp, dirty haze. Lerner had promised to have Harper back by five, so they kept their heads down and their voices low, determined to make it back to the ward without attracting any attention. They had almost made it to the elevator on the ground floor when Harper heard a loud voice behind them.

"Son?"

Shit. Busted.

"Son? Is that you?"

The voice sounded familiar. Harper slowly turned around.

"Son. I knew it was you. I recognized you even without the beard."

Harper could hardly believe his own eyes. It was Muller, the goddamn butterbar from Hill 842.

"Lieutenant. Good to see you again, Sir." He put up a salute.

Muller looked much the same as he did in Khe Sanh, though instead of utilities he was wearing his service uniform, his peaked cap tucked under his left armpit.

"It's good to see you, Son. Hanson, wasn't it?"

"Harper, Sir. James Earle Harper."

"Harper, yes of course. Harper. How's the injury, Son?"

"Oh, getting there. How about yourself, Sir?"

"Me? Oh, I'm fine. In fact I just got my orders home. This time next week I'll be stateside."

"Good for you, Sir," Harper said.

There was a moment's silence. Then Harper said, "Sir, I just wanted to thank you. For the citation, I mean. It means a lot to me."

"Oh, it's nothing, Son. The least I could do. I appreciate what you did for me that day."

Then, without warning, Muller stepped forward and reached out his right arm and clasped Harper's left shoulder, squeezing it tightly. Harper was taken aback by this show of affection and wasn't sure how to respond. U.S. military rules of conduct demanded that officers and enlisted men keep a certain distance between them. In fact, out of the field and off duty there would normally be no contact between the two groups. Muller would have been in a ward for officers, which explained why their paths hadn't crossed until now. Needless to say, Muller's repeated use of the familiar "son" also flew in the face of Marine Corps protocol.

Harper stood stiffly, leaning on his crutches, and eventually Muller relaxed his grip and took a step back.

Harper said, "Well, have a safe journey home, Sir."

"Thank you, Son. I'm sure you'll be heading stateside too, once you're well enough. Just hang on in there."

"Yes, Sir."

Harper and Lerner briefly exchanged glances before Harper pressed the elevator call button. It seemed to take an eternity for the car to arrive, during which time no one spoke. Eventually the elevator doors opened and Harper turned and stepped into the waiting car, with Lerner close behind him. They both turned to face Muller. The uncomfortable silence continued as they waited for the doors to close.

As soon as the elevator car started moving, Lerner turned to Harper and said, "Shit, man, I thought for a moment there he was going to kiss you."

"Goddamn butterbar. Did you hear that? Stateside in a week. And barely a goddamn scratch on him."

"Hey, don't sweat it, man. Remember what the doctor said. The sooner you're better the sooner you'll be heading home yourself."

"Yeah," Harper said.

But it was Lerner who got his orders first. Not home, but back to Vietnam. There wasn't even time for a proper send-off. The orders came in on Monday, and on Tuesday morning Lerner was bundled onto a bus bound for the naval air station at Atsugi, where he would be put on the next Starlifter to Da Nang.

Lerner's bed was soon taken by another Army grunt, a young hillbilly who had stepped on a mine and lost a leg. Or so the hillbilly told him. Harper later heard the truth, that he had been admitted with a gunshot wound, that the doctors had saved his leg, but that the kid was so scared of going back to Vietnam he began dabbing his own piss on the wound until it got infected. The doctors were puzzled as to why the wound wouldn't heal. Eventually gangrene set in, and the poor kid had to have his leg amputated. At least they wouldn't be sending him back to the Nam.

The train pulled into Tokyo Station exactly on time at ten minutes to two. Harper followed Yumi along the platform and down a flight of stairs to a crowded underpass. He thought Yokohama Station had been busy, but it was nothing compared to this. It wasn't just the number of people. The preponderance of men in gray suits all with short black hair gave him an uncanny feeling, as if there was no room for differentness.

Before exiting the gate, Yumi spoke to a uniformed station attendant who confirmed they were at the correct exit and gave them directions to the restaurant. Outside the station, they crossed a busy street choked with buses, streetcars, taxis, and private automobiles and entered a multistoried building. The Western-style restaurant was on the second floor, overlooking the station. A waiter greeted them and took Harper's coat and hat and showed them to a table by the window.

Crossing the room, Harper looked around and saw that the only other customer was a serious-looking young man, also sitting by the window. The man had his head buried in a book and hadn't even glanced up as they passed. They sat down and looked through the menu. A few minutes later the waiter returned and Yumi ordered two coffees.

Harper waited until the waiter had gone and said, "Are you sure this is the right place?"

"Positive," Yumi said.

Harper glanced up at the clock on the wall and saw that it was already five minutes after two. He had been in Japan long enough to know that the Japanese were usually punctual. He tried to put his mind at rest by reminding himself they had been kept waiting for nearly a quarter of an hour outside Yokohama Station, but he remained anxious, continually glancing up at the clock and over at the entrance to the restaurant.

Just before two thirty, by which time they had each drank two cups of coffee and even Yumi was looking agitated, Harper noticed the young man sitting by the window stand up and approach them. The man, who looked a few years younger than Harper and was at least a foot shorter, stopped beside their table, clutching his book to his chest with one hand.

"Mr. Harper?"

Harper glanced across at Yumi before nodding.

"My name is Natsume. I'm from Beheiren."

Harper looked from the man to the table where he had been sitting and back at the man, his mouth open in an expression of bewilderment. "But you've been here the whole time."

"Yes. I had to make sure you weren't followed."

Harper was dumbstruck.

The man sniffed loudly and said, "Now, if you would please come with me." He looked at Yumi before adding, "Alone."

Harper stiffened and was about to protest, but Yumi quickly reached across the table and placed a hand on his forearm.

"No, it's okay," she said. "Please, go with him."

Harper looked into her eyes, but she wouldn't meet his gaze, and instead looked down at the table.

He turned to the man again. "Can you give us a few minutes alone?"

The man nodded, took the bill from their table and went over to the cashier.

Harper got to his feet and walked around to Yumi's side of the table. She stood and reached up and put her arms around his neck as he took her in his arms and pulled her tightly against his body. He kissed her on the lips and then put his cheek against hers and whispered into her ear, "I'll come back, I promise. I don't know when, but I'll come back."

She nestled her head against his chest, burying her face in his jacket. He felt her quiver. Eventually he placed his hands on her shoulders and, ever so gently, pushed her away. She stood with her head bowed, sniffing and dabbing her eyes with the back of one index finger.

"Be strong, Yumi," he said. "I know you can be strong."

After a few seconds she looked up at him and forced a smile.

"That's my girl," he said. Harper slowly stepped back. He released his grip on her shoulders and ran his hands down her arms until he held her hands in his, and then just her fingertips between his, and then they were no longer touching. He picked up the overnight bag she had given him and turned and walked over to where the man was waiting by the door. Only when he reached the other side of the room did Harper turn to look at Yumi for what he knew deep down would be the last time.

CHAPTER 11

The journey by train from Nara to the city of Kagoshima near the southern tip of Kyushu, the most southwesterly of Japan's four main islands, took Masuda and the three deserters the best part of two days. Things got off to a rocky start even before they left Musubi no Ie. In line with Tsurumi's instructions, Masuda had told the Americans they could carry just one overnight bag between the three of them. Anything that couldn't fit in the bag would have to be left behind. All three objected; they wouldn't be going anywhere without their belongings, they insisted. Masuda didn't know how to respond. It was Sakurai who broke the deadlock, by offering to take some things to Tokyo and return them later. As the deserters were organizing their belongings, she turned to Masuda and winked. He realized he would miss her, and not only because of her negotiating skills.

They traveled as far as Hiroshima on the first day, changing trains at Kyoto, Osaka, and Okayama. The following evening they boarded a blue night train bound for Kagoshima. Having spent all day chaperoning the three Americans around Hiroshima, during which time they bickered and talked loudly with hardly a moment's letup, Masuda was looking forward to spending the night in the relative privacy of a sleeping car berth. But on learning the price he realized that the money Tsurumi had given him in Kyoto wouldn't be enough to cover such luxuries. Instead he paid for four seats in a normal car. The Americans slept soundly for most of the journey, unlike Masuda, who remained on edge and was woken by the slightest movement or sound around him, fearful that it might have been the deserters getting up to no good.

The next morning at Nishi-Kagoshima, bleary-eyed from a lack of sleep, Masuda led the three Americans out of the station building and across the road to a streetcar stop. Minutes later they were clattering and rocking their way over a bridge and down the busy main street toward the harbor district.

It was too early to check in to their *ryokan*, so they got off near the Yamagataya department store and walked toward Shiroyama, the forested mountain that bounded the downtown area to the west. At the top of the mountain was a lookout. Before beginning the climb, however, they stopped to rest by a small park where there was a towering statue of Takamori Saigō. The Americans were curious about the figure in Western military uniform, in real life a giant of a man with a massive head and a neck like that of a bear. Recalling what he had been taught about him at school, Masuda explained how Saigō, a native of Kagoshima who admired the West and played a leading role in the Meiji Restoration that overthrew the Tokugawa shogunate and restored imperial rule to Japan in 1868, had become disillusioned with the new regime. When it failed to back his plan for an invasion of Korea, Saigō left the government and returned to Kagoshima, sparking a rebellion that ended with a battle to the death at Shiroyama. The Americans' eyes lit up when Masuda described how Saigō was wounded during the battle and committed ritual disembowelment, or *seppuku*, rather than fall into the hands of the enemy.

The climb up the winding path to the top of Shiroyama took twenty minutes. Thick subtropical vegetation blocked their view for most of the way, but at the summit it was clear. They stood in silence as they looked out over the downtown area and the harbor, and beyond it the calm blue waters of Kagoshima Bay.

Clearly visible in the middle of the bay, less than three miles away, was the city's most famous landmark, Sakurajima. The volcano, Masuda explained to the deserters, was one of the most active in the world. It was an island until just over fifty years ago, when lava flows resulting from a major eruption filled in the narrow stretch of water separating it from the peninsula to the east. As Masuda spoke, plumes of white smoke rose from the top of the volcano.

"It's not unusual for ash thrown into the air from explosions inside the crater to land in downtown Kagoshima," Masuda said. "There are shelters all around the city where people can seek refuge in the event of a major eruption."

"Why don't the people move somewhere else?" Sullivan asked.

Masuda shrugged his shoulders. "Because it's their home, I guess. There are even people who live on the slopes of Sakurajima itself. The volcanic soil, along with the subtropical climate, provides ideal conditions for growing citrus fruits and other crops."

"Crazy," Santiago said, shaking his head.

"Tourists visit Sakurajima too," Masuda said. "Mainly to soak in the hot springs. It's just a fifteen-minute ferry ride from downtown Kagoshima."

This information drew further looks of dismay from the Americans.

"I wouldn't go there in a million years," said Santiago, eliciting nods of concurrence from Roberts and Sullivan.

They spent that night in a *ryokan* just off Tenmonkan-dōri. After breakfast the next morning, Masuda walked alone to a nearby supermarket, where he found most of the items on the list Tsurumi had given him in Kyoto, including brown rice, potatoes, onions, miso, and two large bottles of *shōchū*. On the way back to the *ryokan* he stopped at a clothing store and bought three pairs of identical red swimming trunks, choosing the largest size he could find, and three small white towels. Back at the *ryokan*, the Americans watched curiously as one by one he set the items he had bought at the supermarket on the table. Santiago's eyes lit up when he saw the *shōchū* bottles.

"Don't get any ideas," Masuda said. "These are gifts for our hosts."

"Is it saké?" Santiago asked.

"It's *shōchū*."

"*Shōchū*?"

"It's a kind of liquor made from sweet potatoes. It's distilled, like whiskey."

"It must be pretty strong, then."

"About twenty-five percent alcohol. They make *shōchū* from other stuff, too, such as rice, but sweet potato *shōchū* is a local specialty."

Masuda then remembered the items he had bought at the clothing store.

"Actually, I have something for you three, too."

He opened the bag, pulled out the red swimming trunks and handed one pair to each of the deserters. Masuda watched as they unfolded the garments and inspected them. Expressions of curiosity gave way to looks of dismay.

"It's the only color they had," Masuda lied.

"Where is it we're going exactly?" Roberts asked, pressing his swimming trunks to his pelvis now to check the size.

"We're going to an island south of here. We leave on a ferry tonight."

"How long will it take?"

"We should arrive tomorrow night."

"Tomorrow night?" Roberts exclaimed. "You mean it takes twenty-four hours to get there?"

"Weather permitting."

"What's the matter, Eugene?" Santiago interrupted. "You don't get seasick, do you?"

"You're the one who's sick, Santiago. Still taking your meds?"

"Okay, knock it off," Masuda said, although as usual he knew he had no hope of curbing the bickering between Santiago and Roberts. He tried to think what Sakurai would have done. But he lacked her mediation skills, and the sniping continued on and off for the rest of the morning.

Later that afternoon they checked out of the *ryokan* and wandered down to the waterfront. There they spotted a group of around fifteen young men and women sitting cross-legged on the wharf looking out to sea. Having met Pran, Masuda knew what to expect, but he still felt uneasy at the sight of so many youths with long hair and beards dressed in T-shirts and shorts. Some had headbands tied around their heads to keep their hair in place. Others wore bead necklaces. The women, too, were scantily clad in short-sleeved tops and shorts, revealing nut-brown arms and legs.

Their attention still focused out to sea, none of the hippies had noticed Masuda and the three deserters approach. Masuda called out to Pran, who turned and smiled through his scraggly beard.

"Kawabata!" he said, jumping to his feet and bounding over to greet him. "You made it."

"It's good to see you again," Masuda said, relieved that Pran had remembered to use his alias. "These are my friends," he added, gesturing to Santiago, Roberts, and Sullivan.

Pran turned to the Americans. "Welcome to Kagoshima," he said in English.

The three stood silently, acknowledging Pran's effusive greeting with only the faintest of smiles. Given his own surprise at the sight of the unusual congregation on the wharf, Masuda could hardly blame the Americans for their less than enthusiastic response, and for a moment he regretted not telling them more about their hosts in advance. But looking into their faces, he thought he detected not so much surprise as hostility.

It was Roberts who broke the silence. "Are you all going with us?"

Masuda was not sure if Pran recognized the almost menacing tone of Robert's voice. If he did, he didn't show it.

"No, only four of us are taking the ferry to Suwanosejima. The rest live elsewhere. We gathered here for a festival. We've been camping over at Sakurajima." Pran turned and gestured at the volcano behind them. In the fading light they could just make out the clouds of smoke gently rising from the peak.

"You camped over *there*?" Santiago asked, incredulous.

"At the shrine. The one that was buried in ash and pumice during the last big eruption."

Santiago didn't reply. Instead he turned to Roberts and Sullivan and made a face.

"That was back in 1914," Masuda said, hoping to quell their anxiety.

"Anyway," Pran continued, "the ferry to Suwanosejima leaves in about half an hour. You're welcome to wait with us if you like."

"Thank you," Masuda said quickly, so that none of the Americans would have time to reply.

Masuda waited until Pran was out of earshot and turned to the deserters.

"What's wrong? Why were you so rude?"

"They're hippies," Roberts said, as if it explained everything.

"So?"

"Do you know how hippies in America greet Vietnam veterans when they get back from the war? They spit at them."

Masuda had heard stories about this, though he didn't know if they were true and, if so, how common the practice was. He thought a while before replying.

"They're Japanese hippies."

"So?" Roberts said.

"So, they're different from American hippies. Surely the fact that they've offered to help you should make that obvious."

Roberts looked over at the hippies and back at Masuda. He seemed to be thinking carefully about what Masuda had told him. Eventually he said, "I guess so."

"Good. Now, can you try to be a little friendlier? Because we're going to be spending a lot of time together on a very small island."

"How small?" Sullivan asked.

"Just under twenty square miles."

"Has it got a beach?" Roberts asked.

"Of course it's got a beach, numbnuts," Santiago said. "It's an island."

Masuda stood silently as Santiago and Roberts continued their squabbling. In a sense he was grateful that their discussion of Suwanosejima had been cut short. It meant he could delay sharing with his charges one other important piece of information about the island: that it's most distinctive geographical feature was an active volcano.

CHAPTER 12

Flynn felt at ease riding the Yamanote Line. A full circuit of the railway loop line around central Tokyo took just over an hour, and for thirty yen he could make as many circuits as he liked. The cars were maintained at a comfortable temperature, and the padded seats were a luxury compared to the concrete or bare earth on which he rested his tired body at night. He liked to sit and observe people getting on and off at each station, and to watch the scenery go by between stops. Anything to take his mind of his predicament.

After leaving Kamakura, Flynn had continued north on foot, sustaining himself with *onigiri* and green tea that he bought at roadside stores along the way and sleeping rough. As he walked his mind drifted. He thought of all the people down through history who had embarked on epic journeys across America. Of Lewis and Clark, who traversed Idaho in 1805 on their way to the Pacific, of the pioneers who crossed the prairies in their Conestoga wagons. Of the Okies of the Dust Bowl era, driven off their land and joining the great migration along Route 66 to California. Of Sal Paradise, on the road, bussing and hitchhiking from New York to San Francisco.

And then, early on his second day on the road, the rain came. It fell gently at first, though steadily enough to soak him through. Reluctant to stop, he took an umbrella and a pair of sturdy-looking boots he saw outside the entrance to a farmhouse and continued walking in the rain. He passed avenues of gnarly old pine trees, some so lopsided they seemed on the verge of toppling over. Several times he stopped in the rain to admire the hydrangeas that residents had planted in front of their properties, the pinks and purples and blues a welcome change from the omnipresent gray.

After a sleepless second night under a tree, Flynn got up feeling confident that by the evening he would be in Tokyo. It rained on and off throughout his third day on the road. He passed through hilly Yokohama and the flat industrial belt of Kawasaki, stopping once or twice to ask people if he was heading in the right direction. When he crossed the Tama River he saw a sign indicating he was crossing from Kanagawa Prefecture into Tokyo Prefecture, whereupon he began asking for directions to the Ginza, legendary among the Navy personnel at Yokosuka for its shopping and nightlife, and the only part of Tokyo whose name Flynn knew.

The rain had stopped by the time he reached the district of Shinbashi and he was able to lower his umbrella for the final push into the Ginza. Dusk was falling and dark clouds hung low over the city, but the main street was aglow, the wet asphalt reflecting light from streetlamps, vehicle headlights, neon signs, and the windows of the multistoried commercial buildings all around him. For a moment, Flynn forgot all his troubles, from his blisters and his aching legs and his poverty and his empty stomach to the fact that he hadn't washed in days, that his clothes smelled and that he was a fugitive in a foreign land, and lost himself in the crowds of shoppers and revelers.

He continued walking until he came to a busy intersection, which he recognized from postcards as the heart of the Ginza. Stopping at the edge of the sidewalk, he looked up at the glittering glass cylinder that was the San-ai Building and across the street at the far more sedate but no less imposing stone facades of the Wako and Mitsukoshi department stores. Then he rejoined the flow of pedestrians and was carried northwest up another busy street to the Sony building, where he wandered through the showrooms admiring the very latest radios and televisions and tape recorders.

Further up the same street he entered an arcade full of counters where all kinds of foods were for sale, and the aromas reminded him that he hadn't eaten since lunchtime. He bought some grilled chicken skewers and ate them as he continued to explore the arcade, which seemed to go on for miles.

He felt safe among the anonymous crowds, and was confident that he could have continued walking all night. As he was passing a nightclub, however, he almost collided with a group of American sailors who came stumbling out of the doorway onto the pavement. Though they paid him no attention, their foreignness and the sight of their white Navy uniforms unsettled Flynn, and he was suddenly overcome with physical and emotional exhaustion. He walked on until he came to a park and lay on a bench and slept until dawn.

Flynn was still tired when he woke up the next morning, but the fear that had gripped him since his narrow escape in Kamakura and impelled him to stay on the move had waned. Realizing that the chances of his being recognized in such a crowded city were slim, he decided to stay put, abandoning for the present the idea of fleeing Japan. In the days that followed he continued to wander the streets of Tokyo. He slept in parks and under bridges and railway viaducts, never in the same place twice in case someone reported him to the police or the military authorities. He ate at only the cheapest restaurants and washed himself in rivers. Even so, he knew the money he brought with him would soon run out.

One evening, exhausted and all but broke, Flynn sought refuge in a temple compound. As he was looking for a place to lie down, he remembered seeing people throwing money into offering boxes in the temples he had visited in Kamakura. He crossed to the main hall and, sure enough, at the top of the steps in front of the building's entrance he saw a large wooden box. He climbed the steps and inspected the container. Though his view was partially obscured by a row of wooden slats near the top, he could clearly make out the metallic coins at the bottom.

He tried to move one of the slats, but it was securely attached at both ends. He then tried to squeeze his hand through one of the gaps between the boards. Though it was wide enough for his fingers to pass through, he was unable to get his whole hand inside. Frustrated, he lay down beside the box and went to sleep. He woke the next morning to find a coat draped over him. In the pocket was a thousand-yen note.

On other occasions Flynn woke to find boiled eggs, plates of vegetables, even bowls of boiled rice, by his side. He quickly became used to such acts of generosity. Strangers offered to take him in or wash his clothes. Office workers offered to pay for his food and drinks in bars, in return for which he had only to speak to them in English and praise their attempts to converse with him. Later he discovered the student quarter of Kanda, which abounded with secondhand bookstores and coffee shops and mahjong parlors, but also cheap restaurants where, despite their poverty, students from the nearby universities proved no less generous than the office workers in the business districts of Shinjuku and Ueno.

But Flynn was a country boy at heart, and as the weeks went by he found that living rough in the city was taking its toll on his mental and physical wellbeing. He began to spend more and more time on the trains, going around and around on the Yamanote loop line, one circuit every seventy minutes. He realized that his life was going nowhere, that one day the MPs or the Japanese police would catch up with him. He dreamed of escaping Japan, of going somewhere where he could settle down and live normally without the threat of arrest hanging over him.

Flynn felt the train decelerate and heard the squeal of the brakes. He sat up and peered out the window on the opposite side of the car. The signs on the platform with the bold black letters in Japanese and English flashed by, too quickly to read at first, but as the train slowed further he recognized the name AKIHABARA. The train came to a stop and the doors rumbled open and, without thinking, Flynn stood and joined the throng of alighting passengers. Once on the platform he remembered he hadn't eaten since morning. He changed to the Chūō-Sōbu Line, the line that snaked through the heart of Tokyo, getting off two stops later at Suidōbashi Station. He intended to follow Hakusan-dōri, the broad avenue that led to Nihon University, around which there were a number of cheap eateries frequented by university students. He had only walked a matter of twenty yards, however, before he noticed something odd. Unusually, there was very little traffic in the two right-hand lanes heading toward him, and the traffic in the two left-hand lanes had come to a complete standstill.

He continued walking until he saw the cause of the traffic jam. Up ahead, stretching from one side of the road to the other, was a line of police in full riot gear, including visored helmets and large rectangular shields that rested on the ground and came up to just below their shoulders. They were standing three deep with their backs to Flynn. But the road in front of them was empty. Flynn could not make sense of the scene.

But then he heard shouting and, moments later, a column of helmeted demonstrators appeared from a side street between two large modern-looking buildings on the far side of the road, part of the Nihon University campus. They poured onto Hakusan-dōri in front of the line of police, the column zigzagging from one side of the road to the other as the demonstrators quick-marched in time with whistle blasts, chanting as they went.

Flynn counted half a dozen demonstrators in the front row. They clutched a long pole at waist height to keep the line even. Many of those in the rows behind also carried long wooden poles, which they held aloft over their shoulders. Others held flags or placards. All the demonstrators wore helmets, similar to those worn by the legions of construction workers on the many building sites around Tokyo, except they had been painted different colors and emblazoned with Japanese writing. Their mouths and noses were covered with white towels secured by feeding the ends through the helmet ear loops so that only their eyes were visible.

At first it seemed to Flynn that the movement of the column of demonstrators was totally haphazard, as if it were one of the toy snakes he had seen in a market that you held by the tail and watched wriggle from side to side. But inexorably the column drew nearer and nearer to the line of police just in front of Flynn, until eventually the demonstrators and police were just yards apart.

And then there was contact. Flynn was unsure who initiated it, but suddenly all hell seemed to break loose. Demonstrators broke ranks and began using their poles to rain blows onto the police. The police quickly responded, some raising their shields to protect themselves while others lunged with them to repel their attackers.

There were more shouts and whistle blasts from the students, more urgent than before and chaotic, all sense of rhythm and order having been lost. Police snatched poles out of the hands of demonstrators. Protestors wrenched shields free from policemen, holding them aloft like trophies. Occasionally a student would stumble back, hands clutching a bruised body or bloodied head, into the arms of comrades who would escort them back to the main body of demonstrators.

It soon became clear that the police were outnumbered, and before long they were forced to retreat toward Suidōbashi Station. They did so slowly at first, maintaining their line as they walked backward, continuing to fend off blows from demonstrators. Then one policeman stumbled and fell and was set upon by two students. The police line broke apart as some policemen went to the aid of their colleague while others continued the retreat.

By now the police line was nearly even with Flynn, who was standing on the sidewalk with a small group of bystanders. Fearing they would be caught up in the melee, the other bystanders turned and hurried back toward the station. Flynn considered following them, but someone in the entrance of a noodle shop to his right shouted and beckoned to him and he darted inside.

When he turned and looked outside, Flynn saw that, instead of pursuing the retreating police, the demonstrators had themselves pulled back. Some of those who had lost their poles gathered in a group by the side of the road. At first Flynn couldn't see what they were doing. Then one of them stepped forward and threw what looked like a rock in the direction of the police. When he looked more closely at the group of students, he saw they were ripping up square paving stones from the sidewalk and breaking them into fist-sized pieces by raising them to shoulder height and dropping them. One by one, other demonstrators abandoned their poles, flags, and placards and joined the rock-throwers.

Flynn looked up the road and saw that the police had reformed their line just in front of the station and were facing the demonstrators again with their shields raised. The distance between the two sides was now so great that few of the missiles found their mark, but amidst the shouts and whistle blasts and the dull thuds of rocks hitting asphalt, Flynn could hear the occasional metallic crack as a rock struck a police shield.

But not all of the police had made it. Across the road from the noodle shop from where Flynn was viewing the action, some ten officers were huddled in a group behind their shields with their backs to the wall of a Chinese restaurant. It seemed that the rock-throwers, too, had spotted the stragglers, for as Flynn looked on they turned their attention away from the line of police in front of the station to the police across the road.

Their new targets were well within range. Flynn could hear the clatter of rocks hitting shields and see the protective devices tremble as projectile after projectile struck home. Emboldened by the effectiveness of their onslaught, some of the rock-throwers began to advance on their victims, the accuracy of their throwing increasing the closer they got. Other students positioned themselves between the stranded police and the station, effectively blocking their retreat.

Flynn's heart raced. He was certain that the group of police across the road couldn't withstand such a sustained barrage for long. He looked at the rock-throwers, wondering if they had it in them to maim or kill, but their body language betrayed no clear intention.

He looked back at the group of policemen, and to his surprise he saw a gap slowly open in the wall of shields and from it emerge a figure in darks trousers and a white shirt. There was shouting from the demonstrators and the barrage of rocks subsided.

Flynn looked carefully at the figure, a young male. He seemed barely conscious, and from his ragdoll-like posture it was clear to Flynn that he was not so much standing as being held up by the police behind him. He was bareheaded and there was a wound on his forehead from which blood had spilled down the front of his shirt. Flynn drew in a breath as the reality of the situation dawned on him. The police across the road had a hostage, a demonstrator they had snatched during the initial assault on the police line, and were using him as a human shield.

There was more shouting from the demonstrators, and shouted replies from the police. Flynn couldn't understand what they were saying, but he guessed that some kind of negotiation was underway. The shouting stopped and in the silence the policemen began shuffling up the road toward the station, facing their assailants with their shields raised. They took their hostage with them, his heels dragging on the sidewalk as he was carried along in a semi-upright position. The rock-throwers stood their ground, watching helplessly as their prey slipped from their grasp.

Sensing an opportunity to escape, Flynn ducked out of the noodle shop and gingerly made his way along the sidewalk toward the station, hunched over to present as small a target as possible. He had made it halfway when he looked up and saw that the retreating police on the other side of the street had reached the main police line. At about the same time he heard the first thud of rocks hitting pavement as the demonstrators resumed their bombardment.

Within seconds rocks were raining down all around him, and with only yards between him and the safety of the police line he broke into a run. He remembered seeing a policeman pointing to him, his lips just visible behind the Perspex visor of his helmet, forming words that were drowned out by the shouting and whistle blasts and crashing of rocks. And then everything went black.

CHAPTER 13

"Where is it we're heading again?" Harper asked.

"Nishikiyama," Natsume replied. The young Beheiren operative sniffed noisily, dabbing at his nose with the back of his hand, before adding, "In Shizuoka Prefecture."

"Nishikiyama," Harper repeated. "Shizuoka Prefecture." But the names meant nothing to him.

They were on a train hurtling south along the Tōkaidō Main Line. They had been traveling for more than an hour. It was still light outside, but the day would soon be ending.

"We're going to be staying in the country for a while," Natsume said, his voice barely above a whisper. "On a kind of farm. We need some time to organize your escape."

Harper nodded.

"We'll be riding this train for a while longer, so you're welcome to take a nap. I'm sure you're exhausted."

Harper was indeed tired, but he had no intention of sleeping. He figured that the Beheiren operative wanted a rest, though, and so he settled back into his seat and turned his head toward the window. He heard rustling as Natsume took a newspaper out of his bag and unfolded it. Harper willed himself to stay awake, but the rhythmic sound of the wheels on the tracks and the swaying of the car had a soporific effect, and before long he lost the battle to keep his eyes open.

Harper woke up with a jolt. He opened his eyes and looked to his left, relieved to see the Beheiren operative still sitting in the seat next to him. He turned to his right and looked out the window, but it was pitch black outside and he couldn't see a thing. It took him a moment to realize they were inside a tunnel. He checked his watch before casting his eyes around the car for a clue as to where they were. Seconds later he felt the train decelerate. The PA hissed to life and the conductor announced in a nasal voice, "Nishikiyama. Nishikiyama *desu*." He felt a hand on his shoulder and turned to see a bleary-eyed Natsume looking at him.

"Quickly," Natsume said. "Get your things. We get off at the next station."

Once they had gathered their belongings, Natsume led Harper to the end of the car, reaching the doors just as they emerged from the tunnel and pulled into the station.

They were the only passengers to alight. It was noticeably colder than it had been in Tokyo, and their breath formed clouds in the air as they made their way along the platform and climbed up the pedestrian bridge and down the other side. They passed through the wooden station building and found themselves in a small parking area. Harper spotted a white van. The front passenger's door opened and a man in his forties wearing a padded navy blue jacket and black woolen ski hat got out and approached them. The man's left arm was missing, the sleeve folded at the elbow and pinned to his shoulder.

Natsume and the man exchanged a few words in Japanese. Then, turning to Harper, the man said in English, "Welcome to Nishikiyama."

"Thank you," Harper replied.

"My name is Ikeda," the man said. He smiled, revealing a mouthful of shiny silver teeth.

"Pleased to meet you," Harper replied. "My name is Harper. Most people call me Harpo."

Natsume and Ikeda exchanged more words. As the two men talked, Harper glanced at their host's left shoulder, at the gap where his arm should have been, and wondered how he had lost the limb.

"Now," Ikeda said in English, "I'm sure you're both tired from your journey, so please, if you don't mind, follow me."

Ikeda led Harper and Natsume to the van and they climbed in, Ikeda in the front passenger seat and Harper and Natsume in the back. At the wheel was a woman around the same age as Ikeda, who

Ikeda introduced as his wife. The inside of the van reeked of stale cigarette smoke along with another, more pungent smell.

Harper turned to Ikeda and asked, "What is it you grow on your farm?"

"Chickens, mainly," Ikeda replied.

They drove out of the parking area and turned onto a road that ran south along a river valley. The valley was surrounded by steep hills to the east and west, and though the sun had not yet set, a false dusk had descended, making it difficult to see much on either side of the road.

After about five minutes they came to a small hamlet comprising a dozen or so old two-story houses with weathered wooden walls and tiled roofs. They passed through the settlement and continued along the main road. A few minutes later Harper saw a large sign on the side of the road with Japanese writing on it. They took the next turn on the right and climbed a hill covered in a vast pine forest, the engine snarling as Mrs. Ikeda struggled to find the right gear to negotiate the incline. Near the top of the hill, Harper noticed that the forest had been cleared to make room for several large single-story wooden structures, all of the same design, which he assumed were poultry runs. To the left of these, directly in front of them as they crested the hill, were two smaller buildings around twenty yards apart. As they got nearer, Harper realized that this was where the road ended.

Mrs. Ikeda brought the van to a stop in a parking area in front of the two smaller buildings. As they got out, her husband gestured toward the building on the right and said, "That's the administration building. Inside there's an office along with a common room and a dining room." He then pointed to the building on the left. "That's one of our accommodation buildings. It's where you'll be sleeping."

Harper and Natsume followed Ikeda into the accommodation building and down a corridor and into a medium-sized room with *tatami* flooring. Harper looked around the room. In one corner stood a gas stove, on top of which sat a copper kettle from which steam was gently rising. Next to the stove were two piles of neatly folded futon, each topped by a buckwheat pillow. In another corner was a trashcan fashioned from a gasoline can and next to it a broom. The room was lit by a naked light bulb that dangled on the end of a fly-blown cord over a low table in the middle of the floor.

Harper and Natsume took off their hats and coats and the three men sat cross-legged around the table. Moments later, Mrs. Ikeda appeared carrying a lacquer tray on which sat a ceramic teapot and three cups, which she transferred to the table. After preparing and pouring the tea, she bowed and turned and padded across the *tatami* floor toward the door.

When she had left, Ikeda turned to Natsume and said in English, "I trust Tsurumi is well?"

Natsume glanced at Harper before responding in the affirmative.

"We haven't forgotten the support he gave us after that messy business in 1959," Ikeda continued. "It was a brave thing to do. It could easily have cost him his job, not to mention the damage it could have done to his reputation."

Ikeda paused to drink his tea, whereupon Harper and Natsume each took a sip from their own cup. Then Natsume glanced at Harper again before asking Ikeda, "How much do the others know about our guest?"

"Only a few know that he's a deserter. We've had foreigners stay with us before, so they won't be suspicious. And even if they were, our history is such that it's highly unlikely anyone among us will go to the authorities. You can be assured of discretion."

Natsume nodded. "Are there any rules we should be aware of?"

"No," Ikeda replied. "You're free to spend your time here as you please. Meals are served in the dining room twice a day, at ten in the morning and five in the evening."

Harper glanced at his watch. It was nearly six o'clock.

"Though I'm sure we could get you something to eat now if you're hungry," Ikeda added.

"Yes, that would be good," Natsume said. "If it's no trouble, of course."

"No trouble at all," Ikeda said, standing. "I'll have my wife bring you something shortly." He then turned and left the room.

Sitting next to Natsume on the *tatami* floor, Harper realized it was

the first time he had been completely alone with the Beheiren operative. He watched him out of the corner of his eye as they sipped their
tea. After a few moments, he asked, "What was the messy business?"

"Pardon me?"

"Mr. Ikeda mentioned it just now. 'The messy business in 1959.'"

"Oh, that," Natsume said. He took another sip of tea. He seemed
to be considering what exactly to tell Harper. "One of the people
working here died in circumstances the police regarded as suspicious.
There had been complaints that people were being held against their
will. So the police raided the farm. No charges were made, but the
media continued to run articles critical of the Ichihashi-kai, the
group that runs the farm."

"So this place. It's no ordinary farm, is it? It's more like a
commune?"

"I guess you could call it that."

"And the group that runs it. What are they called again?"

"The Ichihashi-kai."

"Yes, the Ichihashi-kai. What's the connection between them and
Beheiren?"

"There's no connection as such. Shunsuke Tsurumi, who is one
of Beheiren's founders, thought the media was treating the Ichihashi-kai unfairly. He visited the farm to see for himself what things
were like and wrote about it in a magazine."

"I see. So what do you think?"

"What do I think?" Natsume paused again. "I respect Tsurumi,"
he answered eventually. "And I trust his judgment."

"Aren't the police keeping an eye on this place?"

"I don't think so. It was all a long time ago."

"Do you think the police are looking for us?"

"It's hard to tell," Natsume said. "Legally, U.S. military authorities
can ask the Japanese police to search for, take into custody, and hand
over any deserter. Once this request is made, it becomes the duty of
the Japanese police to make such an arrest. Of course, the Japanese
police can also arrest any member of the U.S. military who breaks
Japanese law. But if requested to by the U.S. military, they have to
hand them over to American custody."

There was a gentle knock at the door, which slid open to reveal

Mrs. Ikeda again carrying a tray, this time laden with food. She set the meals down on the table before exiting the room.

Harper looked at the array of dishes. He recognized the rice and the miso soup, but most of the other items were unfamiliar to him. Yumi had made Japanese-style food for him once or twice, but it was nothing like this. He noticed an egg in a bowl next to the rice. Natsume must have seen the puzzled expression on his face, because he said to Harper, "It's a raw egg. We put it on the rice."

"On the rice?" Harper said, the look of puzzlement turning into a look of dismay.

"Look," Natsume said. "I'll show you."

The young Beheiren operative took his egg and cracked it on the side of his rice bowl and emptied the contents over the top of the rice. Then, after pouring a small amount of soy sauce over the top of the egg, he used his chopsticks to mix the rice, egg, and soy sauce together. He scooped some of the eggy rice into his mouth with his chopsticks and looked across at Harper, who repeated this procedure with his own egg. Harper chewed it several times before swallowing. He was prepared for the worst, but it wasn't as bad as he expected. He smiled, and thought he saw a look of relief cross Natsume's face.

Shortly after Harper and Natsume finished their meals, the Ikedas returned. Mr. Ikeda sat at the table and waited while his wife collected the dishes. He took a packet of cigarettes out of his shirt pocket and proffered it to his two guests. Both Harper and Natsume declined, whereupon Ikeda lit a cigarette for himself. After Mrs. Ikeda left the room, Harper turned to their host and asked, "Do you mind if I ask a question?"

Ikeda looked across the table and smiled. "Not at all."

"How long have you been a member of the Ichihashi-kai?"

Ikeda took a pull on his cigarette before answering. "Nearly ten years now. I was one of the first to answer the call of our group's founder, Keisuke Ichihashi, to help set up the farm. Soon members had gathered from around the country, and together we built everything you see here today."

"But why chickens?" Harper asked. "I mean, why did this Mr. Ichihashi want to establish a poultry farm? Why not grow rice or raise pigs?"

"That's a good question," Ikeda replied. "From a young age, Ichi-hashi was intent on finding the answer to one fundamental question: How can people be happy? His rebellious nature soon brought him to the attention of the authorities. This was during the war, when those in power took a dim view of anyone who questioned the status quo. The young Ichihashi was placed under surveillance. At one point he fled and took refuge in a chicken coop, where he whiled away the hours observing the chickens. He began to wonder what it was that made them happy. He came to the view that to be happy, people, like chickens, needed the right surroundings, but they also needed to control their selfish urges and, above all, their anger. That way, they could work together more effectively to solve society's problems. These ideas became the pillars of Ichihashi's philosophy. And what better environment to put these ideas into practice than a chicken farm?"

"I see," Harper said, though having helped raise chickens on the family plot in Redville, he didn't have a particular regard for the critters, and failed to see what humans could learn from them.

"By working together on a farm," Ikeda continued, "people not only learn how to get along, but they also come to appreciate the ideal relationship between people and nature, which is one of mutual support. One thing Ichihashi always stressed is that nature and people are one, that nature is not man's possession. Ichihashi called his philosophy Ichihashism, and later published a book about it. He died in 1961, but we're committed to practicing his teachings here and at other farms around the country."

"So this Ichihashism," Harper said. "It's a kind of religion, is it?"

Ikeda took a long pull on his cigarette, exhaling the smoke through his nose. "No, not a religion. Though like all the great religious leaders, Ichihashi wanted to change society. Above all, he was committed to scientific principles. In fact the application of scientific principles in the pursuit of happiness is central to Ichihashism.

"We have none of the strict rules normally associated with religions. Commune members lead a simple lifestyle with minimal possessions and no money. The community and nature satisfy all the needs of the people here. We eat together twice a day in the communal dining room, and we have communal bathing facilities, but the family unit is still the basis of our community life. There are no bosses and no set work hours. Decisions are made by what we call the 'Ichihashi process.' Proposals are put forward, and these are discussed until agreement is reached. Decisions are made, and disputes are settled, by consensus at meetings."

"You make it sound like utopia," Harper said.

"It was far from utopian at first. The soil was terrible and needed a lot of work to make it productive. Trees needed to be cut down to make room for the chicken runs. We had to work very hard to build everything you see here. That's not the case now that the community is established and the farm is a going concern. But there's a new problem."

"What's that," Harper asked.

"The tendency among newcomers is to work too hard. People attuned to life in the cities aren't used to working without a boss and without set work hours. They find it difficult to learn to rest when they need to. It takes a while for them to adjust to the pace of life here, and to the freedom."

Harper nodded. But then another thought struck him. "When people come to live here, what happens to their property?"

"It becomes the property of the commune."

"And what happens when they leave? Do they get their property back?"

Ikeda smiled and said, "I'm afraid not." He then leaned over and stubbed out his cigarette in the metal ashtray on the table in front of Harper.

CHAPTER 14

The two-hundred-and-fifty-ton *Dai-ni Toshima-maru* sailed south toward the mouth of Kagoshima Bay, her running lights illuminating her passage across calm seas silvered by a near-full moon. With room for just sixty in the ship's cabins, the bulk of the one-hundred-and-fifty-or-so passengers were strewn over her decks. Masuda and the deserters sat huddled in a group with Pran and his three fellow Tribe members on rush matting on the large open foredeck. Soon after setting sail they had opened one of the bottles of *shōchū* Masuda had bought in Kagoshima, and they shared it now, each of them upending the heavy bottle and taking a swig before passing it on to their neighbor.

Presently Pran produced a small drum from his bag, and after wedging it into the well formed by his crossed legs, he began to beat it with his hands. One of the hippies stood up and started to dance. Before long the others joined in, clapping and shouting in time with the drumming. Masuda looked around self-consciously, concerned at how the other passengers would react. At first they seemed unsure of what to make of the hippies' antics, but they soon relaxed, with some of them, old women and children included, even joining in the merrymaking.

Masuda took another mouthful of the *shōchū* and passed the bottle over to the Americans, who had formed a little group of their own. Santiago and Roberts seemed ill at ease, though their faces revealed little emotion. Only Sullivan seemed to be enjoying the festivities. Usually the least animated of the three, he was slapping his knees with both hands, his upper body twisting in time with the rhythm of Pran's drumming and the clapping and calling of the other passengers.

As Masuda looked on, Sullivan smiled and closed his eyes and slowly tilted his head backward. The moonlight caught his upturned face, illuminating his pale features and revealing to Masuda an expression of what he could only describe as ecstasy. And at that moment, for the first time since leaving Nara, Masuda felt that things might just turn out all right after all.

The hippies and their fellow merrymakers, Masuda among them, partied late into the night. The next morning, tired and hungover, they moved gingerly and spoke sparingly as the *Dai-ni Toshima-maru* continued her voyage south. The ferry called at several islands before reaching Suwanosejima, the smallest of these, Gagajima, home to just a handful of families. As they dropped anchor off Gagajima, Masuda got to his feet and wandered over to the side of the deck where the three deserters were standing. They were all looking in the same direction, so riveted by something that they didn't notice him approaching. When he drew alongside them he immediately saw what it was that had captivated them. Surrounding the island was a reef so white it was almost dazzling. Masuda had never seen anything like it.

"It's beautiful, isn't it?" he said.

"We think it's guano," Santiago said.

"Guano?"

"Bird shit," Roberts said.

"Excuse me?"

"The white stuff," Roberts continued. "It's bird droppings. Built up over years. It makes good fertilizer, apparently."

"He's right," came a man's voice.

Masuda and the deserters turned to see Pran standing behind them.

"The reef is home to a colony of *ōmizunagidori*," the hippie said.

"*Ōmizu*-what?" Santiago asked.

"Streaked shearwater. A type of seabird."

Santiago nodded and the deserters turned their attention back out to sea, where a small boat was making its way toward them through a gap in the reef.

Pran turned to Masuda and said, "I've made this journey a number of times now, but this sight still amazes me."

Masuda nodded. "When was it you first visited Suwanosejima?"

"Two summers ago. It's strange. To think I lived in Kagoshima all those years and never even knew it existed."

"Were you born in Kagoshima?"

"Yes. My father was a tea merchant. My elder brother was going to inherit the family business, so at the age of twelve I left school and went to work as an office boy. When the war broke out I was drafted and joined the Naval Preparatory Flight Training Program. It was this program that supplied many of the pilots that carried out kamikaze attacks on Allied ships toward the end of the war."

Masuda nodded. Below them, the small boat from Gagajima had drawn alongside the *Dai-ni Toshima-maru*. Two of the larger vessel's crewmembers, bearing bags of rice and other provisions, carefully descended to the bottom of the gangway and began loading the items onto the smaller craft.

"Thankfully I showed little promise as a pilot," Pran went on. "So I became a radar specialist. I was posted to a remote forward base in southern Kyushu. The work wasn't demanding, and I had a lot of free time. I used this time to read. Schopenhauer, Nietzsche, Marx and Engels, Kropotkin. As the war drew to a close, I saw more and more activity in my sector, mostly kamikaze planes flying south in the direction of Okinawa. It pained me to think that some of those planes would have been piloted by young men I trained with, and that they probably wouldn't be coming back."

The engine on the small boat roared to life, and Masuda and Pran watched as the lone helmsman maneuvered his craft away from the *Dai-ni Toshima-maru* and back through the gap in the reef.

"What did you do when the war ended?" Masuda asked.

"I moved to Tokyo. Like many others who drifted there at the end of the war looking for work, I had nowhere to live, so at night I slept on the street. I eventually found work in a foundry. Later I got a job in a publishing company. When the company collapsed, I dropped out and traveled up and down Japan, visiting wilderness areas in the country and laborers' ghettoes in the cities. I developed an interest in primitive art, especially sculpture. I was also inspired by my travels to write poetry."

There was a loud clanking as the *Dai-ni Toshima-maru* weighed anchor. Masuda waited for the noise to stop and then said, "And that's how you met Gary Snyder."

"And that's how I met Gary," Pran affirmed. "He encouraged me to pursue a career in poetry. He even used his connections to try to secure a creative writing post for me at a university in the United States, but my lack of formal education ended those plans. By this time I was living in Shinjuku, where I became involved in the underground scene. A group of us got together and published a magazine. It was out of this group that the Tribe emerged."

The *Dai-ni Toshima-maru* was moving again, and with nothing but ocean to see over the side of the vessel, Masuda and Pran wandered back to where the rest of their party were sitting on the foredeck. There they continued their conversation, Pran regaling Masuda with stories of his adventures up and down the country, of how the Tribe set up its first commune in Nagano, and of life on Suwanosejima.

Suwanosejima, Pran explained, was part of the Tokara Islands, a link in the chain of islands stretching from Kyushu to Taiwan. Collectively known as the Ryukyu Islands, the island chain once formed an independent kingdom. The Ryukyu Kingdom was unilaterally abolished by Japan in 1879 when the islands were annexed by the Meiji government, who recognized their strategic value as a buffer between mainland Japan and potential enemies to the south. This role was highlighted during World War II, when the largest of the Ryukyu Islands, Okinawa, was the scene of a last-ditch attempt by the Imperial Japanese Army to prevent American forces reaching the Japanese mainland. As many as one hundred and fifty thousand Okinawan civilians died during the Battle of Okinawa, many at the hands of the Japanese military.

There was a shout, and first one and then all four Tribe members on board the *Dai-ni Toshima-maru* were pointing in the same direction. For some time the four had been standing in a group at the vessel's bow, talking loudly among themselves and moving restlessly as they eagerly awaited their first glimpse in more than a week of the island they now regarded as their home. Masuda roused Santiago, Roberts, and Sullivan and led them over to where the hippies were standing. In the distance, barely visible in the fading light, was a roughly conical landmass, dark gray-brown around its circumference where sheer cliffs more than three hundred feet tall rose out of the ocean, emerald green in the middle, and almost maroon toward the top. Swirling clouds and mist masked the island's highest peak, but there was no hiding the thick column of smoke that rose menacingly from it into the darkening sky.

"Is that what I think it is?" Santiago asked.

Masuda turned to the American, whose eyes were fixed on the volcano, which seemed to bear down on them as they drew nearer to the island.

"Don't worry. There hasn't been a major eruption for hundreds of years."

"It sure looks pretty active to me," Roberts said.

As if to verify this observation, there was a loud boom and the outpouring of smoke from the volcano grew more vigorous, its color turning from light gray to black.

"There's nothing to worry about," Masuda said. "People wouldn't be living here if it was dangerous."

What Masuda didn't mention was that the island had been abandoned in the fifteenth century after a major eruption, and only repopulated, by people from the Amami Islands to the south, fewer than one hundred years ago.

"Come on," Masuda said, eager to take the deserters' minds off the volcano, "we'd better get ready to disembark."

He led them over to where the Tribe members were gathering up their possessions and the provisions they had secured in Kagoshima. The smiles on their faces could not have presented more of a contrast to the grim expressions on the faces of the Americans.

Like Gagajima, Suwanosejima was surrounded by a reef that prevented the *Dai-ni Toshima-maru* approaching closer than a few hundred yards from the island. There it dropped anchor, and as Masuda and the other disembarking passengers assembled at the top of the gangway they heard the ship's whistle blow. Looking toward the island, Masuda noticed figures scrambling over the rocky beach at the base of the cliff. A small boat was launched from a breakwater, and soon the helmsman was steering it through a gap in the reef toward the *Dai-ni Toshima-maru*.

At first Masuda thought the steersman was the sole occupant of the boat, but as it drew nearer he noticed movement behind him. Straining his eyes, he made out two bodies in what looked to be woolen coats. They were moving more vigorously now, struggling to stay on their feet as the small boat pitched on the choppy waters outside the reef. When the boat pulled alongside the *Dai-ni Toshima-maru*, Masuda identified horns and small bearded faces, and when the drone of the boat's engine subsided he heard bleating, confirming the identity of the two passengers.

As well as the goats, the boat carried produce, including more than a dozen shiny watermelons. It took several minutes to unload these goods. Only then were the passengers disembarking from the *Dai-ni Toshima-maru* allowed to board.

Such were their numbers and the amount of cargo that needed to be ferried ashore that the smaller boat had to make three round trips. Masuda and the deserters were part of the second contingent, sharing the boat with six large propane gas cylinders and a dozen sacks of fertilizer.

When they reached the island, they were greeted warmly by a group of local residents, and by Pran and the hippies, who had been part of the first contingent. They climbed out of the boat and waded through the shallow water to the beach and scrambled over ropes and cables and fishing nets to the bottom of the cliff from where they watched the boat's cargo being unloaded.

It was dark by the time the final load of passengers and provisions made it ashore, and the residents used lanterns and flashlights to guide them as they helped the last of the passengers out of the boat. The final person to disembark was an elderly woman, whom Pran carried ashore on his back.

Once the boat had been hauled out of the water and up the beach, the Tribe members joined Masuda and the Americans at the bottom of the cliff. After doling out the provisions (Masuda volunteered to carry a sack of rice), they set off in single file up the steep pathway that switchbacked up the cliff. Masuda found the going tough, and soon fell behind the other, fitter members of his party. While stopping to catch his breath at the apex of the first switchback, he looked out over the ocean. The moon had disappeared behind a thick bank of cloud, and in the darkness he could clearly make out the running lights of the *Dai-ni Toshima-maru* receding in the distance.

Though the gradient decreased once they reached the top of the cliff, the path continued to climb. Having fallen even further behind the others, Masuda trudged on alone in the dark, the sack of rice, which he carried slung over his right shoulder, feeling heavier with every step.

After passing the island's only village, Masuda noticed the track became less defined and the surroundings more rugged, grassy meadows giving way to bamboo groves and semi-jungle. Then he was in the open again, and when he saw a large banyan tree and an abandoned farmhouse, Masuda knew he was nearly there. Earlier in the day, during his conversation with Pran on the *Dai-ni Toshima-maru*, the commune's founder told him how the islanders gave permission for the Tribe to use the farmhouse as their headquarters when they first arrived here, until they could build more suitable accommodation. They had since moved out, and the islanders now used the building as a makeshift barn to house cattle during inclement weather.

Soon after passing the farmhouse, Masuda saw an orange glow up ahead. Moments later he came to a clearing ringed by several huts with thatch roofs. Around an open fire, the source of the orange glow, stood a group of men and women of various ages, the men all naked from the waist up, some wearing only loincloths. Their tanned bodies shimmered in the firelight.

Masuda was the last of the new arrivals to reach the clearing. He walked over to where Pran and the others had gathered and unshouldered the sack of rice and lowered it to the ground by his feet. The three deserters were standing off to one side, looking slightly apprehensive.

"Welcome," came a woman's voice. "You must be hungry."

The deserters all looked in the direction of the voice, and Masuda saw the expressions on their faces lighten almost instantaneously. He followed their gaze and saw a young woman wearing blue shorts and a white T-shirt coming toward them from the direction of one of the huts. She was carrying a large pot. Two more figures, a man and a woman, emerged from the hut carrying a rice pot and bowls and chopsticks, and together they walked over to the fire where people were now busy laying rush mats on the ground. Once the mats were down, Masuda and the deserters were invited to join the hippies, and they all sat in a rough circle.

Miso soup was ladled from the large pot into bowls and handed around, together with bowls of brown rice and chopsticks. From somewhere a large bottle of *shōchū* appeared, and it too was passed around the circle. As he ate the food and sipped the smoky liquor, Masuda felt the fatigue from the long boat ride and the climb up to the commune seep away.

A quick round of self-introductions followed dinner. The Tribe members introduced themselves using Sanskrit nicknames, as if to underscore the fact that by joining the Tribe they had cast aside the trappings of modern Japanese society and taken on new identities. Pran went first. He was followed by Karon, Gati, Daksha, Tarun, Bandhu, Jahnu, Mohana, Chapala, Ganak, Anala, and Nanda. Several introduced themselves in English as well as Japanese for the benefit of their American guests, with Masuda translating for those who did not. In all there were twelve Tribe members present, the youngest in his mid-teens. Most looked to be in their late-teens or early-twenties, with a few probably in their thirties. Pran, who was in his mid-forties, was the oldest.

It was Pran who got the evening's entertainment underway. Sitting cross-legged, he began humming, a simple drone at first, with rhythm but devoid of melody. Gradually, as if from nowhere, a tune emerged, and one by one the other hippies joined in. It took a while for all the voices to meld, but when they did the effect was almost hypnotic.

Masuda leaned back until he was lying face up on the rush matting and looked skyward. A patch of cloud veiled the moon, but vast swaths of the heavens lay exposed. As his eyes adjusted to the dark, he saw stars, millions of them, shining with an intensity he had not witnessed for years. In Tokyo, even on the clearest of nights the stars were hardly visible, their brightness overwhelmed by the streetlights and neon signs. For a moment Masuda imagined that he was on another planet altogether, looking up at a completely different galaxy. All around him, voices hummed.

CHAPTER 15

Flynn was used to waking up in unfamiliar surroundings. He was also used to waking up with a sore head. But things were different this time. The pain was not the dull, generalized pain that followed a night of heavy drinking, but sharp and localized. What's more, when he opened his eyes he found he had difficulty focusing. He blinked and rubbed the sockets with his forefingers, but there was no improvement.

He raised his head a few inches and looked around. Slowly things came into focus. He was lying on a thin mattress under harsh fluorescent lighting in what appeared to be a classroom. Beside the mattress lay his rucksack. Around him were other bodies, as many as twenty, also lying on mattresses, some with their forearms draped over their eyes to block out the light. The plaster walls were daubed with Japanese writing in letters three feet tall, all of them unrecognizable except the exclamation marks, of which there were many. Through the uncurtained windows to his right he could see only the black of night.

Flynn noticed that desks had been pushed to one end of the room. On them were strewn white helmets, books, towels, and Thermos bottles. Around one of the desks sat a small group of people talking. He raised himself onto one elbow to get a better look at them, and as he did so they appeared to notice him, for they stopped talking and looked in Flynn's direction. One of them, a young woman with a bob cut and black-rimmed glasses, stood up and walked over to where he was lying. She bent over him and said something in Japanese. Flynn shrugged his shoulders, and she spoke to him again, this time in English.

"What is your name?"

Still confused and in pain, Flynn didn't think before replying. "Edward Flynn, Seaman Apprentice, U.S. Navy."

The woman straightened and looked over her shoulder at the people sitting around the table. She said something and one of them, a man, stood up, walked over and stood beside the woman. He was swarthy with deep-set eyes and bushy eyebrows. In one hand he held a wooden staff, the bottom of which he rested on the floor beside Flynn.

"U.S. Navy?" the man asked.

Flynn slowly nodded. He reached up with his free hand to the spot on the top of his head that seemed to be the source of the pain. There was a lump the size of a rice ball.

"You're an American serviceman?" the man pressed.

Flynn didn't reply. He slowly rubbed the lump on his head.

The man lifted the staff a few inches and, without warning, slammed the end down on the concrete floor. The resounding crack caused Flynn to flinch.

"Answer me!"

"What? Yes," Flynn said, and then quickly, "I mean, no."

The man and woman looked at each other and back at Flynn.

"Who sent you here?" the woman asked.

"No one sent me."

"Don't lie," the man said.

"It's the truth. Where am I, anyway?"

"You're in the main building of the Economics department."

"The Economics department?"

"At Nichidai."

Flynn repeated the name to himself, but it meant nothing. "Who are you?" he asked the man.

"I'm the chairman of the Defense Committee."

"The Defense Committee?" Flynn muttered, again repeating what he had heard, as if doing so might jog his memory.

"Was it the embassy?" the man prodded. "Did the American embassy send you?"

"The embassy?" Flynn repeated. "I don't understand what…"

And slowly it came back to him. Riding the Yamanote Line.

Changing to the Chūō-Sōbu Line and getting off at Suidōbashi. Walking toward Nihon University. He remembered the line of police and the snake-dancing students and the rock-throwers. Nichidai was Nihon University. Students occupied the school, the culmination of months of protests sparked by revelations that university authorities had embezzled billions of yen.

"Yes, I remember now," Flynn said, rubbing his head again. "How long have I been here?"

The man frowned. He was clearly losing his patience. He lifted the wooden staff again and was about to bring it down when Flynn raised one hand in a pleading gesture.

"Wait. I can explain."

The man peered down at Flynn and brought the staff down slowly until it rested on the floor. "It better be good."

"I'm a deserter. From the U.S. Navy. I was in Vietnam. They sent me to the hospital at Yokosuka, but I escaped."

"A deserter?"

"Yes."

The man and the woman looked at each other again and spoke in Japanese. At times the conversation became heated. Eventually the man looked at Flynn and said, "All right, Edward Flynn. Your story's so crazy it's probably true. We'll talk in the morning. Meanwhile, you'd better get some sleep. It's late."

Flynn was woken by shouting. He opened his eyes and sat up. The harsh fluorescent lights had been extinguished, and in the wan light of dawn the room seemed kinder, gentler, the untidiness and disorder less conspicuous. He put a hand to his head and felt for the lump. It was still there, though noticeably smaller than it had been hours before. The pain in his head had also subsided.

Around him, bodies stirred. There was more shouting, closer now. Then the door to the room burst open, a figure appeared and barked an order in Japanese. The bodies around him moved more urgently, flinging aside bedding and rubbing tired eyes and stumbling toward the doorway.

Flynn sat on his mattress and watched as the room emptied of people, unsure of whether to follow or stay put. A minute passed before a light blue helmet poked through the open doorway, and Flynn smiled as he recognized the bushy eyebrows and deep-set eyes. It was the man with the stick.

He came in and approached within a few feet of Flynn. Flynn's eyes were drawn to his helmet. Unlike most of the helmets he had seen so far, which were daubed with Japanese writing or unfamiliar English initialisms, it bore a single English word: FREE.

The man smiled and said, "How's your throwing arm, Edward Flynn?"

"I dunno. Okay, I guess."

"Good. Come with me."

Flynn stood up and went to pick up his rucksack from beside the mattress.

"Leave that here," the man said. "Hopefully we'll be coming back."

He turned and Flynn followed him toward the door. After a few paces, however, the man stopped and looked back at Flynn and then over at the desk he had been sitting at the night before. He walked over and picked up one of the helmets, then brought it over and placed it on Flynn's head, slapping the top of it with his palm as if testing its effectiveness. Flynn winced—the lump on his head smarting from the thumping. The man then fastened the chinstrap and stepped back and scrutinized Flynn, the way a mother might a child in his Sunday best.

"That's more like it, Edward Flynn," the man said.

Flynn smiled. "Call me Eddie."

"Eddie. Good. I'm Yamada. Now, let's go."

They exited the room into an empty hallway, descended a flight of stairs, and entered a corridor identical to the one above, except this one was a hive of activity, with people in helmets all rushing in one direction carrying wooden benches and desks and staves and other items. Yamada led Flynn in the opposite direction, and they struggled to make headway against the onrushing tide.

"Where are they all going?" Flynn asked, shouting to be heard above the din.

"To barricade the stairs."

Eventually they came to another set of stairs. They descended one floor and turned left into another corridor, this one almost deserted. They followed it to the end where there was a large window. On the floor beneath the window were two wooden boxes. One contained rocks, similar to the ones demonstrators had been throwing at the police the day before. The other contained half a dozen bottles stuffed with rags. Flynn knew what they were even before he smelled the gasoline. He stopped in his tracks. Yamada, who had begun to open the window, turned and saw Flynn looking at the box.

"Don't worry. They're just a precaution. Hopefully we won't have to use them."

"What do you mean? What's happening?"

"Riot police. They're trying to get in. It's not a full-scale attack. More of a probing mission to test our defenses. But we need to let them know we mean business."

Flynn looked from Yamada to the box of Molotov cocktails and back to Yamada.

"Come on," Yamada said, "help me get this window open."

As they worked on opening the window, Flynn looked outside. They were at least five stories up. Below them was a narrow street, which Flynn recognized as the same street out of which the snake-dancing demonstrators had emerged onto Hakusan-dōri. Across the street was another building of similar height to the one they were in. Connecting the two buildings was an enclosed overhead walkway, the roof of which was directly below them.

As soon as the window was fully open, Yamada climbed out and jumped down onto the roof of the walkway. He turned and looked up at Flynn.

"Hand me the box of rocks."

Flynn picked up the container and carefully lowered it out of the window into Yamada's waiting arms. He then climbed out and dropped onto the roof and together they walked hunched over until they were about halfway to the other building. Yamada set down the box and they both lay down on the roof and poked their heads over the edge.

On the street below were a dozen riot police. Two of them stepped forward and rested a ladder against the building. A third policeman, his shield in one hand, started climbing. Two more followed as Flynn and Yamada looked on.

Flynn looked at Yamada, wondering what he was waiting for. But the young man wasn't looking down at the policemen—rather, he was looking up at an open window several stories above them. He shouted something in Japanese, and two heads appeared. They were followed seconds later by four hands, each holding a rock.

Seconds later Flynn watched the rocks plummet toward the policemen. The first three missed, but the fourth struck the lead policeman on the top of his helmet, throwing him off balance. He clung to the rail of the ladder, at the same time raising his shield above his head.

By this time the second volley of rocks plunged down. Two of them struck the lead policeman's shield in quick succession, only to slide off and fall to the street below. Alerted to the threat from above, the remaining officers were prepared, and the third volley, though better aimed than the first two, caused no damage.

"Time for some fun," Yamada said.

He raised himself onto one knee and removed two rocks from the box. After taking aim, he let fly with the first. It struck one of the policemen on the leg, but it was only a glancing blow. The officer turned and scanned the windows of the building on the other side of the street, but his shield restricted his vision skyward and he didn't spot Yamada and Flynn.

Yamada waited until all the policemen had turned the other way before letting fly with his second rock. But his aim was off and it sailed past its target and struck the concrete balcony, shattering into pieces that fell harmlessly to the ground.

"Oops," Yamada said. He looked at Flynn. "Your turn, Eddie."

Flynn raised himself into a crouching position and reached with one hand into the box. He picked up and discarded a number of the rocks until he found one that was more or less spherical and roughly the size of a potato. He tossed it in the air a couple of times to gauge its heft, then crept forward to the edge of the roof, stood up and drew his right arm back. He paused for a second or two, his eyes focused on the unprotected torso of the policeman at the top of the ladder. Then his arm shot forward, catapulting the rock at its target.

It was a throw that would have made his high school baseball coach proud. But there was no time to admire his handiwork. When taking his stance, Flynn had failed to make allowances for his follow through. His right foot came to a stop on the edge of the roof, but his momentum carried his upper body forward. As the rock sailed through the air Flynn windmilled his arms in a desperate effort to prevent himself falling off the roof.

He had almost resigned himself to this fate when he felt a hand grip the waistband of his trousers and pull him back to safety. He turned to thank Yamada, but as he opened his mouth he was interrupted by a loud yell from below. Flynn and Yamada scrambled to the edge of the roof and looked down just in time to see the policeman at the top of the ladder tumble backward, the hand that had been holding the ladder rail now clutching his kidney area. On his way down he collected the officer directly below him. There was a cacophony of shouting and clattering and, moments later, all three policemen lay in a crumpled heap on the ground, with a fourth pinned underneath them.

None of the fallen officers appeared seriously injured, but as others went to help them the students in the building resumed their attack, landing several blows on the helmets and unprotected bodies of the would-be intruders before they managed to get to their feet and raise their shields in a kind of tortoise formation. Maintaining this configuration, they slowly began to shuffle backward in the direction of Hakusan-dōri as rocks rained down on them. Only when they had rounded the corner and were out of sight did the students break off their attack, at which point, almost in unison, they raised their fists in the air and let out yelps of delight.

CHAPTER 16

The next morning, Harper and Natsume arrived in the dining room to find around sixty commune members seated along rows of trestle tables. They included several people of Ikeda's generation as well as younger individuals and family groups. Most were dressed in farming clothes like Ikeda's. Just normal people as far as Harper could tell.

Harper and Natsume sat at their own table at one end of the room with Ikeda. After they finished eating breakfast, which consisted of rice, miso soup, raw egg, and pickles, Ikeda lit a cigarette. Harper watched, fascinated at how he managed to complete this task, as he did other routine activities, with one arm in a way that seemed completely natural.

Ikeda took a puff on his cigarette and looked across the table at Harper and Natsume. "You're both probably wondering how I lost my arm."

Harper looked down, embarrassed at the thought that Ikeda had noticed him staring.

"Like you," Ikeda continued, looking at Harper now, "I was wounded in combat."

"You fought in World War II?" Harper said.

"In the Philippines."

Harper was taken aback. "The Philippines? My uncle fought in the Philippines, under General MacArthur."

"Well, well," Ikeda said, looking earnestly at Harper now. "General MacArthur. Such a formidable foe in wartime, and yet so benevolent during the occupation as Supreme Commander of the Allied Powers. When the war ended, most Japanese were terrified at the prospect of being occupied by Westerners. We were convinced the Allied soldiers would be out for revenge. But from General MacArthur down, the occupation forces were considerate, even compassionate, in their dealings with us. They gave hope and happiness to a people who had endured nothing but struggle and privation under a ruthless military regime. And to think we had been such bitter enemies."

Ikeda went on to explain how difficult things were immediately after the war, when malnutrition was widespread and city dwellers were forced to go out into the country to exchange watches, jewelry, and clothes for food. As their host was talking, Harper glanced across at Natsume, and noticed a frown on the young Beheiren operative's face. It was the first sign of friction between the two Japanese on whom Harper now relied for his own safety. And it made Harper extremely nervous.

After breakfast, Natsume and Harper set off for a walk around the farm. Their late arrival the previous afternoon had prevented Harper from gaining his bearings, and so he welcomed the opportunity to survey the surrounding terrain in the morning light. If the police did turn up, Harper knew he might have to get away from the farm on his own. He needed to have an escape route.

After stopping briefly at the office to inform Ikeda of their plans, Harper and Natsume climbed the hill behind the administration building, passing the poultry runs before entering the pine forest that encircled the farm. They followed a track that led up to the crest of the hill. From time to time, Harper directed his gaze skyward. Ikeda had warned them that the weather was likely to turn nasty around midday, and while there were still patches of blue visible through the lattice of pine tree branches, they were getting smaller, squeezed by the gathering dark gray clouds.

The path grew steeper as it rose, and at one point Harper had to stop to catch his breath. Although his body had healed, he was still not as fit as he had been before he suffered his injuries. Strenuous exercise left him exhausted. At the top of the hill, the trail they had been following intersected another one. They turned right, and after walking mostly downhill for a few minutes they came to a clearing. Here the pine forest ended, giving them a clear view of the valley below. Harper saw the river and in front of it the road that led to the train station, out of sight up the valley to their left. He looked for and located the hamlet they had passed through the night before. He had found his escape route.

Natsume drew up beside Harper, his gaze also directed down into the valley. After a few moments Harper turned to Natsume and said, "Do you have beef with Mr. Ikeda?"

Natsume looked at Harper, a puzzled expression on his face. "Beef?"

"A grievance, a gripe."

Natsume didn't answer for some time, and stood there sniffing and staring out over the valley. He seemed surprised that Harper had sensed the underlying discord between Natsume and their host. Eventually he said, "It's just that for all his talk of hope and happiness, like most Japanese of his generation, he did nothing to prevent Japanese aggression and the misery it caused. In fact, by fighting for Japan he aided and abetted that aggression."

Harper thought carefully before answering. "Do you think you would have acted differently? You may think you would have, but unless you lived through that era, I don't think you can say so for sure. It takes a lot of courage to take a stand against something when everyone around you supports it."

Natsume didn't answer. His gaze remained fixed on the hills on the other side of the valley.

Harper said, "I mean, what's the difference between Ikeda's actions during World War II and my actions in Vietnam?"

"They're completely different. For a start you deserted. You did something."

"You make it sound so high and mighty," Harper said. "Maybe I got scared. Maybe I was just trying to save my own ass. What's more courageous: me staying by my brothers' side during combat or sneaking out and hiding in the mountains of Japan?"

"But I know you. I know that's not how it was."

Something inside Harper snapped. "You don't know shit about me!"

Natsume looked at Harper, clearly shocked at the outburst.

Annoyed with himself for having lost it, Harper took a moment to calm down before continuing. "What do you really know about what I did in Vietnam? For all you know I could have killed scores, hundreds of people. Innocent people like down in that hamlet."

"But you didn't," Natsume said. And then, "Did you?"

Harper looked from Natsume to the valley below. Someone was burning rubbish in a yard behind one of the houses. The white smoke rose lazily in a single ghostly column before being caught by the breeze and carried down the valley.

"We were in a valley just like this," Harper said, "on a search and destroy mission. I was a cherry. FNGs they called us. Fucking new guys. I was assigned to a platoon at the United States Marine Corps base at Chu Lai, about fifty miles south of Da Nang. I'd been there about a week when we were choppered inland, way out west, to search for Charlie." Harper looked at Natsume. "That's what we called the Vietcong or the North Vietnamese Army. Civilians were 'slants' or 'slopes.' All Vietnamese were 'gooks,' though we weren't supposed to call them that. We were also supposed to be nice to civilians, but a lot of the time we couldn't tell who was a civilian and who was a combatant."

Harper noticed Natsume wince on hearing these epithets, but the Beheiren operative said nothing. Eventually Harper looked away from Natsume back down into the valley.

"Our platoon leader was a brother, a veteran lieutenant who'd been wounded twice. That's two Purple Hearts. One more and he'd be sent home for good. I wasn't sure about the other members of the platoon, but I looked up to the lieutenant.

"Anyway, we humped out of the LZ and before we knew it we walked straight into a minefield. Funny thing was, they were ours. American mines laid by South Vietnamese soldiers. We called the mines 'Bouncing Bettys.' They were triggered by a pressure mechanism that was activated when you stepped on them and released when you stepped off of them, launching a canister into the air that exploded about three feet above the ground. A normal mine would take your legs off, but a Bouncing Betty would cut you in two. Right through here."

Harper placed his right hand in front of his stomach and drew it across to indicate the height.

"The point man was the first to go. Up in a flash, blown into so many pieces you couldn't count them. The rest of us froze. The lieutenant came up and got us out of there. The trick was to walk back over your own footsteps. That way you could avoid the mines. But there was this one guy, another cherry, who was so scared he couldn't move. We were all telling him to take it easy, just to relax and walk back over his footsteps, but he just stood there looking straight ahead into the jungle.

"The lieutenant went as close as he could by stepping on other guys' footsteps and tried to talk to the guy, but he still wouldn't respond. So the lieutenant went a step closer. He was just a few feet away, and that's when the cherry turned around and ran toward the lieutenant. We all heard the click as he stepped on the trigger. If he'd stopped and kept his foot on the detonator he'd have given the lieutenant time to get out of there, but he kept on running. That's when the canister flew up and exploded. Neither of them stood a chance."

Harper looked across at Natsume. Unable to hold the American's gaze, Natsume sniffed and stared down at his own feet.

"We secured the area and gathered up what remained of the dead guys, took them back with the wounded to the LZ and arranged a medevac. Then we continued with the mission. But something had changed. You could see it in the guys' faces. Most of them were as young as me—nineteen, twenty—but I'm telling you, there was nothing like youth in their faces. One of the squad leaders, a corporal, took command of the platoon. He said we owed it to the lieutenant to carry on. He didn't say as much, but we all knew he wanted revenge. And he wasn't the only one. He was twenty-one-years old.

"We continued heading west. Everyone was itching for a fight, but Charlie was nowhere to be seen. Either he wasn't there or he was hiding real well. When it got dark, we dug foxholes and set up a perimeter. One of the things you learned pretty fast in Vietnam was that you didn't pick a fight with Charlie after dark. We had the days, but he had the nights.

"We broke camp early the next morning, and a short time later we came across a village with about ten hootches. The new platoon leader ordered our squad to hold the perimeter while he took the rest of the platoon in to check it out. A few minutes later we heard gunfire. The platoon leader radioed through and told us to shoot anyone who tried to get past. The last words we heard before the radio went dead were, 'Waste them.' There was more gunfire, more sustained this time. Soon we saw smoke. They were torching the hootches. The guys in my squad all looked at each other, but nobody moved and nobody said anything.

"The shooting died down. Then we heard someone coming from the direction of the village. They were coming fast. We all waited until we could see who it was. It was a gook, a kid of about twelve. We were hunkered down so he didn't see us until he was just a few feet away.

"I was the closest. I saw him look right at me. He stopped for a moment, looking right into my eyes. I pointed my M-16 at him but I couldn't shoot. He must have known, because he started running again. Just as I put my M-16 down I heard a burst of gunfire behind me and the kid went down. I turned around to see our squad leader standing there with his M-16 raised. His face was red and his eyes were bulging. I'll never forget his crazed laughter.

"Later the platoon leader radioed through and told us to join him inside the village. Some of the hootches were still burning. There were bodies piled up in the flames. They'd herded people into a hut and set it on fire. If anyone ran out they shot them. But they didn't just shoot people. They shot everything: chickens, dogs, even a water buffalo. Nothing was left alive. It wasn't until later, much later, that I realized a part of me also died that day."

Natsume was still staring at his feet. Without looking up he said, "But *you* didn't kill anyone, did you?"

"I didn't stop it, either. And who knows what I'd have done if I'd been in the village with the others. They were just following orders. That's what we were trained to do. You have no idea what it's like unless you've been through it. They strip you of your values and your individuality, and turn you into a group of the same people. Even when you know something's wrong, you're afraid to speak up, because you don't want to stand out. You know that you have no power as individuals. And you're afraid you'll be accused of shirking your duty, your obligation. It's the same in any army, and in any war. They take away your humanity."

Harper and Natsume remained silent for a long time before Natsume eventually said they should get going again and together they set off down the hill. They continued walking until they came to yet another path on their right that Natsume said would lead them back to the farm. After following this trail for a minute or two they saw a *torii* on their right. On either side of the gate stood two large cherry trees whose blossoms were just starting to lose their color.

Natsume noticed Harper looking up at the blossoms. "They're coming to the end of their life," he said. "Soon the petals will fall."

Harper nodded.

"They say one of the reasons we Japanese admire cherry blossoms so much is because they're so short-lived. In the Heian period people regarded the cherry blossoms as a metaphor for life itself: beautiful yet fleeting and ephemeral."

Without saying anything, Harper passed through the *torii* and walked up to a stone trough beside the pathway. He scooped up water using the ladle and washed his mouth and hands. Then he turned, approached the small worship hall, took a coin out of his pocket and threw it into the wooden box in front of the building before climbing the steps and ringing the bell. He bowed, clapped his hands, and bowed again.

Surprised at Harper's actions, Natsume followed him into the shrine and stood behind him at the foot of the steps.

"Where did you learn to do that?" Natsume asked.

"Yumi taught me."

Natsume was silent for a moment. Then he said, "Will you miss her?"

Harper didn't answer, but even a fool could have read the truth in his eyes.

CHAPTER 17

Masuda woke to the tintinnabulation of a hand bell. It was faint at first, but grew louder before fading off into the distance again. He patted the rush matting and found his glasses. Santiago, Roberts, and Sullivan were still asleep. Wan light seeped through the cracks in the bamboo walls, casting zebra stripes of light and shadow over their prone bodies.

Masuda got up and went outside. Tribe members were emerging from the other huts, some rubbing their eyes, others looking skyward and stretching their arms above their heads. They set off in ones and twos in the direction of the outdoor dining area, exchanging muted greetings as their paths crossed.

Masuda followed them to the dining area and saw others, the early risers, already sitting on benches on either side of a long, narrow table fashioned from an enormous piece of driftwood.

Masuda recognized the bearded figure of Pran, who looked up as he approached.

"Good morning," he said.

"Good morning," Pran replied. "I trust you slept well?"

"Yes, thank you."

"Please, have a seat," Pran said, gesturing to the space on the bench next to him.

"And what of our American guests?" Pran asked.

Masuda looked over his shoulder in the direction of the hut where he had left the three deserters and then back at Pran. "Still sleeping," he said. "I don't think they're used to drinking *shōchū*."

Pran gave a knowing smile.

"Good morning, Kawabata," called a high-pitched voice. Masuda looked to his right and saw the woman in blue shorts who had greeted them so warmly the night before, and who had later introduced herself as Anala. She approached carrying two mugs that she set down on the table. The familiar aroma came as a pleasant surprise to Masuda.

"Coffee!" he exclaimed. Then, looking up into the face of the woman, barely able to contain his glee, "*Real* coffee!"

"It's Kilimanjaro," Pran said. "One of the few luxuries we permit ourselves."

Masuda took a sip and looked up at Anala again, his smile even broader now. "It's good. I can't wait for breakfast."

"You'll have to wait a little longer, I'm afraid," Pran said. "We don't eat breakfast until nine o'clock."

"Nine o'clock?!" Masuda looked at his wristwatch. It was still only twenty to six.

"Our routine is different here. We work from six until nine, while the temperature is at its coolest. After breakfast we relax until three in the afternoon. We then have a snack, usually noodles or bread, and work again until six in the evening. Between six and seven we practice yoga and meditate. Dinner is served at seven, after which we sing, dance, and so on until bedtime, much as we did last night."

Masuda had assumed the previous night's festivities were a special event, a welcome party for the benefit of him and the deserters, as well as the hippies who had returned from Kagoshima. He was surprised to hear they were a regular affair.

"So you work six hours a day?" Masuda pressed.

"There's a lot to do. From clearing bamboo, cutting timber and gathering firewood, to working on the huts, fishing, and tending to the fields. But six hours is as much as anyone should be expected to work in one day. Especially in a place with this sort of climate."

"What about the cooking? I hope poor Anala here—" he cast a glance in the direction of the woman standing beside them "—doesn't cook every day."

"Certainly not," Pran said. "We have a roster, with two people assigned to the cooking duties each day. The same people are also responsible for deciding the menu. Within certain limits, of course. We try to eat mostly what we can grow or catch ourselves, so our diet mainly consists of fish and vegetables. Due to the scarcity of water, rice isn't grown on the island. We rely on the ferry for our supply of rice, just like all the other residents."

"So it's true there are no stores on the island?"

"None. No cars or televisions, either."

"What about telephones?"

"Telephone," Pran said. Then, for added effect, "Singular."

"One telephone. Between how many households?"

"Nine."

Pran paused and took a sip of coffee before continuing. "With the exception of rice and a few other things, we hope to become completely self-sufficient. We've cleared around two and a half acres of land where we've planted or will eventually plant pumpkins, sweet potatoes, watermelons, tomatoes, spinach, daikon, and so on. The land isn't ours, though. It belongs to the islanders. They kindly allow us to use it for free."

Masuda had been wondering about relations between the locals and the hippies ever since boarding the ferry at Kagoshima. Even given that the islanders' way of life was undoubtedly more relaxed than that of people on the mainland, they must have regarded the ways of the hippies as alien. But everything he had seen and heard since arriving, from the way everyone worked together to unload the ferry to how the hippies had been granted use of the abandoned farmhouse and land, indicated that relations, far from being strained, were amicable.

As he was pondering this, Santiago, Roberts, and Sullivan emerged from their hut and gathered in a row in front of it. Masuda looked over and saw that all three were wearing the red swimming trunks he had bought for them in Kagoshima. They were naked from the waist up. Masuda beckoned them over. The Americans exchanged words before setting off across the clearing. They stopped a few feet away. Almost in unison, the hippies turned their heads to scrutinize the new arrivals. Twelve pairs of dark eyes, all staring in the same direction. Masuda followed suit, trying to see the deserters as the hippies did.

Roberts had by far the most impressive physique of the three: tall and well built, the body of an athlete. Santiago, thin and bespectacled, was no Adonis, but he projected the kind of cool confidence that women found attractive. Confidence was something Sullivan, on the other hand, seemed to lack. The pinkness of his skin was all the more striking next to the tanned bodies of Santiago and Roberts. He looked uncomfortable under the inquisitive gazes of the hippies, and shuffled nervously from foot to foot, his head cast downward.

Santiago glanced up and down the long table in front of Masuda before speaking. "Are we too late for breakfast?"

There was an uncomfortable moment's silence, during which Masuda considered how best to break the news to Santiago that breakfast was three hours away. In the end, it was Pran who answered.

"Breakfast is at nine."

The tone of Pran's voice and the bluntness of the reply surprised Masuda. He regarded Santiago's face, curious as to how the Americans would react, but before he had a chance to respond, Anala said, "Would you like some coffee? It's Kilimanjaro."

There was sultriness in her voice that Masuda had not picked up on during their earlier conversation, most likely because it had been absent. Santiago's eyes lit up as he looked at Anala, as if noticing her for the first time.

"Yeah," Santiago said, smiling lasciviously. "Coffee would be nice."

"Make that three coffees," chimed in Roberts.

Anala turned and headed across the clearing toward the shed that served as the commune's kitchen.

"Sit down, guys," Masuda said, squeezing up next to Pran to make room on the bench for the Americans.

Roberts and Sullivan obliged, but Santiago remained standing.

"Hey, Richie," Roberts said. "Get your ass down here."

But still Santiago didn't move. Masuda looked up to see what the problem was, and noticed Santiago's gaze was fixed on Anala's retreating figure. Alarm bells immediately started ringing in his mind. As if things weren't difficult enough, he thought.

After they had finished their coffee, Pran showed them to an area by the cooking hut where there were basins to use for their ablutions.

"Make sure you use as little water as possible," Pran said in English, directing his gaze at the Americans. "We have to carry it from a stream about half a mile away near the foot of the volcano."

Masuda nodded.

"The scarcity of water is one of the main drawbacks about this place," Pran continued. "Although it does bring one benefit."

"A benefit?" Masuda said.

"No mosquitoes."

"Ah, of course."

"Just watch out for the *habu*."

"The what?"

"Venomous snakes."

Masuda looked at the deserters, concerned at how they might react to this new information. But the Americans took the news of killer snakes with shrugs. After all, it was nothing compared to what they faced in Vietnam: guerilla fighters more numerous and deadly.

At six o'clock, everyone gathered in the clearing to discuss the morning's work. It was a surprisingly informal process. No one was ordered or in any way pressured into doing anything they didn't want to do. Instead, people simply volunteered, and off they went in groups of two or three to the fields, the forest, the beach, or wherever it was there was work to be done. Those on cooking duty ambled over to the cooking shed to wash up and prepare breakfast.

Soon only Pran and Masuda and the deserters were left standing in the clearing.

Pran turned to the Americans. "What say we go fishing?"

Their eyes lit up.

"Great. I'll get the spears."

"Spears?" Santiago said. "I ain't never fished with no spear."

"I'll show you," Pran said. "There's nothing to it."

"If you say so," Santiago said, his enthusiasm no longer apparent.

Pran glanced over at Masuda, who was wearing the same long trousers and T-shirt he had been wearing the night before. "You might want to change into something more appropriate before we leave. I'm sure we could rustle up a loincloth if you want one."

"No, thanks," Masuda said. "I'll just watch if that's all right."

"As you wish," Pran said, and he turned and left.

Masuda looked at the deserters in their red bathing trunks and smiled. He had been on the verge of confessing to Pran that he couldn't swim. Thinking that the Americans would interpret this as a sign of weakness, he thought better of it. He had an idea that he would be called on to exert his authority over Santiago and the others in the coming days, and showing weakness was the last thing he wanted to do.

They left the commune and headed west, in the opposite direction from the beach where they had landed the night before, walking in single file along a pathway through bamboo thickets and semi-jungle. Pran led the way, followed by Santiago, Roberts, and Sullivan, with Masuda bringing up the rear. All except Masuda carried long bamboo poles with sharpened tips over one shoulder.

After forty minutes of trudging through thick undergrowth it came as a relief to Masuda when they found themselves in the open. Moments later they arrived at the top of a cliff. Masuda looked over the edge and saw an emerald blue ocean and a reef. At the bottom of the cliff was a narrow rocky beach strewn with white seashells and driftwood. Pran led them to the head of a trail that twisted down to the bottom of the cliff, and they began the descent, again in single file. The trail was steep and included several switchbacks, and Masuda was already dreading making the return journey. At least this time he wouldn't be lugging a ten-pound sack of rice.

Near the bottom they passed an opening in the cliff face. Pran waited for the others to catch up, then gestured toward the opening with his spear.

"There's a cave there. Sometimes we use it for fasting."

"Fasting?" Masuda said.

"We come down here alone, with nothing but water and a blanket, and sit inside the cave and meditate."

"For how long?" Santiago asked.

"Two, three days. Sometimes longer."

Santiago looked at Roberts, his eyebrows raised in an expression of disdain.

Pran ignored the Americans and said to Masuda, "You should try it once while you're here. It can be a life-changing experience."

"I'll think about it," Masuda lied. He had no intention of taking up Pran's offer. In fact, having spent a week chaperoning the Americans, the idea of spending two or three days completely alone, even if it meant not eating, appealed to him greatly, but he knew that leaving the hippies to look after the deserters on their own would be tantamount to a dereliction of duty.

As it turned out, the fishing required no real swimming ability. The sea was so shallow and the fish so plentiful that all Pran and the Americans had to do was plant themselves on one of the rocky outcrops that extended out from the shore and thrust their spears into the water. Pran demonstrated how it was done, successfully spearing a colorful reef fish on his third attempt, and before long the Americans were achieving a similar success rate.

Once, more out of curiosity than necessity, it seemed to Masuda, or perhaps because he wanted to show off, Roberts waded out a few feet until he was waist deep in the churning water and speared a dozen or so fish, removing each one after he caught it and lobbing it into the waiting arms of Masuda, whose job it was to collect the catch in a woven bag Pran had brought along.

By eight thirty the bag was full. Pran and the Americans went for a final dip in the ocean to cool off, and after gathering their belongings they set off up the trail to the top of the cliff. With the others having to carry their spears, Masuda was stuck with the bag of fish. Although it was nothing like as heavy as the rice sack he had carried the night before, he was struggling by the time they were halfway up and falling behind, so much so that at one point the others felt it necessary to stop and wait for him to catch up. It was almost a relief when he heard the Americans resume their bickering, sparked by a comment Santiago made about Sullivan's complexion. After more than two hours in the sun, the skin on Sullivan's shoulders and back, normally pink like the rest of his body, had turned bright red.

"Wait till they find out what we caught for breakfast," Santiago said, laughing. "I bet they've never seen a lobster so big."

"Shut up, Santiago," Sullivan whined.

And so it continued, back and forth, all the way to the top of the cliff and back along the trail to the commune.

They ate breakfast seated at the same table where earlier they had coffee. It was a simple meal of brown rice and miso soup that was fortified with their morning catch. Anala had managed to seat herself next to Santiago and was constantly turning her head in his direction, making no effort to hide her interest in him. Santiago seemed to be playing it cool for now, ignoring Anala for the most part and focusing his attention on his countrymen, but Masuda thought this was a ruse. He had seen the way Santiago had looked at Anala, and knew it was just a matter of time before they consummated their relationship.

Given the language barrier, it was difficult to imagine that the attraction was anything other than purely physical. Yet Masuda was puzzled as to what it was about Anala's appearance, other than her coquettish manner, that appealed to Santiago. She was short and dumpy and bow-legged. Her skin was dark, and her flat face was framed in a mane of hair that was long and unkempt and unfashionably parted in the center. Certainly, there was nothing about her physical appearance that the average Japanese would find alluring.

Having observed all this, Masuda was not the least surprised when, during the free time that followed breakfast, Santiago and Anala both disappeared. Masuda had helped clear away the dishes before returning to their hut to find Roberts and Sullivan sitting on the rush matting. When he asked where Santiago was, the two looked at each other and smirked.

"He's gone for a walk," Sullivan said.

"With his girlfriend," Roberts added, gleeful at the opportunity to rat on his colleague. Clearly, he still resented Santiago for revealing to Masuda that Roberts had stabbed an MP in Yokohama.

"Is he still taking the penicillin?" Masuda asked.

Roberts and Sullivan traded glances again before shrugging in unison.

Masuda looked at the two for some time. Realizing that they weren't going to be of any further help, he let out a sigh and turned and exited the hut.

It was more than an hour before Santiago and Anala returned, their faces still flushed from their lovemaking. They continued to flirt openly throughout the rest of the day, even holding hands and nuzzling up to each other. Occasionally Santiago's ministrations elicited squeals of delight from Anala that Masuda found increasingly irritating, especially as the camp was relatively quiet during this period, several of the hippies having gone for walks in the forest or swims, while those who remained whiled away the time reading, drawing, or sleeping. No one except Masuda, however, seemed concerned at the antics of the two lovebirds, least of all Roberts and Sullivan, who spent the entire time in their hut, Sullivan nursing his sunburned body and Roberts scheming Santiago's downfall, or so Masuda imagined.

CHAPTER 18

Peals of laughter erupted from the group of students gathered around the desks at the front of the classroom. Several of the students turned and looked admiringly at Flynn, who smiled self-consciously.

Yamada, the chairman of the campus occupation Defense Committee, was giving an account of the events earlier that morning, and of the part he and Flynn played in repelling the police assault. He had been speaking in Japanese, but from his gestures and the number of times he mentioned Flynn's name, Flynn gathered that Yamada was painting him as the story's hero.

It was clear to Flynn that the audience, which included the woman with the black-rimmed glasses, looked up to Yamada and, by praising Flynn, Yamada had seen to it that some of that respect had rubbed off on him. When Yamada finished talking, the gathering broke up. Yamada and the woman then walked over to where Flynn was standing. Smiling, Yamada reached across and clasped Flynn's upper arm.

"That's some throwing arm you've got there, Eddie."

"Nonsense," Flynn said, blushing. "If it wasn't for you, I'd be lying dead on the pavement out there."

Yamada smiled. "Anyway, you're welcome to stick around. We could do with more people with your skills. In the meantime, if there's anything we can do for you..."

Flynn thought for a moment. Then he said, "Actually, I was wondering if you knew anyone who helped people like me."

"People like you?"

Flynn paused. "Deserters."

"What sort of help do you want?"

"I want to get out."

"Get out?"

"Out of this city. Out of this country. Don't get me wrong. I love Japan. Everyone's been really kind. But it's not safe. And I'm tired of being on the run."

Now it was Yamada's time to think. He did so long and hard. Eventually he said, "Let me ask around." He looked at his watch before adding, "We'll talk again later. Right now, I have to get ready for a class. Yonekura here—" he gestured to the bespectacled woman "—will look after you while I'm gone." And with this Yamada walked over to one of the desks, gathered some papers, and turned and left the room.

Flynn turned to Yonekura and said, "A class? But I thought the students were on strike."

"Normal classes have been suspended. But we've organized classes of our own."

"Classes of your own? But who takes them?"

"We take them ourselves. Though we also invite teachers from outside the university to take some. We show films, too. Life here is a lot more satisfying now compared to when the Board of Trustees ran things. Then we were treated like commodities instead of human beings, always taught to obey, never to think for ourselves. In a sense, this is what we're revolting against. The corruption that sparked the protests was bad enough, but it's nothing more than a symptom of our capitalist society, a society that's rotten to the core. We've come to realize that we're fighting not just the corrupt university leadership, but state power itself."

Flynn was lost. "State power?"

"Yes," Yonekura said. Her English was superb. "Let me give you an example. The president of the university's Board of Trustees is also president of the Nippon Kai, a fascist organization whose members include some of the country's most powerful businessmen and politicians. Its chairman is none other than the prime minister, Eisaku Satō. So by challenging the status quo at Nihon University, by demanding freedom of speech and autonomous student associations, we're challenging those elites and the structure they're seeking to impose on Japanese society. The stakes couldn't be higher. And both sides know it."

"I see," Flynn said.

"But enough of politics," Yonekura said, smiling. "You must be hungry."

In all the excitement of the morning's events, Flynn had forgotten that he hadn't eaten in nearly twenty-four hours.

"Now that you mention it, yes," he said. "I could eat a horse."

"Come on then," Yonekura said. "I know just the place."

She led him out of the classroom to an elevator bank. Yonekura pressed the button to take them to the ground floor. As they stood side by side in the elevator looking up at the floor indicator, a thought occurred to Flynn.

"How long has it been since you occupied the campus?"

"Over a month now," Yonekura said.

"And the authorities haven't cut off the electricity?"

"That's right. The water and gas are still on, too. Sometimes we prepare our own meals in the basement cafeteria."

"Don't you think that's odd? I mean, if they wanted to force you out, the obvious thing to do would be to make life as uncomfortable as possible."

"We wondered the same thing. The conclusion we came to was that the university authorities don't want to upset our parents. After all, they're the ones who pay our tuition fees, and in so doing line the authorities' pockets."

The elevator stopped and the doors opened. Yonekura and Flynn stepped out into the lobby, only to find their way blocked by a wall of wooden tables and desks and benches and other bits and pieces that had been stacked almost to the roof. It was obvious there was no way through.

"That's strange," Yonekura said, glancing at her watch. "The barricades should be down by now." She turned to Flynn and added by way of explanation, "We put them up at night to deter unwelcome visitors."

"I see."

"Never mind," she said, turning and heading back to the elevator. "There's another way out."

They rode the elevator to the second floor and Flynn followed Yonekura out and along a corridor and through a door that led outside to a balcony, which Flynn immediately recognized as the one the police had been trying to reach earlier that morning. Sitting on chairs outside were two bored-looking students. They sat up as Yonekura approached and on her instructions one of them stood and walked over to the edge of the balcony, where a crudely fashioned rope ladder lay in a tangled heap. He picked up the free end and hurled it over the balcony wall. Flynn heard a dull thud as it hit the ground below.

"I'm sure it's not up to U.S. Navy standards," Yonekura said, smiling, "but it suits our purposes."

She strode forward, clambered over the wall and quickly disappeared over the edge. Flynn crossed to the wall and looked over. Yonekura was already halfway down, negotiating the descent with ease. When she reached the ground she looked up and signaled to him and he gave the rope a quick tug to make sure it was securely fastened and climbed up and over the wall. The ladder swung precariously as he neared the bottom, and he was relieved when his feet eventually touched the pavement.

In front of them was Hakusan-dōri, the scene of the previous day's confrontation between demonstrators and riot police. Now, however, there were no police in sight and traffic appeared to be flowing normally. It occurred to Flynn that the fight had happened somewhere else, or even that he had imagined it. Then he noticed the gaps in the sidewalk where the students had ripped up paving stones to fashion into projectiles.

They crossed Hakusan-dōri and entered a side street and continued walking until they came to a small coffee shop. Inside, a tall man in a white apron smiled and greeted them as if they were regular customers. Yonekura led Flynn to a table by the window. She picked up the menu and handed it to him.

"Order anything you like," she said.

He glanced at the menu, but was unable to make heads or tails of the Japanese writing. What really concerned him, however, was the cost. He couldn't remember the last time he had had a proper breakfast. He considered it a luxury.

She looked at him, sensing something was wrong.

"It's just…" He paused, uncomfortable at having to explain. "I don't have much money at the moment."

"Don't worry. It's on the house. The owner is a supporter of the occupation, as are most of the small business owners in the area."

As if on cue, the tall man arrived with two glasses of iced water and set them down on the table.

"If you prefer I can order for you," Yonekura said.

"Yes, please," Flynn replied, relieved.

Yonekura spoke to the man in Japanese and he smiled and nodded and disappeared behind the counter. Minutes later he returned with two plates of thick toast and a pair of boiled eggs. As they ate, Yonekura asked Flynn about Vietnam, and he told her about his experiences on the *Respite* and in Da Nang, omitting any mention of his drug addiction and his feud with Petty Officer Dawkins and the reason he was sent to Yokosuka.

When they had finished eating, they thanked the owner and retraced their steps to Hakusan-dōri, but instead of entering the Economics department building through the front door, Yonekura took Flynn around to the back of the building. There a group of six students sat under a lean-to that had been erected on the sidewalk outside the rear entrance.

As they neared the students, Flynn's eyes were drawn to a shiny black sedan approaching from the opposite direction. It slowed as it drew alongside the lean-to, and Flynn tensed as he noticed the rear window open. He hurried to catch up with Yonekura, positioning himself between her and the car. She stopped and looked at him and then at the car, but her expression registered neither fear nor surprise.

By this time the car had stopped and, as Flynn looked on, still unsure of what was unfolding, one of the students sitting in the lean-to stood up and walked over to the vehicle. Out of the open window appeared two hands holding a package. The student took the package, bowed, and the window closed and the black sedan edged away from the sidewalk and disappeared down the road.

"Bento boxes for the lookouts," Yonekura said. "We don't know who he is, but every day he comes at the same time to deliver them. And every time he says the same thing: 'Good on you. Keep it up.'

The first time he delivered them we threw them away. We thought they might be poisoned. But they looked so delicious, on the second day one of the students couldn't resist. He said it was the best bento he'd ever eaten."

By this time the boxes had been distributed to all six lookouts, and Flynn watched as they ripped open the packaging and tucked into the meals with relish.

"Rumor has it they're from an expensive restaurant in Akasaka," Yonekura continued, "and that the mysterious benefactor is a company president. One thing's for sure: we never have trouble finding volunteers to man this lookout."

Flynn laughed.

"Well," Yonekura said, glancing at her watch, "I'd better be going. Can you find your way back on your own?"

"Sure," Flynn said, smiling.

Flynn returned to the classroom on the sixth floor to find it empty. Tired after the morning's dramatic events, he lay down on his mattress to rest. His discussion with Yonekura had stirred forgotten memories of his time in Vietnam, and in the brief period of semi-consciousness before sleep overtook him, his mind went back to an episode that had occurred while he was assigned to the *Respite*.

It was a much-anticipated day of liberty in Da Nang, and he had decided to join a group of crewmembers on a trip to China Beach. With no room at Da Nang's deep-water pier at the base of Monkey Mountain, the hospital ship had anchored in the middle of the harbor. From there they rode an LCM-8 landing craft to the headquarters of Naval Support Activity—NSA—which were housed in an old French colonial-era hotel dubbed the White Elephant on the banks of the Han River. The seamen bused the rest of the way, crossing the Han River and continuing east until they eventually passed through a gate and parked under a clump of tall, windswept trees. Once on the white sand beach, a handful of the men stripped down to their shorts and ran down to the water like excited children, only to be beaten back by the pounding waves. Others gathered in small groups, joining the many other servicemen sunbathing or standing admiring the view.

The beach seemed to extend forever in both directions. For a moment Flynn imagined he was on a beach in Hawaii. But the barbed-wire fence behind him and the almost total absence of females quickly ruined that fantasy. To the north Flynn could make out the rugged silhouette of Monkey Mountain, which they had passed on the boat ride in from the *Respite*. To the south was a cluster of dome-shaped limestone hills called Marble Mountains, home to the U.S. Marine Corps' Marble Mountain Air Facility.

Later, Flynn went off exploring on his own, further down the beach and nearly out of sight of his crew. When he arrived back he was shocked to find the bus had left. He set off on foot, hoping to catch a ride on one of the numerous U.S. military vehicles that plied Da Nang's streets. Several vehicles passed without stopping, each one leaving behind a cloud of reddish dust that made him blink, but eventually an M35 six-by-six cargo truck pulled over. As Flynn approached the passenger door, the driver, a burly Marine with a cigarette hanging from his mouth, leaned over to address him, sprinkling ash into the lap of the Marine in the passenger seat.

"Where are you heading, squid?"

"Do you go past the White Elephant?"

The driver laughed. "Missed the bus, have you?"

Flynn smiled sheepishly. "Yeah."

"Come on then. Jump on the back."

"Thanks," Flynn said. He turned and climbed up onto the truck bed, where two Marines were sitting on a load of produce in hessian sacks. He sat down, and immediately recognized the familiar lumpiness under his buttocks.

"Spuds!" he shouted.

"Yeah, they're potatoes," the Marine closest to him said. "So what?"

"I'm from Bingham County, Idaho. It's the potato capital of America. We grow them on our farm."

"No shit," the Marine said. His cap was pushed back on his head, revealing a curly blond fringe. He reminded Flynn of a character from a comic book he had read as a child. The other Marine, who was unhealthily thin and pale, looked earnestly at the road behind.

Noticing one of the sacks was open, Flynn crawled over and looked inside. He dug his hand in and removed one of the potatoes.

Almost instinctively he gauged its size, shape, and weight, savoring the snugness with which it sat in the palm of his hand, securing it there by wrapping his fingers around its girth. He felt a small lump of dirt on the surface and without thinking removed it with a prod of his thumb. It resisted momentarily before giving way and crumbling into dust, filling Flynn with a warm feeling of satisfaction.

"NSA?" the blond Marine asked.

"No, I'm with the *Respite*," Flynn said. "We got in last night."

"Ah, the hospital ship."

"Yeah."

The blond Marine seemed to think for a moment. Then he said, "Someone told me you treat gooks. Is that true?"

"Yeah, there's an International Ward where we take care of sick and wounded civilians. Sometimes we get some pretty badly shot-up kids. And when it's not busy, when there's a lull in the fighting, the docs do operations to fix cleft palates, that sort of thing."

"You don't look after Charlie, though, do you?"

"Sure, we get some wounded VC come in. Sometimes you can't tell the difference between VC and civilians."

"That ain't right, man," the Marine said, and looked over at his partner. "Sledge, that ain't right, is it?"

Sledge's eyes remained fixed on the road as he spoke. "Hell, ain't nothing right about this war."

The truck crossed the Han River and entered the outskirts of Da Nang proper. The traffic was busier than earlier in the day, and there was an almost constant stream of people on the side of the road, some riding bicycles, most on foot. Some of the pedestrians had poles balanced on one shoulder with woven baskets filled with all kinds of produce hanging from each end.

At one point it became so congested that the truck driver had to slow down to a crawl. Flynn noticed people looking up as the truck passed, and without thinking he tossed the potato that he still held in his hand over the side. A young woman with hair down to her waist caught it and raised her hands in the air in triumph. Flynn crawled over to the open sack, dug out another potato and threw it over the side. This one was caught by an old man in a dirty white shirt, who examined it curiously before looking up at Flynn, a toothless grin on his face.

Before long a small but boisterous crowd of locals was walking alongside the slowly moving truck, their arms extended in front of them, hands open, faces upturned imploringly. Flynn continued to gently lob potatoes in their direction, trying his best to ensure no individual got more than one. Flynn's fellow passengers heard the commotion and crawled over to see what was happening. For a while they sat and watched Flynn lob the potatoes one at a time over the side of the truck. Then the blond Marine said, "No, man, you're doing it wrong. You gotta pull the pin."

Flynn looked at him and cocked his head to one side.

"Like this," said the Marine. He took one of the potatoes from the sack and put it to his mouth. After miming pulling a pin with his teeth, he hurled it at the feet of the crowd of pedestrians.

"Boom!" he said, smiling malevolently.

"Fuck this," the other Marine said. After scooping up a handful of potatoes, he raised himself to a kneeling position and began to throw them as hard as he could at the civilians alongside the truck. There were cries of surprise and shouts of anger from below as the spuds bounced off heads, shoulders, limbs, and torsos.

A few people continued to follow the truck, some raising their hands to fend off the tuberous projectiles, others scrambling to pick the fallen potatoes up off the street. Most, however, fell back and simply watched until eventually the truck found a gap in the traffic and accelerated away, leaving behind a thick cloud of exhaust fumes. Amidst the mayhem, Flynn spotted a woman in black trousers and a pale blue short-sleeved top standing in a doorway holding a baby. There was something serene about her, and for a split second an image of the Madonna and child flashed through Flynn's mind. Then she noticed him looking at her and turned away. Her hand curled around the back of the baby's head, pressing its face to her bosom.

"Eddie."

Startled, Flynn sat up and turned his head in the direction of the voice. Through bleary eyes he saw a figure standing in the doorway. He smiled when he recognized Yamada and got to his feet. Yamada returned the smile, walked over and placed a hand on Flynn's shoulder. The gesture was at once reassuring and unsettling. Yamada was the same age as Flynn, yet his manner was that of someone many years his senior. Anyone watching would be forgiven for thinking that Yamada was the war veteran, and Flynn the unworldly college kid. He had met his fair share of young university graduates in the military in Vietnam, but few of them had Yamada's gravitas or self-assurance. Perhaps it was true what they said; that leaders were born, not made. Or perhaps there was something in Yamada's past, Flynn thought, something unrelated to his education that made him what he was.

"Good news," Yamada said.

"What is it?" Flynn replied, his spirits lifted by Yamada's more than usually enthusiastic manner.

"I've been in touch with someone from Beheiren, and they've agreed to meet you."

"Beheiren?"

"The Citizens' Federation for Peace in Vietnam. They're an anti-Vietnam War group that helps deserters like you."

"And they're willing to meet me?"

"Yes. You're to be at the Fūgetsudō coffee shop in Shinjuku tomorrow morning at ten. Someone from Beheiren will be waiting for you. Do you know where it is?"

Flynn nodded. Then he asked, "But how will I recognize them?"

"Don't worry," Yamada replied. "They will recognize you."

CHAPTER 19

Harper and Natsume arrived back from their walk just as it started to rain. No sooner had they dried themselves off than Natsume excused himself, explaining to Harper that he had to go to the office to make a phone call. Probably a report to his handlers in Tokyo, Harper thought. As he stood by the window of their room staring out at the rain, Harper contemplated the young Beheiren operative. He seemed friendly enough, certainly compared to the dour individuals who had interviewed him back in Yokohama. But when Ikeda mentioned his war service something seemed to come over Natsume. Harper had tried not to let it bother him. He prided himself on his self-control and his ability to project a cool, calm exterior. But Natsume's disrespect for Ikeda's sacrifice and his holier-than-thou attitude tried his patience. He wasn't proud of his outburst earlier, but he was glad he had brought the matter into the open. He hoped that he and Natsume could start afresh. If for no other reason than that his future depended on it.

In addition to his strained relationship with his handler, Harper also had to cope with the fact that he was already missing Yumi. After weeks living in her apartment, he had gotten used to seeing her off as she left for classes or work each morning and having to face the rest of the day on his own, but always in the knowledge that she would return again in the evening. Now it was different. Despite the promise he had made to her at the restaurant in Tokyo, that he would return some day, he knew it was unlikely they would ever see each other again.

They had met at a club in Yokohama's main shopping district of

Isezakichō. It was one of the places Lerner, the air cavalryman he met at the hospital in Kishine, had taken him to back when he was still on crutches. They invited two young women who were passing their table to join them. The women were both around the same age—Harper guessed they were in their early-twenties. Eiko, the prettier of the two, wore a skirt and a white blouse, while Yumi had on slacks and a red sweater. They barely had time to introduce themselves before Lerner asked Eiko to dance, leaving Harper alone with Yumi. At first he was annoyed at being left with the plainer of the two women, but as he chatted with Yumi he found himself relaxing and enjoying himself. She told him she was a university student, but that she worked most days as a waitress at a restaurant not far from the club. Harper felt comfortable in her presence. Her English was good, and the conversation flowed freely. Despite her somewhat homely appearance, there was something unique, intangible about her. After they left, Harper regretted not having asked if he could see her again.

It was soon after this that Lerner was sent back to Vietnam. A few days later, Harper was moved to another ward, this one for patients who needed less care. The atmosphere there was more buoyant, though the downside was the return of military discipline in the form of morning roll calls and the occasional detail. It was only Army discipline, though, nothing like the Marine Corps, and Harper had plenty of free time, which he mostly spent shooting pool and watching movies.

He continued with the physical therapy. Soon he could walk reasonably well unassisted. Two weeks to the day after his first visit to Isezakichō he went back, this time alone. As he was making his way toward the club, his eyes were drawn to a woman in a red sweater crossing the street in front of him. Seeing her enter a restaurant, Harper followed her in. He looked around the room but there was no sign of Yumi. A waitress in a uniform greeted him and showed him to a table. He sat down and ordered a coffee, and while he was waiting he looked around the room again. He noticed another waitress enter from a side door. It took him a moment to realize the woman in the uniform with her hair up was Yumi. He looked at her and smiled as she passed his table. Their eyes met, and by the look of surprise on her face, it was clear that she recognized him too. Instead of acknowledging him, though, she walked straight past, her expression normal again.

A few minutes later she returned with his coffee. As she set it down on the table, he looked up at her and said, "It's Yumi, isn't it? Don't you remember me? We met at the club up the road last week."

"Yes, of course I remember you." She looked around nervously before adding, "But I can't talk now."

"I'm sorry," said Harper. "I don't want to get you into any trouble."

"I finish work at four. Do you want to meet me then?"

"Sure. I'll be waiting outside."

"Not here," she said, looking around furtively. "Wait for me outside the club."

Yumi had changed back into her slacks and red sweater. Her hair was down, framing her heart-shaped face. Harper complimented her on her appearance, and she smiled demurely.

"Shall we go somewhere and sit down?" she said. "Your legs must be sore."

"Oh, they're much better," he replied. "As you can see," he added, indicating his legs with a sweep of both hands, "I don't need the crutches anymore."

"Yes, I noticed. What about your friend? Is he not with you today?"

"Bunny? He was shipped back to Vietnam."

"Really?" she said, a shadow crossing her face. "I'm sorry to hear that, Harpo."

"It's an occupational hazard," he said.

She furrowed her brows.

"The guys with less serious injuries accept they'll be sent back once they recover."

She nodded slowly. Then, smiling, she said, "Would you like to go for a walk? If you're feeling up to it, that is. There's somewhere special I'd like to show you."

"Sure," Harper said.

"It's this way," she said, gesturing up the arcaded street in the opposite direction from the restaurant where she worked.

"You must be looking forward to going home," she said as they set off.

"Yes, I am."

"Will you go back to live with your family in Mississippi?"

Harper remembered telling her about Redville, but not about moving to Washington, D.C. "Actually, I was living with my uncle in Washington, D.C. when I joined up. I was training to be a mechanic."

"You volunteered?"

"Yeah. I was going to be called up anyway, so I figured I might as well. There are benefits you get from volunteering that you miss out on if you wait to be called up."

"Your family must be worried about you."

"I'm not so sure about that," Harper said. "Let's just say we're not all that close."

They reached an intersection and turned right onto a busy street. As they continued walking, Harper noticed a hill up ahead.

"What about your family?" he said. "Do they live here in Yokohama?"

"My mother died during the war. It was just after I was born. My father never remarried. He still lives in Yokohama with my older brother and his wife."

"I'm sorry about your mother."

"It was during the big air raid in May 1945. Many thousands of people died, and the firebombs destroyed much of the city. There were many other, smaller air raids too. By the end of the war, the city's population was cut in half."

"That's terrible," Harper said, unsure of what else to say. He was hardly going to apologize for America's actions in the war. Not after hearing the stories his uncle told him about the way the Japanese treated American POWs.

"Unfortunately," Yumi continued, "Yokohama is accustomed to such tragedies. Twenty-two years earlier, it was devastated by a massive earthquake. Some people think Yokohama is cursed."

They continued walking in silence. At the foot of the hill was a canal. On the other side, the street curved gently as it rose. After climbing for a few minutes they stopped so that Harper could rest and he turned to see the harbor spread out before him, the ocean shimmering under the still blue sky. In silence they continued ascending. Eventually Yumi pointed to a stone stairway, which they climbed until they reached a stone archway consisting of two round columns, one on either side of the stairway, supporting a square cross beam. Harper, who had never seen such a structure before, stopped to look at it.

"It's called a *torii*," Yumi said. "It marks the entrance to a Shinto shrine. The path running through the *torii* is called the *sandō*, or pilgrimage route. We never walk along the center of the *sandō*. That route is reserved for the *kami*, the gods, and people are not supposed to walk there."

"Wait. You said 'gods.' So the Japanese believe in more than one god?"

"Yes," Yumi replied, smiling. "In fact, there are so many we cannot count them."

Yumi led him through the gate and they continued up the steps, doglegging to the left before passing through a second *torii* that led to an area of flat ground. To their left was a stone trough of water on which rested two bamboo ladles. Harper watched Yumi take one of the ladles and scoop up water from the trough. After sipping the water, she scooped up some more and washed both hands methodically. She turned around and offered him the ladle, whereupon he did his best to mimic her actions.

"This is the Iseyama Kōtai-Jingū shrine," Yumi said as they crossed the flat ground. "It was built in 1870, just a few years after Japan reopened its doors to the West after three centuries of seclusion during the Edo period. At the time Yokohama was one of only a handful of cities where foreigners could settle and conduct business. These foreigners also built Christian churches. This worried the Japanese who lived in the area, and so the local officials built this shrine and dedicated it to the Sun Goddess, Amaterasu, as a kind of talisman, to counteract the influence of the Christian churches."

"Did it work?"

"It seems not. The original shrine was destroyed in the 1923 earthquake. It was rebuilt five years later. And then came the war..."

It always puzzled Harper how people could believe in the power of supernatural forces when there was no evidence that they existed.

What little faith he had retained since childhood had been destroyed by his experiences in Vietnam. Nothing he witnessed there suggested the existence of God, certainly not the loving, caring God his mother had brought him up to believe in. Though if he were to be honest he would have to admit he had always been skeptical, even as a boy when he had been forced to go to church every Sunday with his family.

They came to a large wooden building, which Yumi explained was the *haiden*, or worship hall. Behind this was another building, the *honden*, which contained the object of worship representing the *kami*, which in this case was Amaterasu. Yumi stopped a few feet from the *haiden*. She opened her handbag, took out her purse and fished out a coin, which she threw into a wooden box in front of the *haiden*. It clattered several times as it struck the wooden grill on top of the box and clinked as it hit the bottom. She stepped forward and pulled a rope that caused a bell above her head to ring, bowed twice, clapped her hands twice, and bowed again once. She turned to Harper, who again did his best to repeat Yumi's actions, though when she laughed he knew he had done something wrong. Was it one clap of the hands and then two bows, or two claps and one bow? He was grateful that there were no other worshippers around to witness his faux pas, whatever it was.

To the right of the *haiden* was an office. Yumi wandered over and returned a short time later holding two folded strips of paper. She handed him one and told him to open it.

"What is it?" he asked.

"*O-mikuji*," she said. "It tells your fortune."

"So it's like a fortune cookie," said Harper as he unfolded the strip of paper, "but without the cookie."

They both laughed. He looked at the paper, but the writing was in Japanese.

"How do I know if it's good or bad?" he asked.

"Let me see," Yumi said.

He handed the strip of paper to her and she looked at it for a few moments. A shadow crossed her face.

"It's bad, isn't it," he said.

She appeared to hesitate before looking up. "No, it's very good. It says your chances of achieving your goals in life are extremely high."

"Then why the sad face?"

She replied, without hesitating, "Because I know you'll be leaving soon."

She folded the strip of paper, walked over to a wall of metal wires next to the office and tied it to one of the wires before repeating this procedure with her own *o-mikuji*.

When she returned he asked, "What's that for?"

"If the fortune is good, we tie it there to increase its effect," she replied.

Harper nodded, though something about Yumi's explanation didn't ring true.

"And if it's bad?"

Yumi didn't answer. Instead, she led him over to a viewing area on the other side of the *haiden*. Harper was unprepared for the incredible panorama that stretched out before him. Yumi stood beside him and pointed out the cities of Kanagawa and Kawasaki to the north and the Bōsō Peninsula to the east, on the other side of Tokyo Bay. In the foreground was the busy waterfront area with its shipyards and piers, and next to it the green expanse of Yamashita Park, at the south end of which stood the Marine Tower. Topping out at three hundred and thirty feet, the structure contained a museum and viewing platform, explained Yumi, and served as the port's lighthouse.

"And down there is Chinatown," Yumi said, pointing to the southeast. Harper remembered Lerner telling him about Chinatown on the streetcar the day they went shopping, and after scanning the area he eventually spotted the tunnel they had passed through and the road leading from it.

"You were right," Harper said. "This is a special place. Thank you for bringing me here, Yumi."

She turned to him and smiled. "You're welcome, Harpo."

Before parting later that afternoon, they arranged to meet again two days later. Harper could hardly take his mind off Yumi. In the short time they had spent together, he had learned more about Yokohama and Japan than in the weeks he had been at Kishine. It was as if she had given him a glimpse of a whole new world, the real Japan behind the façade most foreigners saw, and he couldn't wait to see more.

She was waiting for him in front of the club when he arrived. From Isezakichō they rode the streetcar to Sankei-en, a forty-seven-acre preserve on a peninsula not far from Honmoku where there was a Japanese garden, a park, and a collection of historic Japanese buildings in different styles. Together they explored the narrow paths that wound through the woods in the outer garden, stopping on the log bridges to admire the colorful carp and feed them morsels of cookies that Yumi brought with her wrapped in a large cloth.

After their next outing together to the nearby seaside town of Kamakura, Yumi invited him back to her apartment for dinner. She was quick to explain that she wasn't a very good cook. Harper replied that he had been living on hospital food for the last two months, and before that combat rations, and that the mere mention of a home-cooked meal made him salivate.

While preparing the meal on a small bench-top gas range in the tiny kitchen-slash-dining room in her apartment, Yumi asked him again about his family. He told her about growing up in Redville with his parents and his younger brother and sister, about his father's battle with alcoholism, and about his leaving home after graduating high school to live with his uncle on U Street, Washington, D.C., where he was training to be a mechanic.

Occasionally there were breaks in the conversation, during which he silently watched Yumi as she prepared dinner, her slippers swishing across the linoleum floor as she moved from the stove to the tiny refrigerator and back again. She had donned the slippers after removing her red pumps at the entrance to the apartment, a maneuver she completed in seconds as if it were second nature, unlike Harper, who struggled not only to remove his heavy boots with their long black laces, but also to squeeze his size eleven feet into the second pair of slippers, identical to Yumi's, that she had placed on the edge of the raised floor. Eventually, amidst giggles of delight from Yumi, he gave up and was ushered to the table in just his socks.

After they finished eating the meal, a spaghetti dish flavored with ketchup she called "Napolitan," she cleared away the plates and began washing up. Harper stood, walked over and, without speaking, wrapped his arms around her waist and kissed her gently on the back of the neck. Her hair was soft against his face and had a fresh, floral fragrance, as if it had just been washed. She turned to face him and he pulled her closer and they kissed. She relaxed, but instead of holding him she held her arms stiffly by her sides. After a while he pulled back, and she held her hands up to show him the suds. She extended one hand and gently tapped his nose with her index finger. He made a face, scrunching his lips and looking cross-eyed at the suds on the tip of his nose, and they both laughed.

She said he would have to take a bath before they went to bed. It was the Japanese way. She led him to the bathroom, where she removed the wooden slat cover from the bathtub and explained that the tub was for soaking only, and that he should wash himself thoroughly before getting in. After she went out, he took off his clothes and closed the bathroom door. Then he drew a bucket of water from the bath and poured it over his head while balancing himself on the tiny wooden stool. He gasped as the hot water cascaded over his body. He paused and took two deep breaths, trying hard to relax. Steam rose from the water in the bath and swirled around the cramped bathroom, the pungent aroma from the cedar bathtub filling his nostrils.

He had just reached for the soap when he heard the bathroom door open behind him. Moments later, before he had a chance to turn around, he felt her hands on his body. Her fingers gently traced the myriad scars that peppered his back from his shoulders to his buttocks and extended to his left arm and his legs.

"Poor Harpo," she said.

Then she took the soap from his hand and rubbed it against a cloth she had soaked in the bucket of hot water on the floor beside them until a thick lather had formed and began to wash his body, gently and slowly as if they had all the time in the world.

They saw each other often over the ensuing weeks, usually meeting outside the club in Isezakichō or at a coffee shop across the road from the Matsuya Department Store. On Thursdays, Yumi's day off, they would go for walks if the weather was fine, or watch a movie if it was not.

It was following his return to Kishine after one of these outings that Harper received an unexpected visitor. He was relaxing, lying on his bed in the ward reading a comic, when one of the doctors appeared by his bedside. It was the same doctor who had teased him the day he arrived about being a Marine in an Army hospital. It was late in the afternoon, an unusual time for him to be checking on a patient, and Harper sensed immediately that something was up.

"How are the legs, Son?" the doctor asked, retrieving Harper's chart from the foot of the bed.

"The legs are good, Sir. I appreciate all you've done for me."

"Good, good," the doctor said, his head still buried in the chart. "You must be itching to get back."

"Sir?"

Harper had been thinking about all the possible reasons for the doctor's surprise visit, including that he was going to be moved to a different ward or hospital or even that he was going to be sent back home but, deep down, he knew what was coming. Though it did nothing to lessen the shock.

"Back to Vietnam," the doctor said.

Harper's heart sank. "To Vietnam?"

The doctor looked up. "You're in A-1 condition, Son."

"A-1? But you said…" His voice trailed off. "When?"

"When are they sending you back?"

"When are they sending me back?" Harper repeated.

The doctor replaced the chart and looked at Harper again. "You should be getting your orders tomorrow morning."

"Tomorrow? Shit. But…" Harper had lots of things he wanted to say, but he saw no point in arguing with the doctor. Instead he thanked him again, and when he left he sank back in his bed, closed his eyes and thought of Yumi.

Harper's orders arrived late the next morning, just as the doctor had predicted. It was no mistake. It was his name on the cover sheet: James Earle Harper. He was to report to the naval air station at

Atsugi the following morning, where he was to board the next available flight to Da Nang.

He dressed quickly, left the hospital and caught a taxi to the restaurant where Yumi worked. His first instinct had been to go to her apartment, but he knew she would be working at that hour.

Yumi was serving another customer when he entered. Ushered to a table by another waitress, he took a moment to observe her. Not only did she look different in her waitress uniform, but she seemed to move differently. It was as if he was seeing her as a stranger would, and he was filled with a renewed sense of what he could only describe as pride. When she eventually noticed him, she looked shocked. This made Harper feel even worse about turning up unannounced, and so when she came over to his table, instead of going into details about what had happened he simply told her he had to talk to her as soon as possible. She agreed to meet him at the coffee shop across the road from the Matsuya Department Store after she finished work that evening.

Harper had several hours to kill. He briefly considered going to the club in Isezakichō, but instead he started walking south in the direction of Chinatown. Soon, though, any thoughts of heading to a particular destination melted away as he mulled over his orders to return to Vietnam. He was concerned that his first reaction had been to take flight. It wasn't in his nature to run away when things got tough. And the last thing he wanted was for people to think he was scared of fighting or was acting dishonorably. Then again, if he really was being shipped out tomorrow morning, he wouldn't have another opportunity to see Yumi before he left. He owed it to Yumi to say goodbye.

She was waiting for him when he arrived at the coffee shop. It was obvious to Harper that she knew right away that something was bothering him, but he had decided not to say anything about the reason for his sudden appearance until they got to her apartment. He was afraid of how she would react, that she might create a scene in the taxi. But when he eventually explained what had happened and told her that he would probably be leaving the next day, she remained calm, as if she had been prepared all along for this eventuality. It crossed his mind that perhaps he was the latest in a long line of American boyfriends (it was something they had never discussed), and for a moment he felt jealous, even angry that she had not been more visibly upset. But such feelings vanished when, after dinner, she led him to the bath and later to the futon. They made love three times that night, the last time just before dawn. Later, after breakfast, he hugged her and brushed away her tears, promising her he would write. He then caught a taxi back to the hospital.

Back at Kishine, Harper quickly changed into his utilities and packed his gear into a duffel bag before saying goodbye to the other patients in the ward. Inevitably, the farewells took longer than expected, and he got down to the entrance to the hospital to find that the bus to Atsugi had already left. He would have to catch a taxi to Honmoku and catch up with the bus there.

While waiting for his taxi to arrive, he caught sight of his reflection in the glass doors at the entrance to the hospital and was taken aback. For the first time he saw himself as most Japanese people no doubt saw him, as a big black Marine going off to fight an unjust war, and for the first time since the previous afternoon he began to have second thoughts about getting on the plane. Even after the taxi pulled up and he unceremoniously climbed in and was driven away from the hospital, he thought how easy it would be to tell the driver to stop and to get out or to ask him to take him somewhere else. As it happened, the taxi got caught up in traffic and he was late arriving at Honmoku. Harper got to the bus stop to find that the bus had left. It occurred to him that this was an omen, that he wasn't meant to be going back to Vietnam.

With the next bus not scheduled to depart until the afternoon, Harper decided to catch a movie. He then had lunch. It was still only twelve thirty when he finished eating. To kill more time, he wandered around the Naval Area, mingling with the other American military personnel and civilians. He soon found himself on Avenue D, and when a streetcar came rumbling to a halt right next to him he climbed aboard without thinking. He rode the streetcar all the way to Yokohama Station, where he followed the remaining passengers as they got off and headed toward the brick building.

As he approached the station, Harper saw a group of ten to

twenty young people standing in the forecourt in front of the entrance. They were holding placards. Most were in Japanese, but as he got closer he noticed that some were in English. STOP KILLING THE VIETNAMESE PEOPLE, one read. When he drew nearer still he sensed that the people around him were watching him. At first he thought it was because he was a black man in a part of the city where few foreigners ventured, but then he realized it was because he was wearing his uniform.

Harper was now just a few feet from the demonstrators. They had been quietly handing out leaflets to Japanese passersby, but one or two had noticed him approaching and passed the message on to the rest, and within seconds they had all stopped leafleting and were looking at him. A young man in the middle who must have been around the same age as Harper held his placard aloft and began shouting, "Hey, hey, LBJ, how many kids did you kill today?" Harper looked at the man's face, which contorted with anger.

The protestors on either side of the young man soon took up the chant. Those holding placards raised them in time with their chanting, while those without signs thrust clenched fists into the air. Harper's instincts told him to turn around and go back the way he had come, but he was determined not to show any sign of weakness in front of the demonstrators, and so he continued walking straight past them toward the station entrance. As he did so, a girl in a blue dress stopped chanting and held out a paper. Harper looked into her face, took the leaflet without stopping and stuffed it into his breast pocket. As he entered the station the chanting died down and he relaxed as he was quickly swallowed up by the mass of bodies inside.

Harper had some explaining to do that night when he turned up at Yumi's apartment in a taxi. But if her reaction the day before had been unexpectedly cool, this time she was if anything overeager, flinging her arms around his neck before he had even set foot inside the door. When he explained that he wasn't back for good, that he would have to report to Atsugi the following morning, she looked crestfallen. Eager to change the subject, Harper showed the leaflet he had been handed at Yokohama Station and asked her what it was about.

Yumi glanced at the pamphlet and said, "They're protesting against the opening of a hospital for wounded Vietnam War veterans in Ōji."

"Ōji?"

"It's a part of Tokyo."

"Why are they upset about a hospital?"

"Because the Americans opened the hospital without telling anyone. Actually, the Japanese government knew, but they didn't bother to tell the local residents, or anyone else for that matter. The residents are upset because of the noise from the helicopters flying in patients. They're also afraid that diseases might spread from the hospital to the neighborhood."

Later that night they made love again, but without the same ardor as the night before. And when he stood in the entranceway of her apartment the next morning ready to leave, there were no tears. Not for the first time, Harper was struck by the feeling that Yumi was able to read his mind. Though in this case she seemed to know even before he did that he wasn't going anywhere that day.

"Shit," he said.

And he turned around, let his bag fall to the floor and held her in his arms.

CHAPTER 20

At three o'clock, the same hand bell that had woken Masuda in the morning was rung to signal that the afternoon meal was ready. Not that the three deserters needed to be told. They had been waiting outside the kitchen for at least ten minutes, eager to find out what was on the menu, and had followed the two hippies on cooking duty when they carried the steaming pot from the kitchen hut over to the table so that they would be the first to be served. Only when Masuda and the others had joined them, however, was the lid removed to reveal the contents.

"What is it?" Santiago asked as the lumpy mixture was ladled into bowls and handed out.

"*Shiruko*," Masuda said. "It's like a porridge, but sweet," he added, struggling to find the words in English to describe the dish. "It's made from adzuki beans, which are boiled and crushed. The dumplings are made from rice flour."

Santiago, having received his bowl of *shiruko*, dipped his spoon into the reddish-brown mixture. He fished out one of the grayish dumplings and held it up to show Roberts and Sullivan, who screwed up their faces in disgust. When all three had been handed their bowls, they sat down together and Masuda watched as they took their first mouthfuls almost in unison. He was relieved when they actually swallowed, but it was clear from their faces that they didn't think much of the *shiruko*.

Based on the number of hippies who went up for second helpings, Masuda concluded that it was one of the more popular dishes at the commune. The deserters, on the other hand, struggled to finish a single helping each, and when they did they showed their displeasure by pushing their bowls away in a manner Masuda thought was completely disrespectful. Their reaction wasn't lost on their hosts, either, some of whom, it seemed to Masuda, were beginning to tire of the Americans' antics, occasionally even casting disdainful looks in their direction. What really riled Masuda was that he himself seemed to be the target of some of these glances. Eager to distinguish himself from his charges, he made a point of getting up and asking for a second serving of the *shiruko*, even though he was full.

If the deserters had irritated their hosts during the afternoon mealtime, they more than redeemed themselves in the three-hour period of work in the "cool" of the late afternoon. Shortly after three o'clock, Masuda and the deserters again accompanied Pran, this time to the nearby fields, some of which had already been planted, others of which were still in the process of being prepared.

While Pran and Masuda set about tending to one of the planted fields, the deserters were put to work clearing bamboo from the edge of an adjoining plot. They approached the task with genuine enthusiasm, swinging their machetes so vigorously that sweat poured from their naked torsos, drenching their red bathing trunks. It was hard to believe that these were the same three people who less than an hour ago were practically sulking after being presented with unfamiliar food. Difficult they may have been, but lazy they were not. It occurred to Masuda that if only they could be kept busy, be given things to keep their minds and bodies occupied, then their stay at the commune would be, if not pleasurable, then at least bearable for everyone.

Alas, this proved easier said than done. The main sticking point remained the food. Dinner, which consisted of brown rice and fish in a soy broth, was received by the deserters as unenthusiastically as had been breakfast and lunch. Their spirits lifted after the meal when they were offered cigarettes and again when the *shōchū* was passed around. But with the exception of Sullivan, who was clearly enlivened by the evening's entertainment and looked overjoyed when Pran handed him an African hand drum and showed him how to play it, the deserters were reluctant to join in the festivities, and were the first to retire for the night, withdrawing to their hut well before the singing and dancing was over.

When Masuda broached the subject with them the next morning, instead of expressing contrition at their poor attitude, the deserters went on the attack, complaining that they needed to eat breakfast first thing in the morning, that the meals lacked variety, that the brown rice was inedible and, above all, that there was not enough meat. Masuda was not entirely unsympathetic to some of their grievances (he longed for a bowl of plain white rice), but he wasn't about to give in without a fight. The hippies ate exactly the same diet as they did, he pointed out, yet none of them seemed to be concerned at the lack of meat.

"That's because we have different bodies," Roberts explained.

"You grew up eating rice and fish," Santiago added, "so your bodies have adapted. It's the same with the Gooks."

Masuda shot Santiago a menacing glance, whereupon the American immediately corrected himself.

"The Vietnamese, I mean. They survive in the jungle eating insects, leaves, bark, whatever they can get their hands on, and they still have the energy to fight. We're different. Sure, C-rats may have tasted like shit, but at least they gave us the sustenance our bodies needed."

"C-rats?" Masuda said.

"C-rations," Santiago said. "Combat rations. Canned food we can heat up."

"Oh man," Roberts said. "Right now, I could kill for some beanie-weenie."

Masuda didn't bother to ask what beanie-weenie was. Instead he sat silently while the three reminisced about Army food. Listening to them talking, Masuda got the impression they missed life in the Army. He wondered if they might have been having second thoughts about deserting.

Eventually Masuda said, "You're just going to have to get used to it, I'm afraid. At least until we get back to the mainland."

"When will that be?" Sullivan asked.

"A week. Maybe longer."

The three silently exchanged glances.

"Look," Masuda said, eager to bring the conversation to a close, "I'll have a word with Pran and see if we can get some more fish on the menu."

"Fish?" Roberts said.

"It's the best I can do. There's just no meat on the island."

"But I've seen cows," Roberts said, staring at Masuda with an accusatory look on his face.

"They're dairy cows," Masuda said.

Roberts didn't reply, but he continued looking at Masuda, his eyes narrowing and his gaze increasing in intensity, making Masuda feel uncomfortable. Masuda couldn't help but think that this was what it felt like to look into the eyes of a killer.

"What about the chickens?" Santiago asked.

A shiver ran down Masuda's spine. "What chickens?"

"Down in the village. I saw them yesterday."

"Yesterday?" Masuda cast his mind back to the previous day. The only time Santiago had been out of his sight was after breakfast, when he had wandered off with Anala. He had assumed they had spent all of their time together somewhere secluded, but apparently not.

"What were you doing in the village?" Masuda said, staring into Santiago's eyes to impress on him how serious he was.

Santiago met his gaze. "Nothing. Why?"

"Why? Because I'm responsible for your safety, that's why. How can I look after you if I don't know where you are?"

"We're not going to go far, are we?" Roberts said. "I mean, we're stuck on this goddamn island."

"We don't need babysitting," Santiago added. "We survived in shitholes a lot worse than this in Vietnam. We'll be fine."

"I don't doubt that," Masuda said, keen to avoid another argument. "But I don't want any of you going into the village on your own. Is that understood?"

"Okay, fine," Santiago said, a little too acquiescently for Masuda's liking.

It was testimony to the cohesiveness and purposefulness of the Tribe that they continued to function smoothly as a group despite the distractions caused by the presence of Masuda and the deserters. With the exception of Anala, who spent her free time either by Santiago's side or watching him from afar, the hippies seemed intent on going about their lives normally, varying their routines only to the extent necessary to enable the new arrivals to adjust, as when Pran had taught the three how to fish with spears.

And adjust they did. As the days went by, Santiago, Roberts, and Sullivan slept in less, were less inclined to congregate around the kitchen before meal times, and showed more interest in participating in the yoga sessions and other group activities during their free time. Sullivan was by far the most enthusiastic of the three, especially when it came to music. His drum playing had improved remarkably, impressing Pran, who told Masuda the American was the quickest learner he had ever encountered.

One morning, Masuda found himself alone in their hut with Sullivan, who had borrowed a drum and was sitting cross-legged, experimenting with different ways of striking the instrument. Masuda was lying a few feet away with his eyes closed. Suddenly, hearing a familiar rhythm, he sat up and looked at the American.

He listened for a few moments longer, then exclaimed, "Blue Rondo à la Turk!"

Surprised, Sullivan stopped drumming and looked up.

"No," Masuda said, "don't stop."

Sullivan smiled and resumed playing. Masuda closed his eyes again and began counting out loud. "One-two, one-two, one-two, one-two-three, one-two, one-two, one-two, one-two-three." But the tempo was so fast he had trouble keeping up. Then the rhythm changed, and Masuda starting counting again, more slowly this time. "One-two-three-four, one-two-three-four."

After a while, Sullivan stopped playing and set the drum down on the floor beside him. He looked over at Masuda and said, "Some people say Brubeck's compositions are too cerebral, or that he can't swing. But you can't tell me that record doesn't swing."

"The change from 9/8 time to standard swing time for the solos was a stroke of genius," Masuda said.

"We can sure thank our lucky stars Mr. Brubeck didn't follow in his father's footsteps and become a cowboy," Sullivan added, smiling.

Masuda laughed. "But where did you learn to play like that?"

"Actually," Sullivan said, hesitating slightly, "I played the drums in high school."

"You played Dave Brubeck tunes in high school?" Masuda asked.

It was Sullivan's turn to laugh. "No. We played square brass band stuff. But I always wanted to be in a jazz band."

"You can do it," Masuda said. "You've got talent. More than me, anyway."

Sullivan looked at Masuda. "You play the drums?"

"The trumpet."

Sullivan nodded. "I saw Chet Baker play once. It was a couple of years ago in San Francisco. I was only a kid, but my father snuck me in to the club. He used to play with Baker in the 6th Army Band at the Presidio."

"No kidding," Masuda said. "My father was a musician too. He played trombone in a big band in Osaka. But he lost his job when jazz music was banned in 1941."

"Banned?" Sullivan said. "How come?"

"Jazz was American music, and after Pearl Harbor that meant it was the enemy's music."

Sullivan nodded slowly. "What did your father do after that?"

"He gave up music and came home to work at my grandfather's bicycle shop."

Sullivan was silent for a moment. Then he said, "Was it your father who got you into music?"

"In a way. He never played again after the war. But when I was growing up he always had the radio tuned to one of the jazz stations that broadcast live from dance halls and nightclubs in Tokyo or Osaka. So the house was always filled with swing and big band jazz. He started collecting LPs when they were introduced in the 1950s. His favorite was Benny Goodman's *Carnegie Hall Jazz Concert*. He'd play it over and over again. Drove my mother crazy."

Sullivan laughed.

"He never really moved on from the swing stuff. When I started learning the trumpet I wanted to play hard-bop like my own musical idols. Lee Morgan. Freddie Hubbard. He could just about put up with that, but he drew the line at modal and avant-garde jazz."

"Sometimes it's hard for older folk to get their heads around the latest trends. I bet he's still proud of you, though."

Masuda thought about his parents and younger brother back home in Tokushima. His father was furious when Masuda told him of his plan to quit university and pursue his dream of becoming a musician, warning him he would never be welcome at home again if he went through with it. Since moving to Tokyo, Masuda hadn't been in touch with his family at all. And though he had no desire to see his father again, he missed his mother and younger brother.

Masuda considered telling Sullivan this, but thought better of it. Instead he said, "There was this one Stan Getz tune called 'Dear Old Stockholm' that my father and I both liked. I practiced and practiced until I had it perfect. Then I played it for him. It's the only time I've seen him cry."

Neither of them spoke for some time.

Eventually Sullivan asked, "So, are they still your idols? Morgan and Hubbard?"

"I guess my real hero is Clifford Brown."

Sullivan smiled. "Brownie."

"He was such an amazing technician," Masuda continued. "He had the ability to articulate every note, even when he was playing at speed. But he also had this incredibly warm, rounded sound that enabled him to really express himself when he played ballads."

Masuda glanced across at Sullivan, who was looking down at the drum now. He studied the young G.I.'s face a while before saying, "I had no idea…"

Sullivan looked up. "No idea about what?"

Masuda looked away for a moment, adjusting his glasses before focusing his gaze back on the American. "How did you meet Santiago and Roberts? Were you in Vietnam together?"

"No. We met at a club in Tokyo. I overheard them talking about going AWOL, and told them I was interested in joining them."

"Did you know about…?" Masuda's voice trailed off.

"About Roberts stabbing an MP? No. But it didn't surprise me. Nothing surprises me any more about this goddamn war. This god-damn fucking war."

The sudden outburst of anger startled Masuda.

"I mean, what do they expect when they train people to kill and to feel no remorse, no guilt? You never get over that. Once you've killed someone, you can never go back to the way you were before."

Masuda didn't reply. He wondered if Sullivan had killed anyone.

Looking at him now, so vulnerable in his red bathing trunks, he thought it unlikely.

"Anyway," Sullivan went on, "I don't plan to stay with them any longer than necessary. Once we're in Sweden or wherever it is we're going, I'll go my own way. Maybe pursue a career in music. Do they play jazz in Sweden?"

Masuda laughed. "They play jazz everywhere!"

CHAPTER 21

Flynn spent the rest of the afternoon wandering around the Nihon University campus, which included a number of buildings on the other side of Hakusan-dōri. Like the buildings housing the Economics department, those containing the Law, Physics, and Humanities departments had all been occupied and barricaded.

It was soon clear that news of his exploits that morning had spread, for as he walked among the students he noticed people looking at him. Some would interrupt their conversations and nudge each other and exchange whispered words, and in the case of female students, the words would invariably turn into giggles behind open palms.

From time to time a student would stop and talk to him. Once they heard he had been with the U.S. Navy, the conversation inevitably turned to his experiences in Vietnam. The students were surprisingly knowledgeable about the war, but were eager to hear from someone who had actually been involved. What did the average soldier think about the war? Were the stories of atrocities against Vietnamese civilians true? Did the Americans really think they could win? At the Humanities department, Flynn was even asked to speak to a class about his experiences. By this time, however, he was growing weary of all the attention, and he politely declined and made his way back to the Economics department.

That evening, after dinner in the cafeteria in the basement, Flynn retreated to the sixth floor. Although tired, he found it difficult to sleep. His mind raced with nervous excitement at the prospect of the meeting with Beheiren the following day.

When sleep did eventually come, it brought not comfort and relief, but the same recurring nightmare that had bedeviled him since he left the *Respite*. He was in the morgue, his feet stuck in the thick layer of gelatinous blood that covered the floor, preventing him from moving forward. Then he was moving backward toward the body on the gurney, turning and reaching and gripping the edge of the sheet and pulling it away to reveal Huerta's face.

He woke with a start. Looking toward the uncurtained windows, Flynn saw that it was still dark. He closed his eyes and tried to go back to sleep, but despite his best efforts he remained in limbo, neither asleep nor fully awake.

But he must have dozed off, for he woke again, this time to voices and the sound of people moving around him. Turning to the windows, he saw several figures silhouetted against the early morning light, pointing down at the street below.

He cast his eyes around the room. Where people had been sleeping just moments ago lay empty mattresses. He pondered getting up and looking for Yamada or Yonekura. Then, remembering his appointment at the coffee shop later in the morning, he decided it would be best to stay put. Better to lie low rather than risk attracting the attention of the authorities with a repeat of yesterday's foolhardy antics. Besides, from what he had seen, the students were perfectly capable of defending themselves.

One of the figures at the window turned and walked toward him. As it drew near its features became clearer. He recognized the short hair and glasses.

"Eddie," Yonekura said, "you need to get up."

"Why? What is it?"

"The police. They're moving in."

"They're just probing your defenses," Flynn said.

"No," Yonekura said, her voice more insistent now. "There are hundreds of them this time. We need to get you out of here now, before they get inside the building."

From Yonekura's tone and manner, Flynn knew she wasn't exaggerating. He got up and walked over to the window. It didn't take him long to recognize the gravity of the situation.

Six floors below was a sea of blue uniforms and riot shields. The officers, hundreds of them as Yonekura had said, were stationary and in a tight, orderly formation facing the occupied building. Those near

the front had their shields raised as students on the second-floor balcony and on the floors above showered the police with rocks, empty
bottles, chairs, and desks. Debris lay scattered on the pavement.

As he looked on, Flynn saw the nozzle of a fire hose appear from
a window three floors below them and, within seconds, a thick jet
of water was trained on the policemen. They were soon soaked, their
shields and helmets along with the asphalt around them glistening
in the sun.

Flynn had seen enough. He turned back to Yonekura. "How do
we get out? Aren't all the exits barricaded?"

"We can get out through the exit at the rear of the building, the
one we came in through yesterday."

Flynn considered his options. Although he supported the students and didn't doubt their bravery and determination, he knew
their resources were limited and that they couldn't hold out for long
against such a large-scale assault. Once they ran out of rocks and
other ammunition, the police would be able to dismantle the barricades and get into the building. If he were caught inside he would
be arrested and handed over to the U.S. military. Much as he wanted
to stand and fight alongside Yonekura and the other occupiers, the
only sensible thing to do was to get out while he still had the chance.

"Quickly," urged Yonekura, "you need to get out of here."

"Okay. Let's go."

He walked over to his mattress, picked up his rucksack and
took one last look around the room before hurrying over to where
Yonekura was waiting by the door.

It seemed to take an eternity for the elevator to arrive. As they
waited, Flynn turned to Yonekura and said, "Where's Yamada? I
need to thank him. I need to say goodbye."

"He's downstairs. Organizing the counteroffensive."

"The counteroffensive?" Flynn said, uncertain that he had heard
Yonekura correctly. Then he remembered the Molotov cocktails.

Neither of them spoke as they rode the elevator to the second
floor. They took the stairs the rest of the way down and ran to the
exit at the rear of the building.

Inside the narrow doorway there was a scrum of helmeted demonstrators. Flynn couldn't understand what they were saying, but it

was clear from their raised voices and the expressions on their faces that something was wrong.

As Yonekura approached the group, one of them saw her and rushed over to say something. Flynn thought he heard Yamada's name. Yonekura reacted immediately, elbowing her way through the group of students and through the open doorway into the street.

Flynn followed. He heard shouting and footsteps and saw a dozen students armed with wooden staves and rocks, standing on the pavement in front of the lean-to near the exit. They were looking up the street.

Flynn followed their gaze. Some twenty yards away was a gaggle of riot policemen. They were slowly retreating, shuffling backward in a tight formation with shields raised. Flynn counted six dark blue police helmets. Then he spotted a seventh helmet. It was light blue, and Flynn could just make out the black lettering on the side. FREE.

Flynn caught Yonekura's attention. "What is it? What's happening?"

"It's Yamada," she replied, her gaze still fixed on the retreating policemen. "The police have taken him."

Flynn looked up the street and back at Yonekura. "We have to do something. We can't just let them get away."

Yonekura turned to look at Flynn, and he thought he saw a tear in her eye. "There's nothing we can do."

Flynn looked up the street again. The policemen were nearly at the corner. Once there they would turn right into the narrow street that ran between the main building of the Economics department and the one next to it. In less than a minute they would be back with the main body of riot police on Hakusan-dōri.

Flynn watched the retreating policemen. He thought for a moment and said to Yonekura, "Get as many people as you can spare out here and follow those policemen. Stay as close to them as you can." He then turned and ran back toward the building.

"Where are you going?" Yonekura shouted, but Flynn ignored her and continued running as fast as his legs would carry him.

Inside, he bounded up the stairs two steps at a time, grabbing at the handrail to pull himself up even faster. By the time he reached the third floor he was out of breath, but he urged himself on, gritting his teeth as he struggled to maintain his breakneck ascent. His thighs burned, and he stumbled twice on the final flight, but he didn't stop, even when he reached the fifth floor. He turned into the corridor, moving so fast that his feet skidded on the floor, and sprinted to the end.

To his relief he saw that the box was still sitting on the floor beneath the open window. He quickly checked the contents. Inside, as well as the Molotov cocktails, there were half a dozen cigarette lighters. He took one of the lighters and shoved in into his trouser pocket. Then he lifted the box, heaved it out the window and lowered it as far as he could reach. He dropped it onto the roof of the walkway, praying that none of the bottles would break. He jumped out and scrambled to the edge of the roof, dragging the box behind him, and looked down onto the street below.

The riot policemen, still formed into a tight knot, had rounded the corner and were steadily making their way down the narrow street. Soon they would be directly underneath the walkway. From his elevated position, Flynn could clearly make out Yamada's light blue helmet in the middle. Following the police were the demonstrators, as many as thirty of them, with Yonekura in the front directing their slow pursuit.

Flynn took several deep breaths to steady himself and dragged the box of Molotov cocktails across to the other side of the roof and looked down. Below him, lying across the street in front of the main group of riot policemen, who were still being kept at bay by the barrage of stones and other missiles from the students inside the building, was a mound of debris including the remains of wooden benches and desks that had been hurled from the balcony and out of the windows. The debris formed a porous barrier that would slow the policemen who had apprehended Yamada. But it wouldn't stop them. Not unless Flynn acted now.

He turned and with one hand lifted one of the bottles out of the box and cradled it to his chest. With his other hand he pulled the lighter out of his pocket.

One more glance down at the street to make sure the policemen had still not reached the wall of debris. Then he lit the rag extending from the mouth of the bottle.

It quickly caught fire, and in one motion he turned and hurled the burning Molotov cocktail in the direction of the pile of rubble, grateful that his target was large and that he didn't need more than a split second to aim.

Amidst the sound of students and policemen shouting and of stones and bottles hitting asphalt and riot shields he heard the glass smash and saw the fingers of flaming liquid spread across the detritus.

He turned and reached for another bottle and lit it and sent it on its way, aiming for a spot a few feet further across the street from where the first projectile had landed. He repeated this four more times until the box was empty.

Below him, a curtain of fire several feet high stretched from one side of the street to the other. The fire was so intense that he had to raise a forearm in front of his face to protect himself from the heat, and even then he couldn't look at it for long.

He scrambled to the other side of the roof and peered over the edge. The policemen holding Yamada were directly beneath him now. On hearing the smashing glass and feeling the heat of the fire they halted their backward shuffling and turned to find their way blocked by a wall of flames.

They pivoted back the way they had come, only to see the group of pursuing students bearing down on them. Outnumbered and with nowhere to escape, the policemen made the only decision possible. They released Yamada, who stumbled forward and lost his footing before picking himself up and running to join his comrades.

Flynn watched as Yamada and Yonekura embraced and turned to face the policemen. The pursuers, who had halted their advance when they saw Yamada freed, began to edge forward threateningly, and for a moment Flynn thought they were going to drive the policemen into the flames.

But Yamada, who now seemed to be in charge, reined in the students by barking an order and spreading both arms. It was then that Yonekura, who was standing directly behind Yamada, tapped him on the shoulder and pointed up to where Flynn was crouched on the roof of the overhead walkway.

Yamada looked up, and a smile broke out on his face as he recognized Flynn. Slowly, Flynn straightened himself, stood tall on the
roof and clenched his left fist tightly and raised it above his head.
Yamada immediately returned the salute. Then, still looking up at
Flynn, he took a few steps backward, and the group of students
followed him, and they all turned and marched back along the street
and around the corner.

CHAPTER 22

The rain stopped soon after midday. Natsume still hadn't returned from making his phone call, and with nothing to do to pass the time, Harper decided to head over to the administration building to see if the Beheiren operative had any news from Tokyo. He found him in the common room, sitting next to Ikeda on a sofa. Both men were engrossed in a newspaper that lay open on the table in front of them. They looked up as Harper approached.

"There you are," Ikeda said, as if he was expecting him. "I was just showing Natsume this article about Martin Luther King. He's visiting Memphis to support a group of black sanitation workers who've staged a walkout in protest at their working conditions."

Harper glanced at the article Ikeda was pointing to but it was all in Japanese. His eyes were drawn to a photograph on the opposite page, which showed a C-130 Hercules cargo aircraft on a runway. He asked what the accompanying article was about.

"It's a report on the Battle of Khe Sanh," Natsume said. He quickly read through the article before continuing. "It says six thousand U.S. and South Vietnamese troops are surrounded by up to three North Vietnamese divisions. Overland supply routes to the base at Khe Sanh have been cut off, but the Americans are flying in supplies by cargo aircraft."

Now Harper realized why the runway in the photo looked familiar. He recalled arriving at Khe Sanh Combat Base before being choppered up to the camp on Hill 842, and the many hours he spent looking down from the camp at the runway next to the base. It seemed so long ago. More than three months had passed since he was medevaced out of Khe Sanh. On the run for about a month now, he wondered how many of the men he served with were still stuck on that hill.

Then, remembering why he had sought out Natsume in the first place, he asked, "So, any news?"

Natsume glanced across at Ikeda before answering. "No news. We're to stay here until further notice."

"Any idea how long that will be?"

"None, I'm afraid. Days, possibly weeks."

"Weeks?" Harper said, unable to hide his disappointment.

"If you're bored," Ikeda said, "there's plenty of work to do outside. If you're feeling up to it, that is."

"I feel fine," Harper said.

"Good," Ikeda said. "Natsume tells me you grew up on a farm."

"It was hardly a farm. Just a small plot of land where we grew a few vegetables, kept a few animals," Harper said. "So I guess you could say I know a thing or two about chickens."

"Excellent," Ikeda said. "What say I meet you outside in half an hour?"

"Sounds good," Harper said.

Harper spent the rest of the afternoon working alongside Ikeda, feeding the chickens and sweeping up manure, which was used as fertilizer elsewhere on the farm. It had been a while since he had done any manual labor, and by the end of the day his body ached. Still, it felt good to be working outside after being confined indoors for so long, in hospitals at first and then in Yumi's apartment.

He had made the decision to lie low at Yumi's place soon after skipping his flight back to Vietnam. He knew it wouldn't be long before he was reported AWOL, and that the Shore Patrol would then be looking for him. It was bearable for a while, but as the days turned into weeks he grew sick of being cooped up inside, and so one Thursday he suggested to Yumi they go to Chinatown. Yumi was reluctant at first, saying that it was a part of Yokohama she rarely visited, but he persisted, confident that being together in an environment where people of different nationalities mixed easily would dispel the gloom that had descended over them. He hadn't counted on the place being overrun by thousands of sailors from a U.S. aircraft carrier that had docked that morning.

The presence of so many sailors, many drunk and stumbling around with their arms draped around each other's shoulders, presented Harper with a dilemma. He had originally intended to take Yumi to the Red Shoes Bar. The establishment was well known for attracting a mixed clientele from all of the services, and he knew he could blend in. But he also knew that it became a bit of a battleground at times, and with so many Navy personnel in town there was bound to be more fighting than usual. So instead Harper decided to go somewhere else.

They wandered the streets of Chinatown, ignoring the touts and steering clear of the nightclubs promising "sexy broads" and "outstanding service," until they found a quiet-looking bar down a narrow alleyway. The only other customer was another brother, a giant of a man in a black suit and tie. Harper walked straight up to the counter, sat down two seats along from the man and motioned for Yumi to sit beside him. He ordered a whiskey for himself and a rum and Coke for Yumi. As the bartender, whose thin face and slicked-back hair gave him an avian appearance, poured their drinks, Harper looked around the room.

It was tiny, even by Japanese standards. There were just half a dozen stools with plump red leather seats in front of the polished wooden bar. Behind him were two wooden tables each flanked by a pair of wooden chairs. The back wall was decorated with album covers, all of them jazz records as far as Harper could tell. As he turned back to face the barman, he noticed for the first time a hi-fi sitting on a low table at the end of the bar, just along from the other customer. He realized this was the source of the jazz music that flooded the room. Behind the barman, bottles of liquor were displayed on shelves in circular recesses in the wall.

Eventually Harper's eyes came to rest on the man next to him. He was looking at Harper through black-rimmed glasses.

"Hey, Brother," the man said.

"Hey," Harper replied.

"Marine?"

"Yeah," Harper said. "You?"

"Navy."

Harper nodded.

"R&R?" the brother asked.

Harper looked at the man carefully before responding. "Hospital."

"You were wounded over in Nam?"

"Yeah, that's right."

The squid slowly shook his head. "You know, Brother, that ain't our place."

Harper took a sip of his whiskey before replying. "What do you mean?"

"I mean it ain't our place."

"But you're in the navy, right?"

"Yeah, I'm in the navy. But I ain't been to Vietnam. I ain't been nowhere except Japan."

"How come?" Harper asked.

"Because I'm a Muslim. A Black Muslim. We're exempted from combat."

Harper had heard of the Black Muslims, though he had never actually met one as far as he knew. And this was the first time he had heard they were exempt from military service.

"War is against the teachings of the Holy Qur'an," the squid continued. "You know what it says in the Qur'an? It's forbidden to take part in any war unless declared by Allah. Vietnam is not our war. It's the white man's war. It's like Muhammad Ali said, 'I ain't got no quarrel with them Viet Cong. They never called me nigger.'"

Now Harper knew the squid was bullshitting. He had read about Muhammad Ali's battle to stay out of the military on religious grounds. It had cost him his boxing license. And he was still fighting in the Supreme Court to overturn the felony conviction they handed him the year before. No, if they wouldn't send this brother to Vietnam, it wasn't because he was a Black Muslim—it was because he was a troublemaker and they wanted him out of the way. Either that or he had managed to slip through the cracks and they didn't know where he was. A ghost. Harper remembered a story he heard in Da Nang about a group of Marines who deserted and were rumored to be lying low in a village just west of the air base known as the Dog

Patch. Some MPs went in after them but the Marines fought them off, and so the brass decided to leave them there. They figured they weren't going anywhere in a hurry. After that the Dog Patch had been placed off-limits to all U.S. military personnel.

Harper took another sip of his whiskey, waiting for the man to speak again.

"The name's Cleveland," the man said eventually.

"Harpo," Harper said. He extended a fist, and Cleveland reciprocated, their hands twisting and swiveling in a ritualized series of moves that ended with a fist bump.

"So," Cleveland said, "when are they sending you back?"

"Back?"

"Yeah. They're sending you back, aren't they?"

Harper slowly nodded.

Cleveland took a pull of his drink and motioned with his eyes toward Yumi. "Is that your girl?"

Yumi smiled and waved her hand.

"Yeah," Harper said, "that's my girl."

"And you're leaving her to go to Vietnam?"

"Orders are orders."

Cleveland slowly shook his head. "Shit, man. Do you have any idea how crazy that sounds?"

The record on the hi-fi had finished playing and Harper watched the barman lift it off the turntable and place it in its sleeve and store it under the bar. He then produced another record, holding the sleeve in front of Cleveland so that he could see it. Only after Cleveland nodded his approval did the barman remove the disk and place it on the turntable. Over a smattering of applause, Harper heard a woman's voice announce, "Art Blakey and the Jazz Messengers." There was an introduction consisting of the same piano chord repeated over a dozen times, then the band seemed to spring into life, all brass and thumping drums.

"*Ugetsu*," Cleveland said, shouting to be heard over the music.

"You-what?"

"*Ugetsu*. The name of the album. It's a Japanese word. Means 'the moon obscured by rain clouds.'"

Harper nodded. They listened in silence to the rest of the track.

When it ended, Cleveland held the album cover up so that Harper could see it. On it was a photo of Blakey performing on stage with the members of his band.

"Now there's a brother who really appreciates this country," Cleveland said. "And they appreciate him. When Art Blakey's band first toured here in 1961 they became the first American jazz band to play in Japan in front of Japanese audiences. There were thousands of fans at the airport to meet them. They even had an audience with the emperor. Blakey said that when they left at the end of the tour, the whole band was in tears. Three members of that band, Wayne Shorter, Lee Morgan, and Blakey himself, later married Japanese women."

"Yeah, well," Harper said. "No offense or anything, but I prefer music you can dance to."

Cleveland laughed. "What, you mean like Glenn Miller?"

"Hell, no. I mean like James Brown."

Cleveland frowned, making clear his disapproval. Then he said, "He's one of us, you know. Art Blakey."

It was Harper's turn to make a face. "Yeah, he's a brother. I can see that."

"No, I mean he's a Muslim."

"No shit."

Cleveland stared at Harper for a moment. Then he said, "You know why jazz is so popular in this country?"

"No, but I've got a feeling you're going to tell me."

"Because as non-whites the Japanese know where we're coming from. They understand the struggles we've been through to have our culture recognized. And make no mistake: jazz is *our* culture. Black culture. Back home, jazz's black roots have stymied its growth. Here, if anything, those roots are helping it flourish."

They listened to several more tracks from *Ugetsu*, Cleveland commenting from time to time on the quality of the playing and the merits of the various band members. Harper was intrigued, not so much by the music, but by the squid's stories about the people behind it, which seemed to bring the music to life.

Cleveland was explaining how Wayne Shorter, who had been musical director of the Jazz Messengers, left the band in 1964 to join Miles Davis's new quintet, when the door behind them swung open and they turned to see three seamen in white sailor suits and marshmallow hats stagger in. Instinctively, Harper sized them up. All three were white, though their faces were rouged from the effects of alcohol, and this—along with their short stature and uniforms—gave them a porcine appearance. For a moment Harper imagined he was looking at the Three Little Pigs. They stood in a close formation by the door, just a few paces from where Harper, Yumi, and Cleveland sat. But they didn't seem to have noticed them, their attention directed solely at the barman. The squid in the middle was the first to speak.

"Hey, barkeep, where are all the girls?"

Practical Pig, thought Harper.

The sailor on the right then took a wobbly step forward. "Yeah, where are you hiding them?"

Fiddler Pig.

"I'm sorry," the bartender said calmly, "but there are no girls here,"

"What's that?" Practical said.

"No girls work here," repeated the bartender.

Practical seemed to notice Harper, Yumi, and Cleveland for the first time. He looked at the two men first, then his gaze fell on Yumi.

"Well, well," he said, smiling lecherously. "Looky here."

Harper tensed and was about to stand up, but he immediately felt a mammoth hand on his shoulder pressing him down onto the stool and he turned to see Cleveland rising and standing in front of him. It was the first time Harper had seen him on his feet. He must have been six and a half feet tall. If the new arrivals were the Three Little Pigs, then here was the Big Bad Wolf.

"I think you boys best head somewhere else," Cleveland said.

"Oh, you do, do you?" Practical said. "And why is that?"

"Just move along, now. We don't want no trouble."

Practical turned and looked at his sidekicks and then back at Cleveland.

"Trouble? We're not interested in trouble. We're just looking for some fun, aren't we, boys? We've spent the last six months in Vietnam. We're entitled to a bit of fun, aren't we?"

"Goddamn squids," Harper said, just loud enough that everyone could hear. "You ain't entitled to shit."

Practical looked at Harper again, more attentively this time, and then looked at Yumi.

"Well, will you look at what we've got here?"

Harper moved to stand up again, but again he felt Cleveland's hand on his shoulder.

"The girl's with my friend here," Cleveland said. "He's a wounded Marine, so you show him some goddamn respect."

"A fucking jarhead," Practical said. "Now why doesn't that surprise me?"

The sailor to the left of Practical stepped forward. Fifer Pig. "Jarhead?" he said in a slurred southern drawl. "Hell, there's another name we used to call folk like him."

This time Cleveland made no effort to restrain Harper as he rose and pushed past the taller man and strode forward until he stood directly in front of the sailor.

He looked into the squid's eyes. "Say it, motherfucker, just say it!"

Harper saw the looping roundhouse punch coming and had plenty of time to react. He bent his knees, ducked and took a step to his left. His assailant's clenched right fist sailed over his head, the momentum of the punch throwing him off balance. In his drunken state he was barely able to stay on his feet let alone respond to Harper's counterattack: a sharp right jab to the squid's now exposed right kidney region. The squid clutched his side with both hands and slumped to his knees, his hat toppling onto the floor.

Harper turned his attention to Practical, who had been observing the brief exchange and now stood staring at Harper, his bloodshot eyes bulging. Behind him, Fiddler tensed, eager to enter the fray. "Come on," the squid said to his buddy, "let's waste the motherfucker."

Harper took a step back to give himself a better view of his two remaining opponents but stayed in a fighting pose; knees bent, right hand formed into a fist and cocked by his right shoulder, left hand open and in front of his chest. Practical, who had now adopted a classic boxing stance, took a step forward. Just as Harper was bracing for the next assault, though, the door behind the squids flew open and another sailor-suited figure appeared. *Shit*, thought Harper. *The pigs have reinforcements.* But instead of entering the bar, the new arrival, who by the look of him was completely sober, stood in the doorway and shouted, "Shore Patrol! A truckload of them!" before disappearing again.

The two pigs froze and looked at each other for a moment before turning to their stricken buddy. They dragged him to his feet and pulled him toward the entrance, but before they could reach it he collapsed again. Panicking, they left him there and headed for the door.

Harper had every intention of following them. He turned to where Yumi was sitting and was about to grab her hand when he noticed that the bartender was standing in the narrow gap between the counter and the far wall. Their eyes met and the bartender waved to him. "Quickly. This way."

Harper took Yumi's hand and led her over to where the bartender was waiting. He had expected Cleveland to follow them but when he turned around he saw the taller man was still standing in the middle of the room.

"Come on, man!" Harper said.

"You go. I'll stall them."

Harper hesitated but, recognizing Cleveland was immovable, he guided Yumi behind the counter where the bartender opened a door that led into a narrow alleyway where crates of empty bottles were stacked high against the wall of the bar and the surrounding buildings. They turned right and ran until they came to a wider thoroughfare. At the corner, Harper stopped and looked back toward the bar. He hesitated for a moment, then he turned to Yumi and said, "Wait here. If I'm not back in five minutes, go back to the apartment."

"Harpo!" she called, grabbing his arm, but he slipped out of her grasp and ran back down the alleyway. He opened the door to the bar, stepped inside and stood behind the counter. Immediately to his right, also behind the counter, was the bartender. Seeing Harper, he motioned for him to keep quiet by placing a finger against his lips. Harper looked over the counter. Near the front entrance, Cleveland was leaning against the wall with his back to Harper, his hands above his head. Behind him, a helmeted Shore Patrolman stood with his nightstick pressed firmly against the back of Cleveland's neck. As Harper watched, the patrolman reached back with his free hand and unhooked a pair of handcuffs from his waist. On the floor, another patrolman sat on top of the squid Harper had decked earlier and was in the process of handcuffing him.

Neither soldier had seen Harper enter. He could still escape. But he had already made up his mind he wasn't leaving without Cleveland. He quietly made his way around to the front of the counter. As he approached the patrolman who was handcuffing Cleveland, his eyes were drawn to the polished black leather holster at his right hip. He crept up until he was directly behind him and in one motion pulled the Colt .45 automatic from its holster and pressed the nose against the back of the officer's neck.

"Don't move," he said. "Turn around and you're a dead motherfucker."

Out of the corner of his eye, Harper saw the other patrolman, who was still sitting on top of the wounded squid, turn and reach for his weapon.

"I'd stop right now if I were you," he said. "Unless you want to see your buddy's brains splattered against this wall."

The patrolman froze.

"Good. Now, get on the floor. Face down."

Harper let a few seconds pass. Then he said, "Do it now!"

Slowly, the patrolman to his right did as Harper ordered.

Harper turned his attention back to the patrolman in front of him.

"You," he said, pressing the nose of the .45 even harder against the man's neck. "Drop the nightstick."

The patrolman released his grip and the nightstick clattered to the floor.

Cleveland, who had remained standing with his hands above his head throughout this exchange, now lowered his arms and stepped away from the wall. With his free hand, Harper shoved the cop forward until his face came into contact with the wall.

"Cuff them," he said to Cleveland.

Without a word, Cleveland took the handcuffs off the standing patrolman and used them to secure the prone patrolman to the foot rail. He then took the prone patrolman's handcuffs, ordered his partner to lie down and cuffed him to the foot rail in the same way. Both sets of keys disappeared into his pants pocket. Finally,

Cleveland took the second patrolman's .45 and tucked it into the waistband of his trousers. Only then did Harper lower the pistol. As he and Cleveland backed toward the rear entrance to the bar, he said, "Remember. Turn around and you're both dead."

Harper and Cleveland sprinted from the bar to the end of the alley-way where Yumi was waiting and Harper took her hand without stopping and together the three of them ran until they came to an intersection. They turned right and continued running until they came to a canal when they turned right again. Without slowing, Harper lobbed the .45 over the railing to his left, hearing a dull plop as it landed in the water. Only when they came to a busy road did they slow to a walk.

"Tell me you wouldn't have shot that patrolman," Cleveland said, still breathing heavily.

"I just saved your ass, man," Harper said. "A simple 'thank you' would do."

"It's just that if you *had* pulled the trigger, my brains would have ended up splattered on that wall along with his."

"Yeah, well, I figure we've got about three minutes to get out of here before the alarm is raised and the hunt is on for two black AWOL motherfuckers. Am I wrong?"

"You're not wrong, Brother. What say we split up?"

"Sounds good to me," Harper said.

"Right," Cleveland said. Then, "One more thing."

"What's that?"

Cleveland reached forward and with his giant hand clasped Harper's shoulder. "Thanks, Brother."

CHAPTER 23

It was late the next afternoon, during the brief period of free time between the end of the afternoon's work and dinner, when things began to spiral out of Masuda's control. Tired from working in the fields, Masuda had curled up under the shade of one of the large trees that encircled the compound and drifted off to sleep. He was woken by the sound of running feet, and opened his eyes to see one of the young hippies, the one who called himself Gati, sprinting from the compound entrance over to the driftwood table where Pran was sitting. The very fact that he was running was the first indication that something was wrong. No one ran in the compound. There was no need.

As Gati drew alongside Pran, everyone in the compound looked in their direction, eager to learn the reason for Gati's dramatic entrance. Everyone except Masuda, who instinctively looked around to see what the Americans were doing. His heart sank. They were nowhere to be seen. He turned his attention back to the driftwood table where Pran and Gati were talking. The conversation was brief, and while he was too far away to follow what was being said, Masuda clearly heard the word *"akapan."* This was the nickname the hippies had come up with for the deserters, a contraction of *akai pantsu*, or red pants. Hearing it usually brought a smile to Masuda's face. Right now, however, it was the last word he wanted to hear.

At the conclusion of the discussion, Pran stood and turned toward Masuda, who had already gotten to his feet and was marching across the compound to meet him.

"Come with me," Pran said, before turning and heading in the direction from which Gati had come. He set off at such a pace that Masuda struggled to catch up. When he did, he drew alongside him and said, "What is it? What's happened?"

"The Red Pants," Pran replied, without turning around. The way he said it indicated to Masuda that he considered no further explanation was necessary.

Masuda walked along quietly for a few moments, trying to decide whether to press Pran for more information. Eventually he said, "Where are we going?"

"The village."

The Red Pants. The village. Now Masuda had an inkling of the nature of the problem.

They continued along the path, past the banyan tree and the abandoned farmhouse, until they came to the village. Pran raised one arm and motioned to a trail that branched off to the left. Masuda followed him down a slope until they came to a clearing, in the middle of which stood an old, wooden, single-story house. Instead of heading for the front door, Pran led Masuda down the side of the house to the backyard, which was fenced off with chicken wire. They entered through an open gate, Masuda pausing briefly to take in the chaotic scene in front of him. It took a few seconds for him to make sense of it.

In the middle of the yard, facing Masuda, stood two men. Their appearance and demeanor suggested to him they were father and son. Masuda assumed they lived at the property. They stood with their feet firmly planted on the ground, their hands held loosely by their sides. Masuda's attention was drawn to the right hand of the older of the two men. In it he held a kitchen knife. Its blade, around six inches long, was covered in blood.

In front of the two men, also facing Masuda, knelt Santiago, Roberts, and Sullivan. Each had his hands clasped behind his head, and the juxtaposition of the near-naked Americans and the two Japanese standing over them reminded Masuda of photographs he had seen of American troops in Vietnam with Vietnamese prisoners. Except here it seemed the tables had been turned.

Masuda looked in turn at the three Americans. Both Santiago and Roberts had what appeared to be blood on their hands and torsos. He looked into their eyes, hoping that they would reveal something about what had happened. Both men looked straight back at him. Sullivan, who appeared unscathed, was staring at a spot on the ground a yard or two in front of him.

Based on the evidence before him, Masuda guessed that the two Japanese had discovered Santiago, Roberts, and Sullivan on their property. They had confronted the Americans and a fight had ensued, during which Santiago and Roberts had been stabbed. But somehow the evidence didn't stack up. Although bloodied, neither Santiago nor Roberts appeared to have any stab wounds or other serious injuries. There was something else about the blood that didn't seem right. It was almost as if it had been smeared on by hand.

Masuda scanned the yard, anxious to find more clues. It was then that he spotted the chicken coop off to his left. The door was open. Masuda's body tensed uncontrollably, but relaxed again as he realized there was nothing moving inside the coop. Among a blanket of white feathers, however, he could clearly make out the bloodied carcasses of three chickens, the heads of which had been removed.

In the few brief seconds that it had taken Masuda to digest all this visual information, Pran had stridden from the gate to the middle of the yard, where he now stood in front of the five men, a sixth figure in the curious *tableau vivant*. Masuda approached as well now, albeit far more slowly and cautiously, his eyes darting back and forth between the group of figures and the chicken coop.

Pran was the first to speak, addressing the older of the two standing men in Japanese. "What happened?"

"We'd all gone down to the beach to meet the *Dai-ni Toshima-maru*. We didn't have enough lanterns for the hike back, so Kinji and I—" the old man gestured to the younger man, the one Masuda assumed was his son "—came back to get some. We heard a noise, and came out here to find these three inside the chicken coop. It was a real mess. They had this with them." He handed the knife, handle first, to Pran, who took it and examined it almost nonchalantly.

Masuda looked at the knife before addressing the Americans. "Where did you get it?"

None of the three spoke. In the end, it was Pran who answered. "It's from the kitchen."

Masuda turned again to the Americans. "How could you? I mean... Why?"

Roberts glanced across at Santiago and shrugged. "We were hungry. We planned to cook them up later, in secret, over a fire."

"How long? How long were you planning this?"

Roberts shrugged again, but this time he remained silent.

Masuda turned his attention to the two Japanese men. He bowed deeply. "These three are my responsibility. The Tribe is not to blame for this."

The two men looked at Masuda, the older man scrutinizing him particularly thoroughly, Masuda thought. It would have been clear from the length of his hair and the way he was dressed that he wasn't a hippie, although Masuda wasn't sure if this worked in his favor or not.

"Please forgive me," he said, bowing again. "I'll compensate you, of course."

"Take them away," the older man said dismissively. "And make sure they never set foot in the village again."

"Of course," Masuda said, bowing a third time.

He turned to the Americans. "Get up. And come with me."

They did as he requested, and he quickly led them over to the gate and out of the yard. He looked over his shoulder and saw that Pran was still in the middle of the yard speaking to the two Japanese, bowing as deeply as Masuda had as he offered his own apologies. Masuda was filled with remorse, particularly after Pran and the other hippies had done so much for them. Secretly, however, he was also relieved. Relieved that there were no police on the island, nor any journalists for that matter.

Having made his apologies, Pran exited the yard and the five of them left the property and silently made their way back up the slope to rejoin the main track that led back to the commune. Masuda had a lot of questions he wanted to ask the deserters, including how Santiago and Roberts had ended up so bloodied while Sullivan appeared completely unmarked. But he decided to wait until they got back to the commune, where he could speak to them in private.

They had just reached the banyan tree when they heard shouts coming from behind them. They immediately stopped and Masuda turned to see a figure running their way. He didn't recognize the voice, and in the fading evening light it was impossible to identify the owner. For a moment Masuda was afraid it was one of the two villagers, having second thoughts about letting the deserters off so lightly. But when the figure got nearer Masuda recognized it as Karon, one of the hippies. Masuda was curious as to why he was running not from the commune but from the opposite direction. Then he remembered that Gati and Karon had gone down to the beach to meet the *Dai-ni Toshima-maru*. They would have been passing the village around the time the deserters were caught in the chicken coop, whereupon Karon must have continued on down to the beach while Gati returned to the commune to raise the alarm.

At first Masuda was unable to make out what Karon was shouting. But as he got closer he thought he could make out the words "camera" and "*akapan.*" By the time he reached them he was almost out of breath. He must have run all the way from the beach. He stopped, bending over and clutching his sides as he struggled to catch his breath. Then he straightened and looked at Pran.

"The Red Pants. We have to hide the Red Pants." He paused to take two deep breaths before continuing. "There's a television crew. They arrived on the ferry. They're here to film some kind of documentary."

Judging from Pran's reaction, it was clear that this news was as much a surprise to him as it was to Masuda.

"They're here to what?"

"To film a documentary. About life on the island. They've started shooting already. They had the camera rolling on the boat as they were coming ashore."

"The villagers must have known about this," Pran said. "Why didn't anyone tell us?"

"I don't know," Karon replied. "I didn't ask. As soon as I found out who they were and what they were doing I decided to come straight back."

"It's okay," Pran said, comforting the younger man. "You did the right thing."

"Pran," Karon said, glancing at the deserters before adding in a hushed voice, "we have to hide the Red Pants."

"Yes," Pran said. "But where?"

The three of them looked around in the growing darkness. Then Masuda had an idea. "What about the barn?"

They all turned in the direction of the abandoned farmhouse, which although visible from the track was far enough away that it was impossible for anyone passing to see inside.

"It's not perfect," Pran said, "but I guess it'll have to do." He thought for a moment longer, then addressed Masuda. "Take them straight there now. Tell them what's happened and make it clear to them that it's unsafe for them to go outside. They mustn't leave the barn, no matter what, until we tell them to. I'll go and talk to the village elders and find out what's happening."

"Understood," Masuda said. He stood and watched as Pran turned on his heels and set off at a jog down the track in the direction of the village. He took a deep breath and turned to face the deserters.

The television crew remained on Suwanosejima for three days, reboarding the *Dai-ni Toshima-maru* when it stopped at the island on the return leg of its weekly voyage to the Tokara Islands. During this time the deserters were confined to the abandoned farmhouse. They complained at first, saying that the smell was unbearable and pleading to be allowed to sleep at the commune at night. But after the episode with the chickens, even the Americans realized they were in no position to be making demands of their hosts, and after the first night they resigned themselves to their incarceration.

In an effort to further placate them, Masuda stressed how lucky they were that the aggrieved villagers had agreed not to take the matter any further. He also hinted that some of the hippies, unhappy at the harm the actions of the three had done to their reputation among the villagers, were out for revenge, and that their enforced separation was therefore timely. This was a lie, of course. While it was true that the chicken episode had destroyed what little goodwill toward the deserters remained among the hippies, he knew it wasn't in their nature to bear any kind of grudge. For the three days of their confinement the deserters continued to be fed, with Masuda and Anala taking turns to deliver meals to the farmhouse. They were also supplied with cigarettes, which were a luxury at the commune and normally rationed, as well as *shōchū*.

Pran met with the village elders the evening the television crew arrived, and later with the television crew itself. They came to an understanding about what could be filmed and what could not, agreeing that the hippies could be filmed working and relaxing, but that their living quarters were off-limits. News of this came as a relief not only to Masuda but to the other hippies, although their relief was tempered when Pran explained that the television crew probably had telephoto lenses that would enable them to film the camp from a distance without them noticing. So although the hippies appeared to go about their normal business for the duration of the crew's stay on the island, they were constantly on guard, making the mood around the camp tense.

The tension eased when the television crew left the island, but only slightly. Their departure prompted the deserters' return to the camp, and the icy reception they received was in stark contrast to the welcome they were given the night of their arrival. During the day, the camp routine appeared to return to what it had been before the chicken episode and the intrusion of the television crew. The deserters worked and dined alongside the hippies and, much to Masuda's consternation, Santiago and Anala resumed their fraternization. After dark, however, the new order was plain to see. Santiago and Roberts had never shown much interest in joining in the music-making, and had always been among the first to retire for the evening. Sullivan, on the other hand, had come alive in the evenings, especially after Pran had taught him how to play the African drum. Intoxicated by the *shōchū* and the music and the liberated atmosphere, he would sing and dance and play the drum, often until he was completely exhausted, whereupon he would lie down on the spot and fall asleep, always with a smile on his face. Now, however, it was as if Sullivan had gone back into his shell. He did stay up late for the first two nights after his return from the farmhouse, but he no longer showed any interest in playing the drum, nor did he join in any of the other festivities. From the third night onward he started going back to the hut with Santiago and Roberts, resigned, it seemed, to the fact that things had changed irredeemably. Masuda would never see that smile on his face again.

They remained on the island another week. Painfully aware that they had more than outstayed their welcome, Masuda would have left earlier had it been possible, but he had no choice but to wait for the *Dai-ni Toshima-maru* to call on its next return voyage to Kagoshima.

On the day of their departure, Pran and Anala accompanied them down to the beach, where the six of them gathered in a small group separate from the main body of villagers. Masuda knew that for Pran the send-off was a token gesture, and that in reality he and the other hippies were looking forward to seeing the back of them. Anala, on the other hand, appeared genuinely sad to see Santiago leaving. As darkness fell, she clung to her beau, who responded in kind, hugging and kissing his mate. Embarrassed as much by their disregard for the feelings of Pran as by their inconsiderate behavior, Masuda turned to Pran and bowed and apologized once again for all the trouble they had caused.

Their farewells completed, Masuda and the three deserters waded out and scrambled aboard the boat. It was so dark now that when he turned and looked toward the beach, all Masuda could see were the glowing points of light of the flashlights and lanterns of the farewell party.

They climbed aboard the *Dai-ni Toshima-maru* to find it filled to capacity, mostly with people heading back to the mainland after spending the weekend with their families on the islands south of Suwanosejima. Resigned to the fact that they would have to spend the night on the ship's deck, Masuda ushered his charges through one of the cabins toward the stairs. The deserters were greeted with cries of welcome from a group of Japanese passengers, obviously emboldened by *shōchū*, who quickly made room for Santiago, Roberts, and Sullivan. There was no room for Masuda, however, and so he continued on alone, climbing the stairs to the deck, where he weaved his way through the prone bodies, eventually finding a place to sleep beside one of the ship's lifeboats.

They arrived in Kagoshima late the next morning. From the dock they took the streetcar to Nishi-Kagoshima Station, where, after buying tickets for the night train, Masuda led the deserters upstairs to a Western-style restaurant. Masuda had hardly slept on the boat and had very little appetite. He ate only half his meal, waiting for the Americans to finish and ordering coffee for them before leaving to find a pay phone. He called the JATEC liaison, Sekiguchi, who instructed him to continue by train as far as Kyoto, where someone would be waiting to take custody of the deserters. He returned to the restaurant to pay the bill and collect his charges, then led them to the platform.

Later, on board the train, Masuda sat back in his seat and closed his eyes, relieved that his mission was nearly over and confident that nothing more could go wrong. He had only to accompany the deserters as far as Kyoto. Sekiguchi hadn't revealed to him the identity of the JATEC operative who would be waiting for him there. He hoped it would be Sakurai. Oh, how he had missed her. He had also missed his jazz music, and had already decided that the first thing he would do in Kyoto after handing over the deserters would be to find a jazz coffee shop, or better still, a jazz club with a live band, and let the music he loved transport him to another, happier place. At some point, of course, he would have to contact Beheiren's co-founder Shunsuke Tsurumi and tell him about the events of the past fortnight. For the moment, however, he pushed such concerns from his mind, determined to get some rest.

He was woken by a gentle nudge in his right side. He sat up, confused at first as to where he was and the time of day. He looked out the window to his left to see farmland flashing by in the twilight. They must have been traveling for more than an hour.

Sitting next to him by the window was Sullivan. The American had his eyes closed, but he wasn't sleeping. Instead, he was gently slapping his thighs with the palms of his hands, beating out a rhythm in his head. For a moment Masuda was carried back to the island, watching Sullivan sitting under the starry sky beating on the African drum.

He felt another nudge and turned to face Santiago, who was

seated across the aisle. Shortly after leaving Nishi-Kagoshima, Santiago had produced a pencil and paper and begun writing. He was holding the sheet of paper now, folded in three.

"Can you mail this for me?" he asked.

"What?" Masuda replied, still half asleep. "I mean, who's it for?"

"It's for Anala."

"Anala?" Masuda said, removing his glasses and rubbing his eyes.

"We're going to get married."

Masuda was wide awake now. He replaced his glasses and looked at Santiago. "Married? What are you talking about?"

"We're going to meet up in Sweden and get married."

"That's impossible. You don't even know if you're going to Sweden."

A look of confusion appeared on Santiago's face. "Where else would we be going?"

Masuda didn't answer. Instead, he said, "Even if you did go to Sweden and get married, how would Anala even get by? She hardly speaks any English, let alone Swedish."

"She can learn. She's smart."

"This is not a good idea. You hardly know each other."

"I'm not asking for your advice," Santiago said. "I'm just asking you to mail this letter." He held up the folded sheet of paper. "I need you to put it in an envelope, write the address, attach a stamp, and mail it. Can you do that for me?"

Reluctantly, Masuda took the letter from Santiago. He was tempted to unfold it and read it right there and then, but he knew this would only antagonize Santiago further. Instead he leaned over, picked up his backpack and tucked the letter into one of the side pockets. He would read it later and decide what to do with it then.

Masuda looked again at Santiago, whose attention was now focused on a *Playboy* magazine. Santiago had bought the magazine from a kiosk at Nishi-Kagoshima Station before they had boarded the train, and immediately waved it in front of his compatriots with a lecherous smirk on his face. He leafed through it now, stopping occasionally to ogle the color photos of semi-naked young Japanese women.

Confounded, Masuda turned his attention to Roberts, who was seated next to Santiago by the window. The window was open, and

Roberts sat with his elbow on the windowsill, the rush of air ruffling his hair as he gazed out at the passing countryside. Masuda looked past the American out the window and saw rice fields and low hills in the distance. In the fading light he could make out figures, farm workers in wide-brimmed hats bent over as they tended their rice crops.

A movement drew his attention back to Roberts. Still looking outside, the American slowly brought both hands up until they were level with his shoulders, his left arm extended in front of him out the open window and his right hand, fingers lightly curled, tucked under his chin.

Masuda tensed as he saw Roberts straighten the forefinger of his right hand and curl it around an imaginary trigger. He held this position for several seconds, then jerked his forefinger back three times in quick succession, simultaneously letting out three muffled cries: "Bang! Bang! Bang!"

Without thinking, Masuda leapt to his feet and lunged at Roberts. His body seemed to move of its own accord, propelling itself forward, knocking the magazine out of Santiago's hands. Masuda was on top of Roberts in a split second, his body pinning him against the wall of the car, his hands, fingers curled into talons, at his throat.

Roberts was caught almost completely unawares. Such was the speed with which Masuda moved that the American didn't see him coming. He was only alerted to the impending impact by Masuda's cry of "*Baka yarō!*" which gave him just enough time to turn away from the window to meet his assailant, but not enough time to defend himself.

Masuda was barely conscious of what he was saying. The words welled up from deep inside him before erupting as he launched himself at Roberts, each syllable enunciated evenly, each louder than the one before, reaching an earsplitting crescendo at the point of contact.

He wrapped his hands around Roberts' throat now, ignoring his victim's increasingly desperate efforts to free himself, impervious to the pain caused by the blows to his body from the American's flailing arms.

"*Baka yarō! Baka yarō!*"

He repeated the words over and over again like a mantra,

tightening his grip around Roberts' neck, their faces just inches apart now.

Masuda looked into Roberts' blue eyes, the eyes of a killer. It was at that point that he seemed to regain control of himself. He relaxed his fingers, and was about to release his grip entirely when he felt an arm come around his own neck from behind, pulling him back. At first he thought it was Santiago. But as he was hauled back toward the aisle, he saw out of the corner of his eye that the bespectacled American was still sitting in his seat.

Sensing that Masuda no longer posed a threat, Sullivan released his headlock and pushed Masuda lightly so that he more or less fell into his seat. Sullivan then bent down and picked up Masuda's glasses, which had fallen to the floor during the fracas, and handed them to him. Masuda put them on, took several deep breaths and looked across at Roberts, who was gently massaging his own neck. The American turned to meet his gaze now, a look of disgust on his face.

"Fucking madman!" Roberts said, still rubbing his neck. "You're a fucking madman!"

Masuda, fully conscious now of the enormity of what he had done, opened his mouth to speak, but he was preempted by Santiago, whose laughter rang out for what seemed an eternity.

They barely spoke for the remainder of the journey. There was nothing to say. Outside Kyoto Station, a fresh-faced young man carrying a copy of the latest issue of the *Asahi Graph* approached them. The two JATEC operatives exchanged greetings. Masuda considered mentioning the incident on the train, but decided against it. He unshouldered his bag, opened it, and pulled out the three red notebooks containing the personal details of Santiago, Roberts, and Sullivan and handed them to his successor.

"Good luck," he said, patting the young man on the shoulder. "They're a handful."

"So I've heard," said the other man, smiling nervously.

Masuda then turned to the three Americans and they exchanged half-hearted farewells. He stood watching as the deserters were led back into the station, waiting until they were out of sight before turning and setting off in the opposite direction.

He had taken less than half a dozen strides before he remembered something and stopped in his tracks. From one of the rucksack pockets he pulled out a folded piece of paper. It was Santiago's letter to Anala. He set off again, opening the letter and reading it as he crossed the square in front of the station. A few minutes later he passed a garbage can. He crumpled the letter into a ball and lobbed it straight in.

CHAPTER 24

Early the next morning, Harper announced to Natsume that he was going for a walk. The Beheiren operative shot him a disapproving glance, but nodded assent after Harper assured his minder he would stick to the same route they had followed the day before. It took him around an hour to walk the loop up to the top of the hill behind the farm, down to the edge of the pine forest, along the track leading past the shrine, down to the road and back up to the parking area in front of the administration building. He spent the rest of the day working in the poultry runs, with long breaks during which he watched television or chatted with Natsume and Ikeda. Heeding Natsume's advice, he kept his interaction with the other commune members to a minimum.

Harper followed a similar routine over the next two days. The following day, the sixth since their arrival at the farm, Harper returned from his walk to find Natsume waiting for him at the entrance to the administration building. He immediately tensed, fearing something bad had happened, but Natsume quickly reassured him that nothing was wrong. It was just that he and Mrs. Ikeda had to go to the station immediately to meet someone arriving on the train from Tokyo. Natsume gave no indication who this someone was. Two possibilities occurred to Harper. Another deserter or a member of Beheiren, relief for Natsume.

Half an hour later Harper was sitting in the common room with Ikeda when he heard the van return, its engine complaining as it negotiated the hill. He heard the van doors opening and closing and, moments later, Mrs. Ikeda announcing their return. There were other voices, male and female, all speaking Japanese, and Harper looked up to see first Mrs. Ikeda and then Natsume walk through the door. They both looked at him. Then his eyes were drawn to another movement at the door. Harper went to stand up, but by the time he had gotten to his feet Yumi had closed the gap between them and was launching herself at him. He barely had enough time to raise his arms and catch her as she reached up and wrapped her own arms around his neck, her feet lifting completely off the floor.

"Harpo," she said into his ear.

"Yumi! Baby, how I've missed you."

If the Ikedas were embarrassed by this display of affection they didn't show it. Both were grinning ear to ear. Even Natsume was smiling. In fact, Harper had never seen him look happier. Eventually Yumi relaxed her arms and Harper released his grip and lowered her to the floor.

"But what are you doing here?" Harper said. "What about your job?"

"It's Thursday, my day off. I'll go back tonight."

"Tonight?" he said, trying desperately to hide his disappointment. "Well, it's so good to see you."

For the next hour they all sat in the common room drinking tea and talking, though Harper had difficulty following the conversation as the Ikedas and Yumi spoke mostly in Japanese for the benefit of Mrs. Ikeda, who spoke no English. Occasionally Yumi would turn to him and give a brief summary of their conversation in English. Mostly they were talking about Yokohama and how Yumi and Harper met. Natsume had very little to say, though it was he who eventually brought the conversation to a close by suggesting Harper and Yumi go for a walk.

In a reversal of the roles they had adopted during their second meeting, when Yumi had led Harper up the hill to the shrine with the view over Yokohama, Harper took Yumi's hand and led her up through the pine forest and down to the clearing where they stopped to look out over the valley. Harper pointed out the hamlet and the river. As usual, someone was burning some rubbish, and with no wind to carry it down the valley, the smoke rose straight into the air.

"He fought in the war, you know," Harper said. "Mr. Ikeda, I mean."

"Most people his age did. Is it a problem for you?"

"It's not a problem for me. But I gather Natsume isn't too impressed."

They stood side by side, neither speaking for some time.

"Anyway," Harper said eventually, "I'm glad you're here. He was starting to get on my nerves."

"Who?"

"Natsume."

"It was Natsume who called me and invited me here. He said you were getting lonely."

Harper looked at Yumi. "Natsume? Natsume called you?"

"Why are you so surprised?"

"No reason. It's just… I don't know, sometimes it's just hard to figure out what he's thinking."

"Perhaps it's the same for him. Sometimes we form images in our mind of people before we meet them, images of how we want them to be, and when the reality turns out to be different we're disappointed. It takes time for us to adjust. Maybe you're not the person Natsume imagined you to be. And now he's adjusting."

Harper thought about what Yumi said and smiled as he remembered their first meeting in the club in Isezakichō.

"Am I the person you imagined me to be?" he asked.

"I try not to form images of people before I get to know them. That way I'm never disappointed."

Harper nodded. "Come on," he said, taking her hand again. "There's something I want to show you."

By the time they reached the shrine, the wind had picked up and was bending the branches of the two giant cherry trees on either side of the *torii*. Harper led Yumi through the gate, being careful to stick to the side of the path. They stopped at the basin to wash their hands and rinse their mouths before approaching the *haiden*.

"I come up here every day to pray," Harper said.

"What do you pray for?"

He paused. "Happiness."

They both stopped to throw coins into the offertory box and together they climbed the steps to the *haiden*. After offering their prayers in silence, they turned and retraced their steps until they reached the *torii*. As they passed underneath, Harper noticed two light pink petals in Yumi's hair and extended a hand to brush them away, but as soon as he did this more petals landed on her head, and before long petals were falling all around them. They stopped and looked up as the shower grew more intense, then looked into each other's eyes and laughed.

"We call it *sakura-fubuki*," Yumi said. "It means 'a blizzard of falling cherry blossom petals.' It signals the end of the cherry blossom viewing season."

Harper reached out and wrapped his arms around Yumi and pulled her to him as they stood looking at the magical scene unfolding around them. Carried by the wind, the cherry blossom petals were falling in a flurry now, forming a swirling pink curtain in front of their eyes and amassing on the ground, slowly obliterating the color of the grass and the earth until everything was pale pink. Just like a snowstorm, Harper thought. Except unlike snowflakes, the petals didn't remain stationary once they reached the ground. Instead, they were picked up by gusts of wind that sent them tumbling and eddying.

Harper was lost in the beauty, but at the same time he felt a tinge of sadness. He remembered what Natsume had told him about cherry blossoms being a metaphor for the transience of life. He was mindful that Yumi would be returning to Tokyo that night. As well, the uncertainty over his future gnawed at him.

The following morning when Harper stopped at the shrine alone during his regular walk, he saw that the two cherry trees were bare. Most of the petals that had carpeted the ground the day before had also blown away. Those that remained had lost their color and had already begun to decay. He prayed as usual and turned to leave. He had reached the foot of the stairs when he noticed a movement out of the corner of his eye. A man had passed through the *torii* and was approaching the *haiden*. Not having come across another worshipper at the shrine before, Harper was momentarily taken aback, and stopped in his tracks. Seconds later the man saw him and froze, a wary look on his face. He was tall and thin and Harper guessed he was around the same age as Ikeda. Harper didn't recognize the man and he was fairly certain the stranger wasn't from the farm. Perhaps he was from the hamlet at the bottom of the hill. Harper smiled, but the expression on the man's face didn't change, his gaze remaining fixed on Harper's.

"Good morning," Harper said.

Silence.

"Do you speak English?"

No reply.

"It's a lovely morning, isn't it?"

Still no reply.

The man was still staring at Harper, his eyes narrowed suspiciously, and the longer this went on the more uncomfortable Harper felt. It occurred to Harper that the man had never seen a foreigner before, let alone a black man.

"It's all right," Harper said. "I'm not going to hurt you. I'm leaving now."

Harper took a step forward, then another. The man stiffened, his eyes widening. But he held his ground, blocking Harper's path. Harper raised his hands in front of his chest, palms outward, in a placatory gesture. He then took another step forward. The man continued to hold Harper's gaze, but as Harper slowly closed the gap between them the man took two steps backward and then stumbled slightly before turning and running as fast as he could down the path and out through the *torii*.

"Goddamnit," Harper muttered to himself.

Harper got back to his room to find Natsume lying on the *tatami* floor reading a newspaper. Harper sat down next to him. Eventually Natsume looked up. Harper had been thinking whether he should tell the Beheiren operative about the man at the shrine. In the end he decided it wasn't important enough to mention, and instead he said, "I wanted to thank you. For inviting Yumi here yesterday."

Natsume didn't reply. He looked down at his newspaper. Then he looked at Harper again. "You seemed to be getting restless. I know it's frustrating not knowing what's happening. But it's the same for me. Believe me. We're doing our best to get you out of the country as soon as possible."

Harper nodded. He was about to speak when he heard footsteps in the hallway outside and they both looked up to see Ikeda standing in the doorway. Harper could tell immediately that something was wrong.

"Please," Ikeda said, "you both need to come to the administration building immediately."

Natsume sprang to his feet. He barked something in Japanese to Ikeda. The reply, also in Japanese, seemed to have a calming effect on Natsume, but as he looked at Harper there was a look of concern on his face.

"What is it?" Harper said. "The police?"

"No, no. It's nothing like that. We're in no danger. It's Reverend King." Ikeda looked over at Natsume and then back at Harper. "He's been assassinated."

They arrived in the common room to find more than a dozen commune members gathered around the television. They quickly made room on one of the sofas for the new arrivals. Harper leaned forward, his eyes glued to the flickering black and white screen. A Japanese newsreader was giving a summary of the events, and every so often Ikeda would interpret for Harper's benefit.

"Reverend King arrived in Memphis the day before to prepare for a march in support of striking black sanitation workers," Ikeda said. "He was shot in the head just after six pm local time as he was standing on the balcony of his second-floor hotel room."

Ikeda was overcome with emotion and had to pause to compose himself.

"A well-dressed young white man was seen running from a hotel across the street. Reverend King was rushed to hospital where he was pronounced dead at five minutes past seven."

Harper turned from Ikeda to the television screen. The talking head had been replaced with shots of buildings on fire and people running from shops clutching merchandise.

"What are they saying?" Harper asked.

For some reason, perhaps shock, Ikeda seemed unable to speak. It was Natsume who took up the commentary.

"As news of the assassination spread, people gathered on the streets of Memphis. There have been reports of arson and looting."

Then a familiar face flashed onto the screen. His hair, still slicked back, looked thinner, his brow more furrowed than the last time Harper saw him. And he wore glasses. But it was unmistakably the same LBJ who, nearly four months ago, had appeared by Harper's bedside. Looking at the television screen, it seemed to Harper as if the president was once again speaking directly to him, just as he had the day he presented him with his medals.

"The president has addressed the nation on television," Natsume said, "appealing for calm."

"A damn lot of good that will do," Harper said. "This is like a spark in a tinder box."

The next shots were of more burning buildings and looting. It took Harper a while to recognize the location. When he did, his heart sank. It was his old neighborhood. U Street, Washington, D.C.

"Crowds began to gather on the intersection of 14th and U streets shortly after news broke of Reverend King's assassination," Natsume continued. "Stokely Carmichael spoke to the crowd before leading them on a march past stores in the area, demanding they close as a mark of respect. The crowd grew angry and started smashing windows. Looting also broke out."

Harper thought it ironic that Stokely Carmichael, the former leader of the SNCC who had rejected non-violence and integration and called for Black Power, was now leading the black response to the assassination of the moderate Martin Luther King. Harper was convinced this was a turning point, perhaps marking the beginning of a new era in race politics in America. Perhaps the brothers he had met in Vietnam who supported the Black Panthers and who had been smuggling mortars back to the States one part at a time were right, and there would be an insurgency. If there was one thing Harper was sure of as he watched the familiar streets of D.C. erupt in flames, it was that things would get worse before they got better.

As if to confirm this prediction, Harper, Natsume, and Ikeda switched on the television the next morning to the news that the riots had spread to Chicago, Baltimore, and scores of other U.S. cities. In Washington, Stokely Carmichael had spoken at a rally at Howard University in the morning, after which as many as twenty thousand demonstrators marched down 7th Street NW to be confronted by police. More rioting and looting ensued, and by midday several more buildings were burning. The police were outnumbered, and thousands of federal troops were called in to assist them. For Harper, the most shocking scene of all was that of Marines setting up an M2 machine gun on the steps of the Capitol. His lingering doubts about deserting vanished.

The television coverage of the rioting lasted for days, during which time the conflict spread to more than a hundred cities across the U.S. In Washington, D.C. alone there were twelve deaths and hundreds of injuries. Thousands of people were arrested. But as the attention of the Japanese media on the unrest dwindled, Ikeda and the other commune members seemed to lose interest, and life at the farm went back to normal. And though King's assassination and its aftermath continued to weigh on his mind, Harper, too, eventually returned to his by-now familiar routine of a morning walk followed by breakfast and work in the poultry runs.

Harper was in such good physical shape now that he had difficulty believing he once found the hike up the hill exhausting. He remembered how he used to arrive back at the farm sweating and breathing heavily. All the walking and working had restored his fitness, and he now arrived back feeling refreshed and relaxed. The walking also aided his mental fitness, enabling him to start each day in a tranquil frame of mind. And so the shock he experienced when, three weeks to the day after arriving at Nishikiyama, he emerged from the pine forest and rejoined the road leading up to the farm and crested the hill to see a police car parked outside the farm's administration building was all the more pronounced.

His first instinct was to run. Down the hill and away from the farm. But where would he go? If the police knew he was at the farm and were after him, then surely they would have the train station staked out as well. Instead he decided to stay put and observe things for a few moments. He retreated to the edge of the forest and took cover behind a large pine tree by the side of the road.

The ground around the tree was higher than the road, and from his concealed position Harper had a clear view of the administrative building on the right and the accommodation building on the left. In front of the administration building, two policemen in dark blue uniforms and peaked caps stood with their backs to him. They were talking to two commune members who stood in the building's doorway. Harper looked in vain at the residents' faces for a sign, any sign, as to why the policemen were there. Then he listened. But though he could hear their voices, he was too far away to make out individual words. And even if he could, he wouldn't be able to understand them.

Then it hit him. What if one of the commune members had informed on them? Ikeda had told Natsume and Harper the day they arrived that the residents of the farm could all be trusted. But perhaps Ikeda wasn't sure, and had only said as much to put their minds at rest. If the police were responding to a tip-off, then Natsume would also be in danger. Harper needed to warn him. And fast.

The young Beheiren operative was asleep when Harper left for his walk. He was a late riser, and chances are he would still be in bed now. Harper had to find a way to get back to the accommodation building without attracting the attention of the police. He looked to his right. If he crossed the road he could make his way through the forest to the back of the poultry runs and then double back without being seen. It was dangerous, but he was confident he could make it. Just as he was about to set off, though, he noticed a movement to his left. Someone was coming out of the accommodation building. It was Natsume!

Harper unconsciously held his breath as he tracked the Beheiren operative, who was heading in the direction of the administration building. He was looking down at the ground as he walked, and hadn't noticed the police car, which was parked in full view just yards away from him. Harper realized that he had to act now to prevent Natsume from walking straight into what could be a trap. He quickly considered his options. He could try and make a dash for Natsume, but he doubted he would be able to cover the ground between them in time. By running, he would also attract the policemen's attention. He could try throwing something at Natsume to make him look up. He immediately cast his eyes around for a small branch or a pinecone, but gave up when he realized that this, too, would alert the policemen.

He looked up. Natsume was passing in front of the gap between the accommodation building and the administration building. As Harper watched helplessly, resigned to the fact that there was nothing he could do, he saw a movement in the space between the buildings behind Natsume. A split second later a figure in a dark blue jacket and black ski hat emerged from the shadows and drew alongside the Beheiren operative. Ikeda!

Harper watched as Natsume, whose body was still facing the entrance to the administrative building, performed a classic double-take, looking ahead of him to where the policemen stood in front of the administrative building, back to Ikeda, and back to the policemen. Then he was gone, disappearing into the shadows with Ikeda, who, Harper was confident, would be spiriting him away to safety.

Harper waited behind the tree until the policemen returned to their car and drove back down the hill. Once the police car was out of sight, he made his way back to his room in the accommodation building. Natsume and Ikeda were sitting at the table. As soon as Natsume saw Harper he jumped to his feet. "Where have you been?" he said.

"For a walk. Like I do every morning."

Natsume glanced across at Ikeda before saying, "There's a problem. The police have just been here."

"I know," Harper said.

"You know?"

"I saw everything."

Natsume and Ikeda exchanged glances again.

Harper turned to Natsume and said, "They were looking for us, weren't they?"

"Not us," Natsume replied. "Just you."

So it wasn't an informer, Harper thought. But how did the police know he was at the farm? Then he remembered his encounter with the old man at the shrine earlier in the week. He told Ikeda and Natsume about it, and the two men slowly nodded.

Ikeda was the next to speak. "Luckily we'd anticipated something like this happening and had a plan. As instructed, the commune members who were spoken to by the police told them there had been a foreigner here but that he'd left for Tokyo this morning."

"And the police believed this?" Harper said.

"They seemed satisfied," Ikeda said. Then, turning to Natsume, he added, "In the circumstances, however, I think it best the two of you leave as soon as possible. You're no longer safe here."

Harper looked from Ikeda to Natsume, whose downcast eyes told Harper that their fate was sealed.

Less than an hour later, Mrs. Ikeda guided the van into the train station parking lot. The Ikedas bought tickets so that they could accompany their guests as far as the platform. There the four of them stood together without talking. When the green and orange train emerged from the tunnel to the west and pulled up, Harper was the first to break the silence, turning to their hosts and saying goodbye. He was surprised to see Mrs. Ikeda's eyes were moist. She spoke not a word of English, but Harper was amazed at how well they had communicated over the last three weeks, mostly through gestures and smiling. Always lots of smiling. Still, he had assumed that his presence was a burden on her more than anyone else, which was why her reaction was so unexpected.

Natsume then launched into a speech of his own that Harper hoped expressed his own gratitude as well as Natsume's for everything the Ikedas had done for them. When he finished speaking, the Beheiren operative bowed and, without any hesitation at all, Harper joined him.

From his seat on the train beside Natsume, Harper looked out the window at the couple, waving as the train left the platform and picked up speed. Moments later they entered the tunnel to the east of the station and were plunged into blackness, the transition from light to dark so abrupt it was as if a curtain had fallen in front of them.

CHAPTER 25

"Given the circumstances, we all agree you performed remarkably well."

Masuda had just taken a sip of coffee, and was so surprised at the compliment that he almost spit the beverage at Sekiguchi.

They were sitting in the Blue Mountain coffee shop in Ginza. It was the same coffee shop where Masuda had met Yoshikawa and Sekiguchi earlier in the year, the day he first heard about JATEC and was invited to join the secretive organization. More than two months had passed since Masuda's mission to Suwanosejima. During that time he had had almost no contact with either JATEC or Beheiren, avoiding the Beheiren office completely. He had busied himself with his trumpet playing and his work at the record store, keen to expunge from his memory the incident involving the chickens and his altercation with Roberts on the train from Kagoshima, events that marred what should have been the adventure of a lifetime.

It was at the record store, five days earlier, that Sakurai had paid him a visit. He was on his own, and he closed the store and the two of them went to a nearby coffee shop. They chatted for more than an hour. Sakurai told him that Beheiren had been contacted by more deserters, and was in the process of organizing their escape. She asked him about the events on Suwanosejima. In the course of the conversation he referred to Santiago, Roberts, and Sullivan as "*akapan*," and then had to explain how the hippies came up with the "Red Pants" moniker. She laughed, and he realized how much he had missed her.

Then, without warning, her expression grew serious. She

explained that Sullivan had disappeared, that there was a rumor that he had turned himself in to the U.S. embassy in Tokyo. She then asked him if anyone had contacted him asking questions about Beheiren or JATEC, and he replied that no one had.

A few days later, Sekiguchi phoned Masuda and asked to meet him at the coffee shop in Ginza. Masuda hadn't spoken to the JATEC liaison since telephoning him upon his return to Tokyo from Kagoshima. By then Sekiguchi had heard all about the antics of the three Americans on the island, and he apologized to Masuda for the trouble they had caused. He hadn't said anything about the incident on the train, which surprised Masuda. It occurred to him that the Americans hadn't mentioned it to anyone.

Since that earlier phone conversation with Sekiguchi, Masuda thought he had put the train incident behind him. But after Sakurai's visit and the request for a meeting from Sekiguchi, he was afraid that the events of that day were coming back to haunt him. On the subway on his way to Ginza, he grew increasingly concerned that he was walking into a trap.

And so it came as a shock to hear Sekiguchi praise him for his handling of the mission to Suwanosejima. The JATEC liaison went on to say that Beheiren co-founder Makoto Oda himself had been asking after Masuda, whose reputation among Beheiren's "cabinet," it seemed, far from being tarnished, had actually been enhanced. There was a lengthy pause in the conversation—Masuda really didn't know what to say. But after taking a sip of his own coffee, Sekiguchi leaned toward Masuda and said, "I understand Sakurai has been in touch with you concerning Sullivan's disappearance."

It dawned on Masuda that this was the real reason for the meeting. He had wanted to believe that it was a coincidence that Sekiguchi's phone call had come just a few days after Sakurai's visit, but now there was no denying that the two were related. In fact, in all likelihood Sekiguchi had sent Sakurai to see him knowing that Masuda had a soft spot for her. He remembered most things about the meeting with Sakurai, which was still fresh in his mind, although he had to think hard to recall exactly what she had said about Sullivan.

"Yes," he said eventually, "she did mention him."

"Naturally, there's some concern within JATEC that he's passed on valuable information about how we operate."

"Yes, of course," Masuda said. This was something he hadn't considered at all.

"Unfortunately," Sekiguchi continued, "there have been other incidents of a suspicious nature. Although we can't prove it, we have to consider the possibility that he was a spy, sent by the U.S. military to gather intelligence on us. In any case, again, we're acting under the assumption that he told the authorities everything he knew about JATEC."

This surprised Masuda. Of the three Americans, Sullivan was the last one he would have suspected of being a spy. But perhaps he had let his fondness for him cloud his judgment. He remembered their discussions on Sumanosejima about Dave Brubeck and Chet Baker, how the two of them had bonded over their shared love of jazz. Eventually he asked, "Why are you telling me this?"

Sekiguchi smiled. "We'd like to ask you to do another job for us."

"A job? What kind of job?"

"A delivery job. An urgent one. We have two more packages bound for Sweden."

Masuda looked across the table at Sekiguchi and took another sip of coffee. Eventually he said, "Why me?"

"We need a fluent English speaker, and someone experienced."

"What about Sakurai?"

"Sakurai is otherwise engaged. Besides, we think it best this mission be handled by an all-male team."

"Oh? Why?"

"Let's just say that suspicions have been raised about one of the deserters in question."

"Suspicions?" Masuda said. "What kind of suspicions?"

"Some of those who've met him suspect he may not be who he claims to be."

"I see. And who does he claim to be?"

Sekiguchi took a sheet of paper out of the inside pocket of his jacket, unfolded it and placed it on the table. Masuda recognized it as a Personal Data sheet, one of which was filled out by every deserter who sought JATEC's help.

Masuda read aloud from the sheet: "Chase Gilroy. Born 1940. Petty Officer First Class, U.S. Navy."

Masuda looked up at Sekiguchi, who nodded.

He returned his gaze to the sheet. The black and white photo showed the tired, unshaven face of a man in his late twenties. His head was tilted forward, but he was staring straight at the camera and grinning, giving him a slightly malevolent appearance. Masuda skimmed through the other details, none of which appeared out of the ordinary.

"Does anything strike you as odd or unusual?" Sekiguchi asked.

Masuda looked at the sheet one more time before answering. "No, it looks perfectly normal."

"Precisely," Sekiguchi said.

"Meaning?"

"Meaning it's too normal, too ordinary. As though it's been made up."

"That's it?" Masuda said. "That's the reason you think he's a spy?"

"No. Gilroy, if that is in fact his real name, phoned us from the Bund Hotel in Yokohama. We sent one of our team to meet him, and his immediate impression was that something wasn't quite right about him. Still, Gilroy said he was in danger and pleaded to be taken in, so we arranged accommodation for him at the home of one of our regular volunteers. He stayed there for two nights. The day after he left, the neighbors all received a visit from the police, asking if they'd noticed anything suspicious in the last few days."

Masuda removed his glasses and placed them on the table and squeezed the bridge of his nose. "But if you all suspect this Gilroy character is a spy, why are you proposing to send him to Sweden? Surely that's playing into his hands."

"That's a good question. Soon after Gilroy showed up, we met with the Beheiren co-founders Tsurumi and Oda to discuss how to handle the situation. Some of us argued that it wasn't worth the risk, that it was unwise to jeopardize the integrity of JATEC and the safety of ourselves and the other deserters for the sake of one individual, even if he was who he claimed to be. But Tsurumi argued the opposite. According to his way of thinking, even if we were ninety-nine percent certain he was a spy, we had to believe in the one percent possibility that he was genuine and act accordingly."

"Interesting," Masuda said.

"According to Tsurumi, it's openness and mutual trust that keep the anti-war movement going. If we treat people we have doubts about as spies, then we'll end up sacrificing that openness and trust, eventually leading to the collapse of the movement itself. In the end, his argument won the day. We decided to go ahead and arrange to get Gilroy out of the country."

Masuda took another sip of coffee and thought about what Seki-guchi had told him. The bitter memory of his earlier mission to Suwanosejima still haunted him, and was reason enough to decline this new mission. On the other hand, here was an opportunity to atone for his earlier mistakes. And though Sekiguchi had made it clear Sakurai would not be working with him this time, the thought that Masuda might rise in her estimation if he succeeded was reason enough to accept.

"You mentioned an all-male team," Masuda said eventually. "Who else are you sending on this mission?"

"You'll be working with Aizawa."

"Aizawa?"

Masuda had heard a lot about Aizawa, although he had never met him. As far as he was aware, Aizawa had never visited Beheiren's Tokyo office, nor had he attended any of the group's regular protests. Apparently this was due to political differences between Aizawa and Beheiren's leaders. Despite these conflicting views, Aizawa was considered indispensable to JATEC, partly due to his vast experience as an activist in various anarchist and communist organizations over the years, but also due to his connections with the fishing boat owners who had smuggled Japanese Communist Party leaders out of Hokkaido to China and North Korea in the 1950s after a government crackdown forced the leaders into hiding. JATEC had for some time been considering asking these boat owners to help them get deserters out of Japan. As a result of all this, a certain aura of mystery surrounded Aizawa, and Masuda couldn't deny that he was excited at the prospect of working with him.

Masuda asked, "And the second package?"

Sekiguchi gave a look of puzzlement.

"You mentioned there were two packages. One is Gilroy. Who's the other?"

"Ah, yes. His name is Flynn. Edward Flynn."

Sekiguchi reached into his jacket pocket, took out another Personal Data sheet and placed it on the table beside Gilroy's.

"Are you sure this one isn't a spy, too?" Masuda asked casually as he skimmed through the information on the sheet of paper.

"He's certainly an interesting character," Sekiguchi said. "He's been on the run since earlier this year, when he walked out of the U.S. Naval Hospital at Yokosuka."

"So he was wounded in Vietnam?" Masuda asked, his eyes still on the Personal Data sheet.

Sekiguchi seemed to hesitate before answering. "He was in the Mental Health Unit."

Masuda looked up at Sekiguchi. "Great. So one's a spy and the other's crazy."

"I wouldn't say he's crazy," Sekiguchi said, chortling self-consciously. "He had some drug addiction issues, but that's hardly unusual for members of the American military. Plus he says he's on top of them now."

"He would say that, wouldn't he? You said he went AWOL earlier this year. So what has he been doing since then?"

Sekiguchi gave a wry smile. "Well, he started by walking to Tokyo."

"Walking? From Yokosuka? That must be over thirty miles."

"Yes."

"He *is* crazy."

Sekiguchi tilted his head to the side.

"And what did he do when he reached Tokyo?" Masuda asked.

"He slept rough, mostly. Eventually he turned up at the Suidōbashi campus of Nihon University. This was during the campus occupation."

Masuda's eyes narrowed. "Doesn't that strike you as suspicious?"

"Not particularly," Sekiguchi said. "From all accounts, his behavior

there was exemplary. He even helped defend the Economics department during an assault by the police."

"Sounds like just the kind of thing a spy would do to gain the
trust of the people he was sent to snoop on."

"You'll change your mind when you meet him, I'm sure. He's
rather affable, and comes across as guileless, naïve even. Not qualities
you usually associate with spies."

Masuda thought Sullivan, too, had been affable and naïve. But
he decided not to share this observation with Sekiguchi. Instead he
said, "When can I meet them?"

"We plan to fly them to Kushiro the day after tomorrow. From
there you and Aizawa will escort them by car to Nemuro, where
you'll rendezvous with another group of deserters who are traveling
to Hokkaido separately. Because of the concerns about Gilroy, we
felt it best to delay his pre-escape briefing as long as possible. They're
staying at the home of a Beheiren supporter in Yokohama tomorrow
night, so we'll do the briefing there with you and Aizawa in atten-
dance. Mori will give the briefing and return the next morning to
drive the Americans to Haneda Airport. You and Aizawa will make
your way separately to the airport and reunite with Gilroy and Flynn
there, after which the pair will be your responsibility."

"And what if, after meeting them, I decide I want to back out?"

"That's entirely up to you," Sekiguchi said.

Masuda nodded.

"One more thing," Sekiguchi said. "Just because we've decided to
put aside our concerns about Gilroy doesn't mean we can ignore our
usual security procedures. I want you and Aizawa to keep a close
watch on him, and if at any time he says or does anything that you
think confirms our suspicions, then you're to abort the mission and
contact us immediately. "I'm sure I don't need to remind you that
your safety and that of JATEC and the other deserters is at stake."

CHAPTER 26

As the taxi gathered speed, Harper swiveled his head and looked through the rear window at Dr. and Mrs. Mizusawa. The couple was the last in a succession of Beheiren supporters to have hosted him since he fled the farm at Nishikiyama. Or at least he assumed they were the last. They were still standing by their front gate, their heads bowed in unison, when the taxi turned the corner, whereupon Harper turned his head to the front and settled back into his seat.

"Where to now?" he asked Natsume, who had been watching from the front passenger seat.

"Back to Tokyo," he replied.

He had enjoyed his time with the Mizusawas in Saitama. Dr. Mizusawa had studied at Yale and had traveled extensively in the U.S. Both Dr. Mizusawa and his wife spoke fluent English, and there was no topic they were not eager to discuss, it seemed, be it sports, religion, or politics. Mrs. Mizusawa was an excellent cook, and Harper almost jumped for joy when he saw the meal she had prepared for him on the day of his arrival: roast chicken and gravy, mashed potatoes, and green peas.

After traveling for just over an hour, the taxi pulled off the main road and entered a sprawling housing complex. They passed rows of almost identical multistoried concrete apartment blocks, each building bearing a letter and number to distinguish it from the others. They eventually found the building they were after and had the taxi driver drop them off at the entrance. As they climbed the stairs, Natsume explained to Harper that the apartment they were going to belonged to a woman who worked as a schoolteacher. A middle-aged man wearing a black beret greeted them at the door. Harper recognized him as the Beheiren operative who had quizzed

247

him in Yokohama. The man showed them into the kitchen-dining room, whereupon Natsume turned to Harper and said, "This is… er… Ōe," struggling, it seemed, to remember the man's name.

"Yes," Harper replied, "we've met."

"Please," Ōe said, gesturing in the direction of the table, "sit down."

The three of them sat around the table and Natsume and the older man began talking in Japanese. Harper assumed it was a debriefing of some kind, and this was confirmed when Ōe switched to English to ask Harper if he had any complaints about his treatment during his time in Beheiren's custody. Harper replied that he did not and said how grateful he was for the hospitality he had been shown.

When it came time for Natsume to leave, Harper stood up and extended his right hand and the young Beheiren operative shook it enthusiastically. Though Harper had been slow to warm to Natsume, and their relationship had come under strain early on in their stay at the commune in Nishikiyama, he had grown to admire the young Beheiren operative, and was grateful for his arranging what Harper suspected would be his last ever meeting with Yumi.

"Thank you," Harper said, still gripping Natsume's hand. "Thank you for everything."

"Don't mention it," Natsume said.

Harper looked across at Ōe, who was grinning broadly.

Harper waited while Ōe saw Natsume out. When he returned, Ōe sat down and turned to Harper, his expression serious.

"As you may have guessed, the time has come for us to get you out of Japan."

Harper found it difficult to contain his excitement. "How? Where?"

"All will be revealed in due course," Ōe said.

Back to the cloak-and-dagger routine, Harper thought. His mind went back to the day he first met Ōe in Yokohama, when he and Yumi were bundled in and out of taxis. Since then he had relaxed, let his guard down. He would have to be more vigilant from now on.

"You won't be traveling alone," Ōe continued. "Two more Americans will join us here this evening. Tomorrow another two will join you. The five of you will escape together."

Harper wasn't exactly overjoyed at this news. Looking after himself had been hard enough. Now he was going to have four others to worry about. Then again, not having seen another American for weeks, a part of him was looking forward to the company.

The first of the Americans arrived early that evening. The doorbell rang, and moments later a white guy dressed in a gray woolen coat like Harper's entered the room. He took it off to reveal an expensive-looking charcoal gray suit. A pair of dark sunglasses rounded off the cool-guy image.

The young Beheiren operative who had shown the new arrival in seemed eager to leave. Ōe saw him as far as the front door, and while they were out of the room Harper and the white guy eyed each other across the table and nodded. Ōe returned and was about to introduce them when they heard the front door open again. Harper expected to see another American, but it was a middle-aged Japanese woman, the apartment's owner. If she was uncomfortable having two strange Americans in her home she didn't show it, smiling as she paused in the kitchen to put away some groceries before Ōe ushered her into a back room.

Left alone with the other American, Harper felt obliged to introduce himself. "The name's Harpo," he said.

"Paul," the new arrival said. "Paul Ferran."

Ferran took off his sunglasses. Seeing the bloodshot eyes and pallid complexion, Harper knew at once that this was a man who loved the juice. He hoped he wasn't a slave to it like Harper's father.

"You been on the run long?" Harper asked.

"Over two years now."

"Two years! Shit."

"I was stationed at Atsugi—"

"You're a Marine?"

"Yeah."

"Me too."

Ferran nodded. "I did one tour of Nam. That was enough. I told them I'd never return. When they ordered me back I went AWOL. Cost me three months in solitary. At the end of it they still wanted to send me back. So I left for good."

"Shit."

"And you?"

"I caught some shrapnel at Khe Sanh in December and ended up at an Army hospital in Yokohama. I was expecting to go home as soon as I was well enough, but instead they ordered me back to Nam. I've been on the run ever since."

The second American, who went by the name of "Pappy" Mayfield, turned up as they were finishing dinner. In contrast to the dapperly attired Ferran, Mayfield looked as if he had dressed in the dark. His baggy gray suit looked like something that had been handed down in the family for generations. Underneath the jacket he wore a wrinkled shirt and tie and a crewneck sweater. Mayfield arrived carrying a suitcase. It was large and heavy, and he struggled to carry it with one hand. Harper had only the cream overnight bag Yumi had given him in Yokohama, and distinctly remembered having been told he could not bring anything larger. He considered mentioning this, but decided if Ōe was happy with Mayfield's luggage then he had no right to intervene.

Mayfield was thirty, yet still a lowly E-4 cook in the Army. This along with his "Pappy" moniker, awkward demeanor, and jug-handle ears suggested to Harper that his elevator didn't go all the way to the top. He knew the Army was desperate for men these days, but he was still shocked that someone like Mayfield was even allowed to enlist. Harper made a mental note to keep an eye on him, just in case he did something stupid that put the rest of them in more danger than they were in already.

With everyone pitching in, the dinner table was cleared in minutes. Their host then retired, leaving Ōe alone with the three Americans. He looked in turn into their faces.

"Gentlemen," he said, "tomorrow you'll be taken to Haneda Airport, where you'll rendezvous with two more Americans, deserters like yourselves."

Harper winced on hearing the word "deserter." Ōe may as well have been calling him a "traitor" or a "murderer." He wondered if he would ever get used to the label.

"The five of you will fly together to Sapporo, on Japan's northernmost island, Hokkaido. There you'll be met by a Beheiren operative, a woman who'll be posing as your tour guide. She'll take you by train to a port on the eastern tip of the island. From there you'll travel by boat to the Soviet Union."

"The Soviet Union?" exclaimed Ferran, so forcefully that everyone else around the table looked at him.

"It's not too late to change your mind," Ōe said. "You're welcome to stay in Japan if you prefer."

Ferran looked at Harper and then at Mayfield, and when it was clear neither of them shared his objection, he signaled his acquiescence by casting his gaze downward like a petulant child.

In truth, Harper shared Ferran's concerns about their destination. But he was pretty sure that the Soviet Union was only a transit point, and that they would eventually end up in Sweden. Then again, nothing seemed certain. But what choice did he have but to go along with Beheiren's plan? The alternative was a stretch in Leavenworth or some other military prison. Besides, if their hosts in Russia were any bit as obliging as Beheiren had been, they had nothing to worry about.

"You'll be picked up at ten o'clock in the morning," Ōe continued. "Until then I suggest you try to get as much sleep as possible. Tomorrow will be a long day."

After Ōe left at the end of the briefing, the apartment owner, who was never introduced by name, showed the Americans to their room. It was Japanese style, similar to the room Harper had shared with Natsume at the farm in Nishikiyama, only smaller. Together the three of them dragged the futon out of the cupboard and lay them next to each other on the *tatami* floor. When Ferran left to use the bathroom, Harper turned to Mayfield, who had taken off his suit jacket and lay stretched out on top of his futon, and said, "How long you been on the run, man?"

"Not long," Mayfield said, frowning as he prodded the buckwheat pillow under his head. "A couple of weeks, I guess."

"You see much action?"

"I was in Hue during the Tet Offensive," Mayfield said.

Harper nodded. He had heard how intense the fighting had been in Hue, but a part of him wondered how much action an Army cook actually would have seen.

Mayfield, looking around nervously, then said in a voice barely louder than a whisper, "These people, Beheiren. Are you sure we can trust them?"

Harper's eyes narrowed as he regarded the cook. "Why's that?"

"I dunno. It's just them being commies and all that."

Harper considered this for a moment. He recalled what Yumi had told him when she first suggested they get in touch with Beheiren, that the organization included communists but also Buddhists and Christians. That they were united by the common desire to see the war end as quickly as possible. He thought about all the people from Beheiren he had met, none of whom had shown him anything but kindness. After all the events of the last few months, he decided he trusted the likes of Ōe and Natsume more than he trusted Ferran or Mayfield.

"Yeah," he said eventually, "I'm sure we can trust them."

When Ferran returned from the bathroom, the three Americans undressed and lay down and Harper extinguished the light by pulling on the cord hanging from the ceiling. Ferran, who had the middle mattress, fell asleep immediately, his loud snoring filling the room and quite possibly the entire apartment. Mayfield, who had the mattress by the window, tossed and turned, obviously disturbed by Ferran's grunting and snoring. To Harper this simply reinforced his first impression of "Pappy" Mayfield as soft, unfit for and unused to the rigors of war. Before nodding off, he again reminded himself to keep an eye on the Army pussy in the baggy gray suit.

CHAPTER 27

"It feels just like a real one," Masuda said, hefting the replica semi-automatic pistol in his right hand. Not that he had ever touched a real semi-automatic. In fact, he had never even seen one. It was illegal for Japanese civilians to possess handguns of any kind. And though the police did routinely carry revolvers, they were nothing like the sleek weapon Aizawa had just pulled out of his jacket pocket and handed to him. The weight and feel of the replica were such that if Aizawa had told him it was real Masuda would have believed him.

"It's a Walther PPK, a German police gun," Aizawa said, leaving Masuda in no doubt about the older man's experience with real firearms. "It's also James Bond's weapon of choice."

"Ah," Masuda said, realizing now why the gun looked so familiar.

"It's a fully functional replica. The only real difference is it can't fire bullets."

Masuda and Aizawa were standing alone in the dining room of the apartment in Yokohama where, a short while ago, Mori had conducted the pre-escape briefing. In the next room were the two Americans: Gilroy and Flynn.

Masuda had arrived late for the briefing. He was greeted at the door by the apartment's owner, who showed him into the dining room where Mori and Aizawa and the two deserters were seated around a table.

During the briefing, which lasted less than half an hour, Masuda observed the four men. Mori, the oldest of the JATEC operatives, whose beard had always fascinated Masuda, did most of the talking. Aizawa, who was tall and thin, said very little, quietly watching from behind tinted glasses. Of the two Americans, Gilroy seemed by far the most at ease. He looked positively relaxed next to Flynn, who grew more anxious as the evening wore on, constantly moving around in his seat, his eyes flitting from one person to another.

When Mori finished speaking, Gilroy asked a number of questions about the timing and route of the following day's journey, matters Mori had intentionally left vague in the interests of security. Mori said as much to Gilroy, who accepted the explanation without further comment.

After arranging a time to pick up the deserters the following morning, Mori then left the apartment. A few minutes later, the Americans bid Masuda and Aizawa good night and retired to the next room. It was shortly after this, as Masuda and Aizawa themselves were preparing to leave, that Aizawa produced the replica Walther PPK. Masuda reacted with surprise, placing a hand on Aizawa's arm as if to restrain him. He listened, and only when he heard voices coming from the next room indicating that Gilroy and Flynn were otherwise occupied did he withdraw his hand.

"It's perfectly safe, then?" Masuda asked now, his eyes still on the gun.

"Perfectly," Aizawa replied.

Masuda wrapped his fingers around the grip and raised the pistol to eye level, careful to point it away from Aizawa. He peered down the barrel. On the wall in front of him was a calendar bearing a photo of Mount Fuji, and he lined the sites up with the mountain's snowy peak.

"It's double-action," Aizawa said, "so all you have to do is squeeze the trigger."

Masuda slid his index finger off the trigger guard and curled it around the trigger. He pulled, watching as the pistol's exposed hammer cocked automatically. He pulled further until he felt the hammer release and heard a clack.

There was a muffled "Shush!" from the next room. The padding of stocking feet quickly followed the whisper, and before Masuda had time to react there was a loud swish as the sliding doors separating the two rooms flew open.

He turned to see Gilroy standing in the opening between the doors. Masuda thought he looked unsettled, even scared. His face was rigid, his eyes wide open, fixed on the Walther PPK.

Masuda looked from Gilroy to the gun, which he still held raised and aimed at the wall, and back to Gilroy before doing a double take, lowering his arm until the gun was by his side and pointing down at the floor.

"Is that what I think it is?" Gilroy asked, his eyes fixed on Masuda's now.

Masuda glanced at Aizawa, who nodded almost imperceptibly. "It's a Walther PPK. For our protection in Hokkaido. Just in case the police show up."

"It looks old," Gilroy said, smiling. It was the same malevolent smile as the one in the photograph Sekiguchi had shown him the day before.

"If it's good enough for James Bond..." Masuda said. He forced a smile of his own, hoping to ease the tension.

"Adolf Hitler owned one too," the American said. "He used it to blow his brains out in his bunker in Berlin."

Masuda didn't reply. Instead, he slowly nodded.

"Just as long as you know how to use it," Gilroy said. He turned to face Flynn, who was standing behind Gilroy peering over his shoulder. "We wouldn't want you to shoot yourself in the foot, would we?" he added. And the two Americans dissolved into laughter.

Masuda waited for the laughter to die down before saying to Gilroy and Flynn, "You two should get some sleep. We've got a long day ahead of us tomorrow."

Gilroy nodded.

Masuda waited, expecting Gilroy to retreat to his room, but the American held his ground. His eyes went to Masuda's side, and Masuda realized that he was still clutching the gun. Nervously, he handed it to Aizawa, who took it and placed it back in his jacket pocket.

"Good night, Kawabata," Gilroy said.

Masuda and Aizawa turned to leave. They were halfway to the front door when they heard Gilroy say in barely accented Japanese, "*Oyasumi nasai*, Aizawa-*san*."

The next morning, Masuda nervously approached the check-in counter at Haneda Airport. He saw Aizawa off to one side, casually leaning against a column puffing on a cigarette. The older man was wearing a different jacket from the previous night. Masuda noticed a bulge in one of the pockets and wondered if it was the pistol.

Aizawa spotted Masuda and beckoned him closer. "Remember," he said, looking around furtively, "first opportunity we get, we search his bag."

This was Sekiguchi's suggestion. If Gilroy was in fact a spy, he would probably have some kind of transmitter enabling his handlers, whoever they were, to track his movements.

"It shouldn't be too difficult," Masuda replied. "He'll have to go to the men's room at some stage."

"What if he takes his bag with him? And what if Flynn stays behind? We can't very well search Gilroy's bag in front of Flynn. It'll alert him to our suspicions."

"You really think they both could be spies?"

Aizawa didn't reply. Instead he took a pull on his cigarette. It crossed Masuda's mind that Aizawa was as nervous as he was. Masuda looked into the older man's face, but his eyes, partially concealed by his tinted glasses, revealed nothing.

"There's something about Flynn that doesn't seem right."

"He's a strange one, that's for sure," Masuda said.

The opportunity came quickly. Mori led the Americans into the terminal. He looked stern and uncomfortable, so Masuda was relieved when he left, his part of the mission over. A few moments later, Gilroy and Flynn asked to use the bathroom. Aizawa followed them, leaving Masuda alone with the luggage.

As soon as they were out of sight, Masuda kneeled down and unzipped Gilroy's overnight bag. He removed the folded clothing, feeling each item to make sure no hard objects were concealed inside before placing it on the floor. He then removed and opened Gilroy's toiletry bag. Inside, along with the usual bathroom items—razor, toothbrush, toothpaste, etc.—he found several small plastic bags containing pills of various sizes and colors. After making a mental note to ask Gilroy what the medicine was for, Masuda closed the toiletry bag and placed it on top of the pile of unpacked clothing. He now turned his attention to the empty overnight bag itself, feeling the bottom to see if there was a hidden compartment. Nothing.

After looking up to make sure there was no sign of Aizawa or the Americans, he carried out a similar search of Flynn's bag, but found nothing untoward.

When he eventually returned with the Americans, Aizawa looked at Masuda and raised his eyebrows inquiringly. Masuda responded with a shake of the head. He thought he noticed a look of disappointment cross the older man's face. Either Gilroy wasn't carrying a transmitter, or he had it concealed on his person.

The ninety-minute flight to Kushiro went without incident. Soon after they took off, Gilroy, who was sitting next to Masuda, began recounting his entire life story, from his birth in Claremont, New Hampshire and graduation from high school to his studying at university to become a teacher, studying he eventually abandoned to join the Navy. He trained at the Great Lakes Naval Training Station in Illinois before entering a Navy medical school. After graduating he worked at an emergency medical center for three years. He then underwent Marine Corps field hospital medical training before being posted to the Navy hospital at Yokosuka. He did one tour of duty in Vietnam, including a stint at the NSA hospital in Da Nang, before returning to Japan.

Masuda watched Gilroy carefully as he spoke, wondering if the American had a tell. He tried to remain alert to any inconsistencies in his story. But the American seemed relaxed and confident, never hesitating to meet Masuda's gaze, and Masuda concluded that his story was either true or extremely well rehearsed.

At Kushiro Airport Aizawa picked up a rental sedan and the four of them were soon heading east on the main highway into Kushiro City. Aizawa drove, with Masuda in the front passenger seat and the two Americans in the back. They reached the city in about half an hour. There they stopped at a restaurant for lunch. When they got underway again, Aizawa drove around the city for a few minutes. Only when he was satisfied they weren't being followed did he rejoin the main highway heading east.

Soon after crossing the Kushiro River they approached a T-junction. The road straight ahead led to Nemuro. When they reached the intersection, Aizawa braked suddenly and turned left without indicating. As they gathered speed again, Masuda glanced in the rearview mirror and saw Gilroy jerking his head from side to side, looking out the windows as if trying to work out where they were.

Eventually the American turned to the front and said, "This isn't the way to Nemuro."

Masuda traded glances with Aizawa before focusing his gaze on Gilroy's face in the rearview mirror. "We're not going to Nemuro."

"We're not going to Nemuro?" Gilroy sounded surprised, but his expression remained calm. "Where are we going, then?"

"Teshikaga."

"Teshikaga?"

"It's a hot spring resort about fifty miles north of here. We'll be staying there tonight."

Masuda scrutinized Gilroy's face in the rearview mirror again, but there was no sign of panic. "Is something wrong?"

"No," Gilroy replied. "Nothing's wrong. I just assumed we'd be heading straight to Nemuro."

"There's been a change of plan," Masuda said. "That's all."

Masuda didn't reveal the real reason for the detour to Teshikaga, which was that it was within two hours' drive of both Nemuro and Kushiro. Depending on whether or not their suspicions about Gilroy were confirmed over the coming hours, they could either continue on to Nemuro tomorrow morning as planned or return to Kushiro. This was Aizawa's idea. As the liaison between JATEC and Toda, the fishing boat owner in Nemuro on whose vessel Gilroy and Flynn were due to make their escape, Aizawa had insisted that every precaution be taken to avoid exposing Toda to any more danger than he was already in. The other advantage of heading north was that the road between Kushiro and Teshikaga included a number of long straight stretches that would enable them to check again to see if they were being followed.

It was dark by the time they pulled up in front of the *ryokan*. As a precaution, they hadn't made reservations in advance. Instead they had stopped at the tourist information center by the train station upon their arrival in Teshikaga and asked the receptionist to recommend a place nearby. After telephoning to make sure rooms were available, they drove straight there, ensuring Gilroy had no opportunity to contact anyone to let them know where they would be staying.

As Aizawa switched off the car's engine, Masuda glanced at his watch for the second or third time in as many minutes, unable to believe it was still only four o'clock. With the sun below the horizon, the temperature had also plummeted, and his body tensed instinctively as he opened the car door and felt the cold air envelop him.

They quickly gathered their belongings and walked the short distance from the car park to the *ryokan* entrance and went in. The proprietress, a middle-aged woman in a kimono with elegantly coiffured hair, greeted them. A younger woman, also wearing a kimono, soon appeared and showed them to two adjoining Japanese-style rooms on the ground floor separated by sliding doors. Along the way she pointed out the location of the bath. She explained that guests were normally assigned bathing times, but that as they were the only people staying at the *ryokan* that evening they could use the bath whenever they liked.

As soon as the woman left, Masuda announced that he would be taking a bath straight away, before dinner, eliciting a look of disapproval from Aizawa. Although perfectly aware that as their guests, Gilroy and Flynn should have been invited to bathe first, the memory of the three deserters he had escorted to Suwanosejima and their disregard for Japanese bathing etiquette was still fresh in his mind. He doubted that Gilroy and Flynn were as disrespectful as the Red Pants, but he was still reluctant to allow the pair to bathe before him.

Masuda returned from his bath to find the table set for dinner and the proprietress and the young woman who had shown them to their rooms kneeling by the table unloading plates and bowls of food from lacquerware trays. When the women had finished, they padded across the *tatami* floor to the entrance and turned and bowed again before leaving.

The four ate mostly in silence. Masuda was reassured to see that both Gilroy and Flynn were not only adept at handling chopsticks, but familiar with the food and how to eat it, correctly dipping the sashimi in the small bowls of soy sauce and the tempura in the larger bowls of *tentsuyu* sauce. If it weren't for the fact that one of them was likely a spy and the other mentally unstable, he felt he could even have gotten along with the Americans.

Flynn, seemingly aware that Masuda was staring at him, looked up and smiled. "It's delicious," he said. At times, Flynn seemed almost childlike. And it wasn't just because of his short stature and freckled face. There was something truly ingenuous about his manner.

"You've hardly spoken since we left Tokyo," Masuda said to Flynn. "Nothing's the matter, I hope?"

"I'm fine," Flynn said. "Just a bit sad about leaving. I'll miss Japan."

"Really?" asked Masuda, his curiosity roused. "What will you miss about it?"

Flynn thought for a moment. Then he said, "The people, I guess. Everyone has been so kind. I had some bad experiences in Vietnam. War brings out the worst in people, and I lost my faith in humanity. By the time I arrived in Japan I had stopped trusting anyone. I made some bad decisions because of that. But I've changed since then. I guess you could say my faith in humanity has been restored."

After the meal, as they lapsed into a postprandial torpor, Gilroy pushed himself back from the table and raised his right knee and began to rub it. The American saw that Masuda was watching and said, "I busted it in Vietnam."

"You were wounded in Vietnam?" Masuda said. "But I thought you worked at a hospital?"

"I did," Gilroy said, his eyes holding Masuda's. "The NSA Hospital in Da Nang. Like I told you earlier."

Masuda didn't reply.

"Don't you believe me?" Gilroy said.

Masuda shrugged, whereupon Gilroy rolled up his trouser leg to reveal two purple scars, each several inches long, on either side of his kneecap.

Masuda looked at the scars and slowly nodded.

"We weren't supposed to leave the hospital because it was too dangerous," Gilroy said. "But, once a week, a few of us would visit an orphanage near China Beach where we held a clinic to treat the local civilians. One day we were coming back in a convoy of jeeps when we were ambushed. Although that's probably overstating things. Someone took a couple of potshots from a hootch by the side of the road. No one was hit, but the driver of the jeep I was in panicked. He slammed on the brakes, then, realizing we needed to hightail it out of there, he planted his foot on the accelerator. I was sitting on the back of the jeep with my feet on the back seat. When the jeep lurched forward I was sent flying backward onto the asphalt."

"Ouch!" Flynn said.

"Yeah," Gilroy said. "Ouch! Anyway, they got me back to the hospital and straight into surgery. They managed to fix my knee up pretty good. I was back on my feet within a week. But it still hurts something bad. It'll be a while before I'm off the painkillers."

Masuda remembered the pills he found in Gilroy's toiletry bag. He had been waiting for the right opportunity to ask him about them. But it appeared as if the mystery had been solved and they were just analgesics. Still, there was something about Gilroy's story that didn't seem right. He couldn't put his finger on it right now but, given time, he was confident it would come to him. Unfortunately, time was running out.

CHAPTER 28

Harper, Ferran, and Mayfield got up just after first light. After the apartment owner left for work, they sat around the dining table waiting for Ōe to arrive to drive them to the airport. As fighting men, they were used to waiting. It's what occupied most of their time in Nam. Waiting for orders. Waiting for action. Now, like fighting men about to go into battle, they talked among themselves, not only to pass the time, but also to allay their fears. None of the three deserters mentioned what was uppermost in their minds, which was their apprehension about the hours and days ahead, and about how they would spend the rest of their lives.

The doorbell rang and they stopped talking. Harper, who had instinctively assumed the role of leader, went to the front door, gently lifted the metal flap covering the mail slot and peered through. He half expected to see a uniform, either the deep blue uniform of a policeman or the olive green uniform of an MP. He relaxed when he saw it was Ōe and quickly opened the door.

"Get your things and come downstairs now," Ōe said, clearly not in the mood for small talk.

All three Americans had their coats on and their bags packed and ready, but Mayfield had chosen this of all times to go to the bathroom, and Ōe, Harper, and Ferran had to wait by the front door until he reappeared, struggling to zip his fly. Together they hurried out of the apartment, Ōe locking the door behind them and throwing the key through the mail slot. Outside, Ōe guided them to a white sedan. They climbed in, Harper in the front next to Ōe and Ferran and Mayfield in the rear.

They had left the housing complex and were on a busy four-lane road when Harper, who was sitting in the passenger seat, noticed

Ōe glancing up at the rearview mirror. Harper wondered if there was going to be a repeat of the cloak-and-dagger routine with the taxis the day he met the Beheiren operative in Yokohama. Then, without warning, Ōe yanked the steering wheel, sending the car lurching to the left. They crossed in front of a taxi in the lane next to them, missing it by inches. Harper heard the screech of brakes and the blare of a horn. By the time he realized what was happening they had left the main road and were hurtling down a side street.

"What the hell!" came a voice from the back seat.

"Hold on," Ōe said.

Again Ōe spun the steering wheel, this time to the right. Harper's body was thrown against the door to his left as they careened around a corner and entered another side street. Ōe changed gears and planted his foot on the accelerator. The engine raced.

Gripping the assist handle with his left hand, Harper turned his head and looked at the two men in the back. Mayfield was glued to his seat, his brow furrowed and his mouth fixed in an O. Ferran had turned around and was looking out the rear window. Following his gaze, Harper spotted a black sedan about twenty yards behind them. Judging from the speed at which it was traveling, he was in no doubt it was following them.

"Who the hell is it?" he asked.

"Plainclothes police," Ōe replied. "Or U.S. military. It doesn't matter. The important thing is we need to lose them. And fast."

Without slowing down they turned right onto a side street and followed it until they rejoined the main road. They wove through the traffic, changing lanes every few seconds. Harper glanced at the speedometer and saw the needle nudge toward eighty kilometers per hour.

Looking behind them again, Harper saw that the black sedan was falling behind, but only slightly. Then he heard a ringing sound. He turned his head to the front and his eyes were immediately drawn to the flashing lights of a railroad crossing just ahead. The long black and yellow crossing arms, one on each side of the road, had already begun their inexorable descent.

The car in front of them slowed. Seeing its brake lights illuminate, Ōe tapped the brake pedal and swerved to the right, steering the sedan toward the gap between the slowing car and a truck that had come to a stop in the next lane. They made it through with inches to spare, but the crossing arms were now almost completely lowered. Ōe sped up, aiming for the center of the road.

Harper ducked and closed his eyes. There was a clatter as one of the bamboo barriers struck the roof of the car, followed by a series of judders as they negotiated the railroad tracks. Harper opened his eyes. In front of them was another set of barriers on the far side of the crossing. Unlike the ones they had just passed, though, they were fully lowered.

"Shit," Harper said.

Harper braced himself, expecting Ōe to stop. But the car continued on. Ahead of them there was a space a few feet wide where the two crossing arms met, too narrow for them to pass through. Still they hurtled forward. Harper felt a jolt as they made contact. The bamboo arms bent, but didn't break, scraping against the sides of the car as Ōe hit the gas. Pedestrians shouted as they broke through. The engine roared as they accelerated along the open road in front of them.

Harper lowered the sun visor on the passenger's side and looked in the vanity mirror. Behind them the road was clear.

"We've lost them," he said. "Whoever they were."

"Can we slow down now?" came a voice from the back seat.

Harper looked in the mirror again, this time directing a glare at Mayfield.

It was Ōe who answered. "We still have a plane to catch."

At Haneda Airport, Harper, Ferran, and Mayfield bid farewell to Ōe before getting out of the car and entering the terminal separately, as instructed by the Beheiren operative just prior to their arrival. Ōe had also told them that another person from Beheiren would be present inside the terminal to make sure their rendezvous with the other deserters went smoothly and that they all got on the plane safely, but that they would only identify themselves if something went wrong. They regathered by the check-in counter and waited for the other deserters to show up. The first to appear was a tall, well-built Army private by the name of Eugene Roberts.

He had a cool confidence about him that belied his youth (Harper put him at around nineteen). A few minutes later the second of the two appeared. Richard Santiago, also in the Army, was about the same age as Roberts but thinner and wore glasses. Harper noticed the new arrivals trading suspicious looks as Mayfield introduced himself. It seemed he wasn't the only one with concerns about the Army cook.

Their introductions complete, the five Americans checked in. A short while later, a woman's voice came over the PA announcing in Japanese and English that their flight to Sapporo was boarding. It took them a few minutes to find the gate, by which time a queue had already formed. Knowing that a group of five foreigners might attract attention, they lined up separately. No one mentioned it, but they also knew this would also make it easier for the others to escape if one of them was busted.

Wary after the incident on the way to the airport, Harper scanned the faces of the other passengers. He had expected them to be the only foreigners on the flight, but he counted half a dozen other non-Japanese in the queue. Four of the six were elderly tourists, two couples traveling together. He disregarded them and focused on the fifth. A woman in her forties. Unlikely to pose a risk, Harper thought. The sixth foreigner, who stood in the queue about halfway between the end where Harper stood and the gate, was a middle-aged man in business attire—a dark gray suit and matching fedora. An alarm bell went off in Harper's head. At first he couldn't work out why, but then it hit him. The short hair, the upright posture. Everything about him except the clothes suggested military. The man turned. Harper was sure the man was going to look in his direction, but instead he directed his attention to the Japanese man behind him. The two men spoke, and Harper realized they were together. The Japanese man also wore a suit. Business associates on a work trip. Or were they? Harper relaxed, but only slightly. He reminded himself to stay vigilant.

Moments later, Harper heard shouting from the front of the line. His heart sank when he recognized the voice. He poked his head to the side to get a better view. As he feared, it was "Pappy" Mayfield. He was standing next to a female airline staffer who was checking passengers' boarding passes, talking loudly and gesticulating at the suitcase by his side. From what Harper could hear, it appeared the attendant was refusing to let Mayfield board the plane with the luggage.

Harper realized he had a decision to make. Intervene and risk not only his own safety but also the safety of the other deserters, or stay where he was and leave Mayfield to his own fate. But it was one of the new arrivals, Roberts, who acted first. Without hesitating, he left his spot in the queue just in front of Harper, strode up to Mayfield and with one hand prodded him in the back.

"Just dump it," he said, the anger palpable in his voice, which was clearly audible to Harper and therefore to everyone else in the queue. "Throw the damn thing away!"

Mayfield was momentarily thrown off balance by the push, but he quickly regained his footing, clutching the handle of the suitcase as if to emphasize his determination to hold onto it.

"No," he said. "I'm not leaving without it."

"Fine. Then stay here!" Roberts yelled, his eyes bulging, his face, florid with rage, a matter of inches from Mayfield's. "Because we're getting on that plane right now."

Afraid that the situation was getting out of hand, Harper decided he had to act. Clutching his own overnight bag, he walked to the front of the queue and flashed a smile at the attendant and in the calmest, politest voice he could muster he said, "Is there a problem, Miss?"

The attendant smiled back. "I'm afraid the gentleman's suitcase is too large to take into the cabin."

"I see," Harper replied, still smiling. "And there's no other way of getting his suitcase to Sapporo?"

The attendant hesitated. Harper believed she was on the verge of surrendering to his charm offensive. Just one more blow.

"I know how much your airline values its reputation for upholding the highest standards of service. It would be a pity to let such a minor incident tarnish that reputation."

The attendant thought for a moment. Then she said, "Strictly speaking it's against the regulations, but perhaps we can have the suitcase stowed at the back of the cabin."

"I'm sure the gentleman would be happy with that," Harper said, staring menacingly at Mayfield.

The Army cook nodded in acquiescence, and with the standoff resolved, Harper signaled to Roberts that they should return to their original places in the line.

Outside, as the five made their way with the other passengers across the tarmac toward the airstair at the rear of the waiting Boeing 727, Harper drew alongside Roberts. After making sure no one else was within earshot he said, "Try another stunt like that and it'll be *you* we leave behind. You got that?"

Harper was woken by a change in the pitch of the 727's engines and, moments later, he felt the aircraft dip. He opened his eyes and peered out the window to his left. They had begun their descent, but below them it was water as far as the eye could see. He glanced at his watch. They had been in the air for around an hour, which meant they were probably flying over the narrow band of ocean separating Honshu from Hokkaido.

Harper looked to his right and was relieved to see that the other deserters were still in their seats. Back at Haneda, even after the doors fore and aft had closed and as they taxied slowly to the end of the runway, he had remained on his guard, half expecting the aircraft to come to a stop, half expecting to be tapped on the shoulder and led off the plane along with Ferran, Mayfield, Roberts, and Santiago, if that's who they really were. He trusted none of them. The aircraft seemed to pause at the end of the runway for an inordinate amount of time before the three rear-mounted Pratt and Whitney turbofan engines burst into life, sending the fully laden 727 hurtling down the runway. Only when he felt the aircraft's nose pitch upward and heard the rumbling of its tires on the runway subside did he allow himself to relax.

They took off to the north. Below them, the sprawling mass of greater Tokyo eventually gave way to the checkered green and brown of the countryside with its market gardens and rice fields. Their flight path took them over the mountainous interior of Honshu, where snow coated the higher peaks. Harper settled back in his seat. His eyelids grew heavy. Despite his best efforts to remain awake, he dozed off.

He looked out the window again now. Still there was no land in sight, but they continued to descend, the plane so low that Harper could see fishing boats on the water below. Then they swooped over the coastline. A vast, barren, brown plain dotted with naked trees. Rounded, snow-capped mountains in the distance. The runway beneath them now, thuds as the tires made contact with the airstrip, the roar of the engines as the pilot engaged the reverse thrust.

Outside, it was noticeably colder than it had been in Tokyo. The five deserters hurried across the tarmac to the terminal. There, a young Japanese woman with a ponytail greeted them. She introduced herself as Higuchi. She spoke almost perfect English with an American accent, which made Harper think she had lived in the U.S. As she led them through the arrival hall she repeated what Ōe had told them in Tokyo, that from now on they were to act as if they were a tour group, and that she would be posing as their guide.

"If anyone asks who you are," she added, "tell them you're American college students on holiday."

Outside they divided into two groups, Ferran, Roberts, and Santiago sharing one taxi and Harper, Higuchi, and Mayfield another. Harper noticed Higuchi frown as she watched Mayfield and the taxi driver struggle to lift his suitcase into the vehicle's trunk. Once the trunk was closed, she gave instructions to both drivers, just in case they became separated during the drive into Sapporo.

It took them just under an hour to reach the outskirts of the city, their journey taking them across the open plain Harper had seen from the window of the 727 just before they landed. Driving through the city center, Harper noticed that unlike Tokyo and Yokohama, it was laid out according to a grid plan, with wide streets intersecting at right angles to form city blocks, just like in an American city. There were also lots of parks and gardens.

"The city of Sapporo has a special connection with America," Higuchi said, apparently warming to her role as tour guide. "When the Japanese were developing Hokkaido last century, they called on the U.S. government for help. Among the special advisors sent by the Americans was a group of civil engineers who were tasked with designing the island's new administrative center. As you can see, they decided to follow an American-style grid plan."

It was just after midday when they arrived at Sapporo Station. The night train to Nemuro wasn't due to leave until that evening, so after buying their tickets and leaving their bags in storage, they left the station and found an Italian restaurant where they had lunch. Higuchi picked up the tab, and also paid their entrance fees at the Botanical Gardens and at the Television Tower, which they visited as part of their afternoon "sightseeing" tour of the city.

Back at the station, Higuchi told Harper and the other deserters to wait while she made a phone call. Judging by the number of coins she fed into the red pay phone, Harper guessed it was long-distance. Probably a progress report to her superiors in Tokyo. He managed to get close enough to hear her voice, but she said very little, and what she did say was in Japanese. When she replaced the receiver he smiled at her and asked, "Everything all right?"

"Yes," she said, smiling back at him. "We're to proceed as planned."

Harper wasn't exactly sure what the plan entailed other than catching a train to Nemuro and continuing by boat to Russia, but he felt reassured nonetheless.

To Harper's annoyance, for the first hour or so of the overnight train journey, Santiago and Roberts behaved like excited children, rushing up and down the aisle and talking loudly and generally making nuisances of themselves. Knowing that tomorrow would be another long day, Harper was eager to get some sleep. But he had lingering doubts about the trustworthiness of his fellow deserters and felt he needed to watch them closely. Above all, he wanted to be awake and ready to act in the event that they caused another scene like the one at Haneda Airport. Partly this sense of responsibility was due to his family history. As the eldest of three children, Harper had often watched over his younger brother and sister, especially when his father was drunk. But it was also a result of his experience leading patrols in Vietnam, where a bad decision could cost the lives of the men under his command. Of the other deserters, only Ferran outranked him, but Harper had seen enough of Ferran to know he had no leadership capabilities.

To Harper's relief, all the traveling and "sightseeing" eventually caught up with Santiago and Roberts, and the pair retired to their curtained berths along from where Mayfield and the loudly snoring Ferran were already sleeping. Harper made his way down to the bathroom at the end of the car and was on his way back when he saw Higuchi coming toward him. They exchanged smiles and Higuchi stopped just in front of him.

"Good evening, James," she said. "May I call you James?"

"Actually, my friends call me Harpo."

"I see. Then I will call you Harpo." She looked around to make sure they were alone before adding, "By the way, thank you."

"What for?"

"For keeping an eye on the others."

"Not at all. It's you who deserves the thanks. I'm sure the others appreciate your efforts too, even if they don't show it at times."

She acknowledged his thanks with a smile and a nod.

"It must be costing your organization a lot of money," he said. "The airfares and the train tickets for the five of us must have cost you hundreds of dollars."

"One thing Beheiren does have experience with is fundraising. We're certainly not a rich organization, but there are many people in Japan who oppose the Vietnam War, and many of them are willing to—what is the expression in English—to put their money where their mouth is?"

Harper smiled at her use of the idiom.

"Is that wrong?" she asked, frowning slightly.

"No, no. That's perfect. To put their money where their mouth is."

"Anyway, I should let you get to bed. Tomorrow will be another long day."

"Now that you mention it," Harper said, "I was going to ask about our plans for tomorrow."

"I wish I could tell you more than I already have," Higuchi said. "But really, the less said, the better. Please understand that it's for your own safety."

Harper didn't believe Higuchi's excuse for a minute. But he was reluctant to press her for more information. "I understand. Well, I guess it's time to hit the sack."

This time it was Higuchi who smiled, pleased, he gathered, at his use of another idiom.

"Good night," she said.

Harper took a step to the side to allow Higuchi to pass him. As she did, he caught a trace of the shampoo fragrance of her hair, and he thought again of Yumi. Of their walks together in Sankei-en and the hills around Yokohama and Kamakura. Of the touch of her soapy hands on his body in the tiny bathroom in her apartment. Of their final moments together at Nishikiyama before she boarded the train for Yokohama, when he kissed her and again promised her that he would come back.

CHAPTER 29

Masuda woke several times during the night, each time looking over at the window to see if it was light, each time lamenting the darkness and the cold before sinking back into his futon and drifting back to sleep. He had just woken for the third or fourth time when he heard a loud swish. He opened his eyes to see the two doors separating the adjoining rooms open and a shadowy figure appear in the gap between them. Masuda reached out, found his glasses and sat up and looked at the figure again. It was Flynn. He was wearing military-issue boxers and a white T-shirt, accentuating his boyish appearance.

"What is it?" Masuda asked, keeping his voice low so as not to wake Aizawa, who was still asleep in the futon next to his. "What's the matter?"

"It's Gilroy," Flynn replied.

"Gilroy? What about him? Is he ill?"

"He's gone."

"He's what?"

"He's disappeared."

Masuda let a few seconds go by. Then he said, "What time is it?"

"It's four-thirty."

Masuda fumbled on the *tatami* for his watch. After confirming the time, he looked at Flynn again and said, "He's probably just gone to the bathroom."

"No, I've checked. His bag's gone too."

There was a rustling noise and Masuda turned and saw that their talking had woken Aizawa, who was sitting up now and rubbing his eyes. He looked at Masuda and said in Japanese, "What is it?"

"It's Gilroy," Masuda replied. "Flynn says he's gone."

Aizawa threw off his top futon, sprang to his feet and stumbled across the room to where Flynn was standing and pushed past him into the next room. Moments later, he reappeared. He turned to Flynn and said in English, "Pack your things. We leave right away."

Aizawa hadn't spoken English in front of the Americans before. Perhaps it was the shock of hearing the language pass his lips for the first time, or perhaps he just didn't understand him, but Flynn didn't move.

"Now!" Aizawa shouted. "We leave now!"

Flynn turned quickly and disappeared into the next room. Meanwhile, Aizawa strode back to his futon, shrugged off his *yukata* and began to put on his clothes. Without stopping, he said to Masuda, reverting to Japanese, "As soon as you're dressed, I want you to settle the bill and go and wait in the car."

"But it's only four-thirty," protested Masuda. "The proprietress will still be asleep."

"Then wake her," Aizawa said brusquely.

"What about you?"

"I have to telephone Captain Toda. It's too risky to do it from here, so I'll go outside and find a pay phone."

Masuda had nothing more to say, so he turned to change and pack his bag.

"One more thing," Aizawa said.

"What?" Masuda said, turning back to face Aizawa.

"Whatever you do, don't let Flynn out of your sight."

Masuda leaned forward, wiped the heel of his hand across the fogged-up windshield and looked out from the passenger seat. Apart from a faint halo of light in front of the entrance to the *ryokan*, it was black all around. He held his breath and listened. Silence. Leaning back, he sat for a moment, shoulders hunched, hands thrust deep into the pockets of his corduroy jacket, before turning his head and looking over his shoulder at Flynn.

"He shouldn't be long," he said, smiling reassuringly.

"Where'd he go?"

"To make a phone call."

The American looked down. "I should have known."

"Known what?" Masuda said.

"That he was a spy."

After a pause, Masuda said, "We don't know that for sure."

Flynn looked up. His eyes held Masuda's. "What will happen if we're caught?"

"We won't be caught," Masuda said, trying his best to sound confident.

They sat in silence, each thinking their own thoughts. After a few minutes, Masuda again peered through the windshield. The darkness and the cold and the early morning stillness unsettled him. But a part of him wished that dawn would never arrive. If someone *were* looking for them, they would be easier to find in the light of day.

Two loud taps on the driver's side window broke the silence. Masuda jerked his head around. He looked through the steamed-up glass and heard Aizawa's voice.

"It's me. Open up."

Masuda leaned across and unlocked the door. "What took you so long?" he said as the older man eased his tall frame into the driver's seat.

"I couldn't find a pay phone," Aizawa said. He paused, cupping his hands over his mouth and nose and blowing warm air into them. "I had to go back and call from the *ryokan*."

Masuda said nothing. They both knew that if the police found out where they had stayed they could search the phone records and work out whom he had called.

They drove back past the train station with the headlights on full beam and soon they were on the main highway leading back to Kushiro. As they continued southeast, the sky ahead of them gradually grew lighter. Eventually Aizawa turned off the headlights and powered down the heater. The cozy fug inside the vehicle had a soporific effect on Masuda, and he felt his eyes grow heavy.

"We've got company."

Masuda woke with a start. He sat up and straightened his glasses before looking across at Aizawa.

"Behind us," the older man added.

Masuda reached forward and lowered the sun visor, adjusting the angle so that he could see the road behind them. In the vanity mirror he could just make out the black and white form of a police car. It must have been about a hundred yards behind them.

"How long has it been there?" Masuda asked.

"About five minutes," Aizawa replied.

"Do you think they're following us?"

Aizawa glanced up at the rearview mirror. "It's hard to tell."

Noticing the activity in the front of the vehicle, Flynn leaned forward and asked, "What is it?"

"Don't turn around," Masuda said in English. "But there's a police car behind us. We might be being followed."

"Shit," Flynn said.

Aizawa turned to Masuda and said, "There's a cigarette lighter in my jacket pocket. Take it and burn his ID and throw the ashes out the window. If you've got anything on you with your name on it, burn that, too."

Masuda did as he was instructed, explaining in English to Flynn what he was going to do before taking the American's ID card, resting it on the car ashtray and setting it alight. When it was completely burned he wound down the side window, scooped up the ashes and dumped them out the window.

Aizawa glanced up at the rearview mirror again and said to Flynn, "Do you think you could field strip a Walther PPK?"

"Yeah," the American replied, his voice tense. "I think so."

"Good," Aizawa said. "It's in my jacket pocket. The right one. Take it and strip it down and throw the parts out the window."

Flynn hesitated. "Won't the police see?"

"Do it!" Aizawa barked.

Flynn quickly leaned forward and removed the semi-automatic from Aizawa's jacket pocket. He sat back in his seat and looked at the gun. Moments later he looked up, his mouth agape. "It's not real! It's just a toy!"

"It's a replica," Masuda corrected.

The American directed his gaze back at the "weapon."

Aizawa said, "You can strip it down just like a real one."

With help from Aizawa, who issued occasional instructions from the driver's seat, Flynn soon had the gun broken down into half a dozen or so parts. He wound down the rear side window and flung them out one by one.

"What do you think?" Aizawa said, peering in the rearview mirror. "Are they getting any closer?"

Masuda checked in the vanity mirror. "Looks like still the same distance."

"If they *are* following us, what are they waiting for?"

"Maybe they're waiting for us to make a run for it."

"That's what I was thinking," Aizawa said. "Which is why I'm watching my speed."

They drove on in silence. Occasionally Aizawa and Masuda checked to see if the police car was any closer, but it remained more or less the same distance behind them. They had just passed through the town of Shibecha, some thirty miles north of Kushiro, when Masuda turned to Flynn and said, "How's your singing voice, Eddie?"

"Okay I guess. Why?"

"Do you know the words to 'We Shall Overcome'?"

"Sure. Everyone knows that song."

And so they began to sing:

We shall overcome,
We shall overcome,
We shall overcome some day;
Oh, deep in my heart,
I do believe,
We shall overcome some day.

They sang to the end, paused, and began singing again from the start. They were still singing as they approached the outskirts of Kushiro.

We shall overcome,
We shall overcome,
We shall overcome some...

Aizawa's voice was the first to trail off. At first Masuda didn't notice he had stopped, so absorbed was he in his own singing. It was only when he heard the gears change down and felt the car begin to decelerate that he, too, stopped singing. He glanced over at Aizawa and saw that he was staring straight ahead. Following his gaze, Masuda looked up the road and saw two police cars parked across the highway, completely blocking their path.

Aizawa brought the car to a stop on the side of the road about a hundred feet in front of the roadblock. Masuda swiveled his head and saw that the police car that had been following them had stopped in the middle of the road a similar distance behind them. Turning his attention again to the road ahead, Masuda saw the front doors of one of the police cars open and two officers in deep blue uniforms get out and adjust their caps before slowly walking down the road toward them.

"Remember," Aizawa said, "they may think we're armed, so keep your hands where they can see them."

Masuda did as Aizawa advised, placing both hands palm down on the dashboard. One of the policemen stopped a few yards in front of the car and looked on cautiously as the other approached the driver's side and motioned for Aizawa to roll down the window. When he did so, the officer bent over and looked in, casting his eyes over the occupants and the bags on the back seat. Then he said to Aizawa, in Japanese, "Ask the American to step out of the car."

Aizawa's reply was curt. "Ask him yourself."

The officer, obviously unused to anyone questioning his authority, appeared taken aback. Masuda fought the urge to intervene, instead putting his trust in the experience and judgment of his senior partner.

"You're already in a lot of trouble," the policeman said. "I advise you not to make things even more difficult for yourselves."

"We've done nothing wrong," Aizawa said.

A silence ensued. Then the officer said, "We believe the American is a deserter. I'm asking you again, please invite him to step out of the car."

"And I'm telling you again," Aizawa said, "we're—"

"It's alright," came a voice from the back seat.

Masuda and Aizawa both turned to face the American.

"It's me they want, isn't it?"

Masuda slowly nodded.

"I don't mind going with them. You've done everything you could. I know it'll only make things worse for you if I stay."

"Stay where you are," Aizawa said in English. But Flynn was already clutching his bag and opening the rear door and stepping out of the car. The officer who had positioned himself up the road approached him. When he reached where Flynn was standing he placed a hand on his arm.

The officer who had addressed them turned to Aizawa again. "If you want to see your American friend again, you'll have to follow us to the precinct in Kushiro."

Masuda and Aizawa remained seated in their own vehicle as Flynn was led away and placed in the back of the police car. There he sat motionless, flanked by two uniformed officers. When the police car eventually pulled away, he turned his head and looked at them through the rear window. He seemed calm, as if he had accepted his fate, and Masuda liked to believe there was even a hint of a smile on his freckled face.

Despite the policeman's assurance, neither Masuda nor Aizawa saw Flynn again. Upon arriving at the police station, they were both taken into custody and placed in separate cells, where they languished until the evening. After their release they were told that Flynn would remain in police custody and that he wouldn't be allowed to see any visitors. Reluctantly, Aizawa and Masuda left the police station and wandered the foggy streets of Kushiro until they found a *ryokan*. Aizawa then went out to phone Sekiguchi to let him know what had happened.

The next morning they returned to the police station and again asked to see Flynn. This time they were told he was no longer there. The officer on duty wasn't sure where he had been moved. Resigned to the fact that there was nothing more they could do, Masuda and Aizawa drove directly from the police station to Kushiro Airport and booked two seats on the next flight back to Haneda.

On the plane back to Tokyo, Masuda mulled over the events

of the last few days. It was now clear to him that Gilroy *was* a spy, and that Oda and the other decision-makers in Beheiren had been wrong to give him the benefit of the doubt. And while Masuda had played no part in that decision, he knew he could have—and should have, given his own suspicions concerning Gilroy's identity—pulled the plug on the mission earlier, preventing Flynn falling into the police's hands. He felt personally responsible for Flynn's capture, and regretted not having done more to avert it. These feelings of remorse would return to haunt him again and again in the years that followed. As would the image of Flynn's boyish face receding into the distance.

CHAPTER 30

Harper had left the blind next to him open a few inches in the hope that he would be woken in the morning by the first rays of sunlight. As it turned out, he was woken not by the sunrise but by the tossing and turning of the occupant of the berth above his. He looked at his wristwatch, its face barely readable in the gloom. It was five twenty-five. Well after daybreak. He opened the blind a few more inches and peered out.

The reason for his sleeping in was clear right away. He could just make out the coastline, where foam-crested sea-green waves crashed onto a black sand beach, but everything beyond that was obscured by a dense curtain of fog. There was a faint glow, and from its position and his knowledge of the geography of Hokkaido, gleaned from a map he had consulted before leaving Tokyo, Harper concluded they were traveling northeast along the island's eastern seaboard. That meant he was looking out over the Pacific Ocean. On the other side of the ocean, more than four thousand miles away, was the west coast of the United States.

After a quick trip to the bathroom, Harper returned to his bunk and lay looking out the window. Away from the coast the fog cleared, and he saw rolling countryside covered in long grass the color of straw, stands of leafless trees with their silver trunks exposed, and the occasional evergreen.

After making a stop at the port town of Kushiro, they headed inland before rejoining the coast near Lake Akkeshi. A short while later they went inland again, following one river up to a plateau where the fog lifted to reveal sweeping pastures and large wooden barn houses, countryside Harper would never have imagined seeing in Japan, and then another river back down to the coast at the base of the Nemuro Peninsula. There they made a dogleg and headed north up the middle of the peninsula.

During this final leg of their journey, Harper glimpsed deer in the woods beside the railroad line. They were never alone. Always in pairs or herds. Most turned and fled as the train passed, presenting their fluffy white rear ends as they scrambled nimbly up banks on their impossibly thin legs, or scurried deeper into the woods. Occasionally, though, a stag—and it was always a stag—would stand its ground, turning to confront the train, its hooves planted firmly on the ground and its antlers erect, demonstrating the stubbornness typical of the males of most species. Fight or flight. The same two options were available to Harper. And every time he saw one of those obstinate stags he was convinced he was making the right choice.

They arrived in Nemuro around breakfast time, the train approaching the town from the south before describing a U and pulling into the station, the terminus of the Nemuro Line, facing in the direction from which it had come. From what he could see of Nemuro through the train window (the fog was as thick, if not thicker, here than it had been around Kushiro, reducing visibility to less than a few hundred feet), it was a largely featureless, desolate place consisting of a congregation of weather-beaten, mostly one- or two-storied buildings strewn over hilly terrain. It was also bitterly cold.

Higuchi led them into the station and out the other side where a white van was parked on the street. She climbed into the passenger seat while Harper and the other deserters piled into the back. There were no seats in the rear, so Harper and Ferran perched on the wheel wells while Mayfield sat on top of his suitcase, leaving Santiago and Roberts to sit on the floor. To add to their discomfort, an unpleasant fishy smell pervaded the van's interior.

"This is Captain Toda," Higuchi said, gesturing to the driver. Harper looked at the rearview mirror but it was too dark to see the man's face. "We'll be staying at his house for a while."

"How far is it?" Mayfield asked. "It's freezing back here."

"Not far," Higuchi replied. "We'll be there in a few minutes."

Five minutes later they pulled up outside a wooden two-story house. Inside, Toda showed them through to a large *tatami* room on the ground floor. In the middle of the room was a low table, around which were arranged eight legless chairs. The boat owner invited Harper and the other Americans to sit before formally introducing himself. As he spoke, Harper regarded him closely. He was short but had the tanned, leathery face and wiry body of someone who had spent his whole life toiling in the outdoors. His hands were large and calloused, the result of years of handling rope and fishing line. But there was something about Toda—perhaps it was his near-fluent English—that suggested to Harper that he was not your average fisherman.

After completing his self-introduction, Toda turned to Higuchi, and the pair spoke with each other in Japanese for a while. It was Toda who eventually addressed the Americans.

"Gentlemen, I invite you to make yourselves at home while I get my wife to prepare something for you to eat."

"Please," Harper said, "tell your wife not to go to any trouble."

But Toda dismissed the suggestion with a smile and a wave of the hand. He then left the room, returning a few minutes later and joining the deserters and Higuchi around the table.

"So," Harper said, "when do we leave?"

"When the fog lifts," Toda replied, making a sweeping gesture of the air.

"When will that be?"

Toda shrugged. "Maybe today. Maybe tomorrow. Unfortunately, fog is common at this time of year."

Ferran said, "Then maybe you should have gotten us out earlier. Some of us have been waiting for months."

It was Higuchi who responded. "Given that you've been waiting for months, I'm sure another few hours won't make much difference."

Harper smiled, impressed with Higuchi's riposte. Then, turning to Toda, he asked, "Exactly how far are we from Russia?"

"The closest Russian territory is an island called Kunashiri. It's just ten miles off the coast of Nemuro. In fact, on a clear day you can see it from the harbor. But we're not going there."

"You mean we're going all the way to the Russian mainland in a fishing boat?" Ferran said, a hint of incredulity in his voice. "That must be hundreds of miles away."

Toda glanced at Higuchi before replying. "Not all the way. Once we're in the open sea, we'll rendezvous with a Soviet Maritime Border Patrol vessel. You'll be transferred to the Russian vessel for the remainder of your journey."

"It might reassure you to know," Higuchi said, "that Captain Toda is not exactly an amateur when it comes to this kind of thing. Smuggling has a long history in these parts, as has contact between Japanese fishermen and the Russians. Fishing boats from Nemuro are often allowed to operate in the Soviet-controlled waters west of here in return for information of value to the Russians, about the movement of Japan's Maritime Self-Defense Force vessels in the area, for example."

"I'm sure we're in capable hands," Harper said with a smile. Though the revelation that Toda was a pragmatist, guided not by ideals like the other Beheiren operatives he had met but by purely practical considerations, made him nervous.

After breakfast, with the fog showing no signs of clearing, Santiago and Roberts retired to a corner of the room to play cards, leaving Harper, Ferran, and Mayfield sitting along one side of the table and Higuchi and their host along the other. Ferran began explaining to Mayfield how he had lain low in his Japanese girlfriend's apartment for more than a year before making contact with Beheiren, after which he had been taken to a safe house in the country. Harper regarded the two Americans. He knew as soon as he met the Army cook that he was going to be a liability. The look on Mayfield's face when Ōe had outrun their pursuers on the drive to Haneda Airport only reinforced this initial impression. And then there was the suitcase. Harper wondered what was inside it. And what about Ferran? Had he really spent all that time in hiding? Next Harper looked over to where the two youngest members of their party were playing cards. Roberts' altercation with Mayfield at the airport could well have compromised the whole operation. And lastly there was Santiago, the quiet one. Too quiet for Harper's liking. Harper wondered if any of these four men were connected to the occupants of the car that had followed them in Tokyo. They must have been waiting all night outside the apartment. How had they discovered the location? Had they followed one of the deserters there? Or had someone led them there?

It was late in the afternoon, during their second meal of the day, that the drinking began. Captain Toda prepared the meal, which consisted of thin strips of meat and vegetables cooked in a broth made by mixing together soy sauce, sugar, and saké, on two portable gas stoves set up on the table in front of them. Harper knew as soon as the saké appeared that it would only be a matter of time before Ferran managed to wangle himself a glass. Even so, he cringed when Toda, noticing Ferran staring fixedly at the large 1.8 liter bottle, asked the American if he wanted some. Once Toda had poured Ferran a glass, as the host he was naturally obliged to offer his other guests a drink. Mayfield declined, but Roberts and Santiago accepted. After they had finished eating, the three drinkers formed a little group of their own at one end of the table where, before long, they were knocking back glass after glass.

It was getting dark when Harper heard a phone ring. Seconds later Mrs. Toda appeared and spoke to her husband in Japanese. He looked across at Higuchi, who rose and followed Mrs. Toda out of the room. Harper thought he noticed a look of concern on her face. He turned to Toda and raised his eyebrows, but the boat captain simply smiled and nodded.

Higuchi was absent for several minutes. When she returned, she nonchalantly resumed her place at the table next to Toda and leaned toward him, speaking quietly into his ear. As Toda listened, his expression sobered, and when Higuchi finished speaking he looked upward as if considering something carefully. A few moments later he addressed the Americans.

"Gentlemen. The fog has lifted. We'll be leaving as soon as you're all ready."

Harper looked into the faces of his compatriots. The significance of the moment was immediately apparent to Mayfield, whose expression was a picture of earnestness. Ferran, Roberts, and Santiago, on the other hand, were slower to react, their senses numbed by the saké they had been quaffing. When it did come, the reaction of the two Army privates mortified Harper. Turning to Santiago, Roberts raised his glass so vigorously that saké spilled from it over his hand and onto the table.

"Here's to freedom!" he declared.

"Freedom!" echoed Roberts, holding his own glass aloft. And after touching glasses, the two deserters knocked back the remainder of their drinks and leaned back smugly against the backrests of their legless chairs.

As Harper and the other Americans began to gather their belongings, Toda and Higuchi left the room. They returned a few moments later with armfuls of wet weather gear that they piled in a heap on the floor.

"You're going to the fishing harbor on foot," Higuchi explained. "Although it's dark outside, a large group of foreigners will still attract attention. Hopefully, with this clothing on, you'll pass as Japanese fishermen."

The Americans rifled through the pile of clothing, picking out items and holding them against their bodies to check their size. Ferran, Mayfield, and Santiago, being below-average to average height, had no trouble finding gear that fit, but Harper and Roberts struggled to find items big enough, and were still looking by the time the others were clothed and ready to leave.

"Come on," Ferran said, "it's not a goddamn fashion show."

Eventually Harper managed to squeeze into a coat whose sleeves barely reached his wrists and a pair of overalls whose legs were at least six inches too short. He quickly found a hat, placed it on his head and tied the drawstring under his chin then looked up, whereupon Mayfield and the still-tipsy Santiago broke into spontaneous laughter. Harper felt aggrieved until he glanced over at Roberts. Roberts, too, had had to settle for a coat and overalls several sizes too small, and if Harper looked anywhere near as ridiculous as the Army private did he could understand the reaction.

"Quickly," Toda said. "We must go!"

The Americans picked up their bags and shuffled across the room, their wet weather gear rustling loudly. Toda stood by the entrance and watched them as they passed, like a schoolteacher watching over a group of unruly pupils. Harper was the last to exit, and as he did so he turned to see Higuchi still standing by the table.

"You're not coming?" he asked.

"No," Higuchi replied. "My job ends here."

"I understand. Well," Harper said, looking into Higuchi's eyes, "thank you for everything."

Higuchi smiled. "Bon voyage."

Harper pivoted and stepped across the threshold into the corridor, then stopped and turned his head to look at Higuchi.

"Please," he said, "would you give my regards to Natsume?"

"Natsume?" Higuchi replied, a puzzled expression appearing briefly on her face, only to be replaced moments later by a smile of recognition. "Yes, of course. Now, please, you must hurry."

Outside, the fog had lifted to reveal a cloudless night sky. After spending so long indoors, Harper was shocked by the cold and he hunched his shoulders and frowned as they exited Toda's house onto the dimly lit street. The six men gathered together in a loose huddle, and with the boat captain leading the way they set off on foot down the gently sloping street toward the fishing harbor.

Harper relaxed when they reached the waterfront, relieved that they had passed no one along the way. Then he looked up and saw that the harbor was awash with bright light from several tall floodlights positioned like sentries around its perimeter, and anxiety again gripped him. He cast his eyes around the docks, counting at least a dozen men on the wharf or on boats. Luckily they were all busy going about their work, coiling ropes, checking nets, and so on, and Harper and the other deserters hardly attracted a glance as Toda led them along the wharf and up a ramp onto the deck of the fishing boat.

The boat was around forty feet long. There would have been plenty of room for them all on deck, but instead Toda led them into the tiny cabin. When he opened a hatch that led down into an even smaller, windowless compartment, those at the front halted, reluctant to go on.

"Come on," Harper said impatiently. "What's the hold up?"

"Why do we have to go down there?" Mayfield asked, peering down into the gloomy compartment.

"You must stay out of sight," Toda replied. "In case we pass a Japanese patrol boat.

A couple of the other deserters exchanged nervous glances.

"How do we know it's not a trap?" Ferran asked, glancing at Toda.

Harper knew that time was of the essence. He had to do something to calm his compatriots' nerves, otherwise there was a real danger of a mutiny, if not now then later out at sea, where the consequences would be even graver. He pushed his way to the head of the group and stood directly in front of Mayfield, his face just inches away from the Army cook's.

"If you're not happy then get off this goddamn boat now! I'm not going to stand by and let you jeopardize this mission and put the lives of these men at risk. Is that clear?"

Mayfield didn't reply. Instead he turned his head to the side, looking in turn into the faces of the other Americans. When even Ferran remained silent, he looked down in defeat.

Harper turned and climbed down into the compartment, followed by Santiago, Roberts, Ferran, and finally Mayfield. There were no seats, so with the exception of Mayfield, who perched on his suitcase, they were forced to sit on the floor.

Toda, who had stood patiently to one side while the Americans sorted out their differences, peered down through the hatch. "Remember, you must stay out of sight and remain quiet until we rendezvous with the Soviet Maritime Border Patrol. When the time comes, I'll come and get you and you'll be transferred to the Russian vessel."

He closed the hatch, plunging the compartment into semi-darkness.

No one spoke. Robbed of his ability to see in the dark, Harper's other senses worked overtime. His ears picked up the waves sloshing against the boat's hull, the creaking of its timbers. His nose the stench of body odor mixed with diesel. His skin the dampness of the air.

Without warning the engine roared into life. Then the boat was moving. It was calm for the first few minutes until they left the safety of the harbor, whereupon the boat began to pitch and toss. As a Marine, Harper was at home in the open sea, but he still found it disconcerting not being able to see outside, which meant there was no way of telling when the boat was about to encounter a larger than normal wave, or when it was about to plunge into a trough.

Harper was curious as to how the other deserters were coping with the conditions. His eyes having adjusted to the dark, he scanned their faces in turn. Ferran, the other Marine, appeared calm. Santiago also seemed untroubled, though this was probably due to the amount of alcohol he had consumed, dulling his senses to the point where he was oblivious to the violent rocking of the boat. The remaining three appeared to be in varying states of discomfort, with Roberts looking the worst. As if on queue, the young Army private doubled over, clutching his stomach and letting out a loud moan.

"For chrissake," said Ferran, who was sitting next to Roberts, "don't go puking on us now."

"Shit!" Mayfield said.

"Keep your voices down!" Harper said. Then, spying a bucket in a corner of the compartment, he turned to Ferran and said, "Give me that."

The Marine did as Harper ordered.

"If you're going to puke," Harper said, leaning over and placing the bucket at Roberts' feet, "do it in here."

Roberts looked up and nodded lethargically. As he returned to his seat, Harper caught a movement out of the corner of his eye, and he turned to see Ferran reaching for his bag and unzipping it. The Marine reached in and grabbed hold of something. Harper tensed, wondering what it could be. He recognized the large cylindrical object almost immediately. It was the saké bottle from Captain Toda's house.

"Who wants a drink?" Ferran said, unscrewing the metal cap and holding the bottle aloft.

Santiago's eyes lit up, but as he reached over to take the bottle off Ferran, Roberts leaned forward, neck extended and mouth open, and after three convulsions, each more vigorous than the one before, he was violently sick. Some of the vomit landed in the bucket at his feet, but a considerable amount ended up spattered across Santiago's right arm.

"Shit!" Santiago said. He jumped to his feet with his arm thrust out to one side, but as he reached his full height his head struck the wooden ceiling with a thud and he was propelled down again. He sat on the mat with his right arm still extended and his left arm bent as he rubbed the crown of his head with his free hand.

"Lucky that coat's waterproof," Ferran said.

Laughter echoed around the cramped compartment.

Harper had had enough.

"Give me that," he said to Ferran.

He took the bottle in one hand, pressed the mouth to his lips and upended it. The saké was surprisingly fragrant, sweet with a dank earthiness. For a brief moment it took his mind off the mayhem breaking out around him.

Harper had experienced discomfort far worse in Vietnam. On Hill 842 he had shared quarters not much larger than the boat compartment with members of his platoon while Charlie lobbed mortar shells onto the roof. And then there were the nights out on patrol during the rainy season. Sitting on their helmets in waterlogged foxholes, often two to a hole, huddled together under makeshift shelters made by snapping together their rubber-coated ponchos. Hoping the trip flares and claymores on the perimeter would take care of any gooks who tried to get too close. But always at the back of their minds: Charlie had the nights.

Perhaps it was the alcohol that brought these memories back. But more likely it was being trapped in a small, cold, dark, damp compartment with four American servicemen, his senses assailed by the fishing boat's violent pitching and rolling, the engine's incessant drone, and the smell of diesel and vomit. And as had so often been the case in Vietnam, although his mind drifted, at its core it was concentrated on just one thing: his own survival.

How long had they been on the boat? An hour? Two hours? Longer? Harper had lost all track of time. The first thing he noticed was the slight change in the sound of the engine as the captain eased off on the throttle. They were slowing. The thrum of the engine subsided. Harper strained to hear other sounds. Anything to give him a clue as to what was happening above them.

"We're stopping," Ferran said excitedly.

"Shh!" Harper commanded. "Stay calm, soldier!"

Muffled voices. Suddenly, a sharp jolt accompanied by a loud bang. All five Americans were thrown to one side, arms flailing in a desperate bid to steady themselves. Moments later a loud scraping noise followed by more shouting.

"There's another boat alongside us," Ferran whispered.

There were more thuds as someone or something landed on the deck above them, then footsteps. Harper recalled Toda's instructions. How they were to stay put until Toda came and got them.

Together they waited. No one spoke. Minutes passed. Noises on the other side of the hatch. Then two knocks. The hatch opening. The familiar face of Captain Toda.

"Everybody out! Quickly!"

The Americans needed no encouragement. They were out of the compartment in seconds. Harper was the last to leave. He stood inside the open hatch to make sure everyone got out safely, offering a hand to Mayfield, who was the second to last out and struggled to get his suitcase through the narrow opening.

They followed Toda through his cabin and onto the main deck of the fishing boat, which was lit up by a searchlight mounted on the Russian vessel. The light was so strong Harper had to squint and hold his hand in front of his eyes to see where he was going.

Toda brought them to a halt by the side of the fishing boat. Harper took the opportunity to size up the Russian vessel, which was considerably larger than Toda's fishing boat. The sea was still rough, and although the two boats had been lashed together, they were not rising and falling in unison. Harper watched, trying to discern some kind of pattern in their movements, but they appeared totally random, one often rising when the other was falling. Getting from one vessel to the other wasn't going to be easy. There was also the difference in height to contend with, the deck of the Russian boat being several feet higher than that of the fishing boat. As if reading his mind, Toda tapped him on the shoulder and pointed to the fishing boat's cabin. A ladder on the side provided access to the roof, which was more or less level with the deck of the Russian vessel. But the cabin did not span the full width of the boat, and the roof was small in area, too small to hold them all at the same time. They would have to take turns.

Ferran was the first to go. He scrambled up the ladder, stood on the cabin roof and threw his bag onto the deck of the Russian vessel. He waited, timing his jump so he left the fishing boat as it was rising and landed on the Russian boat as it was falling. Two burly Russian crewmen in dark uniforms and fur hats with flaps jammed down over their ears were waiting to catch him, but he brushed them aside and quickly turned and beckoned for the others to follow.

Next up was the ailing Roberts. He climbed up the ladder clumsily, his feet slipping off the rungs two or three times, and stood on the cabin roof facing the Russian vessel. Seconds ticked by.

"Jump, you dumb ass."

Harper turned to confront the voice's owner.

"Jump!" Santiago repeated.

Harper looked up at Roberts. "Soldier, get your ass onto that Russian ship. That's an order."

Harper was in no position to be issuing orders to an Army private, but he hoped the command would shock Roberts into action. And it did. Roberts took two steps forward and launched himself across the gap. He landed with arms flailing. But he had timed the jump wrong and made contact with the deck of the Russian vessel as it was rising. The impact sent him backward, toward the edge of the boat.

Harper watched helplessly as Roberts reached out to grab the railing, anything, to steady himself. But there was no railing and Roberts was clutching at thin air. He continued to stumble backward, his feet losing traction on the slippery deck. Harper was certain the Army private was about to fall overboard, where he would likely be crushed between the two vessels. But at the last minute one of the Russian crewmen rushed forward, grabbed Roberts and pulled him to safety.

Santiago was next, followed by Mayfield. The Army cook surprised Harper by making the transfer look easy. Now only Harper remained. He turned to Toda and the two exchanged nods. After climbing up onto the cabin roof and throwing his bag onto the Russian ship, he waited until he saw its deck begin to dip. Then he ran and jumped and landed in the arms of the two Russian crewmen.

Ferran, Roberts, and Santiago had been led down into the bowels of the Soviet vessel. Of the deserters, only Harper and Mayfield remained on deck. Harper turned to the Russians and said, "That's it. Let's get out of here."

"Wait!" Mayfield said. Then, addressing the Russians, "My suitcase! My suitcase is still on the other boat!"

The Russians frowned at each other and shrugged their shoulders.

Mayfield turned his attention to Harper. "Please, Harpo, I need my suitcase."

Harper regarded Mayfield, who looked back at him imploringly. Then he peered across at Captain Toda, who had already begun untying the ropes holding the two vessels together. Harper thought for a moment, then he shouted to attract Toda's attention and pointed to Mayfield and gave what he hoped was the international gesture for a suitcase, curling his right hand into a fist and raising and lowering it beside his hip.

Toda didn't seem to understand at first. Then it dawned on him, and he quickly scanned the fishing boat's deck. He spotted the suitcase and dragged it to the edge of the deck. Looking up at Harper, who had taken up a corresponding position on the deck of the Russian boat, he lifted the suitcase and swung it back and forth three times in increasingly wide arcs. On the third swing he let go. The suitcase sailed in a loop across the gap between the two vessels and landed in Harper's arms. Harper nodded to Toda for a final time. Then he turned and, together with Mayfield, was led inside the Russian vessel by the two Russian crewmen.

EPILOGUE I

New York City, November 1999

Eddie Flynn paused when he reached the top of the stairs at Waverly Place, as much to catch his breath as to get his bearings. He had all but gotten lost in the cavernous, bi-level West Fourth Street subway station and was on the verge of a panic attack when he finally found the Waverly Place exit, one of only two out of the station. He stood leaning against the stone wall of the diner at the top of the stairs until his heart stopped racing and his breathing settled. Then he turned up his coat collar and walked to the nearby intersection of Waverley Place and Sixth Avenue and turned right. He looked up and saw in the distance the lights of the Twin Towers. Confident now that he was heading in the right direction, he lowered his gaze and quickened his pace, getting some small pleasure from the meager warmth the movement of his body generated.

He had spent the day wandering on foot around Midtown in a vain effort to reacquaint himself with the area. It had been a long time since he had last been in New York. Nearly twenty-five years, in fact. He was amazed at how much it had changed. Times Square, a gritty, grimy, crime-ridden neighborhood when he had frequented it in the 1970s, was as safe and clean as Disneyland now, and about as interesting. Gone were the adult movie theaters, peep shows, and sex shops. In their place stood souvenir shops, towering illuminated signs, and theme restaurants.

One thing that hadn't changed much was the Armed Forces recruiting station, which still squatted on the same traffic island between Broadway and Seventh Avenue. Flynn had tensed involuntarily as he walked past the building with its illuminated Stars and Stripes façade, unsettled by the symbolism and by the presence of so many people in military uniform. He had hurried past, keen to put as much distance between himself and the building as quickly as possible.

Now, as he crossed West Fourth Street and continued south along Sixth Avenue, past Minetta Park and the public basketball courts, he felt much more relaxed. Walking was one of the things in life that gave him pleasure. He always walked alone, and always outdoors. Confined and confusing indoor spaces like the West Fourth Street station still unnerved him.

It was his spell on Treasure Island, much of it in solitary confinement, that had caused his claustrophobia. His condition was so bad that after his release in 1974 he had avoided entering buildings of any kind. Even vehicles made him anxious. He had set off for his home in Bingham County, Idaho on foot, sleeping in the open, just as he had done when he walked from Yokosuka to Tokyo. He took a roundabout route, skirting built-up areas to avoid being targeted by overzealous policemen, who, like many Americans, Flynn quickly learned, regarded lone walkers with suspicion. How different it was from Japan. There, the tradition of making pilgrimages meant that people traveling alone on foot were treated with respect, even reverence.

At first he could barely manage ten miles a day, so long had it been since he had done any serious walking. But as the strength returned to his legs and calluses formed on the soles of his feet, the distance he was able to cover gradually increased, until he was regularly traveling twenty-five, even thirty miles before sundown. It was summer when he set off and the days were long. By the time he wandered into Blackfoot, Idaho, however, the days were getting shorter and the nights colder and the leaves starting to turn the color of rust.

The closer he got to home the more he began to worry about the reception he would get, both from his family and from the local community. It was for this reason that he had refrained from contacting his parents to tell them of his impending arrival. His apprehension proved well founded. While his mother seemed pleased to see him, his father, who had never shown much affection toward him in the past, was openly hostile. It didn't help that one of Flynn's brothers, who had joined the Marines not long after Flynn had left for Vietnam, was a decorated veteran and a hero in the local community.

That same community treated Flynn as a pariah. Clearly unwelcome not only on the farm but in the entire county, it seemed, Flynn had little choice but to leave. He decided to head east. He traveled by bus using some of the money his mother had secretly given him before his departure on the fare to New York City. He rented a cheap apartment in the Lower East Side and proceeded to frit away the rest of his money in the go-go bars and strip clubs in and around Times Square.

Six weeks after his arrival in the Big Apple, with his money nearly all gone and his rent overdue, Flynn was resigned to joining the ranks of the homeless in the Bowery, when a chance encounter with a fellow Vietnam veteran in a soup kitchen resulted in him landing a job as a porter at a hospital in the Bronx. Instead of using the opportunity of a steady job and steady income to turn his life around, however, he continued along the same hedonistic path, supplementing the drink with a cocktail of prescription drugs, which were readily available in the hospital wards.

Earlier, soon after arriving in New York, he had phoned home twice hoping to speak to his mother, but both times his father had answered and he had hung up without saying anything. More than a year passed before he plucked up enough courage to phone again. This time his mother answered. Amid sobs she broke the news to him that his father had died of a heart attack a month after Flynn had left. The next day Flynn quit his job and caught a bus back to Bingham County.

Without his domineering father, Flynn found the mood in the Flynn household noticeably warmer. He knew his mother would do her best to make him feel welcome, and in this regard she didn't disappoint. What was surprising was that his brothers, too, seemed more hospitable toward their errant sibling. Over the ensuing months, the three of them worked closely together on the farm, cutting the seed potatoes and loading the pieces onto trucks for transportation to the fields and planting them in the ground. Laboring outside everyday, feeling the warm sun on his face and the damp soil on his hands, Flynn realized that he was happiest when he was working on the land. He grew physically fitter and, having weaned himself off drugs and alcohol, he was generally healthier. He threw himself into the farm work, inspecting the fields first thing every morning and ensuring the rapidly growing potatoes were well watered and receiving the right amount of fertilizer and regular doses of pesticides, herbicides, and fungicides.

In the autumn of 1976, however, after they had harvested and stored the final crop, Flynn decided it was time to move on, time to strike out on his own. So he packed up and moved into an old house on the outskirts of nearby Idaho Falls, where he started his own landscaping business. He met and married a local farmer's daughter, and three years later the couple welcomed a baby girl. Flynn doted on his daughter, and the fulfillment he found both at home and at work brought to his life a degree of contentment that he had not felt since he was a boy.

Flynn and his wife and daughter often spent Christmas with Flynn's family in Bingham County, sometimes staying on to see in the New Year. Such was the case in 1997, when, with the exception of the eldest of his three nephews, who had emulated his father in joining the Marines and was serving in Germany, Flynn's entire extended family was present, including his mother, now approaching her eighties but still in fine fettle, relishing the role of matriarch she had assumed upon the death of Flynn's father.

Flynn was still at the family farm early in the New Year when a letter addressed to him arrived from Japan. He didn't recognize the sender's name: Shinji Masuda. He opened it and began reading, and his jaw dropped when it dawned on him that Shinji Masuda was Kawabata, the young man who had accompanied him to Hokkaido during his failed attempt to escape Japan nearly thirty years ago. The letter mentioned a reunion of former members of the organization Masuda had been a part of, to which Flynn was invited.

Flynn remembered closing his eyes after reading the letter and reliving the days leading up to his arrest in Hokkaido, as he had done numerous times over the intervening decades. His first meeting with Gilroy, whose smooth talking fooled not only him but also the people organizing his escape. The flight to Kushiro and the drive to the hot spring resort of Teshikaga. His waking early the next morning to discover Gilroy missing. Their fleeing the *ryokan* and driving back to Kushiro, breaking down the replica pistol and throwing the pieces out the car window, singing "We Shall Overcome."

He replied a week later, thanking Masuda for his letter but declining the invitation to the reunion, citing financial hardship. In fact, it was the fear of being made to relive the events after his arrest, including his trial and imprisonment in the U.S., events that still haunted him at night just as the death of Huerta once haunted him, that prompted his refusal. He had not spoken to anyone—not even his wife—about this period of his life, and he was afraid that to do so now would trigger a return to those dark days of loneliness and drug and alcohol addiction.

A year later, Flynn received another letter from Masuda, this one informing him that Masuda would be visiting New York in November and asking him if they could meet. Flynn initially balked at the suggestion for the same reasons he had declined the earlier invitation. But his wife, perhaps sensing that a meeting with Masuda might force Flynn to confront the demons that she knew had been tormenting him for years, encouraged him to go, and he eventually wrote back informing Masuda that he could make the journey to New York after all. Emboldened by his decision, Flynn also worked up the courage to fly for the first time since returning from Japan.

Flynn heard a low-pitched grinding sound behind him. It quickly grew louder and he stopped and looked over his shoulder just in time to see a young man on a skateboard, his face concealed by the hood of his dark sweatshirt, bearing down on him. He cursed as he stepped to one side and watched as the skateboarder brushed past him and maneuvered his way through the thin crowd of pedestrians along Sixth Avenue, one arm raised, the middle finger extended in a vulgar parting gesture.

At the corner of Sixth Avenue and West Third Street he turned left. He passed the black façade of the Blue Note Jazz Club with its piano-shaped canopy and continued east for two more blocks, threading the brick canyon formed by the New York University School of Law's main classroom building and the D'Agostino Residence Hall across the street. A short while later he spotted the place he was after. He descended the stairs, past a small blackboard sign with the words BAR OPEN and LIVE MUSIC scrawled in white chalk, and entered through a glass door.

For a moment Flynn was sure he had mistaken the address. There was a bar all right, but the room was small and devoid of a stage, let alone musicians. Flynn's confusion was compounded by the décor, which was all exposed brick, red velvet drapes, and etched glass.

Then he heard music. The dull twang of a double bass. The jangle of brass. The sound was muffled, but judging by the volume and the way the floor reverberated under his feet, Flynn knew that it wasn't far away. He looked at the far end of the room where the music was coming from, saw the drapes part and a figure emerge. In the brief moment before the curtains closed again, the music was louder, more distinct, and Flynn knew he had the right place after all.

Perched on a stool to his left, just inside the door, was a man in a shiny suit. The bouncer gave him a once-over. Having lived in New York, albeit a long time ago, Flynn knew the locals had a seemingly innate ability to distinguish between their own and outsiders. He knew better than to take offense, but he still resented the way the doorman looked him up and down, and took an immediate dislike to him.

"The back's full," the man said, "but if you want to sit at the bar there's no cover charge."

Flynn looked over at the bar, noting that the dozen or so stools were all occupied.

"Actually, I'm supposed to be on the list."

"Name?" the doorman said.

"Flynn. Edward Flynn."

The man turned to his right and consulted a sheet of paper on a lectern, running his index finger down a list of names. Without acknowledging Flynn, he looked over his shoulder and caught the eye of a young African American woman with shoulder-length dreadlocks who was standing a few feet away at the bar.

"Kayla," he said as the woman approached. "Show this man to table two."

Kayla turned, took a menu from a pile on the bar and looked at Flynn. She smiled. "Follow me."

She swiveled on her heels and Flynn followed her down the narrow passageway between the bar stools and the wall to their right. When they reached the velvet drapes at the end of the room, Kayla parted them with one hand and with the other hand motioned for him to enter.

Although on the small side for a live venue, the back room was considerably more spacious than the bar. From what he could see in the semi-darkness, it appeared similarly decorated, with a bank of velvet red drapes covering the back wall. In front of the drapes was a low stage where a group of musicians was playing under the harsh glare of spotlights. The only other illumination came from flickering candles in jars, one atop each of the twenty or so small wooden tables scattered around the room.

Kayla led Flynn to the only free table, by the wall on the left, just two back from the stage. She picked up the RESERVED sign and gestured for him to sit down. She waited for him to remove his coat and take his seat before handing him the menu. "Can I get you something to eat or drink?"

Flynn gave the menu a cursory glance. "Just a Coke, thanks," he said, looking up and smiling. He watched Kayla's own smile wane.

"Just so you know," she said, "there's a two drink minimum."

Flynn nodded, and after Kayla left he turned his attention to the stage.

The band, a quartet, was playing a bebop number that sounded vaguely familiar. Knowing next to nothing about jazz, he had no idea if the quartet was any good, but judging by the applause and the number of cries of "Yeah" that followed each solo, the rest of the audience thought they were.

One thing that did impress Flynn was the multiethnic make-up of the band. The pianist was Latino, the drummer black, the bassist white, and the trumpeter Asian. Their ages also varied. The drummer and bassist looked to be in their twenties, while the pianist was at least forty. The trumpeter was clearly the oldest. He was also the most flamboyantly dressed. Whereas the other members lived up to the New York stereotype in their choice of various shades of black, the trumpeter sported a colorful wardrobe that included a yellow jacket and a blue porkpie hat. The playfulness even extended to his glasses, whose checkerboard frames reminded Flynn of the trim on the Checker Taxicabs that plied the city's streets in the 1970s.

When the band finished the bebop number, the trumpeter approached the microphone and announced they were taking a break. A few moments later, the other three members of the quartet stepped down from the stage. Flynn watched as they set off in the direction of the bar beyond the red velvet curtains, stopping occasionally to chat with appreciative audience members.

Kayla returned with his Coke and, without a word, set it on the table. He took a sip, glanced back at the stage and noticed the trumpeter looking at him. Still clutching his instrument, the man stepped down from the stage and made a beeline for Flynn's table. He stopped a few feet away and said, "Eddie Flynn?"

Flynn scrutinized the man's face. "Mr. Masuda?" he said, slowly getting to his feet. "Or should I call you Mr. Kawabata?"

The man carefully set his trumpet down on the table and extended a hand. "Shinji will do just fine."

Flynn leaned across the table and took Masuda's hand, smiling as he shook it.

"Please, sit down," Masuda said, gesturing for Flynn to resume his seat. He took off his hat and set it on the table next to his trumpet before parking himself opposite Flynn. He spent a brief moment examining Flynn's face. "I see you've lost your freckles," he said, pointing to his own cheeks with both forefingers.

"And I see you've lost your hair," Flynn replied, raising his eyebrows and looking up at Masuda's shiny pate.

They both laughed. Then Masuda said, "I thought you weren't going to make it."

Flynn took a sip of Coke before responding. "I nearly didn't. But it seemed a waste to come all the way to New York and miss the opportunity to thank you."

"To thank *me*?" Masuda said, his brow furrowing.

"For helping me all those years ago."

"On the contrary," Masuda said. "It is I who should apologize to you. Especially for not making the effort to get in touch with you sooner. Although you must understand, we did try."

"We?"

"The surviving members of JATEC."

"JATEC?"

Masuda laughed. "JATEC was the organization that tried to help you escape from Japan."

"But I thought it was Beheiren."

"JATEC was a secret group within Beheiren. So secret we didn't reveal its name to those we assisted."

"I see," Flynn said. Then, remembering Masuda's colleague on that fateful mission, the tall man with the dark glasses, he added, "And was Mr. Aizawa also a member of JATEC?"

"Not officially. He joined us on certain missions. When we required his special skills."

Flynn nodded. He recalled the tall man's face, eyes hidden behind tinted lenses. "Please give him my regards. When you get back to Japan."

Masuda hesitated. "Sadly, he passed away last year."

"Oh? I'm very sorry to hear that."

Masuda acknowledged the expression of sympathy with a slight bow of his head.

"Were you close?"

"Not particularly," Masuda replied, looking up. "He was not an easy man to get on with. We lost touch over the years."

Flynn nodded. He took a sip of his Coke. Then he said, "And what about Gilroy?"

Masuda gave a look of disdain. "The spy? Not surprisingly, we never heard from him again. Although we half expected him to turn up at my trial to testify for the prosecution, which would have been interesting."

"*Your* trial?" Flynn said, confused. "You were arrested for helping me?"

"Not exactly," Masuda said. "It was perfectly legal for Japanese civilians to aid American deserters in Japan. However, it was, and still is, illegal for civilians to possess handguns."

Flynn thought for a moment. Then he said, "The Walther PPK."

"Yes."

"But it was only a toy."

"A replica," Masuda corrected him. "Yes. You and I knew that. As did Aizawa."

Flynn nodded.

"But Gilroy didn't."

"Also, we got rid of it. I threw it out the car window before we were stopped by the police."

"Exactly. They had no evidence at all. Which raises the question: why did they prosecute? The only possible explanation is that Gilroy, believing that he'd seen me in possession of a real handgun, had reported this to his handlers, who then passed the information on to the Japanese authorities. Not surprisingly, the charges against me collapsed. But in the course of the investigation the police searched my apartment as well as the homes of several other members of JATEC. Perhaps that was their aim all along. To gather information and disrupt our activities."

Flynn nodded slowly. "I'm sorry. I didn't know."

"Nonsense," Masuda said. "It was nothing. A mere inconvenience compared to what you went through."

Flynn wondered how much Masuda knew about what he went through. Not a lot, he thought.

"We all felt terrible about what happened to you that day. And about what happened to you afterward. Aizawa and I asked to see you at the Kushiro Central Police Station the day you were arrested, but our request was denied. We returned the next morning and again asked to see you, but this time we were told you'd been moved to Tokyo."

Flynn nodded slowly. "Soon after I arrived at the police station, I was taken to a room and questioned by the police. I refused to tell them anything apart from my name, date of birth, rank, and serial number. They got angry, said I wasn't a prisoner of war and wasn't protected by the Geneva Conventions, but I still refused to talk. Eventually they threw me in a crowded cell full of drunks and vagrants. I spent the night there. The next day I was handed over to the Americans. I was taken to the train station and put on a train to Sapporo. From there I was flown to Camp Zama in Kanazawa."

"The U.S. Army base."

"Yes. I thought things would improve now that I was in the

custody of my own countrymen, but I was wrong. At Zama I was questioned by seasoned interrogators, from the CIA and ONI."

"ONI?"

"Office of Naval Intelligence."

Masuda nodded. "How long did they keep you there?"

"Not long. After a day or two they moved me to the Navy base at Yokosuka and put me in solitary confinement."

"We figured you'd end up at Yokosuka eventually. Which is why we sent Tsurumi to try to get in touch with you."

"Tsurumi?"

"Shunsuke Tsurumi. One of Beheiren's leaders. He managed to speak to your lawyer, but the Navy insisted he couldn't meet with you personally."

"Yokosuka was where things really started to get rough. I thought the Mental Health Unit, where I'd spent time before I deserted, was bad. But that was nothing in comparison.

"There was no bed in my cell, and for the first three days I had no blanket. I had to sleep on the floor. One night I was woken by a voice coming from a loud speaker outside my cell. 'Listen to this,' it said. And then I heard thumps and cries, the unmistakable sounds of someone being beaten. I didn't know if it was a recording or live, but it made no difference. The thuds and cries got worse. Until then, I had no idea it was possible to distinguish between a punch and kick by the sound alone. Before long the victim—I assumed it was another prisoner in a nearby cell—was pleading for his life. His attackers were merciless, laughing as they continued their assault. The cries grew fainter. And then they stopped altogether. The beating, though, continued for several more minutes. There was a brief moment of silence, and then a voice, the same voice that I'd heard at the start, said, 'Did you hear that, Flynn? If you don't follow orders, you'll be next.'"

Flynn took a sip of his Coke before continuing. "I realized this was all part of a plan to soften me up for more interrogation. This time there was no one from the CIA. It was just ONI. They wanted to know how I'd gotten in touch with Beheiren, where I'd stayed while I was on the run, the names of all the people who'd helped me. When I refused to tell them anything, they brought in guards to beat me.

Not as badly as the prisoner I'd heard over the loudspeaker, though. In fact, I'd had worse beatings from my father when I was a kid."

A hint of a smile flashed across Masuda's face, and Flynn laughed, relieving the tension that had settled over their table.

"They tried all kinds of tricks to break me, including hosing me down with cold water. One day I returned to my cell to find a razor blade. After a couple of days the blade disappeared, only to be replaced by a bottle of pills. I had no idea what they were, but I had a fair idea what the result would be if I took them.

"I knew that unless I gave them some information, the physical and psychological torture would continue. So I told them some things, things I was certain they would have known, and made up some names. After two days of interrogation they placed a typed sheet of paper in front of me and told me to sign it. They said it was my confession. I read it, got them to change a few things, and signed it. Three days later I was handed over to the Marines and put on a plane to Hawaii."

"Did things get any better there?"

"They did," Flynn said. "For a start, it was warmer. And the conditions in which I was held were more relaxed. There were no more beatings. I was able to interact with the other prisoners, and even managed to smuggle out a letter to my family. I never heard back from them, though. So either they didn't get it or they chose not to reply. I was just getting used to things when I was moved again, this time to the mainland."

"That must have been just before your court-martial," said Masuda.

"That's right. You heard about that?"

"We found out later by searching the military records."

"Five years hard labor," Flynn hissed, struggling to control his anger. "The trial was a total farce."

Masuda looked down at the table, clearly uncomfortable at Flynn's show of emotion.

"I was sent to a high-security brig on Treasure Island, in San Francisco Bay. Conditions there were the worst of all the places I was held. I spent a lot of time in solitary confinement. And the beatings started again. Sometimes the guards got totally carried away. One day they beat a prisoner so bad he died."

Masuda frowned. "What happened? Were the guards charged?"

Flynn snorted in disgust. "Nothing happened. It was covered up. Obviously it wasn't the first time something like that had occurred."

Masuda nodded. "But you survived."

"I survived five years in that hellhole."

"What did you do after you were released?"

"It'd been so long since I'd had to make any decisions on my own, I had no idea what to do or where to go. So I headed home, to Bingham County. I walked all the way from San Francisco. It took me nearly forty days. It was as if I had come full circle, from walking to freedom in Japan to walking to freedom in America. But I soon realized I couldn't stay at the family farm. Things were too tense. That's when I came to New York. A few years later I moved back to Idaho. I've lived there ever since."

"So is this your first time back in New York since the 1970s?"

"Yes. I arrived last night. I spent yesterday in Washington, D.C., paying my respects at the Vietnam Memorial."

Masuda nodded silently.

"There was one name in particular I wanted to find."

"And did you find it?"

Flynn nodded. He looked down into his glass of Coke for a few moments. Then he directed his gaze back at Masuda. "I also realized something."

"What was that?"

"I realized that if I hadn't deserted, my name would be carved on that wall. I've no doubt about it. I went through hell, but I don't regret what I did for a minute. Not a minute."

Flynn finished his Coke and glanced over at the curtained entrance to the room, where members of the audience were beginning to drift back in. Mingled with the patrons were the other members of Masuda's band, who eventually took their assigned positions on the stage and began fiddling with their instruments.

Flynn looked across the table at Masuda and said, "I think your presence is required."

Masuda turned in his chair, looked at the assembled band members and then at his watch, the expression on his face suggesting to Flynn that for Masuda time had passed more quickly than he expected. He picked up his trumpet and looked at it.

"It was your dream, wasn't it?" Flynn said. "To become a professional jazz musician."

"This?" Masuda replied, raising the trumpet in one hand. "Oh, this is just a hobby. I was never good enough to make a career out of it. The owner of this place is Japanese, a friend of my brother's. I did some work for him once. He knew it had always been a dream of mine to play in New York, so he arranged this gig in return."

"I see. So what *do* you do for a living?"

"I write."

"Really? What do you write?"

"Oh, a bit of everything. Fiction, nonfiction…"

Flynn nodded. "Did you ever marry?"

"Me?" Masuda replied. "No. There was someone once. A long time ago. But it didn't work out."

For a brief moment, Flynn thought he noticed a hint of melancholy in the Japanese man's face.

"Well," Masuda said, looking over his shoulder at the stage, "I hope you'll stay until the end of the next set. It'd be nice to talk some more."

Flynn smiled and nodded, a gesture he intended to be as noncommittal as possible.

Masuda smiled back at Flynn. Then he stood and turned and walked the short distance to the stage. The audience responded with a brief but enthusiastic round of applause as Masuda took his place in front of the other band members. He put the trumpet to his lips and spent a few moments blowing into the mouthpiece and rapidly pumping the valves with the fingers of his right hand. Then he stopped and looked down at the stage, and it seemed to Flynn that he was deep in thought. He went over to each of the band members and briefly spoke to them in turn before returning to the front of the stage. Then, bending over until his face was level with the microphone in front of him, he announced in a quiet voice, "This one's for Eddie."

Masuda stepped back and stood with his eyes closed and head down as his fellow band members started playing. Flynn listened closely, but he didn't recognize the tune. Then Masuda stepped forward and raised his trumpet to his lips, and with his eyes still closed, he played the opening bars of "We Shall Overcome." There was a spattering of applause and several cries of "Yeah" from the audience. Alone at his table, Flynn leaned back in his seat and closed his eyes. For a moment he was sitting in the back seat of a rental car, speeding along the highway north of Kushiro, with Aizawa at the wheel and Kawabata in the passenger's seat. Then he relaxed and let the music wash over him.

EPILOGUE 2

Arlanda Airport, Stockholm, April 2010

Harper heaved the suitcase out of the taxi's trunk and lowered it to the ground. He rolled it toward the curb, skirting the puddles of snowmelt, and stood there for a moment, eyes darting from the suitcase to the trolley on the sidewalk in front of him.

"Let me take that, Dad," Alex said, reaching for the bag.

"I've got it," Harper snapped. "Get out of my way."

He took a deep breath, held it. Then, grasping the handle with both hands, he lifted the suitcase and stepped up onto the sidewalk and hefted it onto the trolley. He winced as a jolt of pain shot through his lower back.

"Are you okay, Dad?"

"Of course I'm okay," he said through gritted teeth.

Alex slid his own suitcase next to Harper's. Then he turned to his father and said, "Didn't Dr. Holgersson say no heavy lifting?"

"Dr. Holgersson?" Harper snorted. "The guy's a quack."

Alex frowned. "Would it be so difficult to take it easy for a while?"

"Take it easy? What, you think I'm too old to look after—"

"Come on, you two," Ingrid said, slipping the change from the taxi fare into her purse as she approached. "If we don't get a move on we'll miss our flight."

Harper looked at Alex's wife. She normally wore her hair loose, but today she had it tied in a ponytail. It was how Anita liked to wear her hair when he first met her. And Ingrid's appearance wasn't the only thing about her that reminded him of his late wife. Anita, too, had been strong-minded and liked to be in control. He felt a pang of sadness, but managed to stifle it before it took a hold of him.

The three of them entered the terminal and found the check-in aisle for their flight. The queue was mercifully short, and within a few minutes they were at the counter, where a young woman in a dark blue Scandinavian Airlines uniform asked them where they were flying.

"New York," Ingrid said, setting their passports on the counter.

As Alex lifted their bags onto the scales, the woman leafed through their travel documents, glancing up as she came to the identity information page in each one to look at the owner's face. Harper noticed her frown slightly when she opened his, and she seemed to study his face particularly carefully. He looked into her eyes and smiled, reminding himself to stay calm. But there was a tightness in his stomach that he had not felt for some time, and it crossed his mind how easy it would be to turn around and walk outside and catch a taxi back home. Eventually, however, the woman nodded and closed his passport, sliding it and the others across the counter together with their boarding passes and luggage tags.

"Your flight is boarding in half an hour through Gate 39," the attendant said. "Immigration and Security can be especially busy at this time of day, so I suggest you head there right away."

"Thank you," Ingrid said.

They gathered their carry-on luggage and set off toward Passport Control. But Harper was still feeling on edge. Seeing a bathroom on the other side of the hallway, he tapped Alex on the arm and told him he had to take a leak.

Once inside the restroom, Harper headed straight for the nearest stall. After relieving himself he lowered the lid and sat down. Then, closing his eyes, he took three deep breaths.

His last long-distance flight had been to Japan with Anita in 1998. He had felt anxious at the airport before that flight, too. It was his first trip abroad since arriving in Sweden thirty years earlier. He remembered breaking into a cold sweat as he stood in the queue at Passport Control with his new Swedish passport. But once he got on the plane he relaxed.

The rest of the trip went smoothly. A Beheiren representative met them at Narita Airport and drove them to Tokyo. They spent three days there, during which time Harper was reunited with "Ōe,"

"Natsume," and "Higuchi," all of them aliases, he learned. Harper and Anita then traveled around the country for a week, Harper speaking at schools and at public meetings organized by their hosts.

From Tokyo they made a day trip to Yokohama. Much of the city still looked familiar, but the area that once housed the Navy Exchange had changed beyond recognition. The shops, theater, and bowling alley were gone, replaced by an up-market shopping center and condominiums. And at Kishine, the land on which the 106th General Hospital once stood had been turned into a park.

Before leaving for Japan, without mentioning it to Anita, whom he had not told of his relationship with Yumi, he had asked Beheiren if they could get in touch with his old flame, since all of the letters he had sent her after arriving in Sweden had been returned unopened. But no one in the organization had her contact details and, though they tried, they had been unable to locate her. Not being able to meet Yumi again had been the only real disappointment of the trip.

Things had gone so well in Japan that after their return Harper thought about traveling to the U.S. to see his family. He had considered it once before, in the late 1970s after President Carter had granted amnesty, first to Vietnam War draft dodgers and later to deserters. But by then Harper had settled down in Stockholm. He had a new wife and plans for a family. And while the African American community in the city was tiny, he felt welcome and had experienced racism only rarely, and never on the scale he had experienced it in America. For all these reasons he had pushed the idea out of his mind. Then, after the trip to Japan, it found its way back.

He later realized that the decision to go was as much Anita's as his. She had been sowing the seeds for some time, dropping hints and making subtle suggestions. Alex was a teenager, she reminded him, curious about the world and keen to learn more about his African American roots. Harper's father had died in 1975. And while his mother was still alive, she wasn't getting any younger. He began making plans. Then came 9/11, putting the idea on ice, where it remained throughout the Bush presidencies. But when Obama became president at the start of 2009, Harper was filled with renewed hope and pursued the idea again with uncharacteristic enthusiasm. He could hardly believe it. A black President of the United States of America! Then, in June of that year, Anita was diagnosed with a brain tumor.

The tumor was malignant and aggressive, and within three months of the diagnosis Anita was dead. Shattered, Harper gave up all thought of traveling overseas. He stopped going out and became increasingly withdrawn, spending more and more time alone. Alex, in his late twenties by then and married himself, was clearly distressed not only at the loss of his mother but at the toll Anita's death was taking on his father. But Harper was as reluctant to talk about his feelings as he was to talk about his experiences in Vietnam, and he rebuffed Alex's attempts to get him to discuss his future. In the end, Alex asked Ingrid, whom he knew Harper adored, to try to convince him that a trip abroad would do him good. But it was news of another diagnosis, this time of Harper's mother, who had Alzheimer's disease, that finally persuaded Harper they should go. And so it was that in early 2010, father, son, and daughter-in-law made arrangements to travel in the spring to New York and Washington, D.C., where Harper's mother was being looked after by his brother's family.

"Dad?"

Harper opened his eyes. How long had he been sitting there?

"Are you in there?"

"Just a minute, Son."

He took another deep breath and rubbed his eyes with the heels of his hands. Then he stood, flushed the toilet for a second time, and opened the stall door.

"We have to go now or we'll miss the flight."

"Okay, okay," he said, brushing past Alex and crossing to the bank of basins on the other side of the bathroom.

"Are you alright?" Alex asked.

As he stood washing his hands, Harper glanced up at the mirror. He saw an old man, his face drawn, gray hair at his temples.

"Yeah, I'm alright," he said, looking at Alex's reflection behind his own in the mirror. "Just an upset stomach."

To Harper's relief they had no problems going through Immigration and Security, but the walk to Gate 39 took longer than they expected.

"Come on, Dad," Alex said, imploring him to walk faster.

But Harper's back was killing him. He rolled his eyes to indicate he was moving as fast as he could. They eventually reached the gate five minutes before the scheduled departure time, only to find that their flight had been delayed. According to the flight attendant on duty, they would not be commencing boarding for another fifteen minutes. Relieved, they found three empty seats by a large window with a view out over the taxiway and sat down.

Harper leaned back in his chair and watched the planes maneuvering on the runway. After a few minutes, he closed his eyes and did a quick calculation in his head. Forty-two years. Was it really that long ago? They had arrived at Arlanda Airport on a Scandinavian Airlines flight from Leningrad and stepped off the plane to be greeted by a swarm of journalists and photographers. Harper still had a copy of one of the photos taken that day, of the five of them standing on the tarmac with the plane in the background. Harper clutching the cream overnight bag Yumi had given him in Japan. Ferran holding a guitar he had picked up in Moscow. Santiago. Roberts. And Mayfield with his goddamn suitcase.

It had been a similar scene, only on a much larger scale, when they had arrived in Moscow four weeks earlier. There were journalists and photographers, but also young girls with flowers. After months as fugitives, trusting no one and continually looking over their shoulders, it was almost overwhelming. After the big welcome at the airport in Moscow they had been whisked away to a hotel in the city. Later they had embarked on a tour of the country by plane and train as guests of a Russian peace group. It was exhilarating at first, but after four weeks of traveling around the country and attending receptions and public meetings they were exhausted, and it was a relief when they reached Leningrad—now St. Petersburg—to be told that arrangements had been completed for their passage to Sweden.

After arriving at Arlanda Airport they had been questioned by immigration authorities before being handed over to the local police. They had entered Sweden without passports, and were told it would take a day or two to establish their identities. Until then they would be held in police cells. The news came as a shock after their treatment as heroes in the USSR, but they were released early the next morning and met by representatives of the American Deserters Committee.

It took a while for their status as refugees to be recognized, and until then they were not permitted to work. The money they had been given before leaving Leningrad soon ran out, and they had to rely on the generosity of their hosts and the other American deserters to survive. There were around eighty of them in Sweden, including more than a dozen brothers.

Eventually Harper got a part-time job as a mechanic and found his own place to live. He established his own circle of friends, and saw less and less of the other deserters. About six months after they arrived, he heard that Mayfield, unable to adjust to life in Sweden, had wandered into the American embassy in Stockholm and given himself up. He was sent back to the U.S. where he was found guilty of desertion and sentenced to four years at Leavenworth. Soon afterward, Ferran was diagnosed with cirrhosis of the liver. He carried on drinking anyway, and died in 1975 at the age of thirty-four. Santiago continued his womanizing ways, and the last time Harper met him, in 1990, he was onto Swedish wife number three. Roberts, too, seemed determined to carry on where he left off in Japan, and had been arrested at least twice as a result of his barroom brawling. Given they weren't exactly the most respectable bunch of people, it's a wonder Sweden let them in to begin with.

As for Harper, when his efforts to get in touch with Yumi came to nothing, he decided to start dating again. He met Anita toward the end of 1970. He had started working as a movie actor to supplement his income. Just minor roles in low-budget films when they needed an African American. Anita, a native of Malmö, was a make-up artist on his second film. She spoke fluent English, which was just as well since Harper's Swedish was rudimentary at best, and they hit it off right away. After a whirlwind romance, they got married in early 1971. Nine years later, Alex was born.

Harper had not been the perfect husband. He had been unfaithful a number of times in the years after Alex was born. It was only when Anita threatened to leave him and take Alex with her that he realized what a fool he had been. After that, their love for each other only grew stronger. He came to realize that he was one of the luckiest men in the world. If only she was still here so he could tell her.

An announcement came over the terminal PA, breaking Harper's reverie.

"We have to board now, James."

Harper opened his eyes and turned in the direction of the voice. His vision was still blurry, and the sight of the woman with the ponytail confused him at first. Then the image sharpened and he recognized the figure of Ingrid and, standing next to her, Alex.

Harper looked at Ingrid and nodded. He leaned forward and gripped the armrest to his left, steeling himself for the pain he knew would hit him when he tried to stand. But then he had another thought.

"Come on, Son," he said, turning to Alex. "What say you give your old man a hand?"

For a brief moment a look of confusion registered on Alex's face. Then he stepped forward so that he was standing directly in front of Harper and extended his right hand. Harper grasped it with his own right hand and allowed himself to be pulled up onto his feet. He felt a twinge in his lower back, but it was nowhere near as bad as he had expected. The two men stood there awkwardly for a moment, just inches apart. Then, still holding Alex's right hand, Harper reached over with his left hand and clasped his son's right shoulder.

"Thanks, Son," he said.

"Don't mention it, Dad."

"No, I mean it. Thanks for everything."

Alex seemed taken aback, unsure how to respond. But after a moment's hesitation he wrapped his own free arm around his father's shoulders and the two men held each other in a clumsy embrace.

"I hate to interrupt you guys," said Ingrid, who was standing off to one side. "But maybe you'd like to continue your little tête-à-tête on the plane?"

Harper laughed and released his son from his clutches. "How long is the flight?"

"Nine hours," Alex said.

"That should just about be enough time. I've got a lot to tell you both."

He turned and picked up his carry-on bag from the seat behind him. Noticing the look of irritation on Ingrid's face, he recalled how when she and Alex had arrived at his apartment earlier that morning to pick him up they had both reacted with shock at the state of the thing, its cream exterior discolored and almost worn through in places. Yes, he had told them, he did have something newer, but this one had sentimental value. Perhaps when they got on the plane he would start by telling them how he came to meet its former owner.

HISTORICAL NOTE

More U.S. military personnel deserted during the Vietnam War
than in any other war in modern American military history. According to the Department of Defense, there were a total of 503,926
desertions between July 1, 1966, when the military began keeping
statistics, and December 31, 1973, by which time U.S. combat forces
had left Vietnam. This compares with an estimated 50,000 desertions during World War II and 13,790 during the Korean War. The
discrepancy is mainly due to the long duration of the Vietnam War
compared to those earlier conflicts. But a comparison of the desertion rates also shows that while at the start of the Vietnam War the
rate was similar to those for World War II and the Korean War, as
the Vietnam War dragged on the desertion rate increased, peaking
at 73.5 per 1,000 troops in 1971, well above the highest figures from
World War II (63 per 1,000 troops in 1944) and the Korean War
(22.3 per 1,000 in 1953).

Contrary to the common characterization of deserters as
endangering the lives of their brothers-in-arms by abandoning
them on the battlefield, during the Vietnam War the overwhelming
majority of desertions occurred on U.S. soil, typically among troops
who had returned after a tour of duty. Moreover, the vast bulk of
deserters ended up returning to military control. A small minority,
probably no more than a few thousand, fled to foreign countries,
including Canada, Mexico, and Sweden, where they joined the
ever-increasing numbers of American draft resisters. Only a tiny
proportion of deserters fled while in Vietnam, while an equally
insignificant number absconded while stationed at bases elsewhere
in the Asia-Pacific region.

In Japan, which hosted more than a dozen U.S. military bases and was a popular R&R destination for American military personnel, circumstances were quite different to those faced by deserters either in Vietnam or at home. Outside places like Okinawa and Yokosuka, where there was a heavy U.S. military presence, foreigners were few in number and English was not widely spoken, making it difficult for American deserters to hole up. Moreover, not only were they unable to claim asylum in Japan, but under Japanese immigration law, once deserters left the armed forces they could be arrested as illegal entrants or residents. The U.S. military could—and did—call on the Japanese police to help them track down and apprehend deserters. Despite all these difficulties, a number of deserters chose to remain in the country, often living with Japanese girlfriends. Others acquired forged travel documents and attempted to flee Japan on their own. At the end of 1967 another option became available when Japan's largest anti-Vietnam War organization, Beheiren, began reaching out to U.S. military deserters, offering to shelter them and to smuggle them out of Japan to countries where they could claim asylum.

The Japan Technical Committee for Assistance to U.S. Anti-War Deserters, or JATEC, the clandestine group whose real-life exploits were the inspiration for *Sweden*, was active for just a few years. In the beginning its very existence was a closely guarded secret, with even those it helped often unaware of its name. Yet it was so successful that the U.S. Senate Armed Services Committee rated it "the most active and effective" of the two dozen or so organizations in seven countries working with American deserters during the Vietnam War.

Formed in early 1968 in the wake of the Intrepid Four episode, which unfolded more or less as described at the start of this novel, JATEC functioned as the underground wing of the Citizens' Federation for Peace in Vietnam, or Beheiren. Beheiren had existed since 1965 as a popular anti-Vietnam War movement. It initially concentrated on organizing largely non-confrontational actions, such as marches and public meetings. By 1967 it had become more militant, staging sit-ins in front of the U.S. embassy in Tokyo and actively encouraging American military personnel to take direct action against the war by engaging in sabotage or deserting. But it remained highly open and inclusive, and these qualities meant Beheiren was ill-suited to the task of assisting American deserters, a task that required a high level of secrecy.

Given this unsuitability, as well as its unpreparedness to act in the event of deserters actually seeking their assistance, the speed and efficiency with which Beheiren organized and implemented the escape of the Intrepid Four were nothing short of remarkable. It was on October 23, 1967 that Beheiren's Tokyo office first learned of the existence of the four American sailors and their wish to desert. Beheiren took custody of them on October 28. Less than two weeks later, on November 11, the four were transported to Yokohama and smuggled aboard a passenger ship bound for the Russian port of Nakhodka. They arrived in Sweden on December 29.

Beheiren's coordination of the escape of the Intrepid Four, details of which became public in the weeks following Beheiren's press conference of November 13, was a major PR coup for the organization and a cause of great concern for the U.S. and Japanese governments, who were worried that others would be emboldened to follow in the Intrepid Four's footsteps. Despite this concern, the American embassy in Tokyo was convinced that Beheiren's success was a "fluke." This conviction proved to be wildly optimistic.

With JATEC now handling the deserter operation and news of Beheiren's success in spiriting the Intrepid Four to Sweden spreading, the organization's continued efforts to reach out to disillusioned American military personnel quickly bore fruit. Over the next twelve months they successfully sent a further dozen deserters to Sweden, most leaving Japan on fishing boats sailing out of the port of Nemuro and being transferred to Soviet Maritime Border Patrol vessels on the high seas in the manner described in the novel. By 1971, when for the reasons outlined below, JATEC's underground railroad effectively ceased operating, this number had doubled.

One of the main reasons for JATEC's success was the widespread opposition to the U.S. war in Vietnam among the Japanese. Polls show that as many as eighty percent of the population opposed American policy in Vietnam. For many older Japanese, the U.S. bombing campaign against North Vietnam brought back memories of the Allied bombing of Japan during World War II. As for the younger generation, many had been radicalized during the struggle against the ratification of the revised Japan-U.S. Security Treaty in 1960, and perceived the U.S. as a bully. It has also been suggested that many Japanese felt an affinity with the Vietnamese people as fellow Asians. Though it cannot be attributed solely to the conflict, anti-American sentiment in Japan grew over the course of the Vietnam War, with the proportion of respondents in polls indicating that the U.S. was their favorite foreign country dropping from forty-nine percent in 1965 to just eighteen percent in 1973.

The Japanese government, on the other hand, remained supportive of the U.S. war effort. Though the Japanese Constitution prevented Japan sending troops abroad, under the terms of their security treaty with the U.S., bases in Japan could be used as staging areas for ground and air operations in Vietnam. This disconnect between government policy and popular opinion worked in favor of Beheiren (and by extension JATEC), who were seen by many as upholding the spirit of the Japanese Constitution. As evidence of this, one need only look at the huge increase in support for Beheiren in the months following the escape of the Intrepid Four. Not only did letters of support and donations flood into the organization's offices, but also dozens of new chapters formed around the country.

Given JATEC's effectiveness in smuggling deserters out of the country, then, why did this operation end so prematurely? One reason is that the Soviet Union, whose assistance was essential to the operation of the Nemuro route, ceased cooperating with JATEC toward the end of 1968 after an American spy infiltrated the group, leading to the arrest of a deserter. Related to this was the increasing cost of JATEC's operations. The number of deserters seeking JATEC's help increased, but the unavailability of the Nemuro route required them to be sheltered in Japan for longer, up to a year in some cases. In addition, there were concerns within Beheiren over the anti-war credentials of some of the deserters. Also a factor was the knowledge that the PR value of providing assistance to deserters in Japan, which had little material impact on the U.S. war effort due to the small numbers involved, had diminished significantly after the initial shock and intense media coverage of the escape of the Intrepid Four.

In the fall of 1970, two American deserters flew out of Japan on commercial flights bound for Europe using forged passports provided by JATEC. They were the last deserters to be spirited out of the country by Beheiren's underground wing, which henceforth directed most of its resources toward supporting G.I. resistance among troops stationed at U.S. military bases in Japan.

It has been called "the year that changed history," "the year of revolt," and "the year that rocked the world." Throughout 1968, in country after country, not only students but also workers, women, and people of color took to the streets en masse to protest injustice, to demand change, and to unite to create a better world. Often rejecting both the status quo and the centralized and authoritarian alternative presented by the Old Left, they sought to usher in a new future based on, and achieved through, methods that were decentralized and anti-authoritarian. Beginning with the Prague Spring in January, the ideas and practices of the New Left took Europe, Asia, and the Americas by storm in 1968, sparking massive street demonstrations and occupations of college campuses in, among other cities, Paris, Berlin, Rome, Tokyo, Mexico City, and Chicago.

In Japan, the growth of Beheiren, support for which swelled early in 1968 following the publicity surrounding the escape of the Intrepid Four and Beheiren's involvement in a large protest in Sasebo over the visit of an American nuclear-powered aircraft carrier, was just one manifestation of the dramatic rise of the New Left in that country. The student movement, which had atrophied and split following its failure to prevent the re-signing of the Japan-U.S. Security Treaty in 1960, experienced a resurgence, culminating in the occupations of the University of Tokyo, Japan's most prestigious university, and Nihon University, the country's largest tertiary institution. Like Beheiren, Zenkyōtō, the coalition of students' councils that spearheaded these occupations, was independent, decentralized, and anti-authoritarian. Over the course of 1968, its influence spread, giving rise to the seizure or occupation of dozens of high school and college campuses around Japan.

Later in the year, on International Anti-war Day, October 21, nationwide protests reached a crescendo in Tokyo where students overran Shinjuku Station, the city's largest train depot, in an attempt to stop a freight train loaded with aviation fuel leaving for the U.S. military base at Yokota. Their numbers swelled by disaffected local residents, the students occupied the station and the surrounding streets, forcing the closure of several major department stores and the suspension of rail traffic. It was not until late in the evening that police eventually quelled the protests using water cannons and tear gas. Five hundred people were arrested at Shinjuku and a further 200 at Roppongi and other locations around Tokyo.

The responses by authorities around the world to the New Left-inspired uprisings of 1968 varied both in their swiftness and in their intensity. In France, after a month of unrest in May, President Charles de Gaulle threatened to implement a state of emergency and call in the army if workers did not return to work. The National Assembly was dissolved and a snap election called, after which the revolutionary fervor of both students and workers subsided. The Prague Spring ended that summer, crushed by the Warsaw Pact invasion of Czechoslovakia in August at a cost of 72 dead and more than 600 injured. The student protests in Mexico City on the eve of the Olympics resulted in police killings of between 300 and 400 civilians on October 2, during what became known as the Tlatelolco massacre.

In Japan, the occupation of Nihon University, which had been ongoing since June, was dealt a blow with the issuing in October of arrest warrants for the student leaders, who were forced underground. Despite this, the occupations at Nihon University and the University of Tokyo continued until January the following year, when the police moved in. Beginning early on the morning of January 18, the police assault on Yasuda Hall, the students' stronghold at the University of Tokyo, lasted two days. Police fired 10,000(!) tear gas grenades from the ground and sprayed tear gas from helicopters. There were 400 arrests, and 270 students and 710 police were injured. Far from abating, however, the student unrest spread, with nationwide campus occupations totaling 127 in 1969, compared to 67 the previous year. By the end of 1969, however, nearly all of the barricades at campuses around the country had been dismantled and the street demonstrations subdued.

ACKNOWLEDGMENTS

Sweden is a work of fiction. With the exception of Beheiren's leaders and other public figures, such as President Lyndon B. Johnson and Gary Snyder, the characters are either fictionalized or entirely products of my imagination. And while many of the events referred to in the novel happened more or less as described, others have been altered or fabricated in the interests of good storytelling. The following is a selection of the main historical and biographical sources I drew on in writing the novel.

Thomas R. H. Havens' *Fire Across the Sea: The Vietnam War and Japan 1965—1975* (Princeton University Press, 1987) is a comprehensive survey of the impact of the Vietnam War on Japan, with a particular focus on the anti-war movement.

"Protesting the National Identity: The Cultures of Protest in 1960s Japan," a PhD dissertation by Peter Kelman (Faculty of Arts of the University of Sydney, 2001), is a scholarly study of the anti-Vietnam War and other protest movements in Japan in the 1960s, and includes chapters on Beheiren, JATEC, and the campus occupations of 1968-69.

Tonari ni dassōhei ga ita jidai: JATEC, aru shimin undō no kiroku (The age when deserters were around: the record of a citizens' movement, JATEC), edited by Shigeru Sekiya and Yoshie Sakamoto (Shisō no Kagakusha, 1998), contains multiple firsthand accounts of the activities of Beheiren and JATEC and includes an exhaustive chronology.

Another valuable source of information on Beheiren is the website maintained by Beheiren's former secretary-general, Yūichi Yoshikawa, until his death in 2015. It can still be found at http://www.jca.apc.org/beheiren/index.html.

On the protests of 1968, I found "Japan 1968: The Performance of Violence and the Theater of Protest" by William Mariotti in *American Historical Review* (February 2009) to be very helpful.

I am grateful to Terry Whitmore's memoir (as told to Richard Weber) *Memphis, Nam, Sweden: The Story of a Black Deserter* (University Press of Mississippi, 1997), which helped me "get inside the heads" of my deserter characters.

I gained further insights into the experience of Americans caught up in the Vietnam War from Michael Herr's *Dispatches* (Picador, 1991).

Navy Medicine in Vietnam: Oral Histories from Dien Bien Phu to the Fall of Saigon by Jan K. Herman (McFarland, 2008) was a mine of information on U.S. Navy hospital ships and U.S. Navy hospitals in Vietnam.

Gary Snyder's relationship with Japan and his involvement with the Tribe are touched on in Timothy Gray's *Gary Snyder and the Pacific Rim: Creating Countercultural Community* (University of Iowa Press, 2006), Gary Snyder's *Earth House Hold: Technical Notes & Queries to Fellow Dharma Revolutionaries* (New Directions, 1969), and *Gary Snyder: Dimensions of a Life* (Sierra Club Books, 1991), edited by Jon Halper.

Life at the hippie commune on Suwanosejima and the encounter between the Red Pants and the Tribe are described in detail in two books by former JATEC operative Fumihiko Anai: *Ahōdori ni ai ni itta* (I went to meet some albatrosses) (Shobunsha, 1975), and *Beheiren to dassō beihei* (Beheiren and U.S. military deserters) (Bungeishunju, 2000).

Kaiya Yamada's *Ai amu hippii: Nihon no hippii mūbumento 1960—1990* (I am a hippie: the Japanese hippie movement 1960—1990) (Daisan Shokan, Tokyo, 1998) was another helpful source of information on the Tribe.

For my description of the occupation of Nihon University, I drew on a variety of online resources, the most comprehensive of which is *Nichidai Tōsō by Nichidai Zenkyōtō* (The Nihon University struggle by the Nihon University All-Campus Joint Struggle Committee) at http://www.geocities.jp/keitoy2002/.

For a recent introduction to the same occupation in English, see

"Japan's 1968: A Collective Reaction to Rapid Economic Growth in an Age of Turmoil" by Eiji Oguma (translation by Nick Kapur with Samuel Malissa and Stephen Poland) in *The Asia-Pacific Journal: Japan Focus* (March 28, 2015).

I am grateful to Wikipedia, from which I sourced information on everything from the history of the Satsuma Rebellion to the engine configuration on a Boeing 727. Please support Wikipedia and keep it free of advertising by making a donation.

I am extremely grateful to the many people who helped and advised me on this book. In particular, I am indebted to Graham Bathgate of Fine Line Press and Dr. Chigusa Kimura-Steven for reading early drafts and providing valuable feedback and encouragement. Thanks to Toby Boraman, Hitomi Mizutani, Frank Prebble, Shaun Randol, Erik Sanner, the New Zealand Society of Authors, and my family for their advice and support. Finally, special thanks to Keiko Turner for her patience, love, and encouragement.

ABOUT THE AUTHOR

Matthew Turner was born in Greytown, New Zealand in 1961. He was educated at the University of Canterbury in Christchurch, New Zealand, where he gained a BA (Hons) in Japanese, and at Nagoya University and Keio University in Japan. *Sweden* is his first novel.

ABOUT THE MANTLE

The Mantle publishes emerging critics, writers, and intellectuals in the areas of Arts & Culture, International Affairs, Philosophy, and World Literature. Online, we foster discourse with a global audience through critiques, essays, and interviews. We pay close attention to voices with limited exposure in their home countries and the English language, as well as individuals experiencing censorship. Our Roundtable debate series allows for deeper engagement on select issues, while our Publishing arm features emerging critical and literary talent in print and ebook form. Learn more at www.themantle.com.